Cover by Nina Patel
Editing by Kate Keysell

Books by Peter Larner

Historical Fiction
Farewell Bright Star

Jack Daly mysteries
Lost in a hurricane
Deathbed Confessions
The Unfolding Path
Harpoon Force

Covenant Series
Covenant of silence
Covenant of retribution

Compilations
The Jack Daly Trilogy
The Covenant Chronicles

One Christmas Past

To
George, Harry and Isobel

One
Christmas
Past

PETER LARNER

una Saturnālia praeterita!
unus nātālis festus praeteritus

One
Christmas
Past

 I saw an angel coming down out of heaven, having the key to the Abyss and holding in his hand a great chain. He seized that ancient serpent, who is the devil, and bound him for a thousand years. He threw him into the Abyss, and locked and sealed it over him, to keep him from deceiving the nations anymore until the thousand years were ended. After that, he must be set free for a short time.

Book of the Apocalypse: 20: 1–3

Chapter One

Courage

One Christmas past, in those distant, unremembered days before the time of enlightenment, a curious story was told of misfortune and great malevolence; a tale of dark deeds driven by envy and the intemperate nature of man. It tells of two young souls conjoined by fate in life and death, though they knew it not. Nor did they know each other, in fact, which makes the tragic tale all the more intriguing in its unfolding.

The first was a boy whose fledgling spirit had latterly departed this earth, though his soul had not yet found peace, nor his body rest. And the second youth, whose spirit still lived, was an innocent stripling sorely tested by providence, and yet he remained indifferent to the misfortune that beset him and was entirely resigned to the will of God. The drama itself is set upon a yuletide fashioned from great portent and conjecture, an epochal hour in fact, forsworn by the Revelator himself.

It is only natural, of course, for every generation since Moses to believe it abides in the wake of enlightenment, but these were indeed dark days, unprecedented in the evolution of mankind.

Obviously, I received the story much later than the events themselves. And yet, in spite of its infrequent retelling, it has avoided embellishments or distortion and endures the manipulation of man and, moreover, woman in its recounting.

This is a story of happenstance and artful conception. And it is the account of one person's journey towards destiny. Wisdom tells us that destiny is not the victim of chance, but of the inevitable consequences of our actions, virtuous or otherwise. Providence may be the product of a decision taken in the face of adversity or opportunity. Or it might simply be the irreversible truth when events are left to their own devices. And our only armour against such ordinance is the sedecim virutum fatum *- the sixteen virtues of destiny.*

Time is the enemy of all remembered things and I am undeniably subject as the next man to Lethe and its destructive draught. But, still and all, I can never forget the haunting account of this strange tale that, at various times and in differing places, has been known by an assortment of titles. 'The Shepherd's Warning', it has been called, or 'The Motherless Son', or 'The Lost Sheep'; and yet it is principally referred to as the tale that begins 'One Christmas Past'. And there is one very good reason for this, as there is a strange correlation between the book and the title, which is contained in its sixteen chapters. Indeed, a riddle is set for the reader to uncover, as to why such a title is so appropriate. The only clue provided by the author is: 'start at the beginning and read each chapter', which sounds not at all cryptic but, on the contrary, a statement of the obvious. Anyway, it is for the reader to consider why this title is so apposite.

That the puzzle refers to beginnings is indeed apt, because the story enjoys a beginning that tells us much of the time in which the events are set. "Una Saturnālia praeterita!" the pagan Romans had said for a thousand years, blessing the god of winter. But times change and with them language and beliefs perish and are reborn. This story is the product of an inconstant age, a time when the church and, in particular, the monasteries ruled the land. In those ancient days, all were subject to the worship of one God, and to do so in a language that the great majority could not even understand, let alone speak. It was a time when there were more saints than days in the year to which to dedicate to their names; a time when men collected virtues as if they were laurel wreaths to adorn their noble brows.

This was a time when the pagan god of winter fell prostrate at the birth of a new God, born a simple peasant baby in an occupied land and laid to rest in a stable stall, one thousand years ago. And so our story begins, not 'una Saturnalia praeterita', but in this new age of 'unus nātālis festus praeteritus'

One last recommendation before I begin. The account is most advantageously told on a bleak advent evening, when one might be wrapped cosily away from a savage north-easterly wind, nestled before an open hearth and a raging log fire. Then, gazing upon the wintry landscape outside, fancy yourself as a callow, yet ardent lad atop a sea-worn cliff on such a midwinter night, abandoned, forsaken and chilled to his nine fingertips.

Thus my story shall begin, not at the beginning, for it is impossible to say where such a place lies. Is it a birth, a conception or, perhaps, dictated by the shaping of the stars? No, we shall start where I have already begun, with the brutal act that took one poor life and will so immeasurably change another. Return now and imagine yourself on that dark winter night, high atop a cliff on a narrow coastal path, subjected to a bitter snowstorm, and you will find yourself as our young wayfarer did that advent eventide, with just the distant light of a church and the virtue of courage to guide his footsteps.

The snow teemed earthward from its heavenly home, sweeping out of a brooding night sky, making it difficult to see the way forward. Tiny, fragile flakes tumbling down in their millions were swept one way and another, blown mercilessly by a turbulent wind, then lay still, crystallized, gratified to find such a steadfast haven at their journey's end. The pale mural that the individual flakes created transformed the untrodden path ahead as the falling snow dissolved into the darkness that crept ever closer as the midnight neared. An ethereal sea wind moaned to an unseen god as a young boy stumbled through the murky gloom, along the cliff-top pathway as it approached Pryklethorn Bay.

Just south of this estuary lay Hollow Hole Cove, a small inlet that was hidden from view, even on a clear day from the cliff top, as the waves that pillaged the sandstone where they met eroded the base of the cliff and had done so for a thousand years, carving into it a small cavern. As he passed this point, the frozen child licked the wind's salty brine from his lips and hunched his shoulders against the reckless power of the storm. And although he could see nothing of the long, sheltered coast below him, he could discern the eerily quiet lapping of the ebb tide, disturbed only by the occasional thump and clump of a small boat striking the rocky shoreline where it was anchored. With each thud, an anchor chain rattled, as if a spirit tried, in vain, to shake itself from this world. Snow billowed and soft echoes of a stolen life were swept aside by the ceaseless thundering of an endless sea.

This was not the kittenish, timorous flurry of snow that accompanied a reticent south-westerly, which may be taken from its course by a wooded copse of ash and elm. This was a tigerish squall, born of an easterly gale, unhindered by land or opposing wind for thousands of miles across an open ocean, unflinching until it reached the vertical cliff of the East Seaxe coast and howled its pain at the world.

"Providence and God's good grace have brought me thus far," shouted the boy through his scarf at the deafening wind. "And they shall accompany me through to my journey's end."

His dry lips cracked as he opened them to shout his defiance at the storm.

As the boy edged his way along the narrow, snow-laden path, the sea slowly retreated in measured steps, and the small craft in the cove below grated and ground its hull on the stony shore beneath the cliff. Unseen by any creature other than the chattering seagulls that clung precariously to the cliff side, an object bobbed at odd times towards the surface of the foaming water, emerging slowly with each surge and backflow of the tide. It was the body of a boy, still years from manhood, a lost soul caught in the River Styx between this world and the next. It dipped below the surf and then, on the waning tide, surfaced again, gently bending at the waist as if genuflecting in an act of penitence. Some nearby sheep in their silent fold looked up at the wayward traveller and seemed to mourn the loss of an unseen child in Hollow Hole Cove.

At the dim twilight of December, swift fell the winter night. It was that time of year and that moment in the dwindling day when the light had left the world in every sense. And what began as an uncommon day, filled with great demands and the prospect of a new life, now ended, full laden with weary bones and an empty stomach. The boy's thoughts sharpened and focused singularly on the last part of his journey, but he struggled in vain to ignore the past twelve hours. Soon all the houses in the small village ahead of him would be shut up for the night; shelter would be scarce and food more so. His empty belly rumbled at his abstinence, for he had not eaten since supper some twenty-four hours past.

Breakfast was a rarely enjoyed feast for him at Shire Farm and the day began instead with the counting of a quartered silver coin. A reluctant morning star rose like a spectre through the grey mists that rested on the flat open fields surrounding the farm and an unending world stretched eastward towards a new life.

That morning, a contemptuous cockerel had greeted the first signs of a rising sun and the boy stirred from his straw cot to face an uncertain world. Mistress Cuddlewick and her husband had said their goodbyes the previous evening but they still came to the door on that grey morning to see him depart. A slave he may have been, but a surrogate child he had become, at least to the Mistress of the household.

The boy was tall for his age and well proportioned, too, for he had laboured each day of his young life on the land. No balls, hoops or spinning tops for him, nor an education. He could read a little but knew no Latin other than *'et cum spiritu tuo'*, which to him seemed a tediously long way to acknowledge the priest's blessing at mass on Sunday.

"*Dominus vobiscum,*" the priest said ponderously, as he turned to look into the boy's heart, like God's own spy. He would find nothing, of course, for the boy had a sinless soul. What opportunity was there for him to steal, covet or kill? He owned nothing and certainly not the graven image of which the holy man spoke; not that Willem knew what a graven image was. And Mistress Cuddlewick would make sure he did not take the Lord's name in vain and that he ceded the Sabbath day to God. Yet, in spite of his innocent soul, there was one such commandment that he could not fulfil. How was he to honour his father and mother when he had neither? It was something he considered often when he went to bed at night to sleep in the barn, alone except for the ox, goats and chickens.

The priest's homily commanded him to support his father in his old age and not to grieve for him during his life.

"For kindness to a father will serve as reparation for sin. On your own day of ordeal, God will remember you. Like frost in the sunshine, your sins will melt away. Whoever deserts a father is no better than a blasphemer."

But it wasn't he who had deserted his father, the boy mused, nor could he grieve for a father in his old age.

Everyone has a mother and a father, he assured himself, as he waved goodbye to the surrogate pair who acted out that part. But he had no knowledge of his real parents, none whatsoever.

At confession, the boy asked the priest how he might fulfil the fifth commandment, and he was told to treat the Cuddlewicks in the required manner.

"But I am their bond servant, Father," he replied a little dispiritedly. "Would a son not eat at the same table as his parents? Does a mother not sing lullabies to her child in his cot each night?"

The priest told him that to receive love was not a right, but a blessing from God; for to receive love, we must first give love.

"Honour your keepers as parents and treat them as you would have them treat you."

And so he did as the priest had instructed him and Mistress Cuddlewick, at least, treated him as a loved one in return. But he was not their son and they did not engage in any conversation about his real parents. Forasmuch as he was without parents, the couple were without children. All parties in this pragmatic arrangement suffered the same loss, the same hardship, and yet neither could see the obvious solution that stared back at them on those occasions when they lamented their misfortune.

Mistress Cuddlewick had given him four farthings, along with his freedom and instructions to use both gifts wisely. Her voice was always melodious and soft, even when chiding or scolding the boy, and yet on this occasion it was even more so. But there was no kiss, no loving touch or kind word, for what purpose would such emotions serve at this late hour?

For his journey, he was to stay on the well-trodden paths, avoiding the temptation of the smaller, but more direct, forest tracks. Forests occupied vast swathes of the land and were often so deep and wide that it was easy to lose your way when trying to transect them. One needed local knowledge and, with no sun in the slate-grey morning sky to guide his way, it would be impossible to keep a straight path in the depths of the woodland that filled the land between here and Ebbsweirmouth. There were dangers too in the wildwood; boar and wolves lurked therein, and in winter, the beasts of the night were forced to join those of the day in their search for a bloody repast.

Only once on the journey did he venture from the main path towards his destination. Far ahead of him, he could see the track winding around the wood in one direction and then appear up a far hill off to the west. It seemed a long and indirect route to take, especially as a much shorter trail ran through an old yew tree wood. In summer there would have been a dark canopy above the twisting branches of the yew but now, in the heart of winter, what light there was found an easy course through the gnarled and leafless wood. No beasts could hide there and the only sound he could hear was the hawfinches feasting on the red berries that hung from the spindly boughs.

The bark and the leaves that had been shed this recently past autumn crackled beneath his feet until there, deep within its midmost trees, the woodland revealed a bowered den and sitting thereby was a woman, as wizened as those spindly boughs that bore the red berries. In her hand she held a stave made from the rowan tree. The barren branches that lay about her lair were covered in lichen and ivy, protecting her from the wind that made it thus far into the wood.

Silence is a field that produces a rich harvest and not least among this is the gift of prophecy. Of course, as the disciple of Tarsus had written, the last of the great prophets had passed from this world, but the gift of soothsaying lived on through those still skilled in the arcane art. The old crone was one of these and yet she knew that what she saw was only what might be, for the gift was being taken slowly from the world.

The sorceress had the patience and wisdom of age but possessed also the agile mind and quick-wittedness of a young cat. It was apparent to all that the boy was both courteous and thoughtful, but she noticed immediately that he was graced also with the gifts of a receptive mind and a pure soul. She handed the boy a cup of water and, pointing to a fallen tree, invited him to sit down. The silence continued for several minutes, while the grey-haired hag looked deeply into the boy's soul.

All the time, as she sat there, the woman scratched strange symbols on the floor of the clearing with a witch's stave and these provoked distant remembrances of Willem's infancy. The boy drank the cold, fresh water that he was offered and he asked many questions of the crone, but she answered none to begin with. Indeed, it was not until he went to leave that she spoke at all.

"Love, honour and courage are the cornerstones of virtue and love stands above all others."

Her words seemed to be taken by the wind, as they were spoken as much to the trees as to the boy. So quickly were the words taken that Willem had to repeat them in his mind, for he knew that he should think on them at some calm moment in the future.

"Thank you," the boy answered, not really knowing what he was thanking her for. As he committed the wise words to his memory, she spoke again, even more quietly, and yet he knew that this time the advice was not for the wind to take abroad, but for him alone. She spoke of providence, but he did not understand, although his inquisitive mind meant that little remained unknown to him for long. The crone explained that providence was fate and

Willem again sought clarification, for he had led a shallow life on the farm.

"Fate is not something that happens by accident," she whispered; and yet her words seemed to be directed at the wind, censuring it like a wayward child.

Then she spoke of destiny and told Willem that their paths had already crossed at the time of Maeldun.

"I was not born at the time of Maeldun," the boy told her, so he was certain they could not have met before.

"But it was already written," she answered.

"What was already written?" he asked.

"Your destiny."

The boy did not understand what she meant and sat back down on the fallen log.

"Your road to destiny is a short one," she said, now speaking directly at the boy. "And yet it is an arduous path that takes you there." She looked deep into the boy's eyes and, in that instant, conjured in her mind a foreordination of hope. She knew her powers were declining, yet gave the gift with a sincere heart.

"You must gather about you the virtues of destiny by the time of the Christ's mass. Most men are granted a lifetime to complete the same task. But your lifetime depends on your ability to garner the sixteen gifts in just ten days."

"Is it written that I shall succeed?" he asked.

"What is written is what might be, not what will be."

"Where do I begin?"

"By choosing the right path and opening your heart to the gifts. But beware," she cautioned him, "for good and evil walk on different sides of the same path."

The boy wondered whether his next step would change his destiny forever but, by now, the woman knew his every thought.

"The first step is courage," she added, but she could see that courage came as easily to him as leaves to a tree in spring. It was as if, by dint of blood, he had been made courageous. The old woman stood up and pointed, in turn, to three paths that led from her curious dwelling place. The boy had not noticed them before and could not even remember what direction he had arrived from.

"For, with courage, all things are made possible," she said, her final words echoing through the trees.

Willem chose the right-hand path and wondered whether this way led to courage. If it did, thought the boy, then what was it that the other two paths led to? Courage seemed such an esteemed virtue to begin his journey with and he felt the need for it in his heart, so he showed no hesitation in taking the trail he had chosen.

Destiny, the woman reflected again as the boy walked off, is not something that happens by accident and she mocked the wind for thinking otherwise. As he left, she reflected on how the world might have changed had the boy taken one of the other paths, for she knew well the fickleness of providence.

The barren fields, bare trees and hedgerows stretched away before him. Only the holm oak and the ivy remained green and, as the day grew long, the crunching leaves would be replaced by icy snow. The threatening sky warned him of the coming storm, as did the absence of sound. No creature stirred in its elfin lay, for the world at the edge of the forest was still subdued by the night's intoxicating potion. Even the bare-branched trees stopped their sway, summoned to stillness by the dormant chill of Boreas himself. No birdsong pierced the hushed landscape either. Only some magpies and crows broke the peace, fighting over the feeding rights at the carcass of a hare left by a disturbed fox, as a great foreboding sky crept over the land.

The short-lived day slowly ebbed away and a darkening sky that continued to mourn the loss of summer was bathed in the ashen clouds of winter. Slowly, by degrees, floating snowflakes masked the night sky and began to veil the earth in mist. Hills and dales alike fell under the season's spell and the trees that had lost their verdant robe longed achingly for spring, yet were trimmed in white.

What began as tumbling, tiny crafted individual plumes of pure white feather soon gathered as drifts of icy shafts that convened as one and flooded the world around the fledgling traveller. Darkness stole down from its hidden lair as the snow billowed in harmonious waves, like a flight of swallows at roosting time, swooping in the wind and crashing through the threadbare branches that sheathed his path towards Ebbsweirmouth.

Apart from the old woman, not a soul did he meet on his way. The fields, once swarming with people at harvest time, now lay barren. The pastures housed scattered cattle and hardy sheep that looked anxiously at an angry sky. But the farmers were in their sheds and barns, well hidden from our pilgrim's path, and their stock was left to fend for itself.

As the night drew on, the boy began to worry that he would not reach his destination before the snow overwhelmed the earth and him with it. Through the storm he could see nowhere to shelter for the night. So, he onward trod until he heard another noise, growing louder than the wind itself. And, thinking he knew what it was, he increased his pace and trudged more purposefully through the deepening snow. The roar of a vast ocean gave battle with an unrelenting easterly wind, as they each struggled to become more raucous than the other. The boy's ears became too cold to distinguish between the two and an otherwise silent world surrendered to their joint enterprise.

Eventually, through the mist, a fork appeared on the road ahead, marked by a sign. He removed his cold hands from the pockets of his coat and rubbed his eyes. Then, stepping up to the wooden pole, he brushed the snow from it with his sleeve. He was relieved to see that his destination was just one mile away, though his happiness was short-lived when he found the well-worn road flooded so deeply that it could not be crossed. Another, smaller path led away towards the sound of the roaring ocean, so he summoned up the last morsels of energy and set off along it, hoping it too would lead to civilisation.

The coastal trail provided the only access to the small town of Ebbsweirmouth, as the ford in the drove road had flooded a few days before. And so the boy took the only alternative track that headed north towards the village. The winding pathway followed the line of the cliff and ran close to its edge, circling the town close to Pryklethorn Bay and passing through a small copse that protected the inhabitants from the eastern sea winds. He thought about leaving the path and making his way across the fields that separated him from his final destination. But he remembered Mistress Cuddlewick's advice. He knew from his experiences at Shire Farm that fields often became dangerous quagmires in winter and it seemed to him that fields so close to the sea were probably more disposed to this.

The drove road flooded regularly at the ford, often forcing the shepherd Abel Cotes to drive his flock through the fields of Holm Farm, damaging some of his lordship's crops in the process and annoying Seth Wainthrop, who managed the land for Lord Scullion. In summer or autumn, a payment would be demanded as recompense by the shire reeve, but not at advent, not this late in the year, for the crops were all harvested by Michaelmas and now lay at his lordship's pleasure in the tithe barn.

The shrill sound of the wind seemed to call the boy's name and he stopped momentarily in the snow to wonder whether it was someone other than the wind that wailed so loudly. At times on the journey, the boy dawdled as he considered whether his name had any significance. He knew of no one else named Willem, nor did he know what the name meant or what significance it might have. Was he named after his father? The name gave no indication of his father's profession or craft. Was his father another drudge, another servant like he was? Had his parents died when he was born, or was he just unwanted? An undesirable wretch, a burden on society, given away, not even sold, to the only person who would accept the burden, because the head of any township, the lord of any village, had that responsibility.

Mistress Cuddlewick told him that he came from Ebbsweirmouth. And it was she who said he had been given, not sold, as a slave at the age of just four years, to work on their farm. It was the most suitable outcome for Lord Scullion, for he could not maintain every waif and stray put under his charge. He had housed and fed the infant since birth, or shortly after; that is what the boy was told when he asked Mistress Cuddlewick. And the boy asked often, much to her annoyance, for she had little or nothing to say on the matter, which was at least five words more than her husband.

"You are what you are," she would say ambiguously to almost every question he raised. "There is nothing that can be done to change that."

She didn't enquire of his ancestry on that spring day when the seeding and planting needed another pair of hands. Her husband had injured his foot in the field; severed a toe when he trod on a newly sharpened scythe that he had left among the stubble as he planted turnips.

It was a rude awakening for such a small child, following the bellowed instructions of the gruff, hobbling old man. But the Cuddlewicks could not afford a full-grown slave; they had no money for a man who would require a full meal each day, then perhaps run off at the first opportunity. In any case, they owned an ox to pull the plough, so it mattered not that the farm serf wasn't big enough to hand-plough a field. Master Cuddlewick knew that and gave his wife instructions accordingly. Yet, for all the hardship that those memories recalled, the boy would have gladly exchanged them for this very moment, as he feared freezing to death on such a fearsomely cold night.

Willem shook the snow from a threadbare scarf and wrapped the dry side about his face before trudging along, barely hearing or feeling the crunching freshness of the snow beneath his feet. Then, as if amused by his distress, the wind howled and turned towards his face. For a moment, the boy laboured against this expression of might. What ails the eastern wind, he thought to himself, that it moans so miserably and bites the flesh so fiercely? Where are its cousins of warmer climes?

He prayed too, as he trudged through the deepening snow, that he might see again the angel that visited him in his infancy. It may have been a dream, he thought, but even a dream might offer comfort against the biting wind. Perhaps it had not been an angel at all. Some months later, a new statue of the Virgin Mary arrived at the parish church near Shire Farm. Willem was shaken by the similarity between it and the woman he had seen. The white headdress was the same and, though the blue tunic was much darker than that of the statue, she looked just the same. And yet he never spoke of this distant memory to the priest, or even Mistress Cuddlewick. It was probably just a dream from his early childhood, for a visit from an angel seemed an unlikely event in the life of a waif; especially an angel who joined him for a picnic. No, he thought, it was certainly a dream, and yet the fragrance of the wild dog rose made the experience so real.

Willem's body and face ached from the relentlessness of a storm that prevented him from thinking of anything else. He looked down at his frozen feet and began to tread heavily, deliberately into the snow with a monotonous routine, not pausing, but continuing as unremittingly as the snow itself. And then he tried to visualise a summer's day, that summer's day, convincing himself for the moment that it was a real one, not a creation of his vivid imagination or a dream. But it was too distant a memory. Too long ago to be sure whether it was real. So he satisfied himself with the last glorious summer day that he could remember.

"'Tis birthright that matters," Mistress Cuddlewick uttered in a convincing tone, as they sat eating their lunch under the shade of that old grey hornbeam that stood by the hedgerow. Its low branches stretched out into the field where they were reaping and Willem could stretch out himself, beneath its long-cast shadow, resting after his hard labours in the field. It was not dissimilar to the place in his dream, except there was no hornbeam, just a flourishing dog rose. Yet dreams are produced from just such resemblances.

It was not birthright that set Mistress Cuddlewick aright, but providence and perhaps a pretty face in her youth, though this was hard to imagine for a boy of Willem's young age.

The good fortune of Mistress Cuddlewick had been to marry the eldest son of the family that owned Shire Farm. He wasn't the most handsome of the Cuddlewick boys, nor did he possess the charm of the youngest son. But he had the farm and that was what mattered in those days, just as it does today in most places.

Willem looked at the farmer's wife and saw a fat old woman, although in reality she was not that old, just made old by circumstance and hard work. But the boy could not imagine her nubile frame and the line-free face of her youth, nor could he know the yearning looks she had attracted from the boys of the village in her younger years. And yet, contentment ages a figure and a face greater than the labours of the field. She was too old to have children, of course. She had babies in her youth, during the early years of their marriage; two girls who died in infancy and two boys who did not carry. She believed she could not carry boys, or that is what she told her husband. She had moist, loving eyes, and would have liked a son, for he would have been a good catch for some lucky girl. The eldest son of a farmer or indeed any tradesman could take his pick. And the most sensible of husbands bought their wives by the pound. A pretty face is a fine thing, Mistress Cuddlewick would say, but a scrawny beauty would not keep a husband warm on a cold winter night.

"Birthright is what counts," she repeated to Willem, after she had stopped laughing at her own licentious quip, adding, "not a handsome face or fine words."

"I have no birthright," Willem answered, a little despondently.

"Then, do as I did," she replied encouragingly. "Marry well. You're a handsome boy and will make a handsome man too."

"Did you know my parents?" was one of the many questions Willem asked Mistress Cuddlewick when they rested from their labours.

"Of course not," she replied.

So he asked about brothers, sisters and cousins, and these questions were met with the same response.

"So I may perhaps have a brother." He paused for a moment, wondering about the possibility. "I would really like to have an older brother," he commented with a smile, because the thought did not make the boy melancholy, as such meanderings on his ancestry often did. Quite the opposite, in fact, because not knowing whether he had a brother or sister meant that he may, indeed, have one, for he had a very optimistic nature. In his young mind, everything was possible. Until he was told, categorically, that the opposite was true, then his parents may still be alive and there may be brothers or sisters. So the boy resolved to continue hoping, for until someone told him otherwise, they were still alive. Somehow, in his innermost being, the boy was convinced that, in this respect, he was very much like his mother.

Whilst the boy discovered little of his origins from Mistress Cuddlewick, he learned much about the self-evident truths of life from her during their days in the field, sowing or reaping. Like the most important thing about falling over is to get straight up again, although he doubted that this was the most practical guidance for someone who had broken a limb. And if you are falling over, try not to do so in a nettle bush. Unfortunately that particular piece of advice was given a few moments after Willem *had* fallen in a nettle bush so, again, it was something that was entirely obvious to the boy when the recommendation was given. The farmer's wife was something of a sage when providing counsel on matters of hindsight.

At frequent intervals his mind was dragged back from summer into the cold winter night. But, Willem decided to ignore the storm, and for that moment he thought only of those summer days in the field or of a fine, dry autumn when the crops were harvested.

Willem enjoyed working on the land. It was hard work for one so small, but seeing the fruits of his labour at harvest time gave him great joy. The ripened oats and barley stood higher than the boy himself and in August and September, when the days began to shorten, he would work beyond dusk to ensure the barn was filled for winter. The

Cuddlewicks grew winter wheat and summer wheat too, and Willem took great pleasure from the constant resculpturing of the landscape.

There was a beehive to manage and a chicken coop, too. And the small river that ran along the border of the property attracted geese and other wild birds at different times of the year. But there were no hedgerows, which convinced the boy that his recurring dream had not occurred here. And whilst he longed to discover his true roots, he never wished to leave Shire Farm, because he found such pleasure in the poetry of the earth.

He should have guessed then that he would not be sharing the fruits of such a sparse reaping. Now there was no work to be done at Shire Farm and he had become a burden for its owners. Once the free hazelnuts had been gathered in during the first week of November, he was no longer required, and he could expect no charity from those who may themselves go hungry in the season of dearth and raw winds. Unable to be fed through the winter, Willem had been granted his freedom and told he must make his own way in the world, to seek his fortune and perhaps find something of his past too.

The snow covered the pathway and he managed to keep to it only by following the cliff edge. Each step dug deeply into the rising bed of snow and his feet had to be drawn from it more wearily as he advanced nearer to the distant light. As he went, he recalled again being told that he had come to the farm as an orphan from Ebbsweirmouth, which stood on the coast, a good day's walk from the farm. He had walked for a day, true, but would not consider it good. And he, himself, stood on the coast so, even without the signpost, he knew he would soon arrive at the town. He remembered nothing of it, of course, as he was only four years old when he left, or so he had been told.

Orphaned at birth, he was raised through infancy by Lord Scullion; not personally, of course, but it was the obligation of each thegn to raise and have suckled those abandoned by their parents and God at birth. And so it was with Willem, but only until that time when he could walk, talk and, more importantly, carry and toil. Then it was time for another home, another life; one of labour and poor reward. Now, through nothing more than a poor harvest, he had the opportunity to return home. Although there was no home, just a village that might remember him better than he remembered it.

The path sloped downwards as it curved past Pryklethorn Bay, and then upwards again as frozen hills and mounds produced an undulating and arduous passage. In a small dell to his right, a flock of sheep, made silent by the cold wind, were folded in kinship against its harshness. And, to his left, he could see the outline of the church steeple. Eventually he crossed a wooden bridge over a stream that ran back down towards Pryklethorn Bay and the ocean beyond. In the other direction, the stream followed the pathway as it coiled along a steep hillside towards the village, supplying the citizens with fresh water.

It was just past this point that the boy came to a crossroads that lay below the imposing height of Apparition Hill. Above him, on the hillside, a well-used gallows stood on a natural ledge near the top of the hill, at a point called Gallows Ridge. So high up the hillside stood the gallows that it could be seen from the turret of Scullion Tower, a mile away on the other side of the village. By God's grace there was no body hanging there, so Willem stopped for a moment in the gusting snow and looked towards the distant tower as it shone, dimly lit, like a faraway star in the southern sky.

To the north-west lay a pathway through a deep forest that dominated the landscape; to the west, a drove road provided safe passage for the stock of Four Thing Farm, and to the south, a more frequented road led into the town. Close to this, just on the other side of a dry stone wall, lay the corpse road, a pathway used to take the bodies of the dead from the widows' hides to the church graveyard. It was no more than an unploughed track that ran alongside the drove roads used by Abel Cotes to move his sheep from one pasture to another. Woe betide the farmer if he allowed sheep to use the corpse road, for many believed that the spirits of the unbaptised and the stillborn dwelt along this path. Moreover, it was this corpse road that was used to transport the many who died at Maeldun. The corpse road straggled along a deliberately difficult way, over styles, or across bridges over streams and then stepping stones across brooks that the spirits could not pass. Any obstacle that could be found was laid along its route, in order to stop the dead from wandering the land as lost souls. Anywhere that a track intersected the corpse road was avoided at all costs, as spirit guardians were known to dwell there to prevent the departed from crossing into the underworld. When all else failed, the whispering rowan tree would be raised to protect the townsfolk from enchantment and the evil wanderings of the dead.

Through the starless sky that stretched to the far horizon, sheltered from the north-easterly winds by the hill, Willem could see the faint light of candles in the distance. He stopped and, shielding his face against the wind, looked up at the gallows and the worn, hollowed-out path that led up to it. If he had waded across the ford he would have been at the church by now, but the freezing water would have reached up to his neck and he had no clothes to change into.

As he approached the village, the boy wondered whether he should continue to the church or make his way to one of the cattle sheds near the farm on the outskirts of town. Convinced he might conceal himself inside the church or, if not, in the churchyard that surrounded it, he continued walking towards the town.

In the long days past, the land had been filled with forest for as far as the eye could see. In a shallow valley where a natural clearing appeared in that forest close to the sea, the first visitors to this place had built a home, and the same trees that had been cut down to expand the clearing were used to build the houses that now stood here and, eventually, a village rose up. Apart from a much-loved old lime tree that stood in the church graveyard, only three trees now stood in the single street that stretched from the inn to the church. An oak tree over-canopied one end of a large stone and timber inn, and two more that rose above the church provided futile shade for the dead whose remains lay in the graveyard that surrounded it.

The first building Willem came upon at the northern edge of the town was the inn, made dimly radiant inside by numerous flickering candles. He could hear the voices of men talking loudly at the bar and he paused outside, wondering whether to enter. His cold fingers fumbled in his waistcoat pocket for the four farthings that Mistress Cuddlewick had given him, but he scorned the thought of wasting the money on some ale that would merely numb the cold and empty his pockets.

Willem stood under the oak for a moment to shelter from the snow when, suddenly, the intensity of the storm halted, as if it had been ordered by some unseen power to be still. The boy stood there wondering what this could mean. He was just about to continue the final part of his journey to the church when, about two paces away, he saw something seeping through the undisturbed snow. The powdery, white flakes turned red, as blood seemed to rise to the surface, and Willem wondered whether some poor animal had met its death on this bleak midwinter night.

Above the sound of a creaking sign that identified the thatched building as The Salutation Inn, the voices grew louder, speaking of ghostly spirits that wandered the dark corpse road outside the town, carrying a coffin upon their shoulders and bewailing their loss.

Willem turned to walk farther and, as he lifted up his eyes, amid the dwindling flurry of winter snow he saw the open doors of a small church, with the congregation gathering therein for a vigil mass. The wind had tempered its fractiousness, so the boy continued down into the vale in which the small village sat. It was less a valley than a shallow dip between two modest hills, and yet the terrain and the dense forest on three sides of the town protected it from the sharp coastal winds.

A light dusting of snow continued to fall, unhindered now by the wind, and a bell heralded a Christmas much talked of and scrutinised by those who assembled there. Two candles were being lit in the church on the road ahead, for it was two days before the third Sunday of advent. The vigil mass of an unremembered saint was about to begin, so Willem quickened his step, and a voice in his head told him to martial his courage with equal vigour. Christ's mass was ten nights hence and shelter waited for him at the end of the street. The power of the wind had abated but there were other forces at large on this advent eve. And one thing could be certain in these uncertain times, that the unbridled power of man is as destructive as any storm and more easily delivered.

Providence may indeed result from a decision taken in the face of advantage or adversity, but it is more likely to be fashioned by our actions in those dire moments of insecurity, when we look fate square in the face, and when all that is required is a little courage.

Chapter Two

Faith

Now, at the time of our story, the power in Ebbsweirmouth rested in the hands of one man or, more correctly, in the hand of one man, Lord Morcar Scullion. And the enforcement of that power was the responsibility of his shire reeve, the Chamberlain Oswald Balliwick, who we now find sitting impatiently in the Church of the Virgin Mary, in a mood we can only describe as vexed, waiting for the Friday vigil mass to begin. The nature of such power is often persuaded by irritation and impatience, and can be either unmoved or unbridled by such disturbances, depending on the character of the individual concerned.

It is a curious thing, I suppose, that the world waited patiently for the coming of a mighty ruler. And yet, it was a child that the angels proclaimed that first Christmas night. What power, what influence could a helpless child exert on such a savage world? In truth, one would imagine no more and no less than the child of our own story.

It is for you to decide whether the power of which we speak is unbridled or not for, nobly undaunted by hardship or hindrance *and with pilgrim's steps, we have arrived at Ebbsweirmouth, a coastal village of humble antecedence and origin, a riverine hamlet of good health and abundant harvest, where steep cliffs provide a little protection from the pillaging hoards that ravage the neighbouring countryside.*

To the south, Scullion Tower stands as a bastion overlooking the great eastern ocean at the edge of the world. A castle of modest proportions, but of great import to the people of East Seaxe, a shire that stretches from that great sea to the River Lee in the west, and from the River Tamesis in the south to the rivers Orwell and Gipping, which separate the shire from the territories of the neighbouring Anglians in the north. Betwixt here and the great Tamesis stands Camulodunon, the fortified town where the occupying Romans built their mint.

It is important that, if you are to understand the events that took place here, you must also learn something of the town where those events occurred. For, although the essence of any place is its people, it will serve you well to appreciate the location too.

The Church of the Virgin Mary, The Salutation Inn and Mardyke House all feature in the tale, as does Scullion Tower, Hollow Hole Cove and the drove roads and pathways that lead from one location to another.

The town of Ebbsweirmouth consists of one hundred hides, but less than sixty souls. The reason for this strange consequence is Maeldun, and you shall be told of that shortly. Forty houses built of timber and topped with thatch form the town, and as many as sixty more, in various stages of disrepair, are spread about the countryside around that original forest clearing of which we spoke previously. Amongst those buildings in the village itself, the largest residence is Mardyke House, the home of the Goodlyheads. The childless Mildred is much loved by her devoted husband, Edwin, who through a sparse education in Latin has built a business with travelling tradesmen in all the merchandise that a thriving hamlet might require.

There are but four stone buildings in the area: the castle, the inn, the church, which is only partly stone, and Mardyke House. The others are wood and thatch, built from the endless forests that reach out across the land towards the kingdoms of the west and another great ocean beyond.

Starting at the southernmost point of the area known as Ebbsweirmouth and heading north from the tower, with the sea to the east, we find Holm Farm, passing first a tithe barn and then the smallholding of Seth Wainthrop, who manages twenty hides of arable land for his master, Lord Scullion. To the west is the dense Ebbs Wood, where the wolf and wild boar abide, and the light appears only when the oak has shed its leaves and the day is at its shortest. The main drove road, used by Abel Cotes to find good pastured land for his lordship's sheep, meanders to our left as we head north, looping past the tiny Wainthrop home and across Holm Ford, which floods when heaven's tears fall.

Along a narrow path to the south of the town lies one of only two buildings that are larger than Mardyke House, with the exception of the tower of course. St Mary the Virgin church is a modest wooden building with a flint sanctuary and belfry, which stands one mile to the east of Four Thing Farm. At the other end of town, heading towards Apparition Hill, the last building in the village and one that is only slightly smaller than the church is The Salutation Inn, beyond which, to the north east, is Four Thing Ford and a pathway towards Pryklethorn Bay and Hollow Hole Cove.

Now you ask, why so many homes, so many hides, and yet less than sixty souls dwell here? The answer I give is Maeldun. And you will ask, what is Maeldun? Or, more probably, who is Maeldun? Well, Maeldun is a shadow that is cast across this land

and has been so for these past eight years. It is the barren wombs and the children conceived only in the hearts and minds of their bereaved parents. It is children born without fathers, and mothers who live without husbands. For I must tell you that there are many widows in this town, and not this town alone, for the whole shire and more was made so by Maeldun.

You shall learn all too soon the significance of Maeldun. For now, let us end our journey in the pathway that runs through the widows' hides, those fields sown and reaped by those who mourn. Let us leave this saddest of places to join our benumbed and frozen traveller and attend, with him, the vigil mass of Saint Lazarus of the four days, that saint of unmeasured faith, the second virtue of destiny.

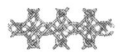

Willem stepped inside the crowded church and the howling whistle of the cliff-top wind gave way to the hushed chatter of nervous voices. With silent steps he made his way as inconspicuously as he was able to the front pew, which was overshadowed by a rickety old pulpit, raised up from the floor and blocking his view of the altar. Yet, more importantly, it also obscured the congregation's view of him. The boy eyed the small space that remained vacant at the end of the pew and squeezed his body onto the rough wooden bench. Gradually he began to thaw a little as the chattering turned into a coherent sound and the words became distinguishable from the mere babble that had welcomed his arrival.

A small, elderly woman sitting next to him was trying to ignore, as politely as she could, the comments of a much stouter woman sitting on the other side of her. She spoke of a fearsome coming and, more vigorously, of how her husband, the butcher, had seen evil spirits in the corpse roads to the north of the town. The smaller woman referred to her neighbour as Mistress Gripple and asked her, in all humility, to temper her words. As she did so, she waved her hand at the woman, suggesting she slid herself along the bench a little, in order that Willem might be more comfortable in the tiny space available to him.

With apprehensive voices, those members of the congregation sitting around the boy spoke hopefully of a blessed intercession, and the man kneeling behind Willem was praying for just such an intervention. Willem tried not to listen to the man's heartfelt plea. Some women he could hear spoke of faith as others did of hope but, just like the shepherds on that first Christmas night, mighty dread had seized their troubled minds and they were fearful and suspicious in equal measure, gripped by the same, single fear. Everyone was affected by what was to come; everyone, it seemed, except the rather serene looking woman sitting by Willem's side, who appeared indifferent to their apprehension. Once she had finished her own silent prayer, she turned to her left and looked directly at the boy with charitable eyes and a generous smile. He pulled his scarf down a little and returned her kind expression.

"Welcome," she mouthed silently, as if she had taken a vow of silence, and his cold face framed another smile. She had clearly recognised the boy as a stranger and, whilst he wanted to be polite, his plan was to remain as anonymous as possible in order that he might take refuge in the church when everyone else had taken their leave. The woman looked him over as tactfully as she could, until her eyes fell upon his hands that rested in his lap, joined in prayer. He then separated them to pull his scarf back up over the lower part of his face, for he was still very cold.

The woman rummaged inside a hessian bag that sat on her lap. She removed a pair of woollen mittens and handed them to the boy. Willem looked at the gloves and back at the woman, before trying to pass them back to her. But she insisted, even to the extent of holding the boy's hands and slipping the mittens on. The gloves had no fingers, just a sleeve for the thumb and a warm pocket for the remainder of the hand to sit in. As she slipped the mitten onto his right hand, something took her attention, and she looked into the boy's eyes questioningly. The tip of the little finger on his right hand was missing, as if it had been cut at the knuckle closest to the tip. The healing was so advanced that she concluded it had happened many years before, in infancy probably, because the boy was certainly less than ten years old. Willem failed to recognise the questioning look and he simply smiled back and held out his gloved hands, palms upright, in order to demonstrate to her that they fitted him perfectly. With his newly gloved hands, the boy struggled a little to remove the scarf from the lower part of his face, but eventually he managed it.

"Thank you," he mouthed silently, not wishing to offend her by speaking in church. They smiled at each other again and waited for the arrival of the priest.

It was not unusual for a mass to be celebrated on the vigil of a saint's feast day. Willem was just pleased that one had happened to arise when he was in the greatest need of shelter. Almost every day was associated with one saint or another and the boy could certainly not remember which saint happened to be blessed on this particular date. Indeed, he was not even sure what the date was. The two lit advent candles suggested that the Christ's mass was imminent. Whichever saint was blessed this day, it was clear he had great power over the devil, for so many people seemed to be greatly feared by the prospect of Satan's appearance, and all seemed to be placing great faith in the name of this particular glorified soul.

Listening to the congregation was a welcome distraction from the icy numbness of his toes, but the boy couldn't grasp why everyone was so afraid. The subject of such fervent, yet subdued, debate by the townsfolk remained a mystery to Willem, although it seemed to involve the coming of a great evil. The controversy that they discussed had occupied the thoughts of them all for some time and had laboured on long before this most nervously anticipated year neared its end.

The parish council had asked Lord Scullion to consider the matter almost two years ago, when that busybody Abel Cotes made reference to the prophecy contained in the Book of the Apocalypse. Of course, he could not read Latin or even Runes, but this did not deter him from speculation. Father Shriver, the parish priest of St Mary the Virgin church, did what he could to dispel the fear and anxiety that spread beyond this small hamlet. Indeed, most folk believed Cotes had come by the prophecy from a stranger, some passing traveller who needed a warm barn to sleep in for the night. For how else would he have come by such a revelation? He is not familiar with the Good Book, for he cannot read, everyone assured themselves.

Abel Cotes was a tenant farmer; he kept sheep and pigs at Four Thing Farm, named so because that was the fee paid by his grandfather many years ago. And he was an illiterate farmer too. The annual fee was much more than a penny now and, in addition, there were tithes to be paid on the sale of the stock. Then there was punitive compensation, as Chamberlain Balliwick called it, whenever the stock wandered into the arable fields of Holm Farm.

Balliwick's position as shire reeve was above everyone in the town, with the single exception of Lord Scullion. Even the head steward at the tower reported to the chamberlain. If his lordship was to lose so much as a lamb, it was the duty of Balliwick to ensure justice was served.

And yet, Abel Cotes had no cause to concern himself with such matters today. Today there was something of much greater import to afflict him. The matter he had been the first to raise, the coming of Satan himself.

Farmer Cotes sat at the end of the rear pew, closest to the door, ready to take his leave in haste should the uninvited guest appear suddenly. He surveyed those gathered in the church and noted the absence of fellow farmer Seth Wainthrop and several tradesmen of the town too. Not everyone, it seemed, was driven to prayer by the prophecy. Cotes knew where Scolop, Byrgan and Gripple were. Their like was neither God-fearing nor fearful of the dark angel, he thought, as he listened to the gossiping hoard who awaited the priest's arrival. Abel Cotes was smug, flushed with self-congratulatory pretension. He had warned them; indeed, he had been the first to warn them. Yet he would never say where he had garnered the information, claiming his late grandfather was a well-read man of good education and

Abel had been favoured with his scholarly doctrine. And though he was harassed and hounded for his source, he would never reveal it, nor even admit there was such a person.

From that day forward, the irresistible subject of the coming, or 'the release from the abyss', as it was referred to, had not been confined to the church. It was increasingly the subject of conversation at The Salutation Inn, led by Aldwyn Byrgan, who tended to the graveyard and buried the dead, as directed by Father Shriver. But just because he served the priest did not mean he had any particular understanding of the Lord's word, yet he had much to say on the matter and was supported in his ranting by Maggoty Gripple, the butcher. Byrgan and Gripple were the subject of another parishioner's meandering thoughts that dark evening at Saint Mary the Virgin church. A parishioner of greater authority than Abel Cotes, yet who shared the farmer's low opinion of the two men.

They were as thick as thieves, that pair, thought Oswald Balliwick as he sat in the church and listened to the gossip that surrounded him. He noted their absence from mass and consoled himself with the knowledge that Aldwyn Byrgan was a simpleton with the intelligence of a chicken. And, if the world ever needed it, Byrgan's two elder sons were living proof that two half-wits do not a full wit make. Balliwick had said as much to Byrgan's face, for he was an outspoken man whose authority in such matters could not be questioned.

In Balliwick's view, the twins shared not only a birth but a brain, too, for they did not have an ounce of sense between them. Quite how Byrgan expected to provide a living for his wife and four sons, two of whom were almost full-grown, would worry anyone with an ounce of intellect, instead of the two beans that Byrgan kept in his head. The older boys were fifteen years old now and they should each be married off to one of the many widows that resided in the town. At least that way they would have some land of their own to sow and reap, instead of digging holes for the dead and giggling like imbeciles. How many gravediggers could make a living in one small town?

The chamberlain sat huddled in the centre of the second pew from the altar and glared at the shaved tonsure on the head of a man sitting in front of him. Balliwick was his lordship's shire reeve, charged to collect tithes and revenue from the tenants of Ebbsweirmouth. Appointed by Scullion as the *probi hominess*, Balliwick was the man made virtuous by his lordship's decree; he was the man who would moderate and make judgement on all legal matters under his lordship's authority. Naturally, no verdict or resolution could be made without his lordship's accord, but he rarely interfered, for it suited him not to spend any time with the people of the village. Indeed, there was not a villager who had seen Eorl Scullion these many years past, for he chose a reclusive life and undertook his many sovereign duties through his good servant, Balliwick.

It was the chamberlain, Shire Reeve Balliwick, who was called upon to make judgement in the matter of the prophecy, too. However, the townsfolk were divided on the issue and Balliwick's master was indifferent to it. So, to keep the peace and wishing to please the shire's ecclesiastical leaders, his lordship had been pleased to give consent to the building of a new church. But there were those who said it would simply provoke the devil when he was freed from the abyss at the end of the thousand years. Others declared that only the Blessed Virgin could protect them from the coming of Satan and so the building of a new church was their only hope of salvation. The arguments continued through the spring and summer, and then came harvest time, when the whole populace was required to labour in the fields. Eventually, when the subject was raised again, the weather had changed and all hope of constructing a new stone church by the year end was lost.

In the end, nothing was agreed, which was why the pews of the small parish church of St Mary the Virgin were packed so fully that advent evening. Their attendance was less in honour of the risen Saint Lazarus and much more about the fears that gathered momentum as the December days rushed by.

One thing was certain, the devil would not be revealed by the 'noel, noel' of herald angels. There was to be a reckoning, was what Abel Cotes had said, which gave credence to the suggestion that he had been told these things by a traveller, for he would not have spoken so eloquently himself. No, there would be no greeting of Christmas joy for the men who feared God. This was a moment for those who feared evil. For there was to be a reckoning.

Here it was, on that cold Friday evening, that the anxious congregation knelt in prayer and Willem's keen eye sought out a place of safety and hiding.

Except for those few men at the inn whose souls had already yielded to a sinful life, the church swelled with every mortal being that dwelt thereabouts. And just a few days separated them from the prophecy of St John, the revelation of the evangelist.

A new face, particularly one so young, attracted the suspicious attention of the regular parishioners. And yet Willem managed to dissolve into the congregation as latecomers added to its number, moving through the transept and sitting in what few spare places there were close to the chancel where Willem sat, in the shadow of the unsteady pulpit.

The twelve tightly packed rows of pews on each side of the aisle were now almost full and the icy breath of an anxious flock rose like pious incense towards the timbered thatched roof above their heads. The boy breathed on his frozen hands, now clad in mittens, and tried to think of warmer days. Alas, the happy days of summer were but a chiming bell, and yet, sheltered from the wind, our suffering child could dream of such cheerful warmth.

The boy was not the only alien face, although it was not unusual to find a visiting friar at mass. The village was more than twenty miles from the next town in any direction and The Salutation Inn provided a welcome resting place for pilgrims and travellers alike. Not that any devout friar would consider staying overnight at an inn, certainly not when there was a parish priest as hospitable as Father Shriver to provide a bed.

Friar Sopscott had never been to Ebbsweirmouth before and was an infrequent visitor to this East Seaxe shire. Like all monks at the time, he lived according to the rule of Saint Benedict, and devoted his life to prayer and to the work of God.

He had spent most of his life at monasteries in France and the western shires. He had studied and prayed in the great temples of Fleury, Worcester, Winchester and Ramsey Abbey, and yet he sincerely preferred the impoverished surroundings of a tiny parish church such as this one. He knelt in the front pew, much to the annoyance of Oswald Balliwick, who normally occupied that seat. The friar's black tunic and scapular were easily recognisable to the chamberlain and indicated a person of high office. Unseen by those behind him, Sopscott's face was cut and bruised, and he removed the hood of his alb reluctantly, for he did not want to draw attention to his injuries. Sitting in the front row, others behind him might not notice the scars, and he chose his position for that very reason. His body, too, was battered and marked with the purple stains of a violent assault, but he turned the pain on itself and offered it up to God.

Balliwick considered his temporarily reduced station and stared unremittingly into the back of the friar's head. He convinced himself that this situation lent itself to his purpose; he was less conspicuous here and, after all, he was only there in order that he might report back to Lord Scullion on what was being said by the villagers. As shire reeve it was his duty to pass judgement on legal matters that did not require the lord's personal attention and, as such, he resolved that he would not socialise or converse with those who may appear before him at some later date. It was a convenience of his office that he enjoyed for, in truth, he despised most of those he now shared the church with.

Behind him sat the remaining members of the congregation, or 'the unwashed', as Balliwick considered them. The chamberlain looked over his shoulder, towards Abel Cotes, and noted that the farmer had placed his own salvation above that of his lordship's sheep, which had been, presumably, left to the mercy of providence. On this dark night, Abel and all the others who gathered there wanted to learn what news there was of the devil's coming, and they hoped to hear it from the priest's mouth, for they were certain he would be the first to know.

A small bell rang in the ante room, the church fell silent in solemn prayer and the heavy wooden doors of the small church were slammed shut. The congregation stood up as Father Shriver, accompanied by the two younger Byrgan brothers, entered through an archway to celebrate the vigil feast of Saint Lazarus, who Christ raised from the tomb after four days. But there were those present who feared the devil much more than God at that time. The virtuous would be rewarded, promised the priest, and the evil doers exiled to a lamentable and unending hell. They were to be the only words the priest would utter on the subject, for Father Shriver was a man of few words, even in terms of his homilies, which made him popular with most parishioners. He was a short man, with long, greasy and straggly dark hair. He grew no beard, which could at least have served to disguise his less than favourable features, consisting of several prominent warts and a particularly unattractive hooked nose.

For his part, Willem remained unseen by the aged priest, who turned from the assemblage and mumbled in Latin of a contrite heart. The two altar servers stood either side of the altar and looked innocently at their mother, who gazed back with pride. She had a good idea of what her husband and two older sons were up to that evening, and prayed for their deliverance from evil.

In the street outside, as the sanctuary bell rang and the parishioners fell silent for the vigil mass, her two older sons approached the inn, opened the door, and called to their father inside.

"The mass has begun," one of them shouted, and Aldwyn Byrgan pulled at the coat of Maggoty Gripple to signal that they must leave.

"We'll see you on the 'morrow, Hoop," called Gripple to the landlord, as they stumbled out of the door, leaving it ajar.

Without getting up from his seat, the fishmonger, Cyrus Scolop, kicked it shut with his foot and bellowed abuse at the departing pair for causing a draught.

The inn was greatly quietened by the men's departure and only Wainthrop and Scolop remained drinking with Leland Hoop. Hoop knew his customers well and found no hardship in ignoring the fisherman, who came to the inn for a single purpose, and it wasn't the idle chit-chat of the landlord. So Hoop continued his discussion with the farmer, keeping his voice low so as not to disturb the purposeful and noisy supping of Scolop, for he could display a violent temper without the need for slight or provocation.

This being so, it came as a surprise to the two men standing at the bar when Scolop began to make small talk, asking, as pleasantly as you like, whether business was good at the inn. Perhaps it is a trick, thought Hoop, expecting Scolop to fashion an argument from such a mundane question. He assured Scolop that business was just as it had always been. The less he said, the more difficult it would be for Scolop to start an altercation.

"No new guests, then?" asked the fisherman, as he returned to the counter to refill his tankard.

"Did you not hear?" replied Hoop, realising that the big man was genuinely wishing to have a conversation.

"What?" came the reply.

"A visitor to the inn died right outside on the porch this very afternoon," the innkeeper continued, pointing towards the door.

And then, much to Hoop's surprise, something even stranger happened. Scolop, who was ordinarily dispassionate on matters that did not concern him directly, became agitated and he began asking questions about the visitor of whom the innkeeper spoke.

"Who was he? What was his business here?"

But, actually, Hoop had not mentioned anything about the visitor being a man, nor that he had been here on business.

Now, it is the nature of an innkeeper to notice the smallest nuance in a conversation, in order that it might be separated from the usual gossip and mused upon later at their leisure and then turned to their own purpose. And Hoop had certainly noticed more than a nuance of suspicious behaviour in his customer's character.

"How did he die?" queried Scolop, not waiting for Hoop to answer the previous two questions.

"He was just a visitor with some business here in town. Nobody I've spoken to knows who he was. Mistress Goodlyhead examined the man and his body has been taken to the church for burial."

"And his name?" asked Scolop, with increasing urgency in his voice.

"Oh, I don't know," answered Hoop, wondering why Scolop was so interested. "He had only just arrived at the inn, when he slipped on the icy snow and struck his head on a rock. That is all we know of him, but Mildred is sure to know more tomorrow, if you are really interested."

All at once, Scolop changed his manner, noticing that Hoop was becoming aware of his peculiar interest in the man.

"Interested?" he replied. "Of course I am not interested in such matters."

Hoop was relieved that Scolop had returned to his normal self; if, indeed, bigotry and aggression could be considered normal. Then, almost as an afterthought, Hoop added that it had been a rarely busy day, as another two guests had arrived.

"Good, noble people," the innkeeper added, believing that the good character of his guests reflected well on his hostelry.

"I don't suppose you know their names either," commented Scolop, irritably.

"Of course I know their names," he replied, "for they at least had the grace not to die on my doorstep."

Scolop waited for him to finish the sentence, but his voice tailed off.

"Their names?" Scolop shouted, unable to conceal his true interest.

"Lord Ravenhead and his good woman, Lady Una," he replied and Scolop smiled. It was another rare event, noted Hoop. But it was a cynical smile of self-satisfaction.

Hoop wondered what was ailing the normally irritable man and would have asked, too, but Scolop took himself off to a dark corner of the room with a refreshed tankard in his hand. With his departure, the remaining pair continued their discussion as quietly as they could.

"And why are you not at the vigil mass, Master Wainthrop?" asked Hoop.

"I shall attend on the Sabbath as I am required to do, Hoop. Hard work is holier than hard prayer."

"Hard work!" barked Hoop. "Farming in winter?"

"'Tis hard work," whispered the farmer meekly, trying to avoid the scowls of Scolop in the corner.

As a sign of his doughtiness and undeterred by Scolop's ill manner, Hoop called into the shadows. "How were the fish today, Scolop?"

"Quieter than you, Hoop," the rude reply came.

"Do not vex him so, Hoop," suggested Wainthrop, but quietly enough so as not to be heard by the fisherman, who he feared beyond most men. "The spirits were heard in the lanes again last night," the farmer added, wishing to change the subject and avoid upsetting Scolop at the same time.

"Are they not affected by the flooding like us mortals?" asked Hoop sarcastically.

"Nay, they be spirits," the farmer assured him. "Four spirits in all, carrying a coffin along the corpse road, if the gossip be true."

Their voices grew louder as they drank and they almost forgot that Scolop still sat in silence, hidden by a shadow in the corner.

"My wife says you can see as many spirits as you wish by standing under the lychgate of the churchyard at midnight on All Hallows' Eve," Wainthrop said, more quietly than before.

"Aye, but nobody has done it, for none have been brave enough. None have seen the spirits of All Hallows. But many have seen the spirits from the drovers' lane, on the far side of the dry stone wall along the corpse road, and more frequently, too, in these few weeks past. Why should that be, Seth? Are they less afeared of one path than the other?"

"Stop your jabbering," demanded Scolop, who had returned from his seat to slam his tankard on the counter.

Hoop filled the tankard with ale again and stared at the scowling face of the fisherman. But the weatherworn face simply sneered back and the tankard was swept up in his craggy and calloused hand as he moved, once more, to the other end of the bar to avoid their tittle-tattle. He aimed another glance at Wainthrop and spat on the dusty floor.

A few minutes later, Scolop finished the remainder of his ale, tied his tankard to his belt, slammed some coins on the counter and exited without a word, deliberately leaving the door open to the cold night air in order to upset the two men who remained.

"He's off for his dinner," said Wainthrop.

"He'll be back later to wash it down," replied Hoop, who then remembered something he had seen earlier. "I saw Scolop arriving in the town early this morning, along the coastal path. Just after dawn, it was," mumbled Hoop, as he walked over to close the door behind his ill-mannered guest. But Wainthrop dismissed its relevance, suggesting that he often fished by the light of the moon.

"Not in the winter, he doesn't," replied Hoop. "I think he was looking for the spirits, because he approached the town from the small copse near Hollow Hole Cove, passing the inn as quietly as you please."

"He fishes off Pryklethorn Bay sometimes and, anyway, Holm Ford is flooded and this is the only way into the village at present."

"He was up to no good, you mark my words," muttered Hoop in a hushed tone. "What time did you arrive in town this morning?" he added.

Wainthrop stuttered and spluttered. "I don't recall. Later, or before perhaps, but not that time."

"What time?"

"At the time you saw Scolop, for I did not see him, that much is certain."

His uncertain words did not alarm the landlord who, on this occasion, failed to notice more than the nuance in the farmer's tone, as he was still wondering about Scolop's uncommon interest in his guests. "He is up to something for sure," he said.

"As likely 'tis something to do with your guests, Hoop. We heard enough questions from Cyrus to be assured of that. What is their business in Ebbsweirmouth in the raw midwinter?"

But the innkeeper simply shook his head, for his guests were people of few words.

"Are they waiting for something?" asked Wainthrop.

"Waiting for what?"

"The arrival of someone else, perhaps."

"Yes and maybe they await the coming of the devil himself, for he is due in a few days hence."

"Aye," laughed Wainthrop, as he opened the shutters and gazed from the open casement towards the church to see if the mass had ended yet. "Unless their prayers are answered, my friend," he added, speaking of those inside the church.

Hoop wiped down the top of the bar and joined the farmer at the window. They gazed down the snow-laden and deserted road, and saw Scolop stumble into his house halfway down towards the church. They both wondered what had taken him so long to make such a short journey, but neither mentioned it.

"What do you think Gripple and Byrgan are up to at this time of night?" asked the landlord.

"Byrgan's son told them that the mass had begun, so perhaps they were going to church?" replied the farmer.

"I think not, Wainthrop. They were up to no good, that's for sure."

"It's about time Byrgan's sons were married off," suggested Hoop, warming himself by the open fire. "I don't know how he makes sufficient to keep them, for they eat like horses."

"I think you mean they eat as much as a horse, Leland."

"They eat as much as one and they *eat* like one too, with their heads planted in their bowls like pigs at a trough."

"I don't know how he affords the cost of their food."

"That's because he doesn't pay his holy tithes like you and I," answered Hoop. "Byrgan and his sons work for the church, digging graves, mending and running errands for Father Shriver. And, for that, they are discharged of their tithes by the monasteries."

"Is that right? I never knew that, Hoop," replied the farmer.

"'Tis an outrage, in my view, because we all serve the parish in our way."

"Your late wife did so more than most," Wainthrop assured Hoop, before remembering that his friend never spoke of his beloved and sadly departed spouse. He swiftly changed the subject, asking whether the priest would make some comment on the coming of the devil. "Will he admit, do you think, that Cotes is right? Is the abyss to be opened?"

Hoop was still consumed with melancholic thoughts of his wife, but recovered himself for his friend's sake.

"No, he will keep silent on the matter. It is not for us peasants to know the will of God. Why else does the church write everything in Latin, which none of us may understand?" He paused and rejoined his friend at the window. "The devil's coming all right. That poor man who died this morning said as much to me. There's to be a reckoning, he said."

Back inside the church, the congregation shared the fears of Leland Hoop. The thoughts of all were not, as they should have been, fixed on the Saviour's coming, but on the lingering shadows of another grave, the deep abyss that held the dark angel himself, Satan. The congregation echoed not the joyous strains of Christmastide, nor were they appeased by Father Shriver's promise of the Lord's annual coming. Such an event, for them, lacked the corporeal promise of the apostle, the evil prophesied for this special year, set aside from all others to receive the ancient serpent. These meek souls remained irreconcilable with the Christmas message, nor could they find any solace to relieve their anxiety, for their grief was not about what had been, nor what was, but of what might be should the abyss be opened.

It was a loose comment in Father Shriver's homily that made Abel Cotes wonder whether the devil could appear as a child too, for even the most mighty of kings begin this life as a powerless suckling child. As the priest spoke, the shepherd farmer caught sight of a new face, an interloper in the guise of a young boy, at the front of the church. He was partly hidden by the pulpit but Cotes was sure he had never seen him before.

"Perhaps the devil will come in the form of a child, as the Christ child came a thousand years ago." Cotes whispered the thought as much to himself as to the widow who knelt praying next to him.

"Or a fierce dragon," the woman replied as she gave him an inquisitive look.

Cotes mused over the image of a dragon and remembered the reference to such a powerful beast sweeping the sky with its tail.

As his mind trembled towards the hastening days ahead, the priest stood with his back to the congregation, chanting in Latin words that they all recognised but few understood. By the grace of God, just as the mass was ending, Abel Cotes stood up and shouted aloud of retribution and the end of days.

"I see the dark angel coming down from heaven," he called aloud. "Holding the key to the abyss. Yeah, that is what Saint John saw. Satan was to be confined for only a thousand years. We are but one week from his coming. What are we to do, I ask, what are we to do?"

As the attention of everyone was turned towards the ranting figure of Abel Cotes, Willem smuggled himself into a narrow hollow beneath the darkened pulpit.

With a disdainful glance at the farmer, Father Shriver instructed his congregation to bow their heads before receiving his blessing. They did so, more in hope of a calming riposte than compliance, but neither came.

"*Benedicat vos Omnipotens, Deus, Pater, et Filius, et Spritus Sanctus.*"

And with this blessing ringing in their ears, the congregation left the church, huddling themselves against the cold night air. Mistress Goodlyhead looked about the departing crowd for the young boy, but he had gone. At the doorway, she stood looking down the street towards the inn, hopeful that she might see him. However, there was no sign of the boy and she made her way home, wondering how late her hardworking husband would arrive home on this cold night.

Outside the emptying church, waiting for Wainthrop to arrive, Balliwick ignored the polite goodnights conveyed to him and, in an effort to avoid any conversation with the peasant townsfolk, he struck up a conversation with the friar who had been sitting in front of him. Even through the dark night air, the observant chamberlain could see the marks on Sopscott's face.

"What happened?" Balliwick asked. "Did you fall on the way here? Mistress Goodlyhead will attend to the grazes if you wish."

"We are afflicted on every side, but we are not crushed; perplexed, not driven to despair," the friar replied, quoting Saint Paul.

Convinced by these words that the visitor was a man of great learning, Balliwick felt obliged to invite Friar Sopscott to stay at the tower, at Eorl Scullion's pleasure. He was surprised when the holy man declined the offer and chose, instead, to stay as he had originally planned, with Father Shriver.

"You will be considerably warmer on this cold night at the tower," Balliwick assured him, thinking that Scullion would be angry with him if he failed to provide the appropriate hospitality to visiting clergy. But the friar was adamant, though polite in his refusal. Sopscott was an abstemious man, who chose at every opportunity to demonstrate his preference for an impoverished life. He took little and gave much. He preferred brevity to loquaciousness, choosing contemplative silence to the rhetoric of the world, and humble and modest surroundings to the grandiose. And yet, he understood the politics that came with his position, so he accepted the chamberlain's alternative invitation to attend mass at the tower chapel on Sunday.

"Will Lord Scullion not be attending mass at the church?" he asked.

"Eorl Scullion attends private mass at the tower chapel. Father Shriver celebrates the mass there after he has done so here each Sunday. He then breaks the fast with his lordship and I hope you will choose to do the same. I am sure that Eorl Scullion would be very pleased if you could join us also."

The friar agreed and, when Wainthrop arrived, the visiting holy man accompanied Shriver to his modest home behind the church while Balliwick left with his companion along the narrow road that led to the coastal path. The tiny thatched houses on each side of the road rested in darkness, as did the street that separated them, except for the hazy moonlight that cast a dim brightness across the peaceful scene. With the exception of young Willem, who remained hidden in the cranny below the pulpit, all but one man went to their beds that night.

Leland Hoop sat in a high-backed chair that stood by the open casement of the inn and gazed out on the dispersing crowd. The innkeeper had struggled to find sleep these past three months, since his wife died. He avoided their marital bed and refrained from changing the blanket that covered it. Instead, he would sit at the narrow casement, keeping his lonely watch over the empty street. He got up from his wooden chair, tossed another log on the fire and went to the alcove room that led from one corner of the bar. He removed the blanket from the bed and wrapped it about him before slumping back into the chair to continue his vigil. He pulled the comforting fleece towards his face and immersed himself in the soft remembrance of her. The redolence of her memory faded all too quickly with each empty day and every lonesome night, and he sat rueing the time that it would be lost to him forever. He, like Willem, sat thinking back on a glorious summer. And, just like the orphan, it had been a harvest like no other.

Fanny Hoop and her husband, like all good servants of his lordship, had joined the harvest as the remnants of that hot summer died like the wilting essence of his wife on the blanket. The gathering in from the fields required everyone to attend. It was a jolly time, a time when the townsfolk were united in their efforts, for all benefited from it. Each family owned one hide of arable land with the required tithe paid to the eorl. But there were also the fields at Holm Farm to be reaped for the benefit of his lordship. Everyone laboured those long autumn days, from dawn to dusk, until the crops were all gathered into the barn. On that final day of the harvest, only Leland had been allowed to depart earlier than the rest, for it was his pleasure to make the harvest punch, filling a large cauldron with the fruits of the fields.

Yet, in that fateful hour after he had left the field, tragedy struck. Fanny had been working as hard as anyone in the afternoon heat. Then, suddenly, without warning, she groaned and collapsed amongst the stubbled corn. Mildred Goodlyhead, who was labouring close by, was called, for everyone around poor Fanny knew she was dead and Mildred was the seeker of the dead, appointed so by Chamberlain Balliwick himself. It was Mistress Goodlyhead's duty to determine the cause of her death and to eliminate foul play, in case Balliwick was required to administer justice to the sad affair.

It was not foul play that had felled the delicate Fanny Hoop, but a faint heart that stopped so abruptly on that once happy harvest day. Her body was wrapped in a sheet, as the labourers had done with the gathered corn all day, and then carried back to the town along the drove roads. It was laid outside the lychgate at the church and Mildred walked as quickly as she could to fetch Leland Hoop, who she could see standing outside the inn, preparing the cauldron of punch. He was staring, in deep contemplation, back towards her, for he knew that matters were not right. Never had he seen a parcel of corn laid so lovingly on the ground. Why was it not being taken to the barn with the rest of the harvest? And why were they laying it there, outside the church? Moreover, why did it look so much like a shroud? And why were the gatherers so silent, why so mournful?

Each evening of the harvest ended with a procession of merriment along the drove roads back to town, with the labourers carousing and ringing bells as they marched. And yet, no such merriment accompanied their journey this day; no carousing and happy laughter, no bells on their ankles, only a mournful procession and a silent column of faces looking towards the anxious Leland Hoop, who now stood awaiting the word of Mildred Goodlyhead. And the word was 'departed', delivered in a sympathetic tone and wrapped in a multitude of other words that Leland did not hear.

The publican gathered his grief away, just as the harvest had been gathered away, and he never showed it to another soul after that day. His grief was one wrapped in privacy, a selfish grief that could not be shared in case it should be diminished or remedied. He did not want it remedied; he did not want his grief to end, for it was his solace, his comfort. He could not return to the marital bed if it was not to be shared with Fanny. So he sat, wrapped in her essence, staring down an empty, snow-laden street, hoping she might one day return.

All the talk of spirits in the corpse road had a greater resonance for Leland. For others, it caused anxiety and fear, but to him it raised hope that he might see her one more time.

So, each day he would act the part. He would join in the jolly banter, fill their tankards and share the bawdy humour of his patrons. But the night was his to share with Fanny and he did not want to waste a moment of it by sleeping.

~~~~~

After the church door slammed and the congregation departed, Willem expected to be drowned in a familiar darkness. But somewhere a light still shone, for this was no time to be extinguishing the light of the world. Not that the younger Byrgan boys knew this; they were just as doltish as their older brothers and had forgotten to snuff out the candles after the mass.

As the people left, an icy wind almost extinguished the advent candles that remained burning on the altar. The congregation dispersed quickly, no one wishing to come upon the spirits of the drove roads at this late hour. Many were certain that it would be these same spirits that would herald the arrival of the devil, not angels singing their noel.

Ten minutes passed and in the street outside a group of men could be heard, stumbling home to their beds. And then, nothing; silence triumphed over the day and flickering shadows were given life by the wavering flames of the tapers.

Willem remained hidden, alone alongside the bones of a long-forgotten saint, who rested beneath the black, purgatorial rails that supported the precariously unstable pulpit. And there the boy sat, waiting to ensure that nobody remained in the church. He looked at his new mittens and rubbed his hands together. He thought about what the farmer had shouted from the back of the church and wondered what the words meant. He was sure he was a farmer for the boy had lived on a farm for the last four years and recognised the drab clothes, the red, scaly granular skin and the unyielding smell of dung and hard work. Perhaps he should have told them about the sign he had seen on his arrival, for it must have meant something. After all, the blood had risen from the abyss that the man spoke of. Naturally, the boy had remained silent, for it was not in his character to speak out. It was in his nature to be inconspicuous, especially today, amongst strangers.

Through a splintered gap in the pulpit frame, two candles still lit the area of the church around the chancel, and another lit the apse where a statue of the Virgin stood gazing down. She looked serene, like the angel he had met that summer day, or perhaps dreamed of, because it was within the power of dreams to make themselves real.

Willem was tired after his long walk and could easily have fallen asleep in the small nook in which he rested below the pulpit. But he was too cold to sleep and, more importantly, there were noises to be identified and dimly lit shapes to be dismissed. They were unlikely to be rats as it was too cold for such creatures and, in any case, no rat would be seeking food in a church, but rather in one of the many tithe barns that littered the fields thereabouts. The sounds were simply creaking shutters and doors, the whistling of the wind through the eaves. Or, perhaps they were something more sinister. What had that man been shouting about as Willem sneaked into his hiding place? An angel coming from heaven. Yes, of course, that much made sense. The angel of the Lord announcing the Saviour's coming to the shepherds in the fields around Bethlehem, even Willem had been taught that much. But he had never heard of an angel holding the keys to the abyss. Why was everyone so alarmed at such words, the boy wondered. What was an abyss? The man had said we were but one week from the coming of Satan and yet that could not happen, not on the day of the Christ's mass.

Once the boy was convinced that everyone had left and the priest was not going to return, he wrestled himself from the small cranny that he occupied beneath the pulpit, and went to the altar to warm his hands on the two candles that stood there. Very little heat was generated by them and so he moved to the Lady altar, which was no more than a small alcove to the left of the main altar. A single but larger candle burned there and, though this produced less heat than the others, he found the sorrowful eyes of the Virgin comforting. He warmed his cold hands against the flame for a few moments and then went to the first pew that faced the statue before kneeling in prayer for a few moments.

Not surprisingly, he found himself seeking her aid and succour and, once he had recited all the prayers he had learned from Mistress Cuddlewick, he sat back on the roughly hewn wooden bench. His head remained bowed for a few moments, but now he was thinking of more practical matters; of how he might secure employment to pay for food and find a more permanent shelter to sleep tomorrow. And, beyond that, he hoped to understand a little more about the time he had spent at this place, before he was taken from here as a small child. He was an orphan, but even orphans have a mother at some time, even if only for the briefest moment at birth. If he came from Ebbsweirmouth, then perhaps his real mother was still here if she lived, or was buried in this graveyard if she had died.

Willem recalled his conversations with Mistress Cuddlewick in those pre-harvest days of summer, when there had been little to do other than watch the barley rise. She had never confirmed that his parents were dead. Nor was she able to say whether he had a brother or a sister.

As the candles flickered on the altar, a grey shadow appeared on the floor beside him. It didn't occur to him that such a shadow could be cast forward by a flame on the altar ahead of him. Nor was he to know that a similar, inverted shadow had been cast by Saint Lazarus on his four-day wait in the dark tomb at Bethany. The daydream of his older brother halted abruptly and he gazed at the shadow on the stone floor of the church.

Willem was still trying to determine, in his mind, where the source of the shadow might be, when he sensed the presence of someone at his shoulder. He had been convinced that he was alone in the church, but someone else was there too and he wondered, for a moment, whether it was the dark angel that the man had spoken of before the mass ended. He didn't want to turn around as he could feel the icy breath of another soul behind him. He pondered, nervously, whether any angel, dark or otherwise, might have such icy breath. The angel he had met that distant summer had the fragrance of green apples and of the wild dog rose.

It was dark and only the light of the candle on Our Lady's altar prevented pitch blackness on that side of the church.

The boy remained sitting and he instinctively returned to his prayer to a not-too-distant God; a prayer for mercy. He wondered whether to kneel but instead, emboldened with courage and without rising from his seat, he slowly turned his head to look over his right shoulder. He gasped and the sharp intake of breath made the candle flicker in the apse where the Virgin stood. The greyish outline of a man appeared behind him.

In truth, the man was less than thirty years old, but he appeared much older. His face was concealed by a hooded tunic and, in the darkness, he was as much a shadow as a human being.

"Are you sheltering from the cold?" the boy asked timidly.

"No, I do not feel the cold," the shadow answered. The voice was hollow, like the shallow breeze that hissed as it passed between the narrow cracks in the church wall. It sounded like the expiring words of a dying man, each word concealed within a rasping breath.

The boy reached out and touched the hand to see if the figure was mortal, for the voice did not appear so. The iciness of the fleshy fingers startled him, but the shadow remained motionless, not moving the hand when it was touched by the boy. Willem went to speak but waited in anticipation that his elder wished to say more.

"Have you travelled far in the storm?" the hoarse voice asked.

"A full day's walk," the boy replied.

"Were you afraid?"

"No, Sir."

The man considered his brief reply, uttered the word 'courage', then asked why his first port of call had been the church.

"For shelter and warmth."

"It is strange," said the man ruefully, "how, when the power of heaven is expressed so fiercely, we seek solace in heaven's earthly home. Do you have faith?"

"I attend mass on the Sabbath, Sir."

"Faith isn't born of compliance, nor in the acceptance of what will be," the man replied earnestly. "But through a fearlessness of knowing that death is not the end."

There was a moment of silence as the boy wondered what to say next.

"Are you a familiar of this town, Sir?" the boy asked eventually, through chattering teeth. He was still so cold that he found it difficult to talk in anything more than short sentences and he clenched his teeth tightly when listening.

"I know only what I have seen here these few hours past and what I might see in the three days yet to come."

"What business do you have hereabouts?" asked the boy.

"I have no business here now," he answered. "I simply wait."

"Wait for what?"

"My guide."

The boy didn't understand the man's answers but felt the need to ask his name.

"Darrayne," the shadow replied, "for my father was a bailiff with jurisdiction over a large shire south of here." He paused, for he did not wish to discuss his own life, but to learn more of the boy's. But Willem was still too cold to speak at length and the man seemed to understand this, so they sat for a few moments in silence.

"So," the older man continued, realising that the boy was too cold to talk. "I am Darrayne and was known as

Darrayne the Younger, or Little Darrayne in my youth." As he spoke, the outline of a man began to take shape from what had been a mere shadow. His breath could be seen in the cold air and rose heavenward like a pious prayer towards the roof beams.

"And when you grew to a man, what were you called then?" the boy asked.

"You ask a great many questions," the man sighed in a questioning tone of his own as if, perhaps, he no longer possessed a name. "I was known as the Watchman, or Watchman Darrayne, for that is what I did and my keen sword favoured me to be the best at my work."

"And what was that?"

"I was the officer of the watch. My father travelled little and believed much in the law. For my part I did not follow where he led."

Each time the man spoke, a draught blew the tiny flame of the candle on the Lady altar. And in that flickering light the boy caught a further glimpse of the man's face. This time it revealed the strange staring of his eyes, as if he gazed unknowingly into the empty space between the two voices.

"Are you blind, Sir?"

"To this world, yes," the man answered reluctantly. "For I do not see the world as you see it." He paused before adding gratefully that he had, with God's grace, seen all he wished to see.

"You are a learned man, Sir," Willem answered, but the man simply shook his head.

"And you," he asked, "what learning have you received?"

"I have learned little and visited nowhere of consequence, Sir," the boy answered.

The man smiled. "I have visited the soul of Christendom itself, the Holy Empire of Rome."

The boy gasped at the thought of seeing the holy city.

"And I have seen the thorn that touched the Christ's brow," Darrayne added, receiving another exclamation of wonder.

"The Glastonbury thorn was planted by Joseph of Arimathea himself, in the kingdom of Wessex, and it flowers every Christmas."

"And you have seen it?" the boy asked, disbelievingly, but regretted his doubting words immediately.

"Yes, I have felt the sharp needles that pierced the head of our Saviour. And I have also felt the pain of the Virgin's heart, just as she did at the loss of the beloved one."

"How so?" the boy asked, looking up at the darkened statue of the Blessed Virgin.

"When you have known love and great friendship, you will know how this is so."

The man's grey and translucent eyes wept and the boy shared his grief.

"Do not be melancholy," the boy said, deflecting the sadness, and the man nodded knowingly. "For I am an orphan, a waif," the boy added, "and yet I am rarely saddened by life's misfortunes. Perhaps I expect little from life, for it delivers little in my experience."

He looked at the man, who was clearly much older than he was, and regretted speaking of experience. He apologised, saying he was too young to speak to one so wise and with such knowledge of the world that he had.

"Experience is not measured by time, young one, but by what is achieved in that time."

"What is there for an orphan to experience, except loneliness and serfdom?" replied the boy and the Watchman responded with the words of scripture.

"Job said, 'is not man's life on earth nothing more than pressed service, his time no better than hired drudgery?'"

"As I say, Master, you are a learned man, as was Job if that is what he said, for he is right."

"He cannot be right," answered Darrayne. "This cannot be all of it; there must be something else."

"Not for an orphan."

"Are your parents dead?"

"I am told so, Sir."

"Did your other relatives not look after you?"

"I have none."

"What of your godparents?"

"I do not know them, Sir."

The statement caused the man to sigh and he looked with benevolence at the boy.

"What is your earliest recollection then?"

"Working in the employ of his lordship at Scullion Tower, before I was despatched to a life of labour at a farm one long day's walk from here."

"You recall nothing before that?"

He shook his head. "I have dreams."

"And what do they tell you?"

"That there is a better life. Or *was* a better life, perhaps."

"I see," he said, the words tumbling reluctantly from his lips. "And you have no memory of Haeferingas?"

The boy returned a quizzical look, for the place the man spoke of was unknown to him.

"Where is Haeferingas?"

"It is a shire, a small kingdom not many miles south of here," he answered, before capitulating to the boy's questions and returning to his own life.

"Who do you serve?"

"I served my lord and was the best watchman; the keenest eye; I travelled afar and yet have far to travel these next three days hence."

"You long to move and I long to stand still," replied Willem. "I simply want to find my home, my true home, my family."

"I have been presented with a homeless child this Christmastide," the man mumbled to himself, as the two sat beneath the shadow of the Virgin. "And I am charged to fulfil my oath."

The building turned quiet as the wind dropped outside and they both sat looking at each other until the older man broke the silence.

"Do you ever wonder why God has created us each in a particular fashion? Each allotted a different challenge in this life?"

The boy simply looked at him, full of wonderment for a moment, before replying. "The world is filled with good and evil, Sir. It has always been so, I believe. We are created that way for a purpose."

"You think God made evil?" The shadow seemed amazed that someone should think so.

"If not, it must be from another world, for God created all things in this one," the boy replied.

"There is no need to seek in other worlds for evil, for there is sufficient here for our fear," the Watchman replied.

The boy gave thought to what he had said and answered that he had seen the power of evil in the storm that evening.

"There was a moment when I could not continue and wished only to die out there on that lonely cliff top."

"Yes, but God intervened and gave you courage, the first virtue of destiny." Darrayne paused for a moment and considered his next words carefully.

"The power of man's evil is greater still than the might of the wind you felt on the cliff top," he added. "Girdle your strength for the tests that are yet to come."

"You speak with certainty of something that you cannot possibly know."

"Arm yourself not with certainty, my young friend, but with the second virtue of faith and a chaste heart. For chastity is the angelic virtue and gives light to understanding, and you will only find what you search for through understanding."

"You speak of faith, chastity and understanding as things to be purchased on our journey through life, Sir." The boy spoke quietly, for the long day was beginning to overpower him.

"The sixteen virtues of destiny are not to be purchased, for they are gifts. Have faith in the courage you have been given and in the creator that gave you that courage."

"Faith to me, Master," the boy replied with a long yawn, "is like a wavering flame, made so by the ill winds of providence."

The boy's words faded into the shadows, sleep overwhelmed his tired body and yet faith rested upon him.

Chapter Three

Chastity

Enlightened and acquainted as we now are with this small town and its arcadian citizens, who wait impatiently for enlistment into our story, we must take a brief sojourn, in order that we might firstly consider the words of the Watchman and then familiarise ourselves with others outside this place who may have some bearing on the events that are to take place. This excursion is, as the fallen snow, a temporary change of landscape and entirely the device of the original storyteller, for the manner and order in which the story is told is of his making. Nevertheless, having now heard from the Watchman of the place called Haeferingas, it follows that we must familiarise ourselves a little with that place also.

In itself, it is not unlike many other small towns that litter the countryside and punctuate the abundant forests of this distant time. It is similar, in many respects, to Ebbsweirmouth, except it is nearly a day's walk from the sea, situated as it is between the great eastern ocean and the Roman fortress city of Londinium, which is now known as Lundenburh.

Haeferingas was so named, I suppose, because it was a pasture where goats, cattle and sheep once grazed, for that is what the word means. It is also the home of the horned church, yet why someone would choose to adorn a holy place with a cow's horn is a mystery to this day. One may only assume that it was in recognition of the beast that provided its inhabitants with their livelihood.

Close to Haeferingas, there is a place called the Ford of Reeds, which was later named Reedford, or the Red Bridge. Hidden by woods, set between this place and the estuary of the mighty Tamesis, stands a small convent named Eling Priory. Unlike many convents of that time, this Benedictine nunnery did not permit the wearing of colourful clothing, or the painting of faces. The accommodation, even for those times, was primitive, and the food was very basic fare.

The place was ruled by a tyrant of an abbess, or prioress to be more accurate, whose principles were based on poverty and an unequivocal submission to the will of God. However, most of its inhabitants were not there through the will of God, but more directly by the will of their fathers who, in all but a few cases, were unable to provide the required dowry in order for their daughters to marry. Of course, the best convents, like a good husband, also required a dowry, but Eling Priory was not considered the best, but rather the most impoverished of convents. Its boarders were required to submit to their newly acquired and greatly reduced circumstances and live a life of devotion, chastity and silence.

Chastity has not been treated well by time and has been diminished by many as simply the moderation of carnal desire, and yet it is a virtue of much greater eminence. Chastity is the cousin of prudence, a cardinal virtue praised highly in the passages of scripture. By some it is often called prudence, but others refer to it as temperance. Under the Roman occupation it was once named auriga virtutum, the charioteer of the virtues, for it guides all other virtues by setting rules and measures. It is chastity, temperance, or prudence that guides the judgement of conscience and moderates the selfish pursuit of pleasure, for temptation lingers in the shadows, which is why abstinence and diligence are its guardians. And it is why the sisters of Eling Priory live their lives exposed to the light of truth. There are no doors to the cells and no secrets from the prioress.

Of course, chastity does indeed moderate carnal desires and, to the sinful, it appears as the enemy of love. And yet it is not, for it is simply the friend of humility and the enemy of indulgence. When chastity is accompanied by silence, as it is in the order of this Benedictine convent, humility is most clearly demonstrated by obedience and by the keeping of any opinions to oneself. The gift of chastity arms us against the influence of hostility, temptation and corruption, and is the third of the virtues of destiny.

Eling Priory was built from the ruins of a deserted Roman villa, much of which remains, including the original gate over which an incomplete Latin inscription is carved that includes the words 'sedecim virutum fatum'. The main building is enclosed within two cloisters that are joined at the front by a large gate and at the rear, where they both lead into the chapel. The cloisters appear like a small piece of Rome left stranded so far from home and abandoned here, close to the Ford of Reeds. The first cloister is called the way of reason and the second is named the way of righteousness. As the sisters walk around this most sheltered part of the priory, they stop to kneel at intervals, to pray beneath a statue or a picture of a saint. On the wall by the gate, two words are inscribed for all to see: 'courage' and 'honour'. At intervals along the way of reason there are six more words written on the wall: 'chastity', 'piety', 'hope', 'knowledge', 'wisdom' and 'counsel'. Similarly, along the way of righteousness there are also *six words: 'patience', 'faith', 'prudence', 'temperance', 'justice' and 'mercy'. Above the door that leads to the priory chapel there are two more words: 'understanding' and 'love'. Both paths lead to the same destination.*

Over the years, the nuns have written their innermost thoughts on the stone work and visitors now have to kneel or bend over to read the words inscribed there. 'Be true unto yourself', says one. 'Be quiet and listen to the silence', says another. 'Every saint has a day' is written beneath one statue and it is possible to read so many meanings into its brevity.

So, this is Eling Priory and we are here to familiarise ourselves with one particular resident. Not the tyrannical abbess of whom we spoke earlier, but a sister who is devout and mute in equal measure.

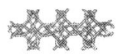

The steps of her unshod feet did not disturb the hushed and darkened surroundings of the priory as Sister Philomena made her familiar way from the small dormitory, around the decorative cloister. Today, she had chosen to take the way of reason. She paused by the word 'hope' and offered a silent prayer, before continuing along the narrow corridor of pillars towards the chapel, which was situated at the far end of the large building.

Hope seemed such an indulgent grace, out of step with her worthier sisters, just as Sister Philomena was. The cold, stone floor added to the chill she felt beneath her thin black tunic. She reflected indulgently on her lost love, who rested in the ice cold tomb, and the all-consuming loss seized her soul. Even now, all these years later, when she woke up in limbo — that realm between heaven and earth, betwixt sleeping and waking — she resided for a moment in a world where he still existed, still lived, still slept by her side; a place where the words of the Watchman had never been delivered. Such a world evaporated so easily, even in that darkest moment before dawn.

Except for the flickering light of the small candle that stood precariously in its holder, complete darkness reigned. She held it upright in one hand and sheltered the flame with the other, for it was in danger of being extinguished by the draughts that made harsh penance of the damp air in the old stone convent.

As she entered the chapel through the archway, the uncertain flame quivered, but still illuminated the frescoes along the far wall. A long-bearded hermit gazed down at her innocence and protected his own from the unveiling light.

Sister Philomena lit the candles on the high altar and checked that everything was ready for the dawn service of lauds. The Bible on the lectern was open at the correct page and she had prepared notes for the priest about Saint Flannan, whose feast day it was. They were brief, for her written word was poor and the prioress criticised her often about her untidy handwriting. 'Irish martyr from Turlough, consecrated by Pope John IV', was all she had written, but it would be sufficient for the priest to test the postulants after the service.

Unlike the earthly quiet of the snow-clad land outside, an unnatural silence filled the chapel and would suffer disturbance only from mortal intervention. The Liturgy of the Hours was a rare opportunity for the daughters of Christ to speak. They would sing psalms as loudly as they could without attracting the attention of the prioress.

Sister Philomena stepped down from the altar and knelt, as if in solemn prayer. In truth, she had succumbed to impure thoughts, for recollections of her past life had appeared in a dream before she awoke and they now continued to haunt her musing. She must caution herself against such inappropriate thoughts, the abbess had said. When a young woman chose to devote herself to the cloistered life of contemplative prayer, she must think only of celestial matters, not of her past experiences. Sister Philomena looked about her and tried to submerge herself in her duties and forget all such remembrances.

A sister of the Benedictine order represented the lowest echelon of the church, a position of choice. Except she wasn't sure it had been her choice. There was no choice. In fact, the only choice she had made was a name. The young novice had chosen not to honour her mother by naming herself Cynthia in her new life. Choosing the saint's name she wished to adopt for the rest of her life had been the final act of self-determination for Sister Philomena.

The abbess, unaware of the dishonour served upon the girl's mother, had considered it a noble choice. To assume the name of a holy martyr demonstrated that the young postulant fully understood the narrow path she had chosen for herself. But then, the abbess did not know the true motive for the young woman's choice of name.

"The feast day of Saint Philomena is the eleventh day of August," declared the prioress from memory. "*Filia luminis,*" she continued, "means the daughter of light. Saint Philomena stands for purity and obedience."

Obedience had little to do with it for, in truth, Sister Philomena desperately wanted to hold on to a small fragment of her past life, one moment that would forever remind her that there was once joy in this lonely world. She knew well the feast day of her chosen saint. It was a day fashioned forever in the heart and mind of this poor nun, just as it was in the hearts and minds of all those who occupied the widows' hides and, indeed, all those who had suffered bereavement on that sad day at Maeldun.

The vow of silence that so many of the postulants raged against suited Sister Philomena, for she never wished to discuss her previous life before Fling Priory. Once she had confessed her sins as a novice, she never needed to speak of those deeds and thoughts again. A visiting friar, of the same order and who had been ordained in the priesthood, as many friars were in these times, had given her absolution. Her sins were no longer to be found in the past, for they were extinguished by the blessed grace of God in a single act of contrition. Whatever had happened during those summer days just before Maeldun had been erased, except in her heart and in her mind. They were a secret, hidden in a place where secrets were not permitted.

As she knelt, she wondered whether she should now confess that she did not want to forget the events in her life before Maeldun. Was it a sin to retain the memory of such things, to hold on to them so selfishly? The abbess would certainly think so, but it was for the priest who heard her confession to decide or, better still, the young acolyte who had stayed here in the company of his renowned master all those years ago, like her, just beginning his long ministry in the faith.

In a very real sense, the young woman's life had been condensed into a single summer filled with previously unknown pleasures and unimaginable grief. Before that, she was a child who had lived, as most girls do, in the shadow of her brother. For a son represents an heir, someone to continue the family line and, perhaps, the family business. A daughter, on the other hand, is but an encumbrance, chattel to be traded or a dowry to be paid.

There were seven sisters who lived at Eling Priory and served in silence alongside Sister Philomena. They were sisters in the order and sisters in life too. Each was placed here by a man lamenting his hardship at fathering such an unfortunate brood.

What harsh penance it must be, thought Sister Philomena, that sisters should be constrained from discourse with their own sister. What good is silence that prevents the declaration of sisterly love? What ill would befall them if they were permitted to utter a simple word of love or sibling kinship? It was not a pleasure she missed herself, but knew how it affected the sisters, for their sadness was apparent each day as they glanced at each other across a silent dormitory or chapel.

Sister Philomena had no blood sisters to further burden her father's purse. Nor was her confinement the fault of an empty purse. Her internment was the result of an empty heart, for she had lost her father's love. She had sinned against both her father in heaven and her father on earth. And so, her earthly father had taken everything from her and placed her at the mercy of the other, to dwell in silence, cloistered from the world forever at Eling Priory. In his eyes, she was less of this world than her deceased brother.

In the eight years she had dwelled here, her father had never visited her once, nor had he sent any message to her, although the prioress believed he had.

Maeldun had changed much for many, but few had suffered so grievously as Sister Philomena. Silence for her was as vast as the snow-driven lands that now surrounded Eling Priory. She wondered whether that young acolyte ever thought of her confession. He did not judge her, nor condemn her.

"Forgive me, Father, for I have sinned," she had whispered through the metal grill that separated them. "I have sinned against my earthly father and my father in heaven." She then told him everything, just as she had been instructed to do. All sins must be wiped from her soul before she donned the back habit of the Benedictine order.

For his part, the young friar had listened patiently, whispering an occasional acknowledgement in return for her impassioned supplication. She spoke of her past life, her status, her circumstances, her previous identity and every small detail of what had happened over those last few months before her father had sent her away.

Her melancholic voice revealed the secrets of her heart and when she finished speaking, he responded, quietly, thoughtfully.

"You seek God's dispensation for your sins and yet I sense no regret in your voice for what happened before you took holy orders."

It was as if he had looked into her soul. She wanted to speak but knew her petition had concluded and she had no right to add a codicil to it.

"However," he continued, "I believe you are truly sorry for offending God and, yes, for offending your father too. It is not a condition of your penance to forget what happened. It is enough that you recognise and repent your sin in the sight of God and I am certain you have done this. As Sister Philomena, you will live a new life. You will not forget your past life, but you must not envy it, either. In envy lies resentment and malice, and there is no room for such vices in the Benedictine order."

The friar paused for a moment and leaned closer to the grill. "Your penance is to think on a different virtue each day and covet each one, rather than your previous life. Silence, in itself, is not a virtue and yet it promotes meditation, and through meditation you shall become virtuous."

He reminded her that Saint Philomena, whose name she had chosen, represented humility, obedience and charity, and instructed her to use these as the foundation for her new life at the priory.

"Your future and that of those you love is etched into the walls of the cloister at Eling Priory. The sixteen virtues of destiny are there to remind you and give you strength," he told her. "Think on these and pray to be blessed by their power."

So, each day, Sister Philomena paused in front of one of the words that were carved at intervals on the cloister wall and considered the merits of it as she prayed. As the days passed, each one became a stone in the new home she had now built for herself. Fortitude and patience were its cornerstones, mercy and chastity its casements, and hope its open door.

Just as the snow lies silent upon the earth, so Sister Philomena remained mute these long years past, and she prayed each day for the silence also of her confessor, for her shame was great. The silence purchased by her father was made less virtuous by his motives and, though he lamented her absence, he slept contented each night that the world would never know the secret shared by them alone.

Secrets only remain so when taken to the grave, unspoken. Whilst people live, their deeds live with them and, yes, their secrets too. Her comfort rested in the inviolability of the confessional and its sacramental seal. A priest, even a monk who has been ordained, is forbidden to betray the words of the penitent sinner. Even then, her confessor had not seen her; they were separated by a metal grill and, moreover, he had been a visiting friar who was unlikely to return to Eling Priory. Nevertheless, the silence of secrets and even those of the confessional, sometimes yields, just as the melting snow does in the warm light of day.

As the young monk had said, silence, in itself, is not a virtue. It is not practised for its own sake, but in the object of some good. Silence should be inconspicuous and yet it was not so in Eling Priory. It was a fabricated silence, born of decree, not the uncompelled silence of true devotion. This silence was absent in the humility that Sister Philomena sought to use as a foundation in her new religious life. And so, each day, as she fulfilled her penitential obligation, she thought deeply on another virtue and pondered on its relationship to silence, then prayed that she might yet find honour and contentment in her new life.

Eling Priory was removed from the world in many senses, yet the walls of a convent are as porous as any other where gossip is concerned; more so, perhaps, when that gossip refers to the very faith and beliefs upon which such an establishment is founded. The Apocalypse of the beloved disciple had been created in just such a forsaken and exiled place as the priory. Alone on Patmos Isle, Saint John had composed his prophetic account of the final battle between good and evil. For this battle to take place, the Revelator knew that evil itself must be released from the abyss. But why one thousand years?

Sister Philomena left the chapel and walked back through the cloister, along the way of righteousness. She paused below the word 'patience', bowed her head in prayer and then returned to her cell and tidied her cot. She brushed the dust from her tunic and white scapular, and knelt to say a prayer of vocation.

The muted glow of the flickering candle cast grey figures on the stone wall of the dank, airless room. She opened a small ornate wooden box that rested by her cot. It was the only personal item she was allowed to keep there. This permission would not have been granted had the prioress known the true significance of its contents. She believed they were just some dried petals to relieve the smell of the damp, stale air. But those petals held much more than the faint odour of a summer these five years past. The box contained memories of a conspiracy of intrigue, designed to satisfy a craving in her heart that would never die.

The plan had been simple. Her co-conspirator would call at the priory with a forged note from her sick father, summoning Sister Philomena to attend his bedside. Even the heartless prioress would not deny such a request, particularly one that came from a generous benefactor to the convent.

Success for the plan had been assured because Sister Philomena's father never had contact with the priory, or indeed his daughter for that matter, so he would not know of her brief sojourn beyond the convent walls.

For his part, the co-conspirator had arranged everything in detail. A meeting place was located and even a small bribe was paid to a maid, who would ensure the attendance of the other party. It could only be for an hour, or perhaps two. But at least she would see him once more.

And so it had been, that blessed day at the onset of summer. A picnic in the sheltered corner of a barley field, protected by two high hedgerows. A still summer day filled with the dusky fragrance of the dog rose that peered from the blackthorn hedge. That same dog rose from which she had plucked the pink velvet petals, along with the cream flowers of the cow parsley that grew in abundance along the field's hedge and promised so much for the summer to come.

Sister Philomena gently closed the lid of the small box and prepared herself for the morning service of lauds. Through the pale light of dawn the cloister outside her cell began to take shape and she paused for a moment to recall that shaded bower of a summer past. She extinguished the flame on the candle and picked up a small hand bell. After genuflecting before the cross on the wall, she began her walk around the cloister, gently ringing the bell to wake her colleagues from their nightly rest. Through a hole in the convent wall, where coal tits nested in the spring, she gazed out upon the fields of cream-coloured snow and, thinking upon the fairy lace and cow parsley that it reminded her of, she was lost in a moment of reflection and transported to a sweet meadow in a land where time passes differently to our mortal world. And then, beyond her timeless journey to that distant land, she was stirred from her wanderings by the sound of morning prayer being resounded by her colleagues. By dint of such fairy power a prayer is whispered and heard beyond this earthly realm, that chastity might be gifted upon a pilgrim soul.

Chapter Four

Patience

Crisp is the winter air and soft the fallen snow. The contrast and contradiction of patience is as discernible as this. And now, our story fashions an unearthly aspect as the sky is blackened by deepening cloud and a waning moon. The cold breath of Boreas relents and an empyrean stillness is restored to the dark December night. And with it a chaste whiteness covers the desolate land that separates Ebbsweirmouth from Eling Priory, where maids in supplicant prayer do kneel.

The blizzard has ceased and the biting wind has lost its sting. The soft murmuring of a shivering boy is persuaded to quietness by sleep, and the earth adopts the pallid hue of death.

And now we see the purpose of the storyteller's diversion. For here is silence of a different persuasion. Not the holiest silence of the virtuous soul, but still one of heaven's making.

There is a patient piety and haunting silence about freshly settled snow. While creation sleeps, the coldest season stills and censors the world to its own design. Winter stands predominant in its ability to alter a landscape so comprehensively in such a short time. The slow onset of spring is tardy by comparison. The long-

anticipated glimpse of fauna on the forest floor, the budding seedtime that sets the harshest seasons apart as spring labours towards the vivid hues of summer, cannot change the countryside whilst the world sleeps. And the dog days of summer made tolerable by the shade of a canopied wood are sterile by comparison. For, day by day, all too lazily, the lethargy of summer and the accession of autumn turns the bowered wood to sparse, splintered branches, like witches' fingers, all gnarled and spindly, and laid brittle and naked to a mocking world. Old oaks and saplings too, which took a season's labour to blossom full in their verdant green, are now edged with the whiteness of winter with just a night's work. Lifeless, lingering winter, benumbed and strangely tranquil, demonstrates an energy shrouded in darkness.

And so, heaven's pale gift is bestowed upon the world. The mute serenity and calm reticence of winter made perfect by the virgin snow that covers the land and mourns the loss of another year.

For us, the settled snow provides a fine, blank sheet of notepaper upon which we may pen our ancient story of a Christmas past. Whatever ailed the wind along Willem's long journey that previous evening has now been remedied in heaven. Those that have wares to sell stir themselves from their beds. For all his demonic fears, Abel Cotes has sheep to tend and fields to drain before streams swollen by the melting snow flood the pastures. The industrious Edwin Goodlyhead has orders to take for the supply of candles and salt.

Tuesday and Saturday are market days at Ebbsweirmouth, although some tradesmen, like the butcher and fishmonger, sell their wares every day except the Sabbath. Roughly hewn wooden tables are turned into stalls that are clustered in front of the houses that run along the street, from the church to the inn. Close to The Salutation Inn is a tanner who produces straps, harnesses, saddles and other leather goods. Next to him, an apothecary sits mixing herbs and plants in a pestle and, when there are more people about, her shrill voice will tell all of the miraculously curative nature of her potions. The butcher sells poultry and mutton and, as he trusses up a rabbit, the pigeons that hang from his leather apron are tossed around. The winegrower visits twice each week and sells oils and vinegar along with the produce of his vineyard. Some say his ancestors were Romans who remained here after the army returned home some ten generations ago. He told everyone that the gift had been handed down to him, but few villagers drunk wine, other than Lord Scullion and the Goodlyheads, and fewer still could testify to his heritage. Close by, a woman sits by a small table selling jams and honey, while an old man sells cheese produced by his small herd of goats that tread the rocky cliff above Pryklethorn Bay.

Most people make their own bread at this time, but one woman, a widow of Maeldun, has made extra and is selling this to raise a few pence. The last stall in the street is the fishmonger, who has little to sell this day, as he has been distracted from his work by a matter of greater importance to his greedy soul.

As the village stirs, only the innkeeper Leland Hoop is still abed on this cold and tranquil morning, although he is more correctly asleep, for, as we have learned, he no longer takes comfort in the marital bed, but prefers to slumber on a chair, wrapped in a blanket, where he is taken, unwittingly and unwillingly, by Morpheus to another world.

The silence of snow crafts a landscape of contentment, fulfilment and peace, and yet, we are told, the devil awaits his release from the abyss, malevolent spirits walk the corpse road, nefarious conspiracies take shape within The Salutation Inn and a body stills lies hidden beneath the high tide at Hollow Hole Cove.

Patience is the fourth virtue of destiny, aptly placed, that our traveller may contemplate on the long journey ahead. The ability to achieve much by doing little is the work of the patient man. Courage, faith and chastity must be wrapped in patience, and Willem must use well the enduring gift of patience if he is to find his true self amidst the false and corruptible legacy that loiters on the path ahead.

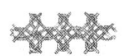

Still wrapped against the frozen dawn, Willem awoke but could find no sign of Watchman Darrayne. The boy's sleep had not been disturbed, nor had he heard the church door open or close, and yet the Watchman had left. The advent candles had burned out and there was just a flicker of a dwindling flame from the candle below the statue of the Virgin. The boy removed his mittens for a moment to warm his hands one last time at the melted candle, before leaving the church as stealthily as he could. It was still dark, with just a faint impression of Aurora's glow through a crack in the door of the church.

The street outside was stirring into life. The impatient artistry of winter was crushed beneath the tireless industry of man, as he roused from his nocturnal rest.

As the morning star signalled the approach of daybreak, Willem opened the door, cautiously looking down the gloomy street, then walked over to the animal trough and, cupping his hands, drank its icy water. He slumped down with his back resting against the trough and his stomach rumbled, objecting to his continued fast.

Directly across the snow-laden road that separated the houses of the town, Cyrus Scolop was setting up a simple wooden table from which he would shortly be selling his wares. His footsteps wedged deep imprints on the snow as he emptied fish from a wooden box onto the table top.

All the time, young Willem continued to sit with his back resting against the trough, watching the stout figure of a man working. Once the other market tradesmen had set up their stalls, the boy would begin to seek work, for if he did not, he would need to spend the four farthings he had been given by Mistress Cuddlewick to feed himself.

As he sat there watching the dawn break behind the houses, Willem wondered about the events of last night. How was it that the shadowy figure had not felt the cold and yet his fingers had felt like ice? And there had been something very curious about the stare from the man's grey translucent eyes, if indeed he was a man at all, for he may have been a spirit. Perhaps, like the angel of a distant childhood memory, he was just a figment of a dream. And yet there was too much detail for it to have been a dream. The man had seen the holy city and touched the Glastonbury thorn, the boy thought. And yet Willem had no concept of how far Glastonbury was, or indeed Rome.

The old woman who Willem met in the yew tree wood had spoken of virtue and courage, and now this shadowy figure had done the same. This strange meeting in the church raised a great many questions in the boy's mind. Why did he think Willem might have memories of Haeferingas, a place he had never visited? And the incisive comments he had made. How true it seemed now, in the dawning light of day, that experience was not the product of days, as the man had said, but of how those days were spent.

Across the road, the two boys who had served upon the altar with Father Shriver at the vigil mass stood whispering to each other. Their furtive actions did little to distract attention from themselves, nor did the shouting of one of them as he pushed the other away.

"Our job is to clear the way. What better way to do it?"

Willem waited a little longer, but the boys made no attempt to clear the path of the settled snow, which was what he assumed they were talking about.

Two young women, as alike as the two boys, passed by and Willem drew his legs back in order that they could do so unhindered.

"What do you think that blood is?" asked one.

"Is it the same as we saw along the drove road outside town?" the other asked.

"Perhaps it is a sign," replied the first woman and, as they walked off towards the churchyard, they pointed ahead of them at something they had seen.

The subdued sky remained charcoal grey. Dawn came, but the feeble sun made less difference to the settled snow than the footsteps of the townsfolk as they rose from their slumbers and began another day. The imprints of their strides gradually carved a narrow and slippery path through the town, past Gripple the butcher, Scolop the fishmonger and the other vendors.

The two women came back from the graveyard and looked at the scant merchandise on Scolop's table before stopping to talk to Gripple.

Scolop looked a fearsome man, thought Willem, and he sought employment from each of the other tradesmen until only the fisherman remained. Still hesitating, the boy sat back down and rested his back against the water trough. In his mind he imagined another three paths before him and wondered if life as a free man was nothing more than a succession of such decisions. At Shire Farm, all decisions had been made for him; he had simply needed to carry out the decisions of others. Providence now instructed him to get up and approach the fishmonger. As he went to do so, a man paused to speak with Scolop, and Willem could overhear him placing an order for fish to be delivered to Scullion Tower. The man looked slightly familiar and the boy wondered whether he knew him from his past life there.

After that man had departed, a well-dressed elderly gentleman examined some large fish as he passed, and spoke briefly to the ill-natured fishmonger as he scraped the scales from his wares. The discussion became heated, with each pointing at the other angrily, but they restrained their voices. Eventually, the elderly gentleman pressed some coins into Scolop's palm and walked off. The boy heard nothing of their conversation until the fisherman shouted after him.

"The deed will be done, Master Goodlyhead," he called, with a tone of contempt in his voice.

What deed, the boy wondered, as the elderly gentleman wandered away past the houses that stood behind the row of market stalls.

Cyrus Scolop was indeed a coarse and violent man. Folk did not question his vulgar manner, nor return his fearsome glance. And least of all did they question his harsh words.

All things about him were large. His build, his great hands and his head, which sat like a boulder on his sturdy shoulders. His ragged beard wrapped itself about his face and little fuss had been made about trimming it.

Eventually, in the absence of any further customers, Scolop leaned back and took something from his apron to eat. Filled with apprehension, the boy crossed the road and stood before the grisly fisherman, who towered above him. His fingers, which were as large as sausages, gripped an apple, from which he took a bite. Then, spitting food ahead of him as he spoke, he asked the boy what he wanted.

"I am seeking a position, Sir; a situation," he answered, standing up straight with his hands placed behind his back.

The immense, bearded face looked back down at him in silence for a brief moment. He wiped pieces of mashed apple from his beard with the back of his hand and flicked them onto the path at Willem's feet.

"Situation? Position?" he questioned, still slobbering food from his open mouth, as if the boy was speaking in a foreign tongue.

"Employment," explained Willem.

"Work!" the reply came, with a loud correcting strain to it as the man looked the tiny boy up and down. "For that's what it is and you naming it something else won't change it."

The man paused for a moment before explaining that a boy he employed had not arrived for work and, as he could not leave the stall unattended, he needed someone to make some deliveries of fish.

"Wait over there," he demanded, pointing towards the trough before continuing to handle a large fish.

The boy looked worryingly at the new mittens on his hands before removing them and stuffing the pair of gloves up the sleeve of his tunic. After all, he would not want his wonderful new gloves to smell of fish.

A few moments later, Scolop called the boy back and instructed him to take one fish to Mistress Goodlyhead at Mardyke House, and deliver the other fish to a man and woman staying at the lodgings in the grounds of The Salutation Inn.

"The name is Ravenhead." He paused and grabbed the boy by his hair. "And make sure you give that one to Ravenhead," he added, pointing to the fish in Willem's right hand.

"Very well," replied Willem, not bold enough to ask how much he might be recompensed for his work.

The boy set off, not stopping to listen to the gossiping women as he went along the slippery street. Just as most of the church congregation had been doing the evening before, the women were speaking of ghosts in country lanes, shrouded spirits carrying a coffin that contained the devil himself. The sign of the beast had been scrawled in blood on the lychgate of the graveyard, the women said. As they spoke, Willem turned around to look back towards the church. He had not noticed when he left the churchyard that the gate had, indeed, been marked in blood. It was difficult to see from this distance, but the writing appeared to be strange markings, not of any language he had ever seen. Not that Willem had seen many languages, actually, just his own and a little Latin.

As he made his way down the street, the snow beneath his feet turned to ice and he trod carefully along his way.

But his care was to no avail when a boy much older than he came running past and knocked him onto the path. He and the fish spilled onto the snow, and he got back up as quickly as he could in order to avoid the attention of the women who were still engrossed in their rumour-spreading conversation. Fortunately, the pair of fish looked no worse for being deposited in the slushy snow, so he brushed them clean and continued on his way to The Salutation Inn.

Just as Scolop had told him, there was an annex building adjacent to the inn that provided accommodation for guests. He approached the door and knocked a little too gently to be heard. Suddenly he heard voices from inside and he was almost toppled again as the door opened and a man stepped out.

"Get out of my way, beggar boy," the red-haired man demanded.

"I am no beggar, Sir."

"Where did you get those fish?" he screamed, assuming the boy had stolen them.

"I'm delivering them, Sir."

"Well, get about your business then."

"I am about my business, Sir. This fish is for yourself, I believe," he continued. "If your name is Master Ravenhead."

The man looked quizzically at the fish and then at the boy who carried it.

"Lord Ravenhead," he corrected the boy, then stood for a moment, before snatching the fish and handing it back inside the room to a young woman who stood there.

"It's a peace offering from that unprincipled oaf, Scolop," he explained to her before returning to the boy. "Well, what are you waiting for, get on your way," he demanded, adding, "about your business," in a most sarcastic tone.

Willem turned and scuttled off towards Mardyke House, where he received a different reception entirely. He knocked on the door and waited, holding the fish up, away from the ground. The door opened and there before him stood the familiar face of the old woman who had given him the gloves in church the previous evening. Mistress Goodlyhead looked at the boy and asked where his mittens were. Willem, fearing that she might think he had sold them, handed her the fish and retrieved the gloves from the sleeve of his tunic.

"I didn't want them to smell of fish, Mistress," he declared and the woman smiled back.

She invited him into the house and led him through to a room that contained no beds. He looked about him and saw a narrow archway that led through to an adjacent room. It was the first time Willem had been in a house with more than one room, well at least since he had lived at Scullion Towers, before going to Shire Farm. And, anyway, he had been too young to remember that part of his life.

"Thank you again for the mittens, Mistress," he said, and his voice tailed away before the woman realised they had not been introduced.

"My name is Mistress Goodlyhead," she stated, placing the fish on the table and wiping her hands on a blue apron. She held out her hand and the boy took it. After shaking it she looked at the hand again, as she had done the evening before, and then looked at the boy. But the boy just replied politely.

"I am pleased to meet you, Mistress Goodlyhead. My name is Willem."

What a strange name," she remarked. "I have met many noble men named William, but none called Willem."

"I have always been called Willem, my Lady."

"Then I am pleased to meet you, Master Willem," she said in a kindly manner, before asking where he was staying and what the purpose of his visit was.

The first part of the question was easy to answer, but he knew not what his purpose was, for Willem had none, except to seek employment and earn enough money to keep himself from starvation. It was too early, he thought, to confess his other reasons for visiting this East Seaxe town.

After hearing his story, the old woman ruffled his mop of tousled hair and told him that he may sleep in the small barn at the rear of the house, where they kept some chickens for eggs and two goats for milk.

"And, this evening," she added, "you shall join Master Goodlyhead and myself for dinner, for it is God's will that we treat strangers kindly."

Her comment brought a large smile to the boy's face, for it resolved his two most immediate problems in one moment of kindness.

"Now, get yourself back to Master Scolop, for he is an intimidating man who defers too easily to his violent temperament." She hesitated for a moment and made the sign of the cross for speaking so reprovingly of her neighbour. "I'm sure that, beneath his rough exterior, Master Scolop has a generous heart," she told the boy. But he looked back at her disbelievingly.

"Although," she added as an afterthought, "he has failed to gut the fish and I will need to begin cooking it long before Master Goodlyhead returns from his business this evening. Are you familiar with the task, Willem?" she asked hopefully.

The boy examined the fish and looked back at the woman.

"I have seen Mistress Cuddlewick do it on the rare occasions that my owners enjoyed fish," he replied. "There was a river close to the farm, but we had little time for fishing," he added.

His comments prompted inevitable questions about the Cuddlewicks and Willem's previous life with the couple at Shire Farm. Only after he had recalled his closeted life in that rustic backwood did Mistress Goodlyhead relax her interrogation. She handed him a sharp knife and encouraged him to try his hand at gutting the fish. Then, placing his left hand on the fish to keep it still, he pushed the point of the knife into the flesh of the fish just below its head and ran the knife along the bottom of its wet body. The fluid-filled carcass of the fish oozed noisily and its contents spilled out on to the wooden table top. As Willem opened up the two sides of the fish, he noticed something strange amongst the purple and bloody organs of the creature. He looked at it curiously and then looked back at Mistress Goodlyhead.

There amongst the innards lay a fragment of paper; a small shred of folded notepaper. They both stared at it in amazement before the boy picked it up and Mistress Goodlyhead swept up what remained of the fish's innards in her hands and threw them into a bucket for the animals to feed on later. Having separated the tiny piece of paper from the gory entrails that stained it, Willem then unfolded it. There, as clear as a summer day, was a message. It contained just two words, 'PAY ME'.

The conversation that followed had Willem and his host exploring how such a note had come to be inside the fish. They had both heard of a message in a bottle, thrown into the ocean by a castaway lost at sea. But this note was not in a bottle and neither of them had ever believed such stories anyway. Perhaps, in the absence of a bottle, which Willem had always thought a strange thing for a stranded castaway to have, someone had tossed the note into the sea, only for it to be swallowed up by the fish?

If so, what did the message mean? It certainly wasn't from Cyrus Scolop because Mistress Goodlyhead was sure that her husband would have paid him for the fish and, in any case, he certainly wouldn't have sent such a demand inside the fish; he would surely have instructed Willem to obtain payment when he delivered it. Neither of them could think of a suitable explanation for the event and both agreed to enquire over dinner that evening to see if Master Goodlyhead could enlighten them over the mystery.

With his task fulfilled, Willem washed his hands and put his mittens back on, before bidding the woman farewell and returning back through the town to the fishmonger for his reward. As he neared the far end of town, where Scolop had set up his stall, the boy was daydreaming about the dinner he would enjoy that evening. Suddenly he was seized upon by the farmer, Abel Cotes, who was remonstrating with Master Balliwick about a certain misfortune he had encountered. The boy was stopped in his tracks by a strong hand on his shoulder, which almost removed the jacket from his back.

"This boy is a stranger," Cotes shouted, pointing a finger towards Willem with one hand, whilst holding him firmly with the other, and all the time urging Balliwick to take action.

"The boy is a waif and stray, Master Cotes, he has nowhere to bed himself, so where would he hide one of your sheep?"

"I can smell it on him," the farmer shouted indignantly and he pulled the newly knitted mitten from the boy's left hand. "Look at his hand," came the accusation and he pulled the boys bloodied hand towards his own face. "He smells of entrails, Master Balliwick. He has been skinning my lamb for sure."

"Unless my senses fail me, Cotes, the boy smells of something other than sheep."

In truth, it was difficult to smell even the innards of a fish over the stink that emanated from the farmer.

"Well, boy?" bellowed Balliwick.

"If it pleases you, Sir," he replied timidly, "I have been gutting a fish for Mistress Goodlyhead."

"Are you a guest at Mardyke House, lad?" the chamberlain asked.

"No, Sir. I was delivering a fish for Master Scolop."

The farmer was deaf to the boy's pleas of innocence and held his arm tightly.

"Let go of the boy, Master Cotes. He no more has your sheep than I do." He turned to look at the boy and waved him on his way.

"Well, who has taken my sheep then?" demanded Cotes, before continuing his unremitting stream of possibilities. "Not a wolf, for I found no carcass. Perhaps it was the devil himself, for the mark of the beast was found on the lychgate at the graveyard this morning, written in blood. Or likely the animal was spirited away by the ghosts who haunt the corpse road at night."

"Nonsense. I shall advise his lordship and make enquiries about town, Master Cotes. Now I cannot be detained any longer for I have urgent business to attend to."

"And I have a living to make too, Master Balliwick, and I am prevented from doing so by villains and ghosts."

In spite of his own dismissal of the farmer's ranting, the shire reeve went directly to the church to see the sign. And there it appeared, strange characters drawn in blood. 'χϛϛ' the word said, if indeed it was a word, for the chamberlain had not seen its like before.

As he stood there examining it from up and down, several women, clad in black widow's weeds, passed him on their way into the church. Each looked at the word, wondering what it could mean. None asked the shire reeve and they simply stood around gossiping, as they awaited the arrival of Father Shriver.

Balliwick left the chattering women, walked through the graveyard around the church and knocked on the small door of the rectory. Father Shriver and Friar Sopscott were preparing themselves for morning mass and had not seen the markings on the gate. The three men walked back to the front of the church and stood there looking at the sign, with the women looking at them.

"It is no Latin that I have ever seen," said Shriver, shaking his head.

"Because it is not Latin, Father Shriver," replied Sopscott, knowingly. "It is Greek and it is something I have some knowledge of."

The friar looked over at the women and whispered to the priest to usher them into the church for mass. The women left reluctantly, as they all wished to know what the learned friar might have to say on the strange blood-coloured scrawl. But Father Shriver insisted that they all went inside to pray to Saint Lazarus, whose feast it was today.

Once they had left, all thinking, of course, that there was something significant in his words, for the saint had risen from the dead, Sopscott examined the lettering before moving closer to the two men. The blood that had been used to write the characters was still wet and was dribbling slowly down the gate. Balliwick made a closer inspection and looked towards Sopscott.

"Blood?" the chamberlain asked. The friar nodded and spoke.

"This," he said in a whisper, "is the sign of the beast. Six hundred and sixty-six."

"But how did it get here?" demanded Balliwick. "Surely only a very learned man could have written it, for who would know how to write six hundred and sixty-six in Greek? Not I, that is for sure."

In the churchyard, some way off, Aldwyn Byrgan and his four sons were busy scraping away the snow in order to dig a grave. Byrgan was a diminutive man and would certainly have had difficulty getting out of one of his own graves. His earthy hands, made coarse by his years of labour, were crusted with soil and his curly rust-coloured moustache betrayed his Norse heritage.

Today he seemed particularly upset with his older sons who, in truth, were always in trouble. The younger sons were considerably better behaved and had enjoyed some lessons from the kindly Mistress Goodlyhead, in reward for their duties as altar servers.

"Did we do it right?" asked the smallest of the boys of his elder brother.

"Yes," he replied, whilst looking about him furtively. "But it is our secret," he whispered.

The two older boys began to dig the ground, but the earth was hard as stone as they struck at it. As they worked, the priest looked over at them and pointed angrily at the bloody message.

"Get this removed, Master Byrgan."

Balliwick looked worriedly at the red symbols that had been scrawled on the gate in blood. Had it not been for Friar Sopscott, the message might not have been interpreted by anyone in the town. So what purpose would it have served?

"I have heard of those words, Friar," Balliwick said. "Yet, what do they mean? What is their significance?"

"Here is wisdom, let him that hath understanding count the number of the beast," he answered.

"Who in our small town would have such understanding, Friar? What is the language of the sign and why is it not written in Latin or some tongue that we might understand it by?"

"It is always written in Greek," he replied solemnly. "It is a number, just a number, and yet it is also interpreted as a reckoning. Someone wants us to believe there is a reckoning to come, for it is written in the Bible as such."

"Abel Cotes!" declared Balliwick.

"How would he write such letters, for he cannot write Latin and so he cannot possibly know Greek?" asked Shriver.

Friar Sopscott responded to the question as he walked away towards the church. "He copied it from a book. Its author probably does not even know its meaning. Wipe it from the gate; it can do us no harm."

"You are right, Friar," Shriver replied. "I have just such a book in the church, but Cotes has never seen it."

By this time, Aldwyn Byrgan had walked across to them and was looking anxiously at the words scrawled on the gate. He looked back at his two sons.

"Get this washed from the gate," demanded Shriver and the gravedigger shouted the same instruction towards his sons.

As he watched the proceedings from the street, Willem straightened his jacket, replaced his mitten and scuttled away towards the market stall of Cyrus Scolop. Yet all the time he kept watch on the chamberlain and observed well the muted discussion taking place outside the church.

"What was he bawling about?" yelled Scolop at the boy as he pointed towards Abel Cotes.

"He has lost a sheep, Sir, and fears it is the work of the devil himself."

"There are devils at work in this town for sure, but Balliwick will never find them. Too busy fawning on his lordship for that. Now, did you deliver the fish as I told you?"

"I did, Sir."

He sneered at the boy and handed him another parcel of fish that had been gutted, sliced and chopped ready for cooking.

"Take this to Scullion Tower and if I am gone home by the time you return, come back on Monday morning and I will find you some more work."

"What am I to be paid for my services, Sir?" Willem asked in a hushed voice, not wanting to provoke the repugnant man's temper.

"Paid?" shouted Scolop, looking at the new mittens on the boy's hands. "Seems to me you've received sufficient reward already today. Who knitted those? Mistress Goodlyhead, was it? Mild and merciful Mildred? Now, be away with you and be back here at dawn on Monday morning and we shall talk of your payment then."

Willem set off across the weald south of the village, hoping to find the ford passable, for the snow had not yet melted. If it was so, then he could be back at Mardyke House in time for dinner.

When he arrived at the ford, with the tithe barn and Scullion Tower in sight, the water level had fallen and the shallow pool that remained had iced over. He looked at it nervously, not knowing just how deep it might be beneath its fragile surface. He convinced himself that there could not be more than a smidgen of water underneath, if there was any at all. He tapped the surface with his boot and it did not crack.

Taking a few steps back, he ran towards it and slid across the ice on the seat of his trousers, holding tightly on to the package of fish as he did so. Then, reaching the other side, he got up and ran off towards the tower, looking forward to doing the same again on his return journey to town.

At the back door of the tower he was met by a woman who served in the kitchen. She looked at him curiously before asking what his name was.

"I am Willem the waif," he answered politely and she asked him how old he was.

When he answered, a look of suspicion entered her eyes, but it left her when she recognised him for who he was.

"Willem, aye, that was it. You left here some four years past. Do you remember me, I'm Mary of the scullery?"

He shook his head.

"Do you remember your time here, boy?"

"No, Madam, but I am told this is where I came from."

"Where you came from?" she repeated in a doubtful tone. "Yes, where you came from," she added, unconvincingly. "Now away with you, boy, before it gets dark. Go across the field and you will be back in the town before sunset."

Willem hesitated. He could not leave without asking the scullery maid the question.

"Are my parents still alive?"

"Your parents? You were a waif and stray. You said it yourself, Willem the waif."

The woman began to close the heavy door, but Willem shouted another question.

"What about brothers or sisters? Did I have a brother or a sister?"

Mary opened the door a little and tried to think back to those times.

"There was another boy who arrived at the same time as yourself. But there were many at that time. The foundlings of Maeldun, people called them."

From inside the building a voice bellowed instructions to the woman and she pushed the door closed.

"Older or younger?" Willem shouted, but his voice tailed off as the door slammed shut. "Still and all," he said to himself, "nobody has said that I have no brother or sister, nor have they said my parents are not alive."

As he continued to think on the possibility, he returned across the fields, stopping only at the water trough to wash his hands, before placing the mittens back on them. Across the road, the two older boys who he had seen digging graves with their father in the churchyard that morning were helping the butcher, Maggoty Gripple, to pack away his stall for the night. One of them pointed towards the church and laughed. Willem looked at their rowdy behaviour and recognised one of them as the boy who had knocked him over in the street, when he was delivering the fish.

Wishing to avoid any further inconvenience, he decided not to cross to the other side of the road. Instead, he continued along the street until he stood opposite The Salutation Inn and crossed the road to walk back towards Mardyke House where, hopefully, his long-awaited supper was being cooked.

As he passed by the inn, he looked again at the spot where he had seen blood oozing from the snow. The red stain remained, but where the snow had melted a little, Willem could see a roughly hewn rock, the size of his own head. He stared at it for a moment before picking it up in his two hands. He felt the weight of the rock and looked at it closely, before turning it over to look at the other side. He replaced it exactly as he had found it and looked at the soil that surrounded the base of a large oak tree. He noted the size and shape of the indentation in the earth and looked back at the rock. Then, suddenly, he heard someone stir inside the inn.

Willem considered the words of the Watchman. 'You will only find what you search for through understanding,' he had said. And understanding only comes through patience, the boy thought, as he moved off before anyone appeared.

The signs that lead to truth often remain unheeded for want of patience and so, as the boy stood their wondering, the gift was bestowed.

Chapter Five

Honour

Honour is all that matters in this life. Ask those who live in the widows' hides; ask the children of the fallen warriors; ask the parents without children, as it is all they have left, for patience and honour are the inheritance of the bereaved.

Our story now takes us to Mardyke House, where the seeker of the dead resides. She knows well the character of sorrow and the curative nature of time. Patience is the enemy of time and the foundation stone of honour. Chill blow the winds of time, casting change and alteration in their wake. For it is with chameleon deftness that time, this inconstant custodian of man's ambition, manifests itself in an altered aspect for each of us to look upon and wonder at its infinite might.

For the infirmed and aged it is a spectre on the road ahead. For the pragmatist and the romantic alike, it is the apotheosis of hope or despair. For the innocent hearts of children it holds the mystic joy of Christmas. And for the inhabitants of Ebbsweirmouth, on this cold advent day, it is a lost sheep, a shilling gained and another lost, a moment to be blessed, a prospect to be feared, a sharp rebuke, an opportunity or a misfortune in the shadows. And *yet time is no more than the waxing and waning of the moon, the rising and falling of the sun and the turning of the tide. Time is the chain, created by man, to bind his soul to the world. But all things perish in its path, all things crumble along its amaranthine passage.*

For Cyrus Scolop, on this sacred Saint Lazarus day, it is an unpaid debt; for Abel Cotes it is both the loss of a sheep and the manifestation of an omen. And, for Edwin Goodlyhead, it is a transaction to be made, an income to be earned.

All humanity is subject to time's triumvirate; some dwell in the past, others in the future and yet, only very few abide in the present day. One of those is our young voyager, who has no choice than to live in the moment, but always with a questioning eye to the past and a suspicious glance towards the future. As he goes about his duties in the present, with all its distractions, Willem can take comfort only in the imminent future: a hot meal, a warm straw bed and the hospitality of the Goodlyheads.

Yet for one poor soul, time is that three-day journey that all shall make, treading in the holiest of footsteps. For him, time is a scratch in the dirt, directed by the will of Rome; a moment when fifteen ill-starred symbols turn to a single letter. And the letter is 'M'. 'M' for Maeldun, he wonders, or 'M' for murder? Or, perhaps 'M' for Meririm, for that is the name that Saint John gave the devil. The children of time are patience, tolerance and forbearance, and one inhabitant of the town is blessed with all three, along with a cheerful disposition and a hospitable nature.

Now, honour awaits; the fifth virtue of destiny and the most challenging to define, for the dark heart of dishonour hides in its shadow. Honour is not measured by the braids of valour, nor the visible laurels of victory, but by inner worth and a noble heart.

Mardyke House, as we have heard, is the largest home in the village except for Scullion Tower, of course. But it is more handsome by far for, unlike the castle, it benefits from a woman's touch and owners with a good income too. Apart from The Salutation Inn, it is the only house with a window; most others have just a smoke hole to release the fumes. Inside it has tapestries and carved ornaments. More importantly, there is a barn so, unlike most others in the town, the animals sleep in a separate building. The building has two rooms, an unusual extravagance in these modest times. And, whilst the wealth of the owners came originally from the wife's late parents, it is now created in the greater part by the business acumen of the husband, Edwin, who we now find arriving home after a long day of trading.

Edwin Goodlyhead was neither a craftsman nor an elderman of the town, yet he was greatly admired and held in high esteem by his neighbours. Perspicacity and intuition kept him at more than arm's length from poverty and, yet, a generous nature ensured he would never be wealthy. The inestimable grace of contentment rested in his heart. Edwin was a merchant, a tradesman, and a simple one at that. "I buy and I sell," he often remarked, when asked about his occupation. His rationale on life was uncomplicated; the appreciation of wealth without causing detriment to others.

As the sun set on the day of the risen saint, Edwin arrived home to find a ragamuffin youth loitering outside the door to Mardyke House. Of course, Edwin would never describe anyone as a ragamuffin. No vagrant or beggar was considered a wastrel in his eyes, for he had a compassionate spirit and a benign temper.

Unaware of the man's approach, Willem was examining his attire and brushing his clothes down. He ran his fingers through his dishevelled hair and was just about to knock on the door. He certainly wasn't paying attention to the house owner, whose arrival was made silent by the carpet of snow on the pathway. That snow had taken hold and now stood as high as the yellow-billed hawfinch that kept a sharp watch on events from the ivy clinging to the house.

The boy removed his mittens to check the cleanliness of his hands when, all of a sudden, Master Goodlyhead was standing over him, offering advice as he was always inclined to do for anyone he was fortunate enough to meet, whether they wanted his guidance or not.

"I should keep the mittens on, young fellow, for it is a cold night."

Willem was startled but recognised the man immediately, for he had seen him arguing with Scolop the fishmonger that morning. The day had not sullied the old man's appearance. He was smartly dressed in tan breeches and a dark green cloak fixed at the neck with a silver brooch. Long gloves stretched almost to his elbows and he peered from beneath a black hat that buttoned under his chin.

As he spoke, the man looked about him, squinting his eyes, trying to make a judgement on the weather, in order that he might prove as useful as possible to the young traveller who seemed to be harbouring under the thatched eves of his house.

"Inclement would underestimate its sharpness and yet freezing might exaggerate its ardour," the man declared as he looked towards the heavens for guidance. "But it is unlikely to improve before the midday sun arrives tomorrow, so wrap yourself up," he earnestly advised, "and get yourself off to your bed, young man."

"But I am a guest, Sir."

"A guest?" Edwin replied, looking somewhat confused by the statement, until Mistress Goodlyhead, who had heard their voices, opened the door and explained what had been arranged.

"This young man delivered our fish earlier today, Edwin," she told him. "And he prepared the creature too." She opened the door wide and introduced the boy.

"This is Willem," she announced. "Not William, as many are named, but simply Willem, which few, if indeed any, are called, my dear."

Willem removed his mitten again and held out his hand. Edwin took it enthusiastically and smiled, impressed by the uncommonness of such a name and the congeniality of the boy who possessed it. His wife went on to explain that the young man had travelled a great distance in the snow to arrive at Ebbsweirmouth and had not managed to arrange any accommodation for himself.

"So he shall sleep in our barn and dine with us on the very fine fish that Master Scolop provided."

"A very fine fish, yet a less than fine man, Willem," confirmed Edwin as he ushered the boy inside and offered him a seat at the table. His wife shook her head at his unkind words.

Edwin was very interested in people and, even before removing his cloak, began questioning the boy unhesitatingly, wanting to learn everything about him. A desire to learn about all things was Goodlyhead's finest asset and it had contributed greatly to the success of his business. At least, that is what Goodlyhead told Willem, and his wife confirmed it was so. Apart from offering this small insight into their nature, neither of his generous hosts spoke very much at all about themselves, for they were earnestly keen to learn about the occupations and interests of other people and they continued their questioning, encouraging him to tell them where he came from and what he was doing in Ebbsweirmouth.

The arduous passage he had made from Shire Farm had been uneventful, apart from his strange meeting with the old woman of the yew tree wood. The journey had required courage, of course, the same courage the old woman had spoken of, but the boy was not one to crow about his own deeds.

Instead, Willem began from his earliest memory of Scullion Tower, where he had lived as an infant, even though this was only a faint recollection. He could remember none of the people who had lived there, or worked there, nor the way the rooms were set out. Only an early impression of his leaving the place had remained with him, for all else had been replaced by new memories of Farmer Cuddlewick and his wife at Shire Farm.

It had been hard work for a boy of just four years old, Willem told the Goodlyheads. But the Cuddlewicks were civil and kindly, he assured his hosts. Willem had slept with the animals and eaten whatever was left once the Cuddlewicks had finished their daily meal. He had worked from dawn until dusk, which resulted in a long day's labour in summer, but less so in winter.

In the four years that followed his arrival at Shire Farm, there was much to do and he grew tall and strong for a boy of his age. But this year's harvest was blighted by an infestation and much of the crop was lost. Once the remaining produce had been gathered into the barn, it became clear that there was insufficient provision to feed all three of them through the winter and so, with much regret, they had told Willem he must leave the farm. Of course, they made great merit of the fact that he would no longer be a slave. Master Cuddlewick even wrote the words on a scrap of paper for him, copying it from a document he kept in a small wooden box. 'Free man' it said and, below this, he made a mark to certify its validity, for the farmer had never been taught how to spell his own name. Yet, the piece of paper changed little and Willem certainly didn't feel free. He didn't feel any different at all, actually, for he had never felt bound to the Cuddlewicks, other than by a sense of indebtedness for their kindness, for where else would he have gone once Lord Scullion had fulfilled his obligation? Indeed, he felt more like a slave today than he had done previously in his short life, for he had worked a day for the fishmonger and not been paid or fed. A pair of mittens provided suitable reward, was his grisly new employer's view, and these had been given to him by Mistress Goodlyhead.

"So you lived at Scullion Tower up to four years ago?" asked Edwin Goodlyhead.

"Four or five years, yes, Sir."

Edwin did not recall the boy living there at that time and asked if he had any memories of his time at the castle.

"I have no memory of the castle, Sir. I know only what I was told of it by Mistress Cuddlewick and she knew very little of my past."

The farmer's wife had collected him from the tower in a horse-drawn cart and she had asked few questions about the boy, other than his fitness to complete a day's work in the field.

Mildred Goodlyhead explained to her husband that Willem was an orphan and had been raised by Lord Scullion from a baby. But, when asked, the boy could not say if his parents were from Ebbsweirmouth or not.

"I think not," replied Edwin, for he was sure he would remember the birth of a baby boy and would have known the parents too.

"For some reason," remarked Edwin, "and we know not why, you must have been brought here from somewhere else. But we know not where or why."

"Perhaps we should call you 'Willem from where'. It is surely to be preferred to Willem the waif."

"Could he not be the son of one of the Maeldun widows, who share the hides on the edge of town?" Mistress Goodlyhead asked her husband.

"Some woman whose husband had died at Maeldun, you mean?"

"Yes, there are many widows. Was one of them perhaps with child, when her husband left for Maeldun?"

"We would have heard," Edwin assured her. "You, yourself, attended many births and I am sure we would have remembered a fatherless child."

"Perhaps Willem was the son of someone at the tower. A maid, whose husband went with the old Lord Scullion to Maeldun."

"It is possible," the old man replied. "But then, why was he sent away to Shire Farm? Would his mother not have wanted him to stay and work at the tower?"

Silence hung momentarily in the air and Mildred Goodlyhead looked glaringly at her husband. She placed her hand across her forehead and gently shook her head from side to side. Edwin realised the callousness of his words and tried to change the subject by asking Willem to enlighten them further of his childhood.

Good table manners were important to Mildred and her own were exceptional in a town that had otherwise not discovered the art of such polite behaviour. She was very learned in the skills required to address illness and injury, and knew the cause of, and cure for, almost every malady. She also cooked well and, much to the pleasure of her husband, was thrifty in her accounts.

A gentle fire burned in the hearth and Willem was beginning to feel warm for the first time in many days. Better still, he was about to be fed, so he did not take offence at the unusually thoughtless words of his host. Indeed, encouraged by Master Goodlyhead, the boy was happy to continue the story of his short life up until the present day, ending with the ten-hour walk from Shire Farm back to the only other place he had known. Not that he intended to return to Scullion Tower itself, he explained, just to the town that lived under its authority, as he held hopes of finding employment here.

"It felt strange," Willem told the Goodlyheads, as Mildred began to retrieve the fish from a large iron cauldron, "when I was charged by Master Scolop to make a delivery of fish to the tower."

"You have already returned to the tower?" asked Mildred.

"I travelled there with a terrible foreboding in my heart. And then, the door opened and I was recognised by a maid there, even though it has been more than four years since I left that place and I must have changed greatly in that time."

Edwin felt compelled to interrupt, even though he was greatly enjoying the boy's engaging manner.

"He speaks well," he commented to his wife as the boy paused for a moment. "He gives a good and interesting account of his day. I like the boy, my dear. I like the boy."

It was true; the boy had a forthright voice and a talent for relating events in an amusing manner. And Mildred agreed.

"He reminds me of you in that respect, dear," she replied, referring to the daily report that Edwin provided at dinner each evening.

"Do you know the maid of whom I speak?" Willem asked. "She has dark hair, like mine, a slim build and kindly eyes."

Edwin shook his head and admitted that he rarely saw any of the servants from the castle. Even when visiting Scullion Tower, Edwin had never been offered any refreshment, nor had occasion to meet any of the maids.

"My business is always with Master Balliwick, the shire reeve, who runs the household for Lord Scullion."

"I think I met Master Balliwick today," the boy answered.

Intrigued by this comment, Edwin asked him to explain.

"He was talking to another man," he began, "who he referred to as Master Abel Cotes."

Edwin and Mildred looked anxiously at each other, as they were very familiar with the wild ranting of the farmer.

"Master Cotes had lost a sheep," the boy continued. "And he suggested to Master Balliwick that I had taken the animal."

"The man is a squirrelly fool, my dear," Edwin told his wife and she nodded. "The boy is not a thief," he added indignantly. "He could no more steal a sheep than you or I."

"Quite so, dear," his wife answered. "As you say, the man is a squirrelly fool."

"Master Balliwick dismissed his claim immediately," Willem said. "And I went upon my way."

"I am pleased to hear it, my boy, and not at all surprised," Edwin replied. "So you travelled here yesterday?" he enquired and the boy nodded.

"Where did you sleep last night?" asked Mildred and Willem hesitated before answering.

"In the church," he confessed, wondering if it was considered a sin to do so.

"No better place to seek succour," she smiled, looking at her husband to ensure he did not scold the boy for the act.

"Willem sat next to me at the vigil mass," she told her husband. "And by the will of providence, we met again today when he delivered our fish."

"Providence indeed," replied her husband.

Willem wondered whether to tell them about the strange man he had met in the church after everyone else had left, but he decided not to do so. He still wasn't sure that the meeting hadn't been a strange dream brought on by an empty stomach and the bitter chill of his journey.

The boy looked about the room that served as the kitchen and main living accommodation. It was separated from the sleeping quarters by a simple partition. There was no evidence of children but he was reluctant to ask if this was the case.

"What has happened to young Eldrik then?" Edwin asked Willem as he drew his chair closer to the table.

Mildred served the fish that had been sitting in simmering water along with some root vegetables. Willem shook his head and said that he did not know anyone of that name. Indeed, he had not even known that his employer was named Cyrus Scolop until the Goodlyheads had told him so, for the vulgar oaf of a man had not introduced himself. Edwin groaned at such ill manners and began to describe Scolop in the worse terms permitted by his own polite nature. In Edwin's view, even someone of the most pious disposition could not avoid speaking ill of Scolop, for he was a most disagreeable man.

"He is," he assured the boy, "an unprincipled individual."

He looked towards Mildred, wondering if she would chasten him for his uncharitable comments, but she was too busy serving the meal.

"And, in spite of his kind nature when he arrived, Eldrik was nurtured in the same misguided way," Edwin added.

"And spent too much time in the company of the Byrgan boys," commented his wife.

"Was Eldrik Master Scolop's son?" asked Willem politely.

"No, he was, like you Willem, a waif and a stray, given to Master Scolop in serfdom, by Lord Scullion, on the presumption that he would feed and raise him to manhood."

"Which he did, of course," added Mildred. "But only to be shown the same coarse ways of his master."

"So where was he today?" asked Willem.

"Too ill to work, I imagine," replied Edwin.

"Or beaten too severely by Scolop," added his wife.

The injurious remark reminded Mildred of her own sinfulness and she placed her hands together in the manner required for prayer. Edwin and Willem followed suit and she spoke aloud a prayer of thanksgiving to God for the food before them.

Prompted by his hosts, Willem began to eat the fish, taking care to remove the bones, which he placed on the side of his bowl. His hosts were pleased to see him enjoying the meal, scooping up the warm broth with his spoon. It was the first hot meal he had enjoyed since the evening prior to his leaving Shire Farm. Normally he would only join the Cuddlewicks at the table on Sundays or a special feast day such as Christmas or Easter. But they had relented for his last supper with them and he had joined them for a farewell meal.

The peasant farming couple did not enjoy conversation the way the Goodlyheads did over dinner. Here, it seemed that a hearty discussion was as important as a hearty meal at the dinner table, and an opportunity to exchange news and tell others how they had spent their day. It was a refreshing change for the young boy, although he did feel the need to defend his life at the farm, for the Cuddlewicks had never done him harm.

"We ate fish at Shire Farm," commented Willem. "Normally on Fridays," he added. "My master and I would fish at the river close to the farm. He spoke even less on those occasions than at other times. He was a man of very few words. Indeed, apart from ordering me to do this or that, he may not have spoken to me more than ten times in all my days there."

Edwin stared in wonder at the boy, more at his stimulating manner of speaking than the content of what he said. He had clearly not been harmed by the unsociable reticence of his employers. Moreover, he appeared, in every sense, to be making up for the silence that had accompanied his time there.

The boy went on to tell them that Mistress Cuddlewick had chatted on occasions, when Willem was helping her with the washing or working in the barn, but not at the Sunday dinner table when her husband was present. Willem was sure that the Cuddlewicks never spoke at supper. Indeed, he was as convinced of this as he was that the Goodlyheads always conducted themselves in this manner at the table. And he was right. Each evening Edwin Goodlyhead would relate to his beloved wife the events of the day and any news from the townspeople. At this time of year it was especially so, for it was too cold on most days for a woman of Mildred's delicate constitution to venture out of the house and learn of events for herself. In winter such occasions were limited to her attendance at mass or conducting her duties as seeker of the dead, a position awarded to her by Chamberlain Oswald Balliwick himself.

In recognition of her integrity in such sombre matters, it was her duty to attend deceased townsfolk to determine the cause of death and liaise with Father Shriver and Master Byrgan to arrange the burial. On these very rare occasions, it was she, rather than her husband, who led the conversation at dinner. However, with the arrival of their young guest, the conversation at supper had been assigned to Willem. So it wasn't until they had heard all about the boy's journey and criticised Cyrus Scolop's behaviour towards him that Mildred finally asked how her husband had spent his day, as she did each evening over supper.

Edwin made himself comfortable at the head of the small oblong wooden table and began his daily chronicle by announcing that Master Willem was not the only visitor to Ebbsweirmouth on this cold winter day.

"There is a mendicant friar in town who would make a fine supper guest if the opportunity should arise," suggested Edwin. "He wears the black habit of the Benedictine order and appears most learned, my dear."

"I saw him at the vigil mass last night," his wife answered. "He was speaking with Master Balliwick when I left the church."

Her husband looked a little disappointed at her last comment.

"He would have been inviting him to dinner, I am sure, my dear," replied Edwin, "and we must do the same. It might provide an opportunity for me to practise my Latin," Edwin suggested, before telling them that Friar Sopscott, for that was his name, was staying with Father Shriver, but would almost certainly be invited to the tower.

"So I shall invite him to Mardyke House at the earliest opportunity," he added, before reciting some Latin to impress his young guest.

"*Sibi, soli vivere sed et aliis proficare.*"

Mistress Goodlyhead smiled proudly, but in total ignorance of what had been said.

"What does that mean?" enquired Willem, much to the pleasure of his guests.

"It is the way of the mendicant friar, Willem. 'Not to live for themselves, but only to serve others', that is their watchword, my boy."

"Has he come to cast out the evil spirits?"

"Evil spirits?" gasped Mildred, almost spilling her spoonful of fish broth.

"Yes, those spirits that haunt the corpse road about the village. I have heard the townsfolk speaking of them."

Edwin and Mildred looked anxiously at each other and appeared lost for words.

"Have you frequented the ale house?" questioned Mildred, knowing that Eldrik had often accompanied Scolop to the inn.

"Have you, young fellow?" her husband asked before the boy could answer the question.

"No, Sir. I first heard of the spirits when I passed the inn last night, but many spoke of them at the vigil mass too. Of how the spirits wander the unploughed path beside the drove roads in groups, carrying their fellow dead."

"Such inconstancy serves only the devil himself," suggested Mildred belligerently.

"I did not mean to offend, Mistress Goodlyhead," replied Willem in an apologetic tone.

"I know that," she replied, placing her hand on his shoulder. "We know that, don't we, Master Goodlyhead?"

"Of course, of course. Scurrilous gossip, as I am sure the visiting friar will confirm, should we have the opportunity to ask his advice over supper."

"But, has the friar not come in response to the farmer's warning?" the boy asked.

"The farmer's warning?" replied Edwin, wondering just how much the poor youth's soul had been corrupted since his arrival in town.

"Yes, the same man who accused me of stealing his sheep today. The one Master Balliwick called Abel Cotes. He spoke of the abyss opening and the coming of the devil himself."

Mildred explained to her husband about the scenes that had ended the vigil mass and told him of the ranting by Abel Cotes, though she tried to avoid the details. Indeed, she hoped it would be left there, but the boy continued his questioning.

"What did he mean about the abyss opening?"

"The man is a fool, as I told you earlier; a squirrelly fool," answered Edwin. "He cannot read and has no knowledge of Latin, so why he believes he is qualified to interpret the words of the Holy Book, I do not know."

The boy hesitated before speaking again, but could contain his words no longer.

"I saw a sign last night,"

"A sign?" asked Mildred apprehensively.

"Or perhaps an omen," the boy said.

"An omen?" countered Edwin anxiously.

"Yes, as I stood at the edge of the town, under the tree by The Salutation Inn, when I first arrived. I stood there looking towards the church and blood appeared to ooze from the freshly fallen snow at my feet. I wondered, when I heard the farmer's words, if it had come up from the abyss."

The elderly couple sat for a moment looking into each other's eyes, wondering how to answer the boy's question. Eventually, it was Mildred who spoke.

"Abel Cotes is a foolish man and people will know that once the year turns and his ill-advised ravings are shown for what they are; calumny, foul calumny." She paused for a moment before adding some words of wisdom that she had learned. "From patience comes obedience and faith in the word of God."

"But," the boy answered, much to the disappointment of his hosts, "does he not speak of the word of God? For he said it was foretold in the Bible."

"There are many contradictory accounts in the Good Book," replied Edwin, hoping to conclude this particular topic of conversation. "They are there to challenge us, for we know not when the Lord shall come, it says."

"Be ever watchful," added Mildred.

Willem thought that he was already being watchful. However, he held his tongue and allowed his hosts to change the subject, for that was clearly what they desired.

The room fell silent for a moment and the three ate some fish, whilst Edwin tried to recover the lost thread of his daily chronicle. But it was Willem who broke the silence.

"It was the same blood that appeared on the lychgate."

"What blood on the lychgate?" questioned Mildred.

"The church lychgate," replied the boy.

"I shall tell you about it tomorrow," Edwin promised his wife. But for now, the old man simply wanted to continue with his review of the day's more mundane events.

Edwin paused for a moment, gathering his thoughts. "Ah yes, yes," he continued, recalling his original point and ignoring Willem's last statement. "And further visitors arrived at Ebbsweirmouth, two days past. A Lord Ravenhead and his fair Lady Una, who have travelled a great distance."

"A great distance, my dear?" inquired Mildred.

"Yes, a great distance, from a land called Haeferingas."

"For what purpose are they here, my dear?" Mildred asked.

As they spoke, Willem recalled the place that had been mentioned by Watchman Darrayne, and his mind searched his memory to recall what had been said of it. He failed to hear that Mistress Goodlyhead had not heard of the place or that Edwin had not visited it. Nor did he hear that Master Goodlyhead knew nothing of the couple's reason for visiting the town.

"My husband has visited many places," Mildred told Willem and confirmed that he was a very well-travelled man. "Perhaps not as many as the mendicant friar, for they travel the world, even to the soul of Christendom itself, the Holy Empire of Rome."

As she spoke, Willem was shocked to hear the very same words spoken by the Watchman the night before. If it had been a dream, then it was a prophetic one, a sign given to him alone. He tried to recall what had been said, but could not remember what the man had said of the place called Haeferingas.

"Where is Haeferingas?" asked Willem, wondering if this had some significance to whatever the forewarning might be.

"As I said, Willem, I have never visited there. It is, I believe, the kingdom of Eorl Haeferingas, a cousin of Lord Scullion."

"And Lord Ravenhead is from this place?"

"So it is said."

Once they had finished eating, Mildred left the table and warmed the broth that remained in the pot, so that they might enjoy a hot drink before retiring to their beds. Her husband joined her on the other side of the room, leaving Willem at the table. He wanted to ask her quietly, beyond earshot of the boy, about a delicate matter that she had attended to the previous day.

"What news of the chandler, my dear?" he whispered.

"I met with Father Shriver, Master Balliwick and Master Byrgan this morning. He seems to have stumbled and struck his head on a rock. The icy conditions have made the pathways treacherously slippery and it is clearly the result of a fall, Master Balliwick says."

"Chandler seemed such a jolly fellow, when we met," her husband replied.

"Yes, Chamberlain Balliwick wishes to speak with you to establish whether the man has kin who should be notified."

"Of course, of course, my dear. And yet, I think he was alone in this world."

Willem overheard the end of the conversation and, thinking they were speaking about him, he assured them that he was not afraid to be alone in the world. Edwin wanted to correct him, but his wife interrupted.

"Indeed, you are not alone, my boy. And you shall join us for the Sabbath feast tomorrow evening."

"You are very kind indeed, Mistress Goodlyhead."

"Now," said Edwin, making himself comfortable in his chair. "You may make restitution for the meal we have provided by telling us a tale."

"But I know no tales," confessed Willem.

"How did you spend the winter nights at Shire Farm, then?" Edwin asked.

"Alone in the cattle shed, with the animals."

"And no tales, no stories to take you to your sleep?"

"The animals knew fewer stories than I," the boy said with a glint in his eye and his hosts laughed and encouraged him to try, for they had both heard their own yarns many times.

The boy relented and began telling them of a strange meeting between a boy, much like himself, and a curious and seasoned traveller who had sailed the seas beyond the distant horizon.

"What were their names?" enquired Edwin, but the boy was concocting the story as he went along.

"The man was called Darrayne," he answered and examined the reaction of his audience closely to see if they recognised it. But there was nothing to suggest they had heard such a name before. Indeed, Mistress Goodlyhead said as much in her response.

"What a strange name for a character," she said. "How did he come by such a name?"

"Let the boy tell the story," insisted Edwin and Willem wondered how he might create a story of interest to them. He also concluded that, if Watchman Darrayne had not been a figment of his imagination, then he was obviously a stranger in town.

"But what of the boy's name?" asked Mildred, ignoring her husband's plea.

"You shall name him," Willem replied, which pleased his hosts very much.

"How jolly," smiled Edwin, "a story with characters that we might name ourselves. You, young Willem, are a fine storyteller. Begin."

"But the name?" asked Mildred.

"Let's call him Willem," Edwin replied and the boy was convinced of celestial intercession.

He then told them of the events at the curious meeting on the previous evening, changing the location from a church to a cattle stall, the description of which was as alike as it could be to the one Willem had learned of at Bethlehem. The Goodlyheads assumed that references to the kingdom of Haeferingas and to the soul of Christendom and the Holy Empire of Rome were not coincidental and simply embellishments of his improvised storytelling. And a large part of it was indeed invention on his part and embellished through the addition of another character fashioned from the statue of the Virgin. The sad story told of how Darrayne was blinded for loving a beautiful lady and it was told with such great conviction that it seized the couple's attention for a full twenty minutes. The tale was finished with a surprise and happy ending, which was considered a blessing by the two enraptured listeners. A providential meeting between the blind man and a boy who turned out to be his own son was as good a story as the pair had heard before.

Once the fish broth had been finished, Mildred furnished the boy with a blanket and directed him to a similar cattle stall to the one he had just described. The beasts stirred at his arrival and took time to settle.

As he lay there, he thought on the words of the Watchman again and wondered how he might find understanding through a chaste heart. Perhaps he should attend confession for, if nothing else, this would protect him for sure if the abyss opened and the devil arrived.

At his last confession he had been told to honour his keepers, the Cuddlewicks, as his parents and treat them as he would have them treat him. He had, he believed, fulfilled that penance and he tried not to harden his heart against the couple when he thought about their rejection of him. They had done what they must, he assured himself. And now the couple's actions had given him reason to search for his own roots, either to find his real parents or, failing that, to find where they were buried.

Willem was tired from his exertions. Here was a soul that slept so soundly it could slip into another world; a world where subtle suspicions of truth lingered and lured one into belief. But tonight it was too cold to sleep in anything but short spells. Yet, when the chickens had quietened for the night, Willem fell into a shallow sleep, nestled in the straw bedding and wrapped in a blanket, with his hands warmed by a new pair of mittens. Honour thy father and thy mother, the commandments said, and he slept thinking on that subject of honour, for it filled the very air that he breathed.

Chapter Six

Temperance

Revered above all things is honour and there are many in our story who would covet such a virtue. Morcar Scullion, an eorl by birthright, knows as much in his heart, for a title may be inherited but not honour. Indeed, the brave deeds of his brother serve only to diminish any claim to the laurel wreath that comes with such a noble title. And his servant too, the virtuous Oswald Balliwick, whose spirit is made weak this night by the onerous responsibilities of his office. With aching persistence, a stolen sheep and a sibylline number scrawled in blood upon the church gate, will unsettle his night's rest.

With measured steps he makes his way along the darkened pathway, imagining the warm glow of the fire in the great hall, where a lion and wolf gaze down and mock his trepidation and the Latin motto beneath the animals speaks of fortitude. It is true, of course, that fortitude cultivates the ability to endure hardship and shape greatness from it, but fortitude is meaningless in this world if it is not accompanied by honour. Sweet harps resonate with the courage spent on Maeldun field and the heavenly choir of angels sings of Morcar's tragic loss when his father and brother fell in *battle there, yet his life is but an echo of their brave deeds, and the loyal Balliwick knows well the lasting injury this causes his master.*

The pathway is dark as Balliwick makes his way home after his business in town and few are still awake at this late hour. The boy Willem sleeps in a cattle stall, dreaming of the shadowy figure he met and wondering whether he might be the one who is to come, the spirit that is to open the abyss, the devil incarnate. The apparition seems not of this world and yet the timbre of his voice is mellowed with compassion and sounds not at all as one might imagine Satan to do. And yet, in spite of such spectral fears, Willem shares the figure's wretchedness, for the sixth virtue of destiny is temperance, which many mistake as the custodian of greed. But no, temperance should not be reduced to the moderation of self-interest, for it is the guardian of the rights and needs of others.

At Scullion Tower, where our story now takes us, nobody is sleeping. Servants do not rest until their master has taken to his bed. And young Morcar, now Lord Scullion, abhors his bed, for with sleep comes accursed dreams filled not with honour but disgrace and self-reproach.

The great hall is used mainly for dining now, with meetings being held in the counting house in order to maintain privacy. The high-lofted ceiling of the Hall gives it grandeur and the large fire that roars every day in the hearth is necessary to make the room habitable in winter. Torches hang from iron grills along each wall, although there is sufficient light cast through the long casement openings on one wall. Escape louvers in the roof remove the smoke from the fire and decorative stone basins stand by the large wooden door. Bowls of rose petals, lavender and fennel stand on pedestals placed around the room and these help to maintain the quality of the air. The rugged stone walls are decorated with several large tapestries, the largest of which depicts the coat of arms of the Scullion family. The lion and the wolf look angrily at each other and their aspect captures well the character of the eorl's late father.

Yes, honour is lauded above all else, and yet honour is more worthily debated and deliberated at The Salutation Inn where, as with the widow's mite, it is more valued and evident, for there is greater honour in a pauper's life than that of a misanthropic eorl who fears the unveiling of both his imperfection and his past frailties.

Through the murky shapeless night outside, the tower appears draped by mist, and Balliwick rounds a clump of trees along the coastal pathway where it joins the road and forks left to the castle or right towards Holm Farm. The chamberlain has spent a long day conducting business in the town and there is much to report to Lord Scullion.

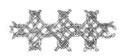

※※※

When the weary chamberlain entered the great hall of the tower to warm himself at the hearth, he found his lordship alone there, sitting in a great throne-like chair, morbidly labouring on thoughts of what might have been and of what should have been. Red-cheeked with wine, he slouched with his limp, lifeless left arm hanging by his side. Balliwick knew it was a sign of his drunkenness that he chose to expose his disfigurement so wantonly.

Scullion looked through bleary eyes at his most trusted aid, then shuffled to make himself more comfortable in the large chair and quaffed wine from a silver chalice. The blustering sound of his voice and the heavy manner in which he returned the cup to the table in front of him confirmed he had been drinking for some time.

"Ah, Balliwick," he declared loudly, adding, "Chamberlain Balliwick," as if the man did not know who he was himself. "Come closer," he said, more in the tone of a request than an order. Balliwick stood beside the chair and Scullion took his right hand in his own. "You are cold, my friend," he said, looking directly into the other man's eyes.

Balliwick could tell from the tone of his master's voice that there was an adjuvant meaning to those five words.

"It is late, my Lord."

"Oh, I call you friend, and yet to you I am your lord." As he spoke, Scullion let go of his hand and reached for the chalice of wine. "The sadness in your eyes matches that in my own heart," he continued as he looked into the chalice only to find it empty.

Balliwick looked down at his drunken friend. "Come, my Lord, I will help you up." He offered his hand again.

"What news of my people?" asked Scullion in a sarcastic tone as he rose from the chair and dropped the chalice.

As his most trusted servant and good friend, Balliwick wanted to tell him about the stranger who had died in town the previous day. But it would do no good to do so at this time. He would wait until morning when a more sensible conversation might be had. Balliwick had seen his lordship like this many times before, undone by drink and reproach for all the faults in his mind and body.

"It is late, Sir, we should be away to our beds."

"Our beds. Yes, yes, our beds. What you really mean, Balliwick, is that I should stop drinking."

The chamberlain shook his head.

"I drink only to forget, my good friend."

"But you do not, Sir."

"Do not? Do not what?"

"Forget, Sir."

As he stood up, the blood rushed from Scullion's head, his humour changed and his eyes became doleful and wayward.

Balliwick took him by his good arm and led him away through the still-open doors towards the stone stairs that led up to the bedrooms.

"Did you know my brother?" the eorl asked as his feet slapped heavily on to each step.

"Of course, my Lord, you know I did."

Balliwick continued to listen as he struggled to help his lordship up the stairs.

"A brave soul. Fearless, absolutely fearless," Scullion added, still continuing to ramble on about his departed brother.

"Yes, Sir," Balliwick answered as he eased Scullion on to the bed and left the room. But, before sleep could overwhelm him, his voice boomed once more.

"I should have gone to Maeldun, you know. I should have ignored my father's instruction. I have one good arm, Balliwick."

"You fight your own Maeldun each day, my Lord," whispered the chamberlain as he closed the door.

"You are a good man," replied Scullion, unheard by the person to whom the comment was directed.

~~~~~

At that moment in The Salutation Inn, his lordship's final words seemed to echo beneath the wooden joists and thatch. Chamberlain Balliwick, the shire reeve of the East Seaxe shire, was the subject of much debate that evening. Aldwyn Byrgan, Maggoty Gripple and Seth Wainthrop stood at the counter, drinking late into the night, discussing the events of the day.

"Balliwick questioned me today about a missing sheep," said Leland Hoop.

"What missing sheep?" asked Byrgan, a little more anxiously than he should have sounded.

"Have you not heard? Abel Cotes has lost a sheep."

"Taken by a wolf," Maggoty Gripple pronounced, as if it was a fact, which is wasn't.

"There were no remains and no blood," the landlord countered.

"Taken by a very hungry wolf then," laughed Gripple.

By his very nature, Seth Wainthrop chose to avoid gossip involving the chamberlain, for he knew it would serve him only ill fortune to do so. And so, to enter into such frivolous debate in the man's absence would count against him for sure, because there were others here who would be pleased to tell Balliwick of the farmer's involvement in the uncharitable words spoken about him. Tenant farmers like Wainthrop and Cotes relied entirely on his lordship for their income and could only enjoy such favour by the grace of Chamberlain Balliwick. Although, it must be said that Abel Cotes clearly took less notice of such matters than the more sensitive Seth Wainthrop, or he would not chant on so about the opening of the abyss. With such thoughts in his mind, Wainthrop took himself off into a corner.

"Perhaps the spirits of the corpse road took the sheep," suggested Byrgan wryly.

"That would account for it," Hoop replied. "Now quieten your voices or you shall frighten off my only guests. Talk of spirits in the corpse road does not encourage visitors to avail themselves of my hospitality."

The innkeeper nodded his head towards a man and woman sitting in the corner by the hearth. The couple tried not to appear furtive, but were certainly speaking very quietly in order that they should not be overheard. Indeed, their behaviour appeared conspiratorial and only added to the interest of the regular customers of The Salutation Inn.

Hoop told his friends at the counter that his guests were Lord Ravenhead and Lady Una, who had arrived on Friday but, as far as he could tell, they had met with nobody and had largely confined themselves to their rooms. He spoke in a lowered tone in order that the couple of whom he spoke would not hear his words. As far as he could see, apart from receiving a delivery of fish, which he had to cook for them, they had said and done very little since their arrival.

"Rooms?" questioned the lecherous Gripple, emphasising the plural nature of the word.

"They insisted," whispered Hoop, "that the room was partitioned by a curtain."

"What purpose does a curtain serve?" asked Gripple, but Hoop was ignoring the licentious suggestions of his customer.

"However," the landlord persevered in a knowing tone and with the intention of telling them of Scolop's unfamiliar interest in the couple when, suddenly, the door burst open and that very man stepped into the room. Hoop stopped speaking of course, for he feared the fiery fisherman as much as all the other men in the town. The only mitigating peculiarity in Hoop's nature was his indifference to death, for he seemed to fear it less than most since the loss of his wife.

Scolop unhitched a tankard from his belt and slammed it on the counter. He didn't speak a word, just sniffed at his hands and wiped them on his leggings before sweeping up the tankard in his large hand and swigging most of its contents. He then turned back towards the man and woman sitting by the fire and stood alongside them, as if to warm his hands at the hearth.

Hoop and the others contrived a conversation about the missing sheep but were, in truth, listening as discreetly as they could to the fisherman, who began, to everyone's surprise, to speak to the couple even more quietly than they did amongst themselves. Forasmuch as his gruff voice would permit, he remained out of earshot of those at the bar, but Wainthrop heard it from his position by the window.

"'Tis done," the fisherman murmured, "now where's my *renoomaration?*"

What deed was done, wondered Wainthrop, and what did Scolop mean by his remuneration? Remuneration for what?

Scolop slurred the final word, not through drunkenness, but because he spoke little and read not at all, so possessed a poor grasp of his native tongue. In his desire to impress his new acquaintances, Scolop had made enquiries with others about an alternative word for money. Perhaps he was persuaded so by the young boy he had met that morning, who had sought alternative words for work and met with

Scolop's disapproval for it. Yet, in the man's annoyance was envy. The five-syllable word should have provoked attention, but most had assumed he was seeking a device to impress Balliwick or, perhaps, Edwin Goodlyhead. It was Hoop who had taught him the word he sought, but the fisherman had little time for learning and rarely managed a word of more than two syllables, so an attempt at one with five was destined for failure. But Lord Ravenhead knew what he meant, as did the prying figure of Seth Wainthrop.

"There are matters to be attended to before any money changes hands, Master Scolop," Ravenhead whispered, before speaking up in a much louder voice. "Come, my good man, take this seat at our table and warm yourself." It was a comment intended to cloak such a meeting with innocence but it only served to attract even more attention from the other customers at the inn that night, for who would want such a foul bedfellow at their table?

Scolop pulled up a chair and sat opposite Lord Ravenhead, ignoring the woman who sat by his side. Each of the two groups that now occupied the inn struggled in their attempts to contrive a discussion that the other party could hear, whilst maintaining a second conversation that could not be heard beyond a whisper. As a consequence, loud and over-emphasised comments about lost sheep and the dangers of sea fishing were batted across the room, whilst covert remarks were passed in more hushed tones.

"In the first part," the smartly dressed nobleman continued in a deliberately legalistic, but lowered tone, "we need to be assured that you have accomplished the agreed task. And in the second part, we must have sight of the agreed subject. Lastly, we must be able to assure ourselves that the aforementioned subject displays the necessary identification. Only then, with all this in place and before any money changes hands, the Lady Una and I need to settle certain matters with his lordship, Lord Scullion." He breathed the last, almost inaudible name mentioned and paused for a moment. And yet he gave no time for Scolop to reply, raising his hand for emphasis. "These are what are called prerequisites," he added.

"'Tis first I've heard of such *prerequedits*. The deed is done and it is now time for payment."

The mispronunciation was ignored. "Within three days, Master Scolop, you have my assurance."

Wainthrop could see that Scolop was becoming agitated by the nobleman and feared being caught up in the argument. So he got up and went to the bar.

"Sunset tomorrow, Ravenhead," the fisherman countered more loudly than he had intended and he rose from his seat in anger. "Or you shall have my assurance," he added, banging his hand on the wooden table and leaving the clenched fist resting there. It was as large as a child's head, rough-skinned, blistered and scarred by a lifetime of misdirected thrusts of a filleting knife.

The noise shattered the covert nature of the two conversations and attracted the gaze of Leland Hoop and Seth Wainthrop, who stood on either side of the counter as the farmer sought to refill his tankard.

"Who are you looking at, Wainthrop? Mind your own business!" screamed Scolop, wondering whether any of his conversation had been overheard. The fisherman made a mental note of where to present himself should he hear any talk of his conversation with Ravenhead.

"Keep your voice down, Scolop, or the town shall know as much of *our* business as we do," whispered Ravenhead.

"Aye and more than I, it seems," replied the fisherman, ignoring the request to be quiet. "But worry not on that score, Ravenhead, your secret is safer at The Salutation Inn than in Shriver's confessional. There is only Hoop, Gripple, Byrgan and Wainthrop here and they are more affeared of me than most in this town, and more than any god or devil that might arrive unwelcomed."

"Let me refill your tankard," replied Ravenhead, trying to calm the situation. "As a sign of good faith," he added generously.

"I have no faith. Not in God nor you, Sir, and I will not take your farthing fill up. Silver is what I was promised and silver it'll be, Sir." The word 'sir' was delivered with abject contempt and the fisherman caught his foot on his seat as he went to walk away. He kicked the heavy wooden bench towards the bar and leaned across the table until his face was an inch from that of Ravenhead.

"Think on it and tarry not."

"You have my word on it," replied Ravenhead.

"I already have your word, now I want your money. No more delays!"

"Tomorrow," came the reply.

"I want my money," the fisherman repeated before stumbling off to the bar and ordering himself another ale. "I'll buy my own ale until this matter is done," he screamed back at them with a frightening glare in his eyes. His mood had changed and his rage made him less inclined to keep their business secret than he had first intended.

Hoop filled the tankard that Scolop slammed on the counter and the fisherman walked off with it to a dark corner of the room to drink it. The change in mood was noticed also by Gripple and Byrgan, who took themselves off to another table to continue their own discussion.

"There is evil being done this night," stuttered Hoop ominously as he returned to speak with Wainthrop.

"There are wicked deeds done by day as well as night, Hoop," replied Wainthrop knowingly. His words hung in the air and, for a moment, he was left wondering whether he had said too much. He regretted his rash words and was relieved when Hoop did not question him further on his wayward comment.

Instead, both men paused, half listening to see if they could hear anything of the exchange between Ravenhead and the woman who accompanied him. Ravenhead was a tall individual, quite handsome with a mop of red hair, a moustache and a thin beard that covered only the tip of his chin. The woman had kept her hood up, but she was not thirty years old and spoke very quietly. She looked at the two men standing on opposite sides of the bar and they averted their gaze.

"You're here late," commented Hoop to the farmer, pretending to take no notice of his other guests, although he could not avoid thinking about their motives. The pair had been less than informative when they arrived at the inn on Friday, and they had left their room only infrequently.

"Aye," Wainthrop replied. "And I've been here all day too. Holm Ford was flooded and I needed to take the cliff-top path, just as I did on Friday before the snow began falling." He supped some more ale. "I had some business with old Goodlyhead and then met with Chamberlain Balliwick."

As they spoke, Ravenhead and the woman stood up and pulled their cloaks about them. Scolop growled from a darkened corner of the room.

"The snow is easing, gentlemen," Ravenhead remarked as he opened the door and left the inn with his female companion.

"Did you hear what Scolop said?" asked Wainthrop, trying to moderate his voice in case the fisherman heard him. "'The deed is done', he said, 'now where is my remuneration?' What was meant by that, Hoop?"

"What could a fisherman do for them? And, if he has done the deed, whatever that might be, then why are they still here?"

Gripple and Byrgan stepped up to the bar to refresh their tankards. So engrossed had they been in their own conspiracy that they had heard nothing of the other conversations taking place that night.

Wainthrop supped his ale. He thought he knew what the deed might have been that Master Scolop spoke of, but his suspicions made no sense to him and he certainly wasn't going to speak of them to anyone, for he knew this would attract the wrath of the fisherman.

~~~~~

Having taken his master to bed, Balliwick returned downstairs and found the fire still burning in the hearth. He picked up the empty chalice and found, on the floor beside the chair, two bottles. One was empty, but the other was still half full. He filled the cup, sat down and drank the wine. He hadn't told Scullion that there would be guests for mass and lunch tomorrow. Still, this did not matter, he thought, for in his drunken condition, his lordship would not know whether he had been told or not.

The chamberlain had invited Friar Sopscott and it would have been impolite to do so without entertaining Father Shriver, too. Furthermore, by celebrating mass at the tower chapel, Balliwick could stay in bed a little longer. Tomorrow's Sabbath bell was already twice holy as it was the feast day of Saint Olympias, the most generous of the saints, and the third Sunday of advent too. It would be too pious, indeed, to attend mass in town and again at the tower chapel. And, most attractively, the visitors would provide a more enlightened conversation at the lunch table than the penitent and monotonous lament of his lordship's past shame. It was a past shame he spoke of only to Balliwick, for it needed to remain secret from the outside world. If the world should know of his disability, then the shire might be forfeited, or at least that was his fear.

Balliwick refilled his chalice with wine and reflected on his long service to the elderman of Scullion Tower. He had just been appointed as shire reeve when the accident had occurred. It was a simple riding accident, but one with far-reaching consequences for the family. The youngest son of that family, who Balliwick had just escorted to bed, had been out horse riding through the forest paths. Lord Scullion, or Morcar as he had been known in childhood, fell beneath his stumbling mount, which crushed his left arm.

Eorl Æthelstan, Morcar's father, had been greatly distressed and searched the shire for someone with the necessary skill to mend the arm, for the village had no apothecary nor even a humble herb beater who might concoct a remedy for his son's ailment. But all who saw the arm shook their heads and said it was beyond repair. Some said it should be taken from him, in case it infected the rest of his body. Most did not even attend on the eorl and simply sent word to his lordship that such cases were impossible to repair. It was a hopeless case, they said, but, in truth, they feared failure, for the old Lord Scullion, Eorl Æthelstan, had been a fearsome man, whose wrath was renowned.

When all seemed lost, word had come to Balliwick that a mysterious old woman, who lived some thirty miles from Ebbsweirmouth, was able to cure all ailments and, in spite of the young chamberlain's pleas to resist false hope, Eorl Æthelstan had sent a messenger to find the woman, who led a reclusive life in a mystic yew tree wood. Some said she was a sorceress, as she had lived there for as long as people could remember and there was great speculation about how old she must be.

And so, the messenger travelled for a full day, just as he had been instructed to do by Balliwick. The following morning, there, far sunk beneath a dark canopied forest roof, the wizened old maid dwelt amidst a mystical yew tree wood, in a shelter created by the naturally winding roots and scaly brown tendrils of an ancient yew tree. The knotted and twisted tentacle roots of the tree rose and fell through the woodland bed around the small dwelling. In the branches above it, deadly red berries hung, to be garnered only by the hawfinches or the most reckless beasts and, in its crooked, empty boughs, only the hardiest of spiders lived, hibernating the long winter through.

On that second day, in that bowered den, hidden in the deepest part of the yew wood, the messenger found the old crone who sat, picking at herb leaves with her spindly fingers.

The woman was impervious to the promises of wealth, but she knew that if she rejected the eorl's summons to attend on young Morcar, her next visitor would kill her, or force her by point of sword. And yet fear, no more or less than riches, made not a shred of difference to her decision to comply with the beckoning. You see, many years before, the woman had taken the spirit of a black cat and with it the nine lives that was its birthright. No, her compliance with the eorl's wishes was the product of destiny, for she knew the events of the coming days were so written.

And so, with nothing more than the clothes she stood up in, the old woman had gone to Ebbsweirmouth.

It had pleased Morcar's father for it to be a stranger who attended on his son, for he did not want news of the young man's condition to become public. The servants had been sworn to silence on the subject, for the old lord knew that his enemies would smell weakness in the shire if the boy's broken arm became public knowledge.

Before beginning her treatment, the old woman had tried to reset the bones, but the pain had been too great for the boy, who was already of feeble frame and greatly weakened by the injury. He screamed aloud until his distraught father instructed the woman to set the bone as it was, for he was tormented by his son's crying.

The woman's name was Silvaria le Fay, for she was reputed to be the daughter of a fairy king who had visited the yew wood in the distant past, although it was clear from her wrinkled face and weak frame that she had not inherited his immortality. For, unlike her father, she had aged but, through guile and use of the arcane arts, she lived on while others had long since perished. The mystical hag spent the first day gathering purple comfrey and other such herbs from the riverbank near Pryklethorn Bay, then wrapped the boy's arm in the muddy sediment she produced from its roots. The leaves of the comfrey were then infused and young Morcar drank this every day that the arm was covered by the mud plaster cast. The fairy's visit was kept secret, but many who saw her in the fields around the tower speculated on who she might be. She spent many hours studying the flora and fauna of the area and often marked the ground with strange symbols.

Before she left, she gathered bishopwort, wormwood and cropleek and, after pounding them up, boiled them with celandine and nettle, and then left the remedy with the servants to be rubbed on to the arm when the plaster was removed.

She instructed the servants that the cast must remain set for no less than six weeks. Eorl Æthelstan had wanted her to stay until Morcar's arm was released from the plaster, but she declined and, fearing her mystical powers, he released her from her duties as he did not wish to upset her, or fall foul of her magic. And, in any case, there was nothing more she could do for the boy.

Yet, for all the treatment Morcar had received, his arm set badly and when the plaster was removed the shattered bones bulged here and there against the taut, young flesh. The remedies the fairy had left ensured that infection did not set in, although this was the only blessing. For, whilst the shoulder and upper arm had some movement, below that only pain existed and after a few weeks the hand began to wither through its idleness.

Fortunately for his father, Æthelstan, Morcar had an older brother. Æryk was already greatly favoured by his lordship and accompanied him everywhere. Morcar, for his part, was confined to the castle. The weak, disabled son had to be kept from the sight of their enemies, as he would be seen as a weakness to be exploited should anything befall Æryk.

A few years later, when the boy first came to manhood, at the time when Æthelred reigned in Wessex, the King summoned to arms the men of the east shires and Eorl Byrhtnoth led what forces could be mustered towards Maeldun, where the army of Norse sea raiders were expected to land. When they arrived and faced their enemy, brave Byrhtnoth was neither shaken by the small number of his men, nor fearful of the massed ranks of the enemy. Æthelstan and his eldest son Æryk responded to Byrhtnoth's call and joined six hundred men near the River Panta. Four thousand Norse warriors landed at Northey Island that August morning and appeared faintly in the mist across the narrow causeway that separated them from the mainland. Their leader, Olaf, was prepared to wait until the tide ebbed and enabled him to cross, but Byrhtnoth gave them leave to cross in order that battle could commence without delay.

Byrhtnoth was killed, slain alongside Æthelstan and his son Æryk in a bloody battle. In the days that followed, King Æthelred paid a fortune in silver to the victorious raiders and those of the six hundred who had not been slain returned to their homes. When word of Lord Æthelstan

Scullion and his favoured son Æryk arrived at Ebbsweirmouth, rule of the East Seaxe shire passed directly to the son who had been concealed from the world these past ten years. And, as a consequence of Maeldun, Morcar became the new Lord Scullion.

Such was the noble respect that the King had for the family, that young Scullion was not even summoned to Wessex to seal his accession. A messenger bringing the King's seal was sufficient to make the youngest son eorl of the East Seaxe shire.

Balliwick finished the second bottle of wine and recalled those last moments before old Æthelstan and his lusty son Æryk had left for Maeldun. The fearful Morcar had wanted so much to please his father and had pleaded with him to let him go. Æryk had thrown a sword towards his frail brother's withered left arm, which obviously fell to the floor, clattering like a leper's bell that signalled the younger son's frailty.

What are endurance, mettle, fearlessness and valour without honour, thought Balliwick. Morcar should have ridden to Maeldun alongside his brother and father, but they would not have him. Even then, when Morcar first received word of his older brother's death, he should have sought vengeance. Pledges were uttered but never fulfilled. Fear and self-loathing, the indignity of a withered arm and the loss of honour had produced a man never seen outside the walls of Scullion Tower for fear the family's vulnerability would be exposed.

Honour is the most noble of virtues and, every day from that day forth, Morcar would wish himself a sea death, or a sword death, and yet he always feared he should endure a straw death in-keeping with his straw life. The past corrupts the future and the present too for those like Morcar, whose vision of honour is corrupted by the absence of truth. Honourable men are led by nature towards the truth and yet truth has the only merit of virtue where it is demonstrated in both words and deeds.

~~~~~

It was late and Hoop would have sent Byrgan and Gripple home by now, but Ravenhead and his lady had returned from their room to warm themselves at the hearth before finally retiring for the night. The pair had waited until they heard Scolop leave the inn and now sat in the shadows, speaking in hushed tones about what needed to be done next.

"We must have evidence and we must have that evidence seen by two reliable witnesses who we might call upon should the need arise," whispered Ravenhead. "I will speak to our man Scolop in the morning. Hopefully he will have calmed down by then."

Ravenhead looked up and noticed that the three men at the bar had stopped talking. Convinced that they were listening, he got up and left, accompanied by Una. The pair stepped out into the cold night air and walked along the side of the inn towards their room. Suddenly, out of the shadows, stepped a large man.

"Did you enjoy your fish?" said Scolop whose sudden movement was entirely designed to scare the two of them in the darkness outside. The slow-minded fisherman had obviously given further thought to his unpaid bill and had returned to wait in the shadows.

"We did, Master Scolop," Ravenhead replied, trying not to appear afraid. He had assumed that the fish was a peace token and that Scolop's anger may consequently have tempered for him to refer to it. From the look on the fishmonger's face it did not appear so.

"Well then, where is it? Where is my money?" Scolop said as he grabbed the man's cloak and fashioned a fierce look.

Ravenhead looked back at him and realised that he needed to act. Scolop's mood had worsened greatly, for here was a man who valued patience as nought and he could not sleep with the account unpaid.

"You shall have it in the morning, my man," Ravenhead offered, more in hope than expectation of a resolution to the matter.

But Scolop was having none of it and demanded immediate payment.

"Here is the trade, Master Scolop," answered Ravenhead, trying to appear bolder than he truly felt. "This is how the scene must unfold if you are to be paid. Tomorrow morning, when everyone is in the church, the body will be washed up on the shore and you shall run to the church and tell everyone that the boy drowned when you were fishing this very night. Balliwick and others must accompany you there. Once that is done and the body is identified, you shall receive your money."

"All of it?"

"All of it, yes. Provided the boy is identified."

"Now you make conditions," Scolop blustered quietly so as not to be heard inside the inn.

"It was always a condition, Master Scolop, that you killed the boy of whom we spoke. It is not enough to produce any body, Master Scolop, it needs to be the child identified as we said. You told us you knew of such a boy."

"Indeed I did and it is he whose body will be on the shore in the morning. And then you shall pay me," he demanded.

"Remember, you must tell Balliwick that the boy went overboard when you were out fishing and drowned."

"He drowned alright. And you will too if you don't pay me my money tomorrow."

As he spoke the door of the inn opened and Byrgan and Gripple stumbled out, almost falling on to the slushy snow outside. They laughed and set off down the road, half leaning on each other for support. The three conspirators leaned back into the shadows and kept quiet until the two men had left. When all was silent, Ravenhead spoke.

"It is the Sabbath tomorrow and we shall be at mass with everyone else in the morning, but you must not be there."

"I pay my tithes and church dues. Is that not enough?" Scolop replied. "Aye and alms to the poor too."

"No, Master Scolop, you will not be at mass because you will be somewhere else, won't you?"

He looked back at them, trying to remember what the plan was.

"Yes, yes. I shall be at Hollow Hole Cove, attending to our mutual friend."

With that, the couple returned to their room and Scolop waited a few moments to make sure that the butcher and gravedigger had gone from the street ahead. Once he was assured of it, he set off down the road, following their footprints. As he did so, the snow began to flutter down, covering his own steps and he hunkered himself against an icy wind and quickened his step.

Leland Hoop looked out from his casement at the falling snow and saw Scolop disappear into his home and off to his own bed.

Close by, Willem was stirred from his night's rest by the rowdy behaviour of Byrgan and Gripple as they returned home. He turned over on the straw and, as the silent footsteps of Scolop passed by, the gift of temperance, the guardian of selfless enterprise, rested upon the boy. The creatures in the stable stirred, for their senses are beyond our imagination.

Chapter Seven

Hope

Imagination stirs when the earth slumbers and the dark night that has now unfolded upon our tale does spawn curious worlds filled with strange meanderings. Troubled minds are eased into the arms of Morpheus and truth is suspended as a raucous world is transported to that silent place that sleeps when we awake. That bower where shapes and shadows dwell, where half-remembered thoughts crash like the foaming sea, endless, fathomless, ungirdled by that other world where we live less fancifully.

This brooding abode of retrospection and contorted thoughts brings drowsy, unreasoned musing to that dark place where now our stray cat of a boy slumbers amongst the beasts and straw, mewing with flickering eyelids. A world of dreams that, even when remembered, make little sense in the real world, encouraging hope to flower once more among the briar and bramble of despair and fear.

Awakening, or perhaps falling farther into the abyss, seduced by the enchantress of dreams, Willem lies in that other world of sleep. With equal licence you may choose; awake or asleep? For our story may be told either way with equal merit. Make of Watchman Darrayne as you will; man or spirit, the figment of a dream, or a mortal like you and me?

Even as he sleeps, Willem is torn on the matter and turns restlessly in his straw cot. The fantasy of dreams may indeed be illogical and so it must remain so in our tale of fortune and fate.

As with the spirits that haunt the corpse road, the Watchman may, if it pleases you, be a direful hallucination, a chimera, an apparition or ignis fatuus, as the learned Edwin Goodlyhead might say. Or the Watchman may be real, whatever real is. Real or not, he is a man who speaks of truth, and what we can be assured of is that dreams, like secrets, lose their power when the truth is spoken aloud.

These are indeed dark days, made so by the disunity of a nation and named so because they stand betwixt two cultured conquests. Some claim to recall those days before Christendom. But they do not, of course. They know only what they have been told. Fragments of that ancient past, handed down from one generation to the next. The world is now less a pattern for Bryttania than the greater realm of Christendom. Where once was Rome, so Normandy will follow and yet neither are held in such high esteem as Jerusalem, the much vaunted centre of the known world.

The barn at the rear of Mardyke House is a fragile wooden structure that needs constant repair and will do so again when the winter snow has melted and left the timbers cracked and loose. Mildred Goodlyhead had insisted on it, firstly to separate herself from the animals and secondly to create her own vision of the stable where the Christ child was born. It is the product of a romantic heart and an impractical mind, for they have no cattle, nor even a horse. So it houses just two goats and several chickens. Mildred does not make cheese, but the goats provide milk and the chickens eggs. No animal she has ever owned has been killed for *food, for she can not bring herself to execute such a deed. Instead, they die of old age and are buried at the rear of the large vegetable plot that stretches out behind the barn. The stable, as she has always called it, is a monument to hope, for it is battered by the coastal winds from the east.*

A flimsy wooden door separates our young pilgrim and his strange bedfellows from the cold night air and a star-filled sky. The rickety building creaks and groans as a sudden gust strikes it and howls to a waning moon. In the crowded cattle stall where now he lies, the clucking of a hen stirs his illusory sleep, where truth is suspended and the seventh virtue of hope dwells among all men.

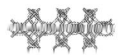

As Willem awoke, his eyes became slowly accustomed to the midnight gloom and the silence convinced him that it was not yet morning. Unsure of what had disturbed his sleep, he looked about him. A chicken fluttered noisily and there, sitting in front of him, was a familiar shape, the same shadowy figure he had spoken with in the church. The man was sitting on a wooden box, his head bowed as if in prayer. It was the same hooded cloak, the same grey face that raised its gaze from the dusty floor of the barn and revealed the same haunted pale eyes. Neither of them spoke for a moment and the Watchman sat, using a wooden twig to scrawl characters in the dust between his feet. 'DCCCCLXXXXVIIIJ' he scratched in the soil. Even looking at it upside down, the boy had learned enough to know what it represented.

Willem was still considering whether the shadow was real and whether it was truth that dwelled in this place or the false illusion of dreams. Then, before he had a chance to speak, he was asked a question.

"Where did you get the mittens?" a voice asked from the shadows. It had the same icy, vapourish sound that the boy remembered from the last time they had spoken. There was so much to discuss that it seemed a tedious subject to begin the conversation with. Surely the Watchman had not searched out the boy to find out where he had obtained his mittens.

"Mistress Goodlyhead," the boy answered, without hesitation or hint of fear, for courage had taken residence in his heart.

"It is a sign," the figure replied.

"A sign of what?" asked Willem, looking at the pair of mittens that stopped his hands from freezing in the cold air.

"Hope," he replied, for he sensed its presence.

"Why hope?"

"Because hope always follows a charitable act, Willem."

There was something wrong with the man's last word. The name 'Willem' jarred and disturbed the boy's thoughts. He could not remember telling the man his name, but thought he must have done so in the church. So he ignored the niggling concern that hovered in his mind and instead asked a different question.

"What are you writing?"

"You ask a great many questions," the Watchman replied. "You need not worry yourself of what I write, for it speaks of times past. Soon you shall write a single character, simply 'M', for a different time is coming, my young friend."

"You are a learned man," spoke Willem. "Is it true, then, that a new world is coming, a new order? Did the farmer they call Cotes speak truthfully?"

"Truth? You ask about truth? What would you have of truth, my young friend? That it be untarnished, unsullied by the world? I can tell you that this world would have it replaced with certainty and to hell with faith and hope. They diminish hope by the way they treat it, for in hope there is aspiration. It is not hope, but fear that stands between us and truth. Truth is unassailable; it withstands derision, malice and ignorance."

"Last night, in the church," the boy said, "you mentioned a land called Haeferingas. Is that where you come from?"

The hooded figure nodded and the boy asked where this place was.

The voice beneath the hood softened as it spoke of its homeland and painted a blissful pastoral scene. Haeferingas, he told the boy, was a large shire to the south of where they were now sitting. The Watchman had been raised on a hill, high above the Ing Valley, which housed the gentlest of all rivers. The valley was surrounded by green forest that ended at the hill top and the moorland gazed down on the grassy verge of the rippling waters. In spring, the edge of the woodland was decorated with brightly coloured wildflowers. Periwinkles and wood lilies littered the shaded brow of the eastern hill and the ground was turned indigo by the hosts of nodding bluebells. Then, as the slope turned from the wood and spilled downward to the River Ing, barrenwort carpeted the earth, its foliage turning the land golden brown long before that colour was adopted by the trees that shaded it. And down by the river's edge, great wreaths of sedge grew more colourful than anywhere else and remained more ardent too, not withering until the cold days of winter.

Winter in Haeferingas, he told the boy, was unlike anywhere else. It was not a time for hibernation but more a coming to life. Gorse lined the narrow Ing River as it became a more ardent stream through the steep valley. The Watchman remembered every detail of his homeland, for even the shattered stone walls around the farms were engraved in the man's memory.

"Winter is the season of survival for both plant and beast, and young and old alike, but in Haeferingas it is a time of beauty."

The boy marvelled at the sound of such a wondrous place and asked if he might accompany the Watchman when he returned. But the man said he no longer lived there, having left to take up the sword and serve his King. The boy wanted to ask why he had never returned, but also wanted to learn about the battles the man had fought in. Yet the shadowy figure would speak of neither.

"I pray that you might find Haeferingas for yourself one day," the man said. "Have you ever been to such a special place?"

Willem then told the Watchman of a place hidden by time in his memory. He was sure he had visited there but, with the passing of each day, he thought it may have been just a dream.

"It is less a place and more a moment in time," said the boy as he began to describe a peaceful, shaded spot where two ancient hedgerows met. He had been taken there for a picnic one fine summer day, or at least that is what he believed.

"I was accompanied by an angel, so it could not have been true. And yet it seemed like a dream that was more real than life itself."

The boy told the figure about the delicate velvet pink flowers of the dog rose, rising above the whitethorn on its precarious stems, with arching briars interwoven among the thicket. And he recalled the intoxicating scent of green apples that filled the air. The honeysuckle, wild violets and the abundant cream flowers of the cow parsley seemed to signal the arrival of summer. The bower of bliss created by the marriage of the two hedgerows shielded the picnic setting from the winds and, for that day only, the tree sparrows, yellowhammers and reed buntings were displaced from their home, disturbed by the happy laughter of the angel and the child.

Such was the place in the boy's dreams that he was unsure of its existence, or whether that summer day had ever really taken place. He wondered whether the place he recalled in his dreams might be the same place that the shadow spoke of. Perhaps this wondrous place was also Haeferingas, although Willem had no recollection of such a place name. More likely, he thought, his dream was of Ebbsweirmouth, as he was sure he had visited here before; at least, that is what he had been told. It had been dark when he arrived on Friday and his arrival was greeted with a blizzard, so he would not have recognised two adjoined hedgerows if he had walked directly past them that night. Anyway, it was winter and the place in his distant memory was always swathed in summer.

"The angel was with me for one day only. I have never truly known what it is like to have a mother, but I did that day, Sir. I never saw her again, even though I hoped to do so each time my head rested on the straw at night."

The boy was disappointed not to learn more of the wonderful place the man spoke of called Haeferingas, although he still had many other matters to question the man on.

"You say that you were a soldier and officer of the watch and yet you no longer carry a sword or bear a soldier's shield. If you are no longer a soldier, then what are you now, if not a watchman?"

"My lord, who I had pledged to serve, was slain on the battlefield eight years past and I chose to trade in blood no more."

The boy listened intently as the shallow voice told him that he had taken up the occupation of a chandler.

"I had brought darkness to many in my life and so I wished only to bring light. I was handed a candle once and instructed to use it to light the way for an infant child. It is an oath that I am foresworn upon."

The boy had an inquisitive nature and showed interest in all matters, without exception. So the man was not surprised when his young friend showed equal attention to the occupation of a chandler as he did to a soldier, wanting to know how candles were made. The man tired of so many questions, but relented, as sleep would not have its way with the boy on this night.

"Candles are simply tallow, or beeswax if there is any to be had. And these are then melted over fibres of flax."

"Did you make the candles at the church we sat in?" the boy asked, remembering how he had warmed his hands upon them.

"No," the cloaked figure answered. "Although I was hoping to do so. I had business to transact with a tradesman in the village."

The boy wondered why he used the word 'had', as if he had not conducted the business that he spoke of.

"It is a worthy and interesting profession," said the boy. "Does it bring financial reward?"

The hooded figure sighed. "Be ambitious for the higher gifts," he advised him. "Truth, honesty, integrity, loyalty, the noble virtues. Relinquish all else for these great treasures."

"What are virtues?" the boy asked.

"A virtue is an impenetrable desire to do good," he replied, as if he had been told this by someone equally learned in a distant time past.

"Like making candles?"

"Higher still."

"But everyone needs candles."

"Poorer people use rushes dipped in animal fat for their candles," the voice beneath the hood replied. And though the boy's questions were endless, the man never tired of answering them.

As the night passed they spoke of many things. The boy pledged to find work in the morning, until he was reminded that it was the Sabbath day, on which all people must rest. Willem's inquisitive nature was discussed and his companion assured him that this was a good thing, telling him that the search for knowledge would find the greater gift of wisdom, and with wisdom came justice.

"Justice is the prerogative of the powerful," replied the boy, but the man shook his head.

"True power dwells in the house of the merciful, Willem."

In that moment, the boy was certain that he had never mentioned his name to the man and he wondered how he knew it. Looking at the shadowy figure before him, the boy became too fearful to ask, but finally he summoned up the courage and put the question.

"How do you know my name, Sir, as I do not recall mentioning it?"

"I knew who you were when I saw your hand."

"But *how* do you know me, Sir?"

"Let it rest for another time. It is a long story."

Childhood innocence treasures truth above politeness and the boy felt an overpowering desire to ask again, for his thirst for knowledge was unquenchable. But, instead, he asked who the saint was whose feast day was being celebrated at mass. When the man answered him, the boy raised another question. Every answer prompted another question, it seemed.

"Why is he known as Saint Lazarus of the four days?"

The Watchman explained how Lazarus had been a friend of Jesus and that Christ caused Lazarus to rise from the dead after he had been in the tomb for four days. The boy admitted that his reading had been limited to the Holy Bible and only then when someone was there to guide him, for he only knew how to read a few words.

"When we met last," the boy said in a halting tone, "you mentioned the sixteen virtues of destiny, which you said are gifts. Who should I look to for such gifts?"

The Watchman then explained that the virtues of destiny are not the gift of our fellow man, but the endowment of God, the product of earnest prayer and a search for truth and justice.

"The gifts begin with courage and end in understanding and love."

He then told Willem that a wise woman had once expressed the virtues as symbols and taught him that only an unwilling heart prevented the many from receiving the gifts that only a few enjoyed. Each virtue must be savoured and made welcome before receiving the next. As the Watchman spoke, he scratched the two or three symbols he could remember.

Willem got up and walked over to stand next to the shadowy figure. The Watchmen knew it had taken courage to stand next to him, just as it had to touch his hand the previous night. And, in that moment, he realised that the boy had begun his journey.

"On my passage to Ebbsweirmouth, I met an old maid in a yew tree wood," Willem confessed reluctantly, believing the man would think less of him for speaking of such matters. And yet, the man sighed heavily, almost moaning into the hands that now cupped his shadowed face.

"What did she say?" he asked through the darkness.

"That courage, honour and love are the cornerstones of destiny and love is above all others."

"And what did she mean by that?"

"I do not know," the boy admitted.

"Then think on it until we next meet."

The boy returned to his straw bed and, just before the night began to close his weary eyes, he was granted the opportunity to ask one final question. Willem thought at length about what one question would satisfy his troubled mind. He concluded that it must be the one that had bothered him since he had awoken from his sleep. Why had the Watchman appeared in the stable here and how had he known that Willem would be there? But that was two questions. So he paused for a moment and spoke.

"What do you want?" the boy asked and he seemed pleased with his question. From beneath the hood of the cloak the boy thought he could see a smile.

"Do you know," replied the shadow, "that was the first question that Christ asked of his first disciple."

"Simon Peter?"

"No, the first disciple was Simon's brother, Andrew."

There was a pause before the boy's question was answered.

"I search for one thing only; justice," replied the shadow.

The boy wanted to ask why the Watchman was seeking justice, but he knew he had already asked his final question and the man would think less of him if he asked another. As he lay on the straw, surrounded by animals made restless by their conversation, the boy considered the last answer he had received. What justice could the shadowy figure desire?

Just before he drifted off to sleep, the boy recalled something the Watchman had said earlier. 'Let it rest for another time. It is a long story.' The boy considered the words and found in them consolation that he would see the man again and might then have an opportunity to question him on his search for justice.

Willem felt no fear in the presence of the strange figure and, as the goats and chickens settled down to rest again, the boy felt himself slipping into a deep sleep. As he did so he heard the faint passing words of the Watchman.

"We all search for justice, my young friend," the voice whispered from the darkness. "But take heed, for the enemy of justice is providence and fate, because fate is what results when men stand by and lose their grip on destiny." The voice tapered away. "Fear fate above all things," he cautioned the boy, for he knew that fate could not rest on hope alone. As his slumbering thoughts took Willem to another place, he heard the final words of the Watchman. "Shrink not from your duty and fear fate above all else."

Chapter Eight

Piety

Shrink not from your duty and fear fate above all else. The Watchman's words echo into the dark night and Willem is still thinking of them as the cockerel crows and ends his dreaming. Yet, fate is not fate when it has a helping hand. And who knows the tides better than a fisherman? So, while the townsfolk of Ebbsweirmouth kneel in prayer on this third Sunday of advent, one unbeliever chooses to use their absence to lay his scene and shape destiny to his own design.

The leaves rustle and the trees bow their heads as the swirling winds take the ebbing tide from Hollow Hole Cove on this cold hallowed morning, leaving a shingle beach that crackles with each foaming wave that pushes the briny main farther away. Rock pools form in the sandy pockets of shell and grit, and these lay hidden from view by the surf. Closer to the cliff, larger cavities and sunken vaults are filled with sea water and creatures of the deep, as life finds a new home against rocks almost hidden by seaweed. In the smaller crevices, tiny crabs peek out and greet the reshaped world that awaits them. Their prehistoric claws stir the sediment of the muddy shore and the strangely shaped creatures search each *watery hole that has been separated from the great ocean that each had once been part of. A group of tiny shore crabs spots the approach of a large spiny spider crab and they try to bury themselves beneath the soft, wet sand. On dry patches of the beach, red fungi rise from the pebbles, as geese and gulls hover overhead before landing and searching the margin land for food.*

As the wind howls its discontentment at the earth, a heavily built man walks and slides down the sloping bank of the cliff and then rests for a moment on the shattered harbour wall. This part of Hollow Hole Cove, where the sea sweeps under and into the cliff, is the final resting place for the abducted waters of the departing tide. The craggy rocks around the cove enslave the ocean, preventing it from leaving its subterranean home. Several large pools of water form and in one of these a tiny fishing boat creaks as it rocks against the iron will of the wind. Next to its battered hull, half sunk in the freezing water, lies the body of a young boy, less than ten years old.

How often the hateful response of fate defies mercy and disguises its hideous face. And yet fate is not the product of itself and, moreover, its true purpose may only be seen from the great distance of time. Despair or joy will change its countenance. Fortitude is a cardinal virtue that, in the pious man, ensures firmness in difficulties and constancy in troubled times. Misfortune cannot disturb the pious heart. But, in the heart of the godless, fate is a heinous endowment. And in the heart of the weak it is accepted as providence; the outcome of fate. As the evil deed is done, so the seeds of providence are sown and silently, in the dawn light, piety the eighth virtue of destiny is bestowed, giving strength to our sleeping pilgrim that he may not yield to submission but accept events and subject them to his own will, for indeed, fate is to be feared above all things.

Piety turns an act of duty into an act of love. Duty is the enterprise of the meek and, whilst they might inherit the earth, it is the pious who shall dwell in heaven.

<hr />

Scolop released the body from the rusty chain and rope that secured it to the boat and examined the boy's hand. The fingers were pale and wrinkled by their long-sunken hours beneath the still, trapped sea in Hollow Hole Cove. The fisherman had hoped for a better outcome, but this would have to do.

Dragging the lifeless, limp body from the pool and lifting it onto his shoulder, he carried it to the widest part of the stony beach. Then, face up it lay, for the fisherman's conscience was no harbour for compunction or remorse. Finally he placed the child's right hand across the chest in order that all might heed the mark that set him apart.

The secluded Pryklethorn Bay formed almost a full circle and on its western shore it was shaded by the cliff from the rising sun. At this time of the year, the sun's ineffective rays brought little warmth anyway and the snow on the ledges, as he clambered up the hill, was unmoved by it. Exposed to the new day, the white blanket that frosted the top of the cliff began to shimmer and melt. In its slow transition, the packed ice was still deep enough to take a footprint, and Scolop buried his heavy feet deep in the watery slush as he made his way back to the town.

As he approached the church, he looked about him and could see nobody. He assured himself that the fools would all be inside the church on this Sabbath morning. They would receive nothing for such labours and even less for their prayers, he assured himself, yet he who made merit from a sinful heart would be ten shillings richer for his efforts on this dour grey morning. Scolop consoled himself with this mercenary thought as he heard reassuring sounds from inside the church.

As the fisherman reached the graveyard at the rear of the church, he could hear the chanting voice of Shriver the priest, pontificating to his fearful flock. Scolop had arrived too early it seemed, so he sat down on top of a grave and leaned his back against the headstone. It had been so recently placed there that it carried no moss or lichen and, unlike most others, remained upright. 'Frances Hoop' was carved on it and he thought for a moment about the pathetic, lovelorn innkeeper, who still mourned the passing of his ill-fated wife.

He rubbed his rough hands together to warm himself, pulled up his collar and listened as the priest blessed his flock and bade them to leave. As soon as he heard the doors open at the front of the building, he feigned a melancholy state and, with heavy breathing as insincere as his mournful look, he ran between the graves until he was face to face with the departing congregation. He leaned down, clutching his thighs as if breathless from running a long distance and then begged their attention.

"Be quick, be quick, where is Master Balliwick, for the boy Eldrik is drowned!" All the time, he looked about him, hoping to see the chamberlain.

Father Shriver stepped through the crowd of people who were gathered about, all jostling to secure a place at the front, and the priest informed the fisherman that the shire reeve was attending mass at the tower that morning.

There was a loud gasp from Scolop, who looked both fearful and surprised at the same time. Surprised, because Balliwick always attended mass at the church and he had been told he would be here by Ravenhead. And fearful, not of the dire consequences of his act, but that he might not get paid for the deed, because of the inexplicable absence of Chamberlain Balliwick.

Mistress Goodlyhead pushed herself to the front of the assembled company and instructed Scolop to take her to the boy.

"No, no," he shouted. "Balliwick must come. Where is Balliwick?"

Deep among the group of people gathered there, Scolop could see Ravenhead and the Lady Una both trying to look as inconspicuous as possible at the rear of the crowd. He looked at them questioningly, hoping that they might intervene, for the plan was now spoiled by the absence of the shire reeve.

"Master Balliwick will be here shortly," replied Shriver. "For he is to accompany Friar Sopscott and myself to the tower to celebrate mass."

"Good," declared Scolop, who looked surprisingly cheered and certainly relieved by the comment. "Then we shall wait."

"Wait?" Mistress Goodlyhead asked in an assertive tone. "Come, we must attend the boy and if he is dead, as you say, then he shall be brought back to the church for Master Balliwick to see and Father Shriver to administer the last sacrament."

"Dead? Of course he is dead," declared Scolop a little too eagerly. "The boy drowned whilst we fished last night. He lies still on the shore at Hollow Hole Cove."

Leland Hoop, who stood close by, observed well Scolop's words. What was being said did not make sense, nor did it reconcile with what Hoop had seen the previous night. The innkeeper was certain that Scolop had gone directly home from the inn and he wanted to say so. But, like most who had gathered there that morning, the reputation of Cyrus Scolop urged him to remain silent.

"Then come with me," Mildred instructed Scolop forcefully, as she feared him not. "And bring some able-bodied men to carry the boy back."

Aldwyn Byrgan stepped forward, pulling the sleeves of his two grown sons, insisting that they would carry the body back from the cove, as it was their responsibility to do so. Unsure of what action to take, Scolop led the group as slowly as he could, with the Byrgans accompanying him and Mistress Goodlyhead following on behind. After a moment's delay, many of those remaining outside the church decided to follow on too and neither Ravenhead nor Una could conceal their desire to join them and see for themselves the dead boy.

And so, the gossiping crowd headed off towards Hollow Hole Cove, not through the town and along the pathway past Pryklethorn Bay, but directly east through the copse of leafless birch and elm trees that, in spite of their empty branches, continued to provided some shelter against the still-ardent easterly wind.

The column straggled out as they confined themselves to the narrow track that was only sparsely dusted with snow, protected as it was by the trees.

Friar Sopscott remained outside the church and pulled the hood of his black habit close about his face. The action was taken as much to hide his wounds as to keep out the cold wind. The friar decided to wait with Father Shriver in order to meet Chamberlain Balliwick. He also wanted to seek assurance that the priest would administer Extreme Unction only if the necessary provisions were met. Sopscott considered the factors that might affect this decision, as he harboured strong principles on liturgical procedures.

"It is the Sabbath and the boy was not at mass," the friar declared. "Can you be sure his soul was in a state of grace?"

The few parishioners who remained, gathered about the two holy men and listened to their learned words, wondering whether the poor boy was to be denied the last rites.

"I am sure he would have been at mass had he not drowned," replied the priest. "Even Cyrus Scolop would not prevent his serf from attending mass on the Sabbath day."

"He had reached the age of reason, then?" came a second question from Sopscott.

"He had."

"How old was the boy?"

"Certainly more than seven years; ten, perhaps," answered Shriver. "But we cannot be sure how long he has been dead. The soul may have left the body."

"If he drowned last night, then corruption of the body has not yet begun. We cannot presume to know the moment when the soul departs, Father."

"Quite so," came the submissive reply. Shriver was entirely happy to defer to the friar's decision in the matter.

The leafless, lichen-clad branches of birch and elm that edged the coastal path stared lifelessly at the low rising sun, as it cast red gauze across the ribboned, sanded beach. As the crowd walked towards the top of the sea cliff, the forest thinned out and the cinnamon-coloured earth not covered by snow turned to sand dunes that swept down towards the shore. The vast ocean view that greeted them denied them its beauty as the bright morning sunshine blinded them. They all moved cautiously towards the cliff edge and looked over. A few paces from where the sea lapped the shingle surface of the cove, the wet sand turned to pebble and shell and there, for all to see, a young body lay still in the morning light, pale white and turning purple in the cold glow of a limp sun.

The slippery pathway down into the cove caused some to lag behind and most remained waiting on the path above the beach. The stragglers, who had left the church after the others, had all arrived by the time the body was finally brought to the cliff top. Mildred was the first to attend the boy, removing what clothes she could whilst allowing the lost soul his modesty. She placed her hands together and said a short prayer before beginning a cursory inspection of the corpse. It was freezing to the touch and Mildred brushed away the sand that had dried on his arms and legs.

Now the body had been moved it could be seen clearly by everyone. But most attending the scene did not notice that the boy was missing the tip of the little finger on his right hand. Moreover, there were enough bruises and scars on the body to disturb the most hardened of hearts, and certainly sufficient to distract them from a missing finger tip. The body's thin frame was marked with reddened skin and large purple bruises that were already beginning to fade. The toneless flesh on his legs was more blue than pink and the glacial eyes were translucent and staring. There was something unholy in those eyes and, before Mildred closed them, she noticed they had turned white to match the paleness of his skin.

It was not the first time that Mildred Goodlyhead had seen a drowned body in her service as seeker of the dead, but it was the youngest she had seen for many years.

"Take him back to the church," she said to Byrgan. "For his life has left this world but perhaps his soul has not yet done so."

The grave digger signalled to his sons to help him, but he was shocked by the texture of the skin as he lifted the body up. Perhaps it was the intense chill of the sea, but the process of cold shortening seemed discrepant with a death just a few hours before. He looked at Scolop and at Mildred Goodlyhead for some comment and yet they remained silent for differing reasons.

As the wandering congregation made its slippery way back to the town, many spoke kind words of comfort to Cyrus Scolop, who received these with unusual grace. The last to approach him was Lord Ravenhead, who removed his glove and shook the fisherman's ruddy hand.

"My condolences for your sad loss, Master Scolop," he said, pressing ten silver shillings into the coarse, yet eager, hand and walking off to rejoin Una.

The fisherman was desperate to look at the coins he had been furtively given but decided to keep a tight grip on them until he was alone. Ravenhead was going nowhere on a Sabbath and would not cross him anyway, Scolop was sure of that.

When the crowd returned to the church, the boy's limp body was laid on the pathway in the graveyard and Father Shriver administered the last rites. He was helped from his knees by Master Byrgan and the priest immediately rested his hand on Scolop's shoulder.

"Trust in God and resign yourself to His will, my son."

Most of those who remained expected Scolop to issue a scolding rebuke and they were greatly surprised by his mournful expression and silent acquiescence to the priest's blessing. And yet, through his sodden beard, some could almost see a smile as the Shire Reeve Balliwick walked towards the crowd, insisting to know what had happened to draw such interest.

"My boy, the serf Eldrik, has drowned, Master Chamberlain," declared Scolop eagerly.

The lifeless corpse lay free of earthly cares on the snow, no longer a child but a limp, sodden body drawn in every sense towards heaven. The priest had opened the boy's eyes to administer the last sacrament and the vacant stare he now bore took everyone's attention, and those of a more delicate disposition were forced to look away. Long faded was any blush in his cheeks and the eyes were white and paler than the ivory skin of his face.

Most of those gathered around had misgivings about Scolop's grief. Indeed, suspicion and surprise were present in equal measure, as many of those present had first-hand experience of Scolop's fierce temper. A few saw the missing tip of the boy's finger and kept silent, thinking it had been bitten off by a fish, or were perhaps convinced that they had not noticed its absence before. Most importantly for Scolop, they kept their counsel, as it seemed an insignificant aspect of such a tragedy and the boy could just as easily have lost the finger tip filleting fish for his master.

Leland Hoop noticed more than the subtle nuance of misplaced grief in the face of his uncouth customer. He had his own reasons to suspect that all was not right, for he had seen Scolop go home to his bed last night and, like most nights, he had kept a constant vigil from his casement window. So how was it that the irascible fishmonger could have been at his business last night?

Willem, too, was full of mistrust, for had Scolop not told him to return to work on Monday? What need would the fisherman have of him if Eldrik had returned to work last night?

This was the first dead body that Willem had seen in his young life. He had seen dead animals of course, but then, all animals on a farm were raised for slaughter. And some humans, also, it now seemed to the impressionable boy. The strangest of deaths he had previously seen was a litter of newborn rabbits, kicked from the warren and left for dead by their mother, who had been overwhelmed by the new sensation of birth, unable to understand what she had just experienced, so the farmer's wife had told Willem. But, even hidden at the back of the crowd, Willem could now see the true horror of human death. And the fact that the boy was about his own age made the scene even more horrid.

By the time Willem glimpsed the limp body of Eldrik, the colourless, pastel transparency of the skin made him feel sick. For a moment it looked to Willem as if the dead boy had the tip of his smallest finger missing but, by the time he looked again, Mildred had covered the boy's body with a cloak.

Out of earshot at the rear of the crowd stood Ravenhead and Una, watching intensely each person's reaction to the boy's death. But suspicion was buried deep within each person's heart and the couple's satisfaction at the outcome needed to be concealed.

"Do you recognise the dead boy?" Ravenhead whispered to his companion.

"I have not seen the child since he was taken from my arms by the wet nurse."

"Is it him?" came the impatient response to her ambiguous reply.

"He has the mark I gave him," she answered, before bowing her head. "God have mercy on me."

The maid's words were enough for Ravenhead and he looked for an opportunity to engage Chamberlain Balliwick. However, the shire reeve seemed anxious to set off to the tower, where his Lordship fasted ahead of the mass, so Ravenhead needed to act swiftly.

Wainthrop, too, considered approaching Balliwick and yet fear gripped his heart, for what proof was there of his own suspicions? What would happen if he stepped forward to make a claim of foul play? What purpose would it serve if there was nobody to second such an allegation? Others may have their suspicions of Master Scolop but, for Wainthrop, it was not suspicion that shaped his face and thoughts, but confirmation of his inner fears and remembrances of what he had seen, or thought he had seen, through the sea haze on Friday morning as he had walked along the coastal path into town. The publican, Leland Hoop, also thought back to the events of the past two nights and wondered whether he should speak up.

Then, just as Wainthrop and Hoop thought upon their doubts, still more uncertainty surfaced in the words of the much sought-after Chamberlain Balliwick.

"Two bodies in a few days, Mistress Goodlyhead. Perhaps we should heed the gossiping voice of Abel Cotes."

Mistress Goodlyhead looked back at him with such a pained expression, as this was an arduous occupation for one of such sensitivities.

Two bodies, thought Willem, as he looked about him in the hope that he could see the Watchman Darrayne. But the shadowy figure had not been at the mass, which could only mean that his guide had arrived and he had now left town, for it was unthinkable for anyone to miss mass on the Sabbath.

Hearing Balliwick's cynical comment, Farmer Cotes turned from the crowd and headed off out of town, mumbling under his breath. Maggoty Gripple cursed the farmer quietly, blaming him for all the fear and trembling that the town now felt.

"He is to blame for this," called Gripple, pointing towards Cotes. "He has caused all this with his unhallowed prophecy."

As the crowd began to disperse, Mildred noticed some small marks on the side of the dead boy's neck. She knelt down and lifted his head, noting that the bruising continued around the back of his neck. This could not have resulted from the body banging against rocks when it was washed ashore. She had seen marks like these on the front of a neck previously, caused by the indentation of fingers used to throttle a victim. But she had never seen them on the rear, as they appeared now, and wondered what it could mean.

Friar Sopscott and Father Shriver began to ready themselves to leave for the tower and, as they did, Byrgan called to Balliwick. His courage had now left him completely and he remained silent about his fears.

"The burial, Master Shire Reeve?"

"Proceed," came the immediate reply, with just a cursory glance towards Mistress Goodlyhead to see if she had any objection. She did not heed the comment, nor see the look from the chamberlain, for she was preoccupied with the boy. She knelt down by the body and folded his arms across his chest. Then, suddenly, she noticed something unusual. She looked at the boy's right hand and subdued a gasp when she saw the missing finger tip. She looked about her, wondering if anyone else had spotted what she had seen. But most people had dispersed and those who had not were simply continuing the argument started by Gripple and Cotes. Mildred stared at the boy's hand. What could this mean? Whatever it was, she feared for the boy Willem, who had only recently arrived in town, particularly as he was now working for Scolop. She turned to the waif and told him to join them at Mardyke House for dinner at dusk. But, much to her surprise, he appeared to decline the invitation.

"There is no work to be had today, Mistress Goodlyhead."

She looked at him, wondering what he could mean.

"Perhaps I can clear the stable for you, or perform some other chores. But I cannot allow you to continue feeding me unless I am able to repay you with my labour."

She stared at him lovingly and instructed him to tidy the stable.

"But, mind you are ready for supper at sunset."

Mildred stood there for a moment wondering what significance the missing fingertip might have. She began to consider who she might confide in. Yet, just for the moment, she wanted to make some sense of it herself.

The crowd dispersed and the priest returned into the church to gather together what he required for the chapel mass. As he did so, a voice called to Balliwick.

"Chamberlain Balliwick, may I have a moment of your time, Sir?"

It was not unusual for those attending mass on a Sunday to wear their finest attire. Indeed, many freemen and women kept clothing solely for that purpose. But Ravenhead's clothing set him apart from even the wealthiest of the townsfolk, like Master and Mistress Goodlyhead. The shirt and tunic he wore were of the finest material, as were the breeches, which were accompanied by wool leggings and leather garters. His cloak was dyed the warm russet of autumn and was secured about his neck by a brooch sporting the symbol of a raven. And the Lady Una was herself as well dressed as anyone of the royal court. Yet, in the turmoil that had greeted Balliwick on his arrival at the church, he had failed to notice the pair, who had been surrounded by locals wishing to see who had drowned.

The man told Balliwick that he was Lord Ravenhead, the son of an eorl in the northern shire of Northumbria, and he wished to meet with Lord Scullion. He then introduced his betrothed, Lady Una Haeferingas, the daughter of Lord Haeferingas, who had recently passed away.

"Lady Una and I intended to marry, but her father passed from this world before I had the opportunity to seek his blessing, Master Balliwick. I was delayed with business at home and failed to arrive before his lordship passed from this life. It was most unfortunate."

Unfortunate for you or him, was what Balliwick wanted to ask, but he suppressed his glib response.

"And how does this involve Lord Scullion?"

"Lady Una is the only surviving child of Eorl Haeferingas, following the tragic and untimely death of her brother, Osmund, at Maeldun. In the circumstances, I am obliged, I feel, to seek the blessing of the Lady Una's cousin, Lord Scullion, before proceeding with the marriage."

Balliwick had never heard of Ravenhead and had certainly never travelled to Northumbria. But he was familiar with Haeferingas, even though he had never visited there either. Nor had Lord Scullion seen his cousin, having been confined to the tower since childhood. But custom and politeness placed certain requirements upon him and, moreover, he was won over by the nobleman's attire and good manners.

"You must join his lordship for lunch at the tower," Balliwick declared, for it was his duty to present any visitors of note to the eorl.

Of course, Balliwick had prepared his lordship that morning for the visiting guests, and it was fortunate then, in his view, that the required hospitality could be extended to all four in one meeting. The servants had been instructed to dice the food so that his lordship might eat with just his good arm and conceal the other beneath his tunic. Scullion had made such arrangements on many occasions, because it was impossible for his master to hide entirely from the world. And, as far as he and Balliwick knew, his ailment remained secret. There were rumours, of course, about his reclusive nature, and yet fear of the chamberlain's reprisal kept the servants from ever mentioning the matter. No slave of Lord Scullion would ever speak to anyone other than another slave and, even then, not on such matters of intimate regard to his lordship.

And so the arrangements were settled. Ravenhead accepted the invitation on behalf of the Lady Una and himself, and even agreed to attend the mass, for he wanted to see the chapel of Scullion Tower. The pious Friar Sopscott reminded the pair that they must forego the Eucharist, for it was not permitted to receive Holy Communion more than once each day and they each acknowledged his ruling, although they had never heard of such a rule, nor tested it for that matter.

Neither Shriver nor Sopscott had seen Ravenhead or Una in town and they and Balliwick assumed that they had arrived late the previous evening.

As the five of them set off towards the tower, ahead of them on the road marched the farmer, Seth Wainthrop, who wondered at intervals whether he should turn around and tell Master Balliwick in private of his thoughts and concerns about what he had seen on Friday morning.

But he convinced himself that nothing could remain private in such a small village as Ebbsweirmouth and he persuaded himself that the shire reeve would not hold the matter private for long. He would demand that Wainthrop stood up and declared his allegiance in public. Then what would happen? In the absence of any other witnesses, his claim would be dismissed. And then he would be left at the mercy of Scolop. What mercy, he thought. For the man had never shown an ounce of mercy in his life. I have mercy, thought Wainthrop, but what good would my mercy do for the dead boy? So he did not turn around, nor did he bear fortitude, but left the matter to providence, for who would want to make an enemy of Master Scolop? It was in the hands of fate, the farmer reassured himself. What happens will happen and it was not for him to divert providence from its natural course. He took consolation in the possibility that his limited knowledge may be flawed. Indeed, was not all knowledge flawed, he asked himself.

It was not fear, he convinced himself, but simply saving the shire reeve valuable time. What good would come of it? He relied on Lord Scullion for his income and his lordship would not thank him for wasting his chamberlain's time.

By the time he had turned and waved goodbye to Balliwick and his guests, Wainthrop held a much improved view of himself. And yet, in spite of his attempts to forget what he had seen, a peaceful mind came reluctantly and troubled thoughts plagued his conscience.

Peace of mind was denied to other residents of Ebbsweirmouth too. Mildred Goodlyhead had much to fill her thoughts, as she returned home to Mardyke House, thinking about the poor soul whose body she had just examined.

Willem tidied the stable with a sense of obligation and duty. But, by now, piety had been added to the seven virtues already bequeathed. With this, his work brought him joy, as it had become a labour of love. And yet the comment that two people had died in the few days since he had arrived haunted his thoughts as he worked.

Chapter Nine

Knowledge

Twice holy is this Sabbath morning. In these most reverential of times it is inescapable for it to be otherwise for, as I have already told you, there are many more worthy saints to be celebrated than there are days in the calendar. Saint Lazarus of the four days, the most blessed friend of the Christ, has seen his feast day pass and now Saint Olympias is celebrated, and it is she who is honoured for a second time on this holy day. This most blessed orphan of the generous heart is remembered this morning at churches throughout the land, at the tower chapel and also at Eling Priory, and most curiously amongst the midmost trees of an old yew wood, for prayer is not diminished by its surroundings and who better to bestow an orphan with knowledge than another orphan.

It is a week and a day before the Christ's mass and at Scullion Tower we find Father Shriver lighting the third candle of advent on the chapel altar. And it is here that we see Forl Scullion, kneeling in devotion to one he considers a cruel God. And yet in spite of his deformities, both in temperament and appearance, he is envied by many for his position and wealth. Such are the gifts of

God distributed and such is the weakness of man that earthly riches are envied by so many.

Not least of these is his chosen shire reeve, who kneels three rows behind, for the first three rows are reserved for family members only. And, even though there are none, protocol must be observed.

Lady Una kneels behind his lordship, but Lord Ravenhead has been directed to sit on the pews to the right of the aisle, symbolising that no blood covenant yet exists between him and Lord Scullion. Balliwick smiles to himself that he should have made such a subtle, yet meaningful gesture. If Lord Ravenhead wants a blood covenant with the East Seaxe shire, he thought, then he must pay for it.

Friar Sopscott sits in the pew behind Ravenhead and removes his hood to pray. He is greatly distracted from his devotion this day and looks curiously at the Lady Una. Is it knowledge or understanding that he searches for on this cold Sabbath morning, or simply an explanation for the troublesome thoughts that now disturb his mind?

Man's appetite for knowledge is surpassed in this world only by the wish of those in power to suppress it. Is the mass not spoken in Latin for that very purpose? Knowledge is a gift held only in part and is, itself, only a step towards the greater gifts of wisdom and understanding. The ninth virtue of destiny is the perfection of faith through knowledge. It is bestowed on each of us in order that we can determine God's purpose for our lives. But it is not God's purpose that Ravenhead seeks this day. His purpose is the selfish product of avarice; it is earthly riches he desires, not the higher celestial gifts that the Watchman commended to Willem.

The ambitions of Ravenhead rely as much on the suppression of knowledge as they do on his own acquisition of it. What has been forgotten is as important to him as that which is eternally remembered. Certainly nobody has forgotten Maeldun, nor the heroism of Osmund, who was mortally wounded fighting alongside Eorl Æthelstan Scullion and his son, Æryk. Nor did any dishonour fall on Eorl Haeferingas, who was too old to serve there. And those matters are never forgotten. Yet, the web that spun from that famous battle stretches beyond those who died and, indeed, those who survived. But, with the dead, memories are buried also. Lord Haeferingas now lies alongside the brave Osmund, who is buried in the graveyard of the horned church. So who is to say who fought and who did not? Morcar, too, shall be buried alongside his father and brother, Æryk. And those who pass their graves will not judge the difference between them. Who carried the banner of honour? Who died? Who lived?

Our knowledge of this world is perishable and is always incomplete. Seth Wainthrop, Leland Hoop, Mildred Goodlyhead, Aldwyn Byrgan and even Willem the waif are each served a portion of information on the death of young Eldrik. Together, these morsels of knowledge do not make a meal, nor do they condemn a man. Young Morcar's knowledge is diminished by his confinement these many years past. He learned of the death of his brother and father only from the few who survived the battle and returned home through Ebbsweirmouth, but not to it, after that long-remembered feast day of Saint Philomena. Eight long years have passed and, for many, memories have departed with them.

Like many others, Scullion believes he remembers too well those past times for, in his heart, they have not gone at all, but they change and lie like a stagnant, poisonous pond corrupting his life. Eight years ago he was Morcar, the second son of Lord Æthelstan Scullion and younger brother of Æryk. His father was only fifty-five years old and his brother was a vigorous youth in robust health. Along with hundreds of others, they were slain on

Maeldun field and the King himself paid ten thousand pounds of silver to prevent the Norse invaders from proceeding further.

For Morcar, the new Lord Scullion, the die had been cast and instead of protecting the east shore with sword and shield, he had simply paid what was necessary, as Æthelred had done. Scullion had so often asked his chamberlain whether the people would prefer to become the spoils of war. It was not a rhetorical question but, of course, they would not.

And so he paid off the raiders and he hid his weakness from the world. Balliwick was his lordship's shire reeve, charged to collect tithes and revenue; designated by Scullion as a virtuous man, the probi hominess of all legal matters under his lordship's authority. It fell to him to collect sufficient revenue to pay the Nordic raiders.

Even knowledge is corruptible and survives according to the garment you choose to clothe it in. Knowledge may bring despair or joy. It leads nowhere of its own resolve, but must be taken steadily towards wisdom, wise counsel and understanding in order to reveal its true value.

"Procedamus in pace," Father Shriver tells them as the chapel mass ends, but peace is not a gift that rests easily on the weak shoulders of the grown Morcar.

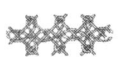

On the chapel altar, Scullion's glittering diptych stood prominently against the dark oak and grey stone surroundings. The shining figures of the Baptist and Saint Peter looked down on the lion and wolf of the Scullion crest and stretched their open palms towards it. And the carved angels too, which hung on the chapel eaves, seemed to conjure a surprised countenance at the rare sight of guests within their hallowed walls.

The mass ended as the servants were preparing lunch. The delayed start of the chapel mass, caused by the events in town, ensured there was only time for brief introductions before they were seated in the great hall. As the small group left the chapel, Balliwick introduced the guests to Lord Scullion, who each thanked him in turn for his hospitality.

"You are very welcome," he said to Friar Sopscott, as he removed his right hand from beneath his cloak to shake that of the friar.

Ravenhead stepped forward and bowed.

"We come to honour thy father's bones," he declared, in a tone that suggested he had rehearsed the words many times. But his kind words were interrupted by Balliwick.

"And I am sure he thanks you for it, Lord Ravenhead. But, for our part, we are less inclined towards fine words. We take greater pleasure in fine deeds, for we have people to feed and tithes to pay."

Friar Sopscott looked a little disappointed at Balliwick's sharp and unprovoked rebuke.

The long wooden table in the great hall was furnished with fine food and wine, and a large log, the size of a hunting dog, burned in the hearth. Friar Sopscott removed his hood, revealing the cuts and bruises he had received before his arrival in town. Of course, this generated much comment and many questions, but the friar was dismissive, saying that he had been set upon by ruffians in a forest a few miles from the town. His lordship was greatly disturbed by such an act of violence, but was relieved to hear that the incident had occurred outside his own shire.

Soon the matter was forgotten and those present were fed on a large fish, which had been sliced for their convenience, followed by a plate of chopped venison. None of the guests realised that the preparation of the food was necessary in order that his lordship could conceal his withered arm. Even following the consumption of much wine, Scullion never lost concentration on this matter and continued to keep his left arm behind his cloak, which lent him a rather dashing air of composure.

They all ate heartily and there was much to discuss. Precedence was given to Friar Sopscott, who was invited to tell his lordship of his service to the church and how this had brought him to a modest East Seaxe shire.

The guests knew from his black alb that the friar was a member of the Benedictine order, although only a very few from this order had ever visited their small town, and the order itself contained several disparate groups. Those present were also familiar with the reputation of the black friars. The *'cani di Dio'* some called them, 'the hounds of God'. And it was true that the monasteries wielded great power in the shires, though it had not been exerted to any great extent in this backwater, where the nearest monastery was more than three days' walk away. So his lordship and, more avidly, his chamberlain listened carefully in order to learn what the purpose of his visit was. But, first, they had to sit patiently and listen of his travels and background.

For his part, Sopscott spoke modestly of what were distinguished credentials. He had been educated at Fleury Abbey before returning to England thirty years ago at the behest of his uncle. But the uncle, a rich benefactor, died before he arrived. Lacking a patron, Sopscott was given a position at Ramsey Abbey and served under a father abbot named Oswald, who applied his efforts to purify the Church from secularism and encouraged his aide to do likewise.

With the determination of a hound of God, Sopscott had set about stimulating a revival of monastic discipline more aligned to the ancient precepts of Saint Benedict. With the aid of other monks and the support of Oswald, Sopscott, who grew in both power and reputation, ejected secular clergy from the churches, sometimes forcefully, and replaced them with unmarried monks sworn to celibacy. Those priests that would not give up their wives were expelled and Sopscott replaced them with monks, who he ordained as priests.

"As a consequence of my work, I have made a great many enemies, but those priests who remain celibate, like Father Shriver here, have nothing to fear from the new discipline imposed by a closer following of the true word."

Oswald, Sopscott told them, died during Lent some seven years ago whilst washing the feet of the poor at Worcester. Since then, Sopscott had lived the life of a simple mendicant friar in search of piety, serving God at Winchcombe Abbey and Westbury Priory before taking to the road.

"Fleury provided me with wisdom; Oswald gave me wise counsel and God rewarded me with understanding. And with these gifts of the Holy Spirit I serve God and search for piety."

While Sopscott spoke, the chamberlain turned over in his mind how he might take full advantage of Lord Ravenhead's visit, and he became impatient to begin the process. Several times, Balliwick tried to cut the friar short, but he continued unhindered, well used to ignoring the secular impatience of the nobility and their servants.

"Men of God should not be confined to a cloistered life behind the walls of a monastery. Instead, they must travel among the people, taking as their example the apostles of the primitive church," declared Sopscott, as he spooned another piece of venison into his mouth.

Balliwick seized the opportunity to move the conversation away from the friar. He and Shriver spoke enthusiastically of their desire to build a new church in Ebbsweirmouth and Scullion asked if some special dispensation may be granted on the holy tithes that were paid from the harvest revenues in order to finance such a project. Sopscott was able to suggest the name of a prominent figure at Worcester Abbey from whom such support might be obtained. And so it was agreed that Balliwick would write to him.

After they finished the fish and meat, servants furnished the table with fruit and a large round of cheese produced, Scullion said, from his own fine sheep. His lordship drank only a little wine, not wanting to lower his guard, for he considered it very strange that Ravenhead should have gone to all this trouble to seek his permission to marry the Lady Una. It had not occurred to Scullion that he might have some claim himself to Lord Haeferingas's seat, for, in the absence of a male heir, someone of good ancestry would need to rule and a cousin might be given preference by the Crown.

A fervent and lengthy discussion on the church continued into the afternoon. The wine flowed freely and it was beginning to get dark outside before the conversation moved to the Lady Una and her consort.

Eventually it fell to Ravenhead to introduce himself and to disclose the purpose of his visit, which Balliwick had only briefly advised his lordship of before the chapel mass had begun.

The brevity of Lord Ravenhead's discourse should have prompted some doubt regarding its veracity, for it contained little of substance and those present simply thought him a man of misplaced modesty. It consisted of little more than the brief facts that he had mentioned to Balliwick outside the church. He was the second of four sons born to the Eorl of Northumberland, far to the north, and had journeyed to Haeferingas in order to request the hand of Lady Una in marriage. But, to his dismay and great sadness, Lord Haeferingas, who had lived to a great age, died before his arrival.

"Much like your own sad journey home to your uncle, Friar Sopscott," said Ravenhead, but the holy man was oblivious to the comment. His mind had wandered far away and his frozen glare was focused on Una. Several seconds elapsed before the friar recovered from his stupor and found himself being stared at by everyone around the table. He apologised for his preoccupation and begged Lord Ravenhead to continue.

"My father is a man of great principles," Ravenhead continued. "And I therefore resolved to do my duty by journeying here to ask for the blessing of Eorl Haeferingas's nearest cousin, bringing the lovely Lady Una with me to, hopefully, receive that blessing."

Balliwick intervened before Scullion had the opportunity to speak. He knew that weakness of character would compel Scullion to simply agree to the entreaty and forego any possible concessions that might reward such a blessing. The chamberlain had already determined that any newcomer to the Haeferingas throne would need to ensure he had the support of peaceful neighbours if he was to succeed in his plans.

"Lord Scullion has not seen the beloved cousin of his late father since he was a small child, but continues, we hope, to enjoy the benevolent friendship of the Haeferingas family." Balliwick glanced at Lady Una before continuing. "Both families lost a son and heir at Maeldun and the Scullions lost a father too, leaving their son Morcar here to rule from a tender age. He has built a great shire that serves the King well and protects the Crown to the west from the raiding Norse sea wanderers. We ask nothing for this, except a pledge of peaceful loyalty from our cousin Una, together with some recognition for the protection we provide." The word 'recognition' was delivered with some consideration. Ravenhead was left in no doubt that the word carried with it financial implications.

Ravenhead looked at Lord Scullion for softer words but none were forthcoming. He then went to respond to Balliwick but the chamberlain raised his hand and directed him towards his lordship.

"I speak for Lord Scullion," the emboldened Balliwick said. "But you should direct your words to him, for it is he whose blessing you seek."

"We hold common ancestry with the King," said Ravenhead, looking directly at his lordship. "As ruling nobility we are entitled to the chartered estates long held by our families."

"But Haeferingas is not *your* family," interrupted Scullion as he sliced a piece of cheese from the platter.

"A woman takes her social rank from her father or her husband after marriage," replied Ravenhead.

"Yes," interrupted Balliwick, "and a husband from his wife if she has no male kin. But you are not married yet, which is presumably why you seek our blessing."

The sentence hung in the air like the blade of an axe. The house of Scullion may not have had sons who wielded an axe in victory anymore, but its power cut as deeply with the incisive words of its chamberlain.

Ravenhead thought for a moment about his next words. 'A man without kinsmen is as vulnerable as a lord without a King', was what he wanted to say. Yet, this would only provoke and antagonise. And, further still, it would not serve his purpose.

"Let us be friends, Cousin," Ravenhead replied.

"He is not your cousin yet," bellowed Balliwick.

"Gentlemen," interrupted Friar Sopscott. "I see no cause for animosity. Does this man not come here in good faith to seek his lordship's blessing?"

Scullion was embarrassed that a friar should need to call for peace in his household. "You give sound counsel, Friar Sopscott," he said in soft tones to quell the storm.

But Balliwick was less patronising. "You preach arbitration, Friar, but you do not practise it. Was it not the black friars that dismissed the married clergy in Kent without arbitration?"

Scullion intervened. "Chamberlain Balliwick, you go too far. Friar Sopscott is a guest in our house and must be treated respectfully."

"We are charged by the King," answered Balliwick, "to equip two ships to guard the coast, but not a soul tells us where the money must come from. At Michaelmas and Martinmas, and Easter too, we pay tax and one hundred sesters of barley to the monasteries, in addition to that which is paid to the King. And, as the easternmost shire, we are left at the mercy of the raiding Nordic hoards, the sea wanderers who, indeed, show no mercy whatsoever in their demands of us."

"How can you say such a thing?" replied Ravenhead, directing his words to Scullion as instructed, but pointing towards Una. "This young woman's brother fought alongside your own kin and fell alongside them too."

"You speak of better men and better times too," answered Balliwick, ignoring his master's plea for calmness. "We had so much that we needed to plough and sow only one field, whilst leaving the others fallow. We had wheat and barley to fill our bellies. The land yielded crops of peas, cabbages, parsnips, carrots and celery. Even in winter, our table was furnished with duck, geese, mutton and venison. Yet now we slaughter our animals and salt them to see us through until the spring." He stood up to emphasise his argument. "Tax does not change and the penalties for crimes remain as ever they were. Five shillings for a stolen sheep and fifty shillings to lay with a virgin of the royal household."

"Calm yourself," demanded Scullion. "What ails you, man, that you rant and rave so? It cannot be the wine for you have hardly touched it."

Balliwick returned to his seat and poured wine into his chalice. Scullion called to the servants to fill the cups and then began to dismiss his chamberlain's dire words. He recalled a time when any thegn with five hides of land was considered a nobleman.

"Now, the lowest of my people have a hide to plough and sow. And there is no cause to leave one field fallow, as everyone must be fed. We have a great many widows in Ebbsweirmouth, since my father ruled. It is for the princes of the blood to inherit and the rulers of the shire to govern. And it is for our good righteous man here, our shire reeve, to administer our laws." He paused and stood up before raising a chalice of wine in his one good right hand. "Let us toast our good, if a little, what shall we say, strident, chamberlain, that he be granted knowledge, wisdom and understanding, along with a little composure for all our sake."

As he spoke, he smiled and the guests raised their cups to Balliwick before Scullion continued his impromptu speech.

"Now perhaps, gentlemen, and Lady Una of course, you will listen with me to my chamberlain and perhaps you might assist me in relieving whatever yoke it is that weighs so heavily on his shoulders. Come tell me, Balliwick, what disturbs you so?"

Balliwick quaffed from his chalice and spoke.

"There have been two sudden deaths in these past three days, a sheep has been stolen and rumours of night spirits in the corpse road only serve to magnify this religious fervour about the opening of the abyss and the coming of the devil. That, my Lord, is what disturbs me."

Scullion drank some more wine, smiled and looked towards his guests for advice, inviting the friar to be the first to speak.

"It is not for me to question the will of God or interfere with the politics of the shires."

The friar's answer provided little help, so Scullion turned to his parish priest.

"Father Shriver, what have you to say on how we might lift Master Balliwick's yoke?"

The priest paused for a moment before speaking.

"It is true what you say, my Lordship, that this town now has many widows and yet it was once a tiny hamlet, consisting of but two small farms. Now the town has its own bee-keeper, a forester, no less than six cowherders and four goatherders, a granary-keeper, two shepherds, a swineherd and even a woman cheesemaker and a corn grinder too. There is a salter, a smith and a weaver seamstress. Indeed, the only items we lack are salt and iron. The community grows beyond recognition and yes, of course, great trials and tribulations follow such growth. Frankly, my Lord, they would laugh in the cities at two deaths and a stolen sheep."

Scullion swigged another cup of wine.

"Better than your normal homily, Father Shriver," he laughed and it was evident to all that his lordship was beginning to drink too much. "And more interesting than Friar Sopscott here, who keeps his counsel as well as Balliwick pins his to his sleeve." He paused once more before inviting Ravenhead to speak.

"From what I learned in the village today," replied Ravenhead, "it seems one man fell and struck his head on a rock. It was unfortunate, but a better death than many others I can think of."

His comment raised another laugh from Scullion, who demanded that the servants provided more wine.

"Another poor soul drowned doing his duty as servant to the town's fisherman. And we should do no more than to toast his bravery for producing the fine fish that we enjoyed as much as your kind hospitality this day."

"And what of Master Balliwick's stolen sheep, Ravenhead, or the spirits in the unploughed paths beside the drove roads? What of them?" demanded Scullion.

"It seems to me that they are one and the same problem, my Lord. The spirits are but thieving villagers who empty the drove roads with their ghostly tales and then steal a sheep when no one is there to see it."

It was a cutting indictment of Scullion's weak authority and his lordship's mood and tone changed swiftly at such an assertion.

"Take care, Lord Ravenhead, these are my sheep you speak of and my people too. And my people would not steal from me." Scullion's words were spoken in a sombre tone at what his guest was suggesting.

"I wager you five shillings," laughed Ravenhead, "that there is cheap mutton being sold by your butcher tomorrow."

Scullion insisted that he had good faith in his people and, in particular, the butcher. "What is the man's name, Balliwick?" he demanded.

"Gripple, my Lord, Maggoty Gripple."

Lord Scullion was tempted to add his own harsh words to those of the chamberlain, but kept his counsel.

The servants drew the drapes and closed the shutters on the windows.

"The day is at its shortest, my friends," his lordship said, still shielding his arm. "You must stay with us this night for it is too dark to travel back to town and there are spirits in the corpse road, remember?" He laughed and any remaining doubt that he was very drunk disappeared.

For Balliwick in particular, his master's inebriation was made obvious by his invitation to his guests to stay, for he seemed to have lost all fear of them uncovering the secret of his withered arm. And yet, throughout, he kept the arm covered by his cloak. He demanded that Balliwick accompanied his guests back to town in the morning and to be sure that he and Ravenhead called at the butcher's stall to enquire on the price of mutton.

"Then," the eorl demanded, "do not forget to retrieve my five shillings from Lord Ravenhead here and return it to me."

With that, his lordship ushered his servants and instructed his chamberlain to escort his guests to their rooms, before slumping back into his chair and looking hopefully into the empty chalice in front of him. The unseasonal death of the boy had unsettled his chamberlain's heart. Scullion had no heir, like his cousin Lord Haeferingas, who had but one daughter. Both families had lost their eldest son at Maeldun. All of these disparate thoughts become muddled in his mind.

Scullion asked no exemption from his portion of sorrow. His family's future was in his hands, for he was still not too old to father a child. Yet, he would first need a woman. He would need to choose wisely too, as Lord Ravenhead had done. This son of a northern shire eorl, who he had never heard of, was soon to marry the only daughter of Haeferingas. With no other children, it was he, not her, who would inherit the title and land. Perhaps he should withhold his blessing and marry the Lady Una himself. But these were all jumbled thoughts that would be forgotten in the light of the morning.

The nature of wine is to embolden the weak heart and harden it to reason. And yet he ordered another bottle and his mind wandered the meandering roads of fortuity and considered what might be. At first, the visit of Ravenhead and Gopscott seemed obvious. One required a blessing and the other simply the opposite. Yet, as he drank, the purpose of both parties came into question. Little maladjustment was necessary for him to develop suspicions and alternative motives for their presence and these destructive thoughts soon began to influence his declining sense of deduction.

He placed the half-empty bottle of wine by the side of his seat with the chalice and, gripping the arm of the chair with his one good hand, he lifted himself from it, swaying forwards and backwards as he did so. For mercy's sake, all the ill thoughts and resolutions he made that night would be forgotten by morning. There is an irrational wisdom to be found in the bludgeoning efficacy of wine and mercy in an equal measure.

Chapter Ten

Wisdom

Mandyke House, or more correctly the stable outside it, was originally the home of a blacksmith, complete with a forge and paddock, but the smithy moved to a new location close to Apparition Hill when Mildred Goodlyhead's father purchased the land and built his elegant new home. It was this same blacksmith's great-grandson, in fact, who told me this winter tale, which is probably why there is no mention of a blacksmith in this version, for he did not want to implicate his ancestor in the plot. The old man had been told the story himself by a traveller or, at least, that is what his young relative told me.

There were many eloquent storytellers around at this time and some made an income from it, trading their tales for something to eat and a place to sleep. The more stories they knew, the longer they could stay in one place, retelling the various yarns to several families in a village before the stories were being passed on by others, less skilled in recounting such fables. And it was not long before everyone in an area had heard them through the grapevine that is village life.

There was little else to occupy the long winter nights, so townsfolk were happy to share a meal and some straw for an evening spent with a minstrel, as they were called, even though few played an instrument. Many of the minstrels were able to invent great yarns that would stretch on for hours and occupy an entire evening, which meant they could eat their fill. But few such stories had the stirring content or indeed the authenticity of One Christmas Past. Some storytellers were less conscientious than others, many changed history with impunity; battles lost were now won and heroes became legends, some in victory and some in defeat, and what remained became reality, for our heritage is not safe in the hands of a storyteller.

The blacksmith's great-grandson related the tale well and, at times, added his own insight on the merits of the people involved, for his father's grandfather had known some of them. The man had been convinced that the beach at Hollow Hole Cove was haunted and would continue to be so, because the dead boy's internment had taken too long to complete. He had received, like everyone at that time, the legends of the corpse roads and how some spirits were separated from the present time only by deception and trickery that had been passed down through the ages. But there was no way to prevent the spirit of the boy from treading the stony beach by the cove.

And so, let us return to our plot, which thickens like a mutton stew left to cool in the pot overnight.

Mercy falls upon this world with the reluctance of tears to an indifferent heart. That same night as the inebriated thoughts of Lord Scullion were laid bare to his guests, and as he checked at decreasing intervals that his elegant brooch held fast the cloak that covered his withered arm, others of less licentious musing enjoyed dinner at Mardyke House. So, let us now join them to see what disturbs their peace this late Sabbath evening and determine how easily mercy is dispensed in enmity's absence.

For Willem and his hosts, the talk is all about the events of the day and each of them have questions they wish to ask and yet dare not to do so. For Mistress Goodlyhead, who has been appointed seeker of the dead, it is her duty to determine the cause of death and liaise with Byrgan and the priest to arrange a burial for the boy. It is to be a simple coffin buried in the churchyard with a small gravestone. The half-filled sandglass carved upon its face will symbolise a life ended too soon. Above this, the stone will show his name and that he had died on Saint Lazarus's day. Nobody knew when he was born, so Master Byrgan will simply inscribe the words 'About nine years'.

Now that the chamberlain has pronounced the cause, without reference to Mistress Goodlyhead, the body may be buried and all the doubt and distrust can be buried with it. And yet, the marks on the back of the boy's neck might suggest that his drowning received some callous assistance. Perhaps the boy had been held below the water by a strong hand placed upon his neck. What other explanation can there be for the bruising that she saw?

What Mildred possesses is knowledge and what she requires is wisdom. Wisdom in order to understand what might have caused the death of this poor soul.

Wisdom is the tenth of the higher gifts and only through wisdom may we find what is divinely decreed. By dint of wisdom, we learn to value properly those things that we believe, for the truths of faith are of greater value than material things. If mercy falls upon the world with the reluctance of tears, then wisdom is delivered with equal reticence. And yet it is bestowed this day on a young boy. It falls to Willem to use such a gift to direct destiny. Each step towards what might become reality is prompted by a *moment of chance and if it is Willem's task to direct destiny, then it is Edwin's role to begin that process.*

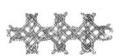

***

Mildred laid the plates of food in front of her husband and Willem, then sat down and, placing her hands together, spoke aloud a prayer of thanks.

"Bless us, O Lord, and these your gifts, which we are about to receive from your bounty. And give peace unto those who have joined your heavenly choir this day. Amen."

As they each placed the palms of their hands together in prayer, Edwin Goodlyhead noticed something that both alarmed and surprised him. The tip of the smallest finger on Willem's right hand was missing, something that had been concealed from most people by the mittens that his wife had given the boy, and it was a deformity that Edwin had failed to notice before.

"Your finger, young Willem, is lost," he declared, stating the obvious.

"Edwin!" Mildred called back. "We must not draw attention to the defects of others."

The tone of her voice revealed that the infirmity was something she had already noticed, as she did not even glance towards the boy's hand.

"Of course, my dear," he answered. "But the boy Eldrik had the same impairment. What can it mean?"

"It means nothing, I am sure," she replied in a less than convincing tone, for she feared it meant a great deal and she did not wish to worry the boy.

For his part, Willem had been pushed to the back of the crowd outside the church and had barely glimpsed the body of Eldrik before Mildred had covered it. So, when he spoke, his voice was as questioning as Edwin's, although the old man's words brought the recollection of a fleeting glimpse of the boy's body outside the church.

"He had a piece of his finger missing?"

Willem's words were spoken in a half-questioning tone, for he was now certain he had seen the shared deformity through the crowd.

The bewildered exression on the boy's face caused great concern to Mildred, who fashioned a disappointed look at her husband.

"It means nothing," she assured the boy, a little lamely, for one could hear the anxiety in her tone.

"His right hand?" the boy asked, in a voice filled with curiosity, and she nodded.

"The smallest finger on the right hand?" he questioned again, as if it didn't make sense at all.

Of course it did not make sense, for how could two boys who, as far as he knew, had never met, be marked with such an unusual impairment? It was a distinguishing feature he had never seen on anyone else before. So how could another boy of the same age be marked in such an unusual way?

Mistress Goodlyhead wished to change the subject, for she had spent several hours wondering about the remarkable coincidence herself, and had reached no conclusion on its explanation. Her husband, however, could not contain his investigative nature.

"When did you lose the tip of your finger, Willem?"

The boy told him that it had always been so from his earliest memory.

"I was born with the missing fingertip, I suppose."

"Was Eldrik born with the same deformity, my dear?" Edwin asked his wife.

She sighed and looked back at him with pursed lips.

"I must admit," she replied hesitantly, "I had not noticed it before I examined his body this morning."

"Do you remember anything of your previous life at Ebbsweirmouth?" Edwin asked the boy. "Before you went to Shire Farm?" He wondered whether there was something in the boy's past that might provide some clue to his connection with Eldrik.

At first, Willem believed he remembered nothing at all about that time, but confessed that when he passed the woodland that sheltered the tower, he recalled gathering winter fuel for the castle as a small boy and seeing strange symbols and patterns etched into the bark of the trees and on the dry, crusty land about their roots. This was all he could remember and none of them could fathom what connection there might be with the poor soul who had been taken to the dread caverns of a watery grave.

"And you recall nothing else?" asked Edwin."

"I was a ward of the eorl, so I was told, born in the lowliest state of serfdom. I was born nought and became nought."

Mistress Goodlyhead chastised him for speaking so. "We are all equal in the eyes of God," she insisted

"And, what of the symbols?" Mildred asked. "What were they, do you think?"

"I do not know, but they remained in my memory for the sake of all else. Strange symbols that mean nothing to me now."

Mildred recalled seeing the same symbols in the woodland and fields around the town some years before. And she remembered how everyone agreed they had been carved there by the old woman who had tended to Morcar's broken arm.

"Is it possible, do you think," asked Willem, hesitantly, "that Eldrik may have been my brother?"

Mildred assured him that, apart from the missing fingertip, there was no similarity of features in the boys' faces, and a missing fingertip was not something that could be considered a family likeness.

"Mary, the woman at the tower," said Willem thoughtfully, "spoke of another boy who arrived around the same time as I did, all those years ago. Perhaps we were brothers and perhaps it was Eldrik."

"Perhaps, perhaps," repeated Mildred, "does not make certitude or truth and you should not dwell on such matters."

"But I came here hoping to find my family and it seems that perhaps I was just too late."

"'Perhaps' and 'it seems' mean little in this world," replied Mildred. Yet, all the time, the expression on her husband's face suggested that the boy's musing may have some substance.

Eventually, Mildred successfully managed to draw this particular conversation to an end. But the boy had not finished with difficult questions, for his mind was full with possibilities.

"Outside the church this morning," he began tentatively, "Master Balliwick spoke of two bodies. Has someone else died here this week?"

Before Mistress Goodlyhead could divert the conversation from further talk of premature death, her husband had blurted the answer.

"Indeed," he bellowed a little too enthusiastically. "He was a chandler, a gentleman who had travelled to our town to seek out my good self, in order to do business, for he made fine-quality candles."

The last word startled Willem. "Candles, you say. How did he die?"

Mistress Goodlyhead explained that, shortly after he arrived in town and had secured a room at the inn, he fell and struck his head on a rock. The footpath around the inn had been made slippery by the snow and ice.

"What was his name?" asked Willem.

"I knew him only as Chandler, for he made candles," Edwin replied. "Indeed, I knew him not at all but had arranged to meet him yesterday morning."

"Yesterday morning?" the boy questioned in an alarming tone. "When did the poor man die?"

"The day before that. He arrived on Friday, the day you arrived too, I believe."

The boy's head filled with questions, for what his hosts were saying made no sense at all. The man they spoke of must be the same man he had met in the darkened church on Friday night, and then again in the barn not twenty paces from here last night. Furthermore, the man himself spoke of being a chandler, visiting the town on business. Willem so wanted to question them further on the matter and yet he knew they would be seriously concerned about his welfare if he did so, because his meeting with the man made no sense at all. How could he possibly have spoken with the chandler these past two nights if he was already dead?

"Why do they call you the seeker of the dead, Mistress Goodlyhead?"

"It is an appointment made by Lord Scullion himself," she replied. "Through the shire reeve, of course."

"But what does it mean?"

"It requires me to attend on each person who dies in the village and attest to the cause of their death, in order that it might be recorded in the parish records."

"And what of the chandler? How did you attest to his misfortune?" the boy asked.

"He fell on the icy pathway near the inn and struck his head on a rock."

The boy hesitated to ask his next question.

"And, was this the place I spoke of before, where the blood seeped through the snow?"

She nodded. "I suppose it could have been."

"So was the blood in the snow an omen?"

"No, Willem. Just testimony to the man's misfortune," she replied, hoping to close the subject for the evening.

For his part, the boy had many more questions to ask, and leaned forward with a questioning expression on his face. But he was stopped in the process.

"You ask a great many questions," Edwin remarked after noticing his wife's expression.

"How shall I learn if not by asking questions?"

"Well, no more, for it is late," replied Mildred.

So, instead, he chose a different course to retrieve the same information.

"I once knew a chandler named Darrayne," he announced.

"Is this another of your jolly stories, Willem?" asked Edwin as his wife got up from the table to pour out three cups of hot broth.

"It seems as though it might be," came the uncertain answer.

"No stories tonight," insisted Mildred. "It has been a long day, filled with the devil's work. We must let the boy go to bed."

Willem was disappointed that he was not given the opportunity to learn more of the chandler, although he was pleased that he was not required to create another story for his hosts. He wished to return to the barn again, in the hope that he might see the mysterious Watchman Darrayne, for he was convinced he and the chandler were one and the same person. He desperately wanted to tell his kind hosts of his suspicions but the risk of embarrassment deterred him. Even a foolish man may speak a wise word, he thought. And certainly a learned man may speak a foolish one. But to speak of meeting a dead person might make him appear as a foolish man speaking foolish words.

Willem left the Goodlyheads with some cautionary words from Mildred. "None of us may yet fully understand the mystery of the missing finger tip, Willem. But there may well be a purpose to it. For the moment, keep the mittens on your hands so that none may see that you bear the same mark as the boy Eldrik."

Edwin nodded in agreement and, although Mildred did not want to cause the boy unnecessary fear or anxiety, she believed in her heart that it could be a sign of some evil intent. Mildred was a practical woman and certainly the last person to place any credence in prophecies of the devil being released from the abyss, but she was equally convinced that there was no coincidence in this matter. So, she kissed him on the forehead, lit a small candle to light his way and sent him off to the barn with instructions that he should not forget to say his night prayers before retiring.

When he arrived at the barn, Willem searched it thoroughly and was disappointed to find no sign of the Watchman. For a moment he wondered whether to walk to the church to see if there was any sign of him there. But he knew the Goodlyheads would worry if they learned of his disappearance. Anyway, the bitterly cold wind howled its own objection to his plan and he drew the wooden door to a close.

With the aid of a rake, he then pulled some fresh straw into the corner of an empty stall. It would be warmer huddled together with the goats, he thought, but the larger of the two stood up and adopted a fierce stance, gazing with glassy green eyes back at the boy.

The dark, moonless night gave no light to the shed and he assured himself that the noises that stirred him as he took to his cot were only those of the beasts that shared the place with him. Convinced of this, he blew out the candle and turned on to his side to sleep, wondering whether he would ever see the Watchman again.

A few hours passed before a fox or wolf that loitered nearby stirred the creatures in the barn from their uneasy rest. A hen fluttered noisily down from a shelf, causing the other chickens to cluck loudly and the goats to bleat in annoyance at being disturbed. Willem, too, was roused by the commotion and threw a large stone towards the door in order to scare any would-be predator. It appeared to work and the creatures began to settle down again.

Just then, a sliver of light from a distant star pierced the narrow gap between the timber wall and the door, and this threw a shadow across the floor where he lay. By now, his eyes had become accustomed to the darkness, yet he could not make out what had stirred him. But he felt a familiar presence and sensed he was not in any danger. Without hesitating, Willem looked up and recognised the shape of the dark figure that sat before him. It could have frightened a child of his age to wonder how the man had gained access to the shuttered barn but, by now, the boy had been blessed with the grace of courage and he convinced himself that he knew how such a thing might be made possible.

"Are you the chandler who was to meet Master Goodlyhead?"

"I cannot speak of that which did not happen, but only of that which has," he sighed. "I must leave soon, for my guide is close by."

"Where are you travelling to, Master?"

"That, I do not know, for I can only trust in faith."

"Faith? Whyfor faith, Sir, should not hope be your saving grace?"

"Faith is of all matters, Willem. It is in good and evil. It is in the past, the present and that which has still to come. But hope provides only for good and is only for the future. Faith is infallible but hope is only made so by faith itself."

"They say you are dead, Sir," the boy muttered reluctantly. "So how is it that I may see you?"

"Show me your right hand."

The boy recalled the warning from Mistress Goodlyhead, but he removed the mitten and extended his arm towards the hooded man. He looked at it and nodded his head gently under the hood before speaking again.

"Before leaving Haeferingas eight years ago, I swore an oath. Then, one month ago I received a message, a note, telling me of the eorl's death and asking me to observe the oath I had given. It seemed my long exile as a chandler was destined to end and yet, strangely, it occurred to me that my simple profession might yet conceal the true intent of the challenge that now faced me."

Willem continued his questions, wanting to know the nature of the oath he had pledged and whether he had succeeded in executing it. But the Watchman would provide no details, only a warning for the boy to be watchful of everyone.

"Tell me who I must be watchful of, Master," the boy pleaded.

"It is not within my power to say, for I cannot speak of what might be, only of what has been."

"Then, for your soul's sake, tell me something that might guide me, as you are to be guided, to a better place."

"Hush now," the Watchman replied, "for there is little time and much for me to tell you."

Still cloaked by a dark shadow, the man told the boy to rest himself on the straw and remain silent while he told him of all that happened at Maeldun more than eight years past and, indeed, on the strange journey that had taken him to that battlefield. The boy did as he was instructed and listened intently to the words of the shadowy figure.

The Watchman began by speaking first of Haeferingas, where his journey had begun. The man's heart leapt and the pale eyes that stared from beneath the hood moistened at the mention of his home. It was here, he explained, that he and his friend Osmund, the son of Eorl Haeferingas, had waited for the arrival of Lord Æthelstan Scullion and his own eldest son, Æryk.

"Æryk and his father rested with us for two nights, as our household retainers gathered and armed themselves for the fight. Æryk possessed a warrior soul and he became good friends with Osmund and me. And Osmund's sister, too."

The Watchman recalled with great fondness those three days, filled with wonder and some trepidation. Willem wanted to know everything about that time, but Darrayne would not speak of it.

"Some memories are best taken to the grave, for if we speak of them, we give them life and we make them real."

"But they were real," countered Willem.

"And yet they are as a dream to me."

The dark figure remained hooded and spoke of the journey to Maeldun.

"We were more than one hundred strong," said Darrayne. "And we expected our leader, Lord Byrhtnoth, to bring many more to the fight."

He then spoke of how they had left their host, Eorl Haeferingas, in the care of his beautiful daughter to mourn his old age and they rode northward to meet the raiding sea wanderers at the place that was to be evermore remembered for the events of a single day.

On the second evening, the group camped by Lavender Wood, for that is what the local people called it. The place was named so because the edge of the wood was lined with the fragrant mauve flower and many thought it would aid their sleep and prepare them for their battle the next day. They were only ten miles from Maeldun but it was too late to continue their journey as the sun had set.

Later that evening, as they sat together eating their supper, a traveller who happened to be passing that way asked if he could share their fire for the night and, once they had agreed, he began to tell them about the mystery of the forest that they had camped beside.

The man was not old and yet he had looked so. He was small, almost like an elfin spirit, slightly hunched, so that his neck extended outwards, rather than upwards from his bony shoulders, and his face peered upwards from his lowly stance. He was dressed in many shades of green. Even the two halves of his leggings were of different hues and he looked like no man they had ever seen before. He spoke in a strange, high-pitched voice, entirely becoming of a dwarf, telling them of how those who lived in these parts had named the place Lavender Wood. Yet, for centuries before, he added, it had simply been known as the old yew tree wood.

Only those who sat around the eorl's fire could hear his absorbing story and, even then, only those who were closest to where he sat, for his voice was shallow. He told of how the ancient yew trees in the forest formed knotted hurdles and obstacles with their winding roots and branches, and how many men had vanished after entering the wood, unable to find their way out of its meandering pathways. There were many explanations given for the disappearance of the men, but none had any foundation.

The wood was and still is, he assured them, inhabited by a venerable old enchantress. Many found the dwarf's words amusing and some, to his annoyance, laughed at intervals but, when he finally spoke the name of the ageless hag, their laughter stopped abruptly and their jolly faces, made red by the fire and wine, turned to trepidation.

"Silvaria le Fay," he said and the name gurgled in his throat as he spoke it. "For she is of the fairies bred."

More than any other, Æthelstan had been greatly stirred by the name, recalling how she had administered to his youngest son, Morcar, those many years past and how, after she had left and the cast was removed, his arm had become limp and withered. The eorl rose to his feet as he spoke and marched around the fire, stirring the men with talk of vengeance.

His son, Æryk, was a brave and strong warrior, but he had never been bold enough to speak against his father. He wanted to remind Æthelstan that it was he who had instructed the fairy, against her wishes, to cast the arm without first setting the bones. But the young man kept his counsel and sat in silence as his father ranted and cursed her name.

By the time the army finally took to their beds that night, Æthelstan had resolved to find and take his revenge against Silvaria. So vehemently did he rage that Osmund agreed to go with him. After all, he was undaunted at the approach of the Norse army, so what had he to fear of an old woman?

The next morning a group of men, led by Æthelstan, Æryk, the Watchman Darrayne and Osmund searched the deep, dark yew tree wood in the hope of finding the crone's fairy grove. They sought her all the tedious day long, often losing their way on the rambling paths that all looked similar, until there, in its midmost trees, they came upon a curious dwelling formed by seven yew trees, whose branches and roots twisted upon themselves to create a dark cavernous den. Some were convinced they had passed this very spot before but had not seen the dwelling, but others said it could not be so. Outside the timber cave, the old woman sat preparing roots and herbs, as she hummed a haunting melody.

There was no trial, no hearing. In fact, she spoke not a single word in her defence as she was seized by Æthelstan's men. The eorl had her bound and tied to a large yew root that stretched upwards from the earth like a pillar. He then instructed the men to gather rocks and stones, before ordering her to be stoned to death. Still, throughout the raucous event, she made no sound; no screams of pain, or shouts for mercy, just silence.

They were like cruel, adolescent boys tormenting a cat, laughing and chiding her, and at one point they did, in fact, hear something cry out like an injured cat that had just been put to death.

So many rocks were thrown at the poor woman that she became covered by them. And it would have formed a suitable burial place if Æthelstan had not demanded that she be uncovered and strung from a tree to be fed to the wild beasts. But when all the rocks were removed, there was no sign of her.

The eorl had the whole area searched without finding her body and, indeed, the only creature they saw all night was a black cat that sat precariously on a high branch of a tree. As they looked for the old woman, the dark night that takes the forest so suddenly lulled their senses and a drowsy numbness encouraged them towards sleep, trapping them in the wood's pitch-black lair.

In this haunted place the men set their camp, thinking themselves a great distance from the forest's edge. By enchantment they had been led to where the fairies dance each midnight and, as the army slept, the fairies frolicked about the trees and the unseasonal budding wreaths of gorse and fern grew about them, turning to great bushes of rampant ivy and sedge that encircled the men who slumbered there.

In the morning, the troop of men awoke and had to cut their way through the binding weeds with their swords, only to find that they had slept just a few paces from where they had entered the wood on the previous day. Having lost many hours in their laboured and fruitless search for the dead fairy witch, they left dejectedly and continued their journey.

"But my mind was unsettled by the ordeal," continued the Watchman. "None of us who had attended the wood that night could explain the extraordinary events, for it was beyond our imagination to do so. In truth, we had simply entered a forest and become lost. None of us had seen or heard anything of the fairies' work that night and yet we all knew of it, so we concluded that it must have been a dream. But, how was it that we should all have been possessed by the same dream?"

Nor could anyone explain what had happened to the old crone.

Darrayne paused for a moment, wondering if the boy had fallen asleep, but Willem lifted his head from the straw to see if the shadow was still there.

"What happened to the elfin man?" he asked.

"When we came out of the wood the following morning, he was gone, though some who had not come into the forest said he spoke at intervals in a strange voice, mumbling a series of words. 'Redress', 'retribution', 'reprisal', 'retaliation', 'revenge' and, finally, 'reckoning'."

"'There will be a reckoning,' were the final words of the dwarf before he simply disappeared. All the men who had remained outside the wood that night appeared as enchanted as we were by the events around the camp fire and, whilst they said they had slept lightly, nobody saw the man leave."

"Perhaps he or the fairy placed a spell on you all," Willem suggested.

"I am certain," the Watchman continued, "that we all felt some strange presence, which stayed with us into battle. Æthelstan sought vengeance for a fault that did not lie with the old crone and this grieved her much, although she did not speak. There is something to be learned from this, I am sure. Those who are capable of such utter revenge never feel the need to declare their intention, but keep it in their heart."

The Watchman paused for a moment and it was clear that, all these years later, he was still disturbed by the events of that night.

"It was Æthelstan who lacked courage," he added eventually, "not his son, Morcar. It was he who could not bear to hear the screams of his son that might have set his bones aright. And, in spite of all that had happened that previous night, it was Æthelstan who stood at the forest edge and swore to the fairy that he would return for her once battle was done."

Darrayne paused before telling the boy yet another strange event from that curious day.

"For all the time we had spent in that strange enchanted wood," he said, "no bird song was heard. Yet, at that moment when Lord Æthelstan swore his revenge on the crone, the mute birds suddenly rose in a deafening chorus of song, the noise of which I had never heard before."

"Was it an omen, Sir?"

"It was certainly not of this world, but whether it was an omen, I cannot say."

"What is an omen?" the boy asked in a softer tone and the man realised that youth often spoke of things that it did not understand.

"It is a sign that warns us of a future event."

"Like blood, seeping to the surface of the snow."

"You speak of things that are not of my time, Willem. Ask me of what has been, for you may learn much from the past."

He thought for a moment before urging the Watchman to tell of how the battle went. And so he did, beginning with their arrival at Maeldun, which had swelled the Seaxe ranks and gave Byrhtnoth new hope. Such was their leader's brashness that he refused to pay tribute to the raiders, calling them heathen sea wanderers and even inviting them to cross the causeway that separated them without challenge, in order that combat may commence without delay.

About a mile outside Maeldun, a fragile finger of shoreline stretches out into the sea. Olaf, the Nordic leader, landed his forces there on Northey Island, which becomes part of the mainland on the low tide, and even then is passable only along a narrow causeway. The two armies stood one hundred paces apart, separated by a stretch of water that was as deep as a man is tall. The old, grey-haired Byrhtnoth accepted the challenge and allowed Olaf and his men to cross the causeway.

"We were about six hundred men and we faced five times as many in the enemy ranks," the Watchman said.

Even then, he continued, the Seaxe company had consisted of little more than household retainers, few of whom were practised in armed combat. Yet they formed a battle wall and met the raiders with great bravery. All, that was, explained the Watchman, except Godric, son of Odda, who fled the battle.

On its own, what did it matter that one coward should escape the battle's roar? It would not have affected the outcome, but Godric chose to steal Byrhtnoth's horse and, with his helmet in place, none could see the young man's flame-red hair. Seeing what they thought to be their leader's steed fleeing the fight, panic spread among the ranks, and many of those at the rear of the battle wall turned and ran. But neither Byrhtnoth, nor Osmund, nor Æthelstan of Scullion, nor his son Æryk, who fought with defiance and determination, left the field. Indeed, when Byrhtnoth fell, his golden-hilted blade pierced the ground by his body and stood like a crucifix, a headstone to a brave warrior. With less than fifty men left standing and perhaps one hundred more that fled with Godric, the battle was done.

So overwhelming was Olaf's victory that he released those who had been taken captive, including Darrayne, and sent a message to King Æthelred that the Norsemen would not return to their homeland for less than ten thousand pounds in silver.

"The sum was paid and what remained of our defeated army returned home."

"But you did not stay at Haeferingas?" asked the tired boy.

"No. I remained there for only two months. Old Eorl Haeferingas became a changed man. With the death of his son Osmund he had no heir, except his daughter. What is worse, to have no heir or to have no inheritance? The ancestry of many emperors has been extinguished by such ill circumstance. What intolerable evil infests a royal house and causes it to be so?"

Darrayne was right. Nobody was left unmarked by Maeldun. It had changed not only those who were there but those who had remained at home, like Eorl Haeferingas and his daughter Una. And it had also affected Morcar, the new fledgling Eorl Scullion. Afterwards, it became more than a place, for just the word 'Maeldun' evoked so much. Maeldun was not just lost friends, or indeed the betrayal of friends, but for each person it came to represent tragedy, heroism, cowardice, an unforgiving foe, a brutal end, surrender and the end of an age.

In the beginning, people had referred to the Battle of Maeldun, but now it was enough to say simply Maeldun, for everyone knew of what you spoke when you said the word.

It was a moment in time, a forlorn day chosen from all time to mourn the loss of youth. Each eorl had been required to provide one fighting man for every five hides of land in his shire, so Ebbsweirmouth was not the only place to have as many widows' hides.

Throughout the tale, young Willem remained silent and when the Watchman stopped speaking, the boy wondered if he was crying for he heard what sounded like sobbing. Willem knew, of course, that the fairy of whom the Watchman spoke was the same one he had met on his journey to Ebbsweirmouth on that cold Friday of advent. He wanted to tell the man that the old woman still lived and yet there was something of greater importance he needed to know.

"When we last met," said Willem quietly, "you told me that you sought justice. Is it justice for Maeldun that you search for?"

The boy spoke as if it was something he could understand. What must it have felt like, the boy thought, to have witnessed the slaying of so many friends and colleagues?

"No, my young friend," the Watchman answered. "It is not honourable to seek justice for our own sake. Take care not to take that path, for there is no honour in retribution and vengeance. No, I seek justice for another."

And with those words, he tried to change the course of the conversation, asking, "what is it that you want?"

"For myself, I simply want to know who I am, because without a mother or a father I am nobody. And yet you are, I am sure, ambitious for a higher gift, so I hope you find the justice that you seek."

"Perhaps our wishes are one and the same, for providence often binds together such things." As the man's voice tailed away, two words came in a different tongue and echoed in the empty barn.

"*Dominus vobiscum,*" the voice said.

"*Et cum spiritu tuo,*" Willem whispered in a weary, involuntary voice, but his tired eyes did not notice that the shadow had disappeared.

Many lay uneasy in their beds that Sabbath night, just as Willem did, puzzling over so many things.

Friar Sopscott was sorely troubled by his short meeting with Ravenhead and Una, but he could not speak of his concerns, for what is said in the confessional may never be revealed.

Leland Hoop wondered whether he should speak up about his certainty that Scolop had not been fishing on Saturday night.

Mildred Goodlyhead slept with her fears and pondered on what had caused the marks on Eldrik's neck. And she and Willem each meditated on the missing finger tip of the dead boy.

Wainthrop, too, was roused from his sleep several times that night, thinking about what he had seen on Friday morning. And Aldwyn Byrgan considered whether he should speak of his opinion on how long the boy Eldrik had been dead.

Silence is the enemy of knowledge and yet wisdom is the gift of prudence, for it exists only where knowledge is worn with discretion.

Chapter Eleven

Prudence

An imprudent wager laid in haste and accepted lightly weighs heavily on the minds of some and it is turned over and over in curious speculation by others. The tide is turning for the events of our story, too. Monday morning brings little prospect of employment for our young pilgrim. In spite of his previous instructions, Cyrus Scolop has no fish to sell and needs to wait for the tide to turn in more ways than one before he can take his boat out to sea. Aldwyn Byrgan has another grave to dig but, with two grown sons to puncture the unforgiving soil, he needs no further help and certainly not from one so small. So there is no work for Willem on this bleak charcoal morning.

Winter is a time of meagre rations and shortened days punctuated with illness and fever, which often results in premature death, for there was little by way of effective medicine at this time. There were many healers of course, but these were often little better than herb beaters, women and some men too, who travelled from town to town selling curative medicines, concocted from plants and insects. Many of these remedies had been passed down through the ages and some were a legacy from the Roman *occupation, the more reliable of which were learned from the Persians and Greeks. Eating venison liver for a fever, taking nettle lotions for aches and pains, and some people, remembering the ancient ways of the Romans, still sacrificed a small animal and examined its liver, as if that had anything to do with the suffering victim. There were probably more healers and herb beaters than there were minstrels and story tellers, making a living as best they could from a meagre economy based on trade, rather than the King's silver.*

Prudence is the child of discretion and wisdom, but little of this was shown when seeking the services of a healer. Aristotle described prudence as 'recto ratio agibilium', or 'right reason applied in practice'. So, it is not enough to be mindfully prudent, but to apply its principles in life.

As we have seen from the imprudent questioning of Edwin Goodlyhead, destiny is changed by the most insignificant of acts. The giving of a pair of mittens may have prevented some of evil intent to observe more than fate had otherwise intended had it not been for this act of kindness and, as we know, hope always follows a kind act.

Destiny is rarely driven by hope, but more often by deed. And so, the seeds of our story are now sown at four locations, where circumstance and foreordination may be amended. At Mardyke House we find Edwin Goodlyhead encouraging Willem to make himself busy, whilst at the church graveyard his wife speaks in confidence to Father Shriver. And, in the main street, the market stalls are being furnished with the tradesmen's wares. But we continue our tale at Scullion Tower, where his lordship occupies his time in the counting house, alone and fearful of his noble visitor's true purpose, which he believes has less to do with marriage and much to do with power.

The counting house is a single-storey stone room with only one door, which leads out to the courtyard. It is an austere space, unembellished by trinkets or tapestries. But, despite its modest simplicity, it is a cheerfully bright cubbyhole full of joyful memories of childhood for Morcar, of those beardless days before the burdensome yoke of duty and obligation was placed upon his weak shoulders.

<hr />

Scullion stared at the bare stone wall and wondered about building a hearth. A childhood had been spent shivering at his studies here and he remembered making such a suggestion to his father. Not that he spent much time here now. Balliwick was the main occupant of the counting house, deciding the amount of tithe that each should pay. His lordship was an infrequent visitor now, except on those occasions when he needed an excuse to meet with his chamberlain alone. And yet it pleased him to sit here reflecting on that lost childhood.

More recently it was a place of refuge, a sanctuary from the responsibilities that lay heavily upon his shoulders. He spent his time here mixing inks and sharpening quills as his father had shown him. Sharpening quills was an arduous task to perform one-handed, so his father had adapted a small vice, which grasped the quill tightly and enabled him to cut and trim the nib. Morcar remembered his father showing him how to complete the task.

The young Lord Scullion was less like his father than he believed or feared. The lukewarm affection that coursed through his veins was less the product of his parentage than his own bitterness would have him believe. It was easier to lay his faults at the feet of a heartless father than accept his own antipathy towards a world that he had eventually become partitioned from. The absolution and pardon of the confessional is remitted only in the truly penitent and he was not that. His penance was one of self-inflicted intimidation. He felt unloved by the world, for who else would love him when he could not love himself? For him, the withered arm was but a physical manifestation of his own perverted love, which was corruptible, ill-founded and contemptible, especially in his eyes. For him, his love was a greater disfigurement than his withered arm.

Scullion wondered why his chamberlain had been in such a foul mood over dinner last night. Surely he was not as concerned about such trivial matters. Two accidental deaths and the theft of a sheep were of little concern to the shire. And talk of spirits in the corpse road or the opening of the abyss was just that, talk, mere tittle-tattle.

When he had finished the task of honing the shafts of the quills, he then took the pastes that he had been preparing and mixed them with the red and black pigments in two small cups. He decided that the black ink would serve well in giving his blessing to the marriage of Ravenhead and Una Haeferingas, as it would add gravitas and authority to the document. And the poisoned red ink, infused with monkshood and hemlock, would be used to condemn some poor soul for the offence of sheep stealing, once the stranger had been apprehended by Balliwick. It had taken little effort to convince himself that it must be the work of a stranger.

The eorl studied the containers of monkshood and hemlock as he had done so often since Maeldun and, yes, even before, when he first realised that his arm had died. Indeed, each time he thought on his injured arm and misaligned heart, he considered the same recourse. He had even brought a chalice here once from the great hall for just that purpose. He did not know how long such a death would take and yet he was certain that it could not be as long as his tortured life. But he simply could not take that first step; he lacked the courage to take such a course of action. He was not his fearless brother; he was Morcar, the ailing, debilitated son of unsound body and malign heart.

Æthelstan, the late Lord Scullion, had always thought it suitably germane to use poisoned ink tinted in the colour of blood to despatch his enemies to the gallows. It was a pleasure that his son rarely enjoyed, for there had been no sea wanderers captured on these shores since before Maeldun; they had all been paid off, bribed and sent home. And so, the gallows on Apparition Hill served only as constant good counsel, a reminder of times past and the immediacy of justice for the townsfolk.

Fortunately, most of Balliwick's employment in the counting house took place in the summer or autumn, when the room provided welcome shade from the hot sun. In the winter it was rarely used by the chamberlain and Scullion could shelter here unhindered. Today, it was especially so. Balliwick and the guests who had attended dinner last evening had set off on foot to town after breakfast, leaving his lordship alone in the tower with his staff.

The great hall would have been warmer, but he found unaccustomed solace in his occupation. He stood up and walked about the room, wondering where the hearth might be situated in order to provide him with the greatest comfort, hidden away from the world. He would commission the work, he decided, before sitting back down and tidying the table he had been working on. The gravedigger, whose name he couldn't recall, was a stonemason; not a good one, but certainly proficient enough to build a hearth and air hole.

As Scullion tidied away his quills and ink wells, he wondered again about Balliwick. Why was he so anxious about such inconsequential matters?

~~~~~

Willem was hard at work in the Goodlyhead's barn. He enjoyed hard work but preferred to labour in the field, surrounded by the pageantry of creation. Edwin had asked him to stack some wooden boxes of nails as high as he could against the back wall of Mildred's beloved stable. And then he needed to do the same with a consignment of salt that had just arrived from Maeldun. He stacked the sacks as high as he could, leaving six to one side for the butcher, Master Gripple, who was to salt the meat to see the village through the coldest part of winter, which was still to come. The boy knew that Mistress Goodlyhead would disapprove of her manger being used as a store, but knew also that she would offer no objection.

The final words of the Watchman continued to haunt the boy's mind as he busied himself in the barn. How could it be possible that the search for his own origins might have the same purpose as Darrayne's heartfelt desire for justice? He was convinced that if he could find out what had happened to the Watchman, it would answer so many questions that still occupied his mind. He was also sure that Edwin Goodlyhead was not the only person to have mentioned a chandler and that could not have been a coincidence.

Willem recalled Mistress Cuddlewick telling him that a travelling chandler had called at Shire Farm one day. He tried to remember when it was. Then it came to him; it was around the time they collected the fruit of the hazelnut tree. It had been in October, about two months before he had left for Ebbsweirmouth. And she said it was not the first time she had seen the man, for he had called on previous occasions too. But Willem had never seen him, just as nobody but he had seen the shadowy figure during this past week.

Perhaps the Watchman was a spirit, Willem thought, as he tried to remember what Mistress Cuddlewick had said about the man. She had told him to trade his wares in town, for country folk had no money for candles. For the most part, the Cuddlewicks slept when it was dark and awoke with the dawn light. On those rare occasions when she did need to light the house, Mistress Cuddlewick had rolled tallow leaves as tightly as she could and bound them with twine.

"I told him," she had said. "I have no money to burn on candles."

And yet, why had he returned on other occasions, if she had rebuked him so fiercely?

It was true, thought Willem, the evenings at Shire Farm had been brief, for the Cuddlewicks lived only in the daylight. They rose at dawn, ate at dusk and retired when the sun set. And Willem did the same. The nightingale sang him to sleep and the cockerel woke him sharply at dawn each day, including the Sabbath.

"God provided long days for our labours in the summer and short ones in winter to give us rest." That was what Mistress Cuddlewick had said, when she worked alongside Willem in the fields.

When he had finished stacking the sacks of salt, Willem decided to take another look at the rock and blood under the oak tree outside the inn. The thought of taking some action, rather than continually dwelling on the matter, fired him with energy and he lifted the final bags of salt with greater vigour.

In the main street outside, Gripple, Scolop and the other merchants were selling their wares, although the fishmonger had only salted fish for sale. At the end of the street, Aldwyn Byrgan and his two sons were trying, with little success, to breach the stone-hard surface of the graveyard. There were two graves to dig and two bodies to be buried, if they could complete the task before the few hours of December daylight had run their course.

As the three worked, the innkeeper, Leland Hoop, knelt on the frozen ground a short distance behind them, tending his wife's grave. If spirits walk the pathways beside the drove roads, thought Hoop, then my Fanny might still return to me one cold night. He consoled himself with his thoughts. Lazarus of the four days rose from the dead, so why not his wife? But it had been nearly four months, not four days, since Fanny Hoop had passed from this world.

"Good 'morrow," called Abel Cotes, a little more cheerfully than usual, as he walked past on the other side of the low wall around the graveyard.

Hoop nodded to the farmer, who thought the better of walking on and decided to tarry a little and perhaps chat a while with Hoop, for the farmer was not a regular at The Salutation Inn and he did not see the innkeeper very often.

"It's not an anniversary is it, Leland? It is not Fanny's birthday until the spring, is it?"

"I need no excuse for placing a posy upon my wife's grave," replied the innkeeper a little indignantly. "If the spirits walk the pathways and corpse roads, as you keep telling people, then my Fanny might walk there also, Abel. And she may see these flowers as she does so."

The farmer feared for his friend's well-being, for he had laboured in this melancholy state for many months. And now he seemed to be taking solace in the most fearsome things.

"It is not I who talks of such matters, but Gripple and Byrgan, although I am taken with their advice. And you should be too, my friend," the farmer warned. "Do not take to the drove roads these winter nights, Leland. I have to use them to take my flock to pasture and I am affeared of the spirits' malevolence more than anyone." The nervous tremble in the farmer's voice did not persuade Hoop towards panic.

"I fear nothing that might prevent me from seeing Fanny again," called Hoop, so loudly that he could be heard by others nearby.

The farmer, the innkeeper and the gravediggers were not the only occupants of the churchyard on that cold winter morning. Mildred Goodlyhead had decided to speak directly with Father Shriver about at least one of the matters that had kept her from sleeping the previous night. So she knocked on his door and was disappointed and surprised to receive no answer.

As she left the churchyard, Father Shriver approached from the pathway that led to Scullion Tower. He could see the woman was anxious about something and rushed forward to see her, leaving his companions to amble their way into town.

Mildred was indeed distressed and, dispensing with the formality of a good morning, she asked the priest to accompany her to the room where the two bodies lay, awaiting burial.

"Do you recall seeing this before?" she asked, looking down at the pallid body of the boy Eldrik. The priest wasn't sure what she was referring to, so she lifted the boy's hand and showed him the missing finger tip.

"Do you recall seeing this injury before, Father?"

"No, but then it is not for me to examine the hands of my parishioners."

"This injury is new, Father." Her voice suggested that this fact had some relevance to the boy's death.

"Perhaps a fish took it off," replied Shriver a little unconvincingly. Mildred responded with a derisory glance, knowing that this was what others would say too if they were asked.

"Do you think it is a sign?" she asked, but the priest just sighed, wondering whether Mistress Goodlyhead had come under the influence of Abel Cotes. Surely she did not believe this was the harbinger of greater evils to come. So, without even considering the woman's proposition, he resolved to dismiss it out of hand.

"No, certainly not," he replied, trying to sound as credible as possible. But his refusal to consider the matter only made her more certain of its significance.

"Something is amiss here, Father, and someone needs to question its meaning."

As she spoke, she lifted the boy's head up and pointed to the pressure marks on the back of his neck.

"I think he was held under the water, Father."

"What is the point of delaying his burial, Mistress Goodlyhead?" the priest replied. His voice sounded tired and he was indeed becoming wearied by the constant talk of auguries and signs.

"The boy is a serf, a slave, so nobody can be prosecuted for his death. And it matters not whether he died by his master's hand or simply drowned, as Master Scolop says he did."

"It matters not?" Mildred boomed in a tone that left Shriver in no doubt she was about to take the moral high ground on the matter under discussion. He was right, for she was about to remind him that everyone was equal in the eyes of the Lord. He needed to either concede the argument and apologise for his reticence, or take a more entrenched position. He chose the latter, if only because it seemed the quickest way to end the argument.

"Do not seek to chastise my words, Mistress Goodlyhead. You know very well what I mean. There are no good consequences to come from continuing this line of enquiry."

The priest's words were chosen to bring the conversation to an end but, in his heart, he knew that Mildred would not leave it there.

"This boy has been taken from his watery grave and is to be given another in holy soil." She paused, expecting some reaction, adding, "he is not a slave in the eyes of the Lord."

What Mildred really wanted to do was to tell him her thoughts on Willem's missing finger tip, but she chose not to do so, knowing he would simply continue to reject her suggestions of impropriety; he would only dismiss it as irrelevant. More importantly, he might mention it to someone else and place Willem's life in danger by doing so. Instead, she decided to walk away, back towards Mardyke House, passing the market stalls and the loud bellowing of the vendors, before stopping only briefly to speak with her husband, who was heading in the direction she had just come from.

Father Shriver looked down at the body and thought on the woman's words. He knew she and her husband still had some influence and he could not dismiss her wishes so easily. Mildred's father had been a cousin and good friend of Morcar's grandfather. It was he who had helped in the construction of Scullion Tower. The reward for his friendship had been Mardyke House, named after Mildred's father. Both the men were long dead but their reputation still cast a great shadow over the town.

As he reached the end of the main street, near the church, Edwin Goodlyhead came upon a group of people heading in the other direction. Oswald Balliwick, Lord Ravenhead and Lady Una had stopped briefly to say their goodbyes to Friar Sopscott, who was keen to rejoin the parish priest for morning mass. Edwin intervened before the opportunity had passed.

"I am so pleased to have seen you, Friar Sopscott," said Edwin smilingly. "I wondered if you would do my wife and me the great favour of joining us for dinner at Mardyke House this evening."

The black-robed monk hesitated, hoping to find a reason to excuse himself. But none came to mind and so he accepted as gracefully as the delayed response would permit.

As they spoke, Lady Una continued her way back towards the inn, whilst Balliwick and Ravenhead set off towards the market stalls. Cyrus Scolop was sitting on a wooden box behind the table that he used for a market stall. He was busy contemplating how he might spend the ill-gained ten shillings he had been given by Lord Ravenhead. As he smiled through his overgrown beard, he heard the approach of footsteps from the church. He recognised the two men, whose movements were purposeful, and for a brief moment Scolop considered escaping. He looked about him to see how far he might run before he was captured. Chamberlain Balliwick was stepping stridently towards him and Lord Ravenhead was at his heels. The fishmonger resisted the temptation to abscond and decided to stand his ground. He looked at the long-bladed knife lying on the table before him and felt for it with his right hand. The shire reeve was now only twenty paces away and heading directly for him.

"I have only salt fish today, my Lordships," Scolop called in an unusually polite tone towards the two men. "For I cannot fish on the Sabbath." His heart was pounding as he spoke, but the decision was made; he would face them and deny everything.

As he approached, Balliwick fashioned a curious expression, then looked away and marched farther along the street in the direction of the inn. The sigh of relief was almost audible when Ravenhead followed him and smiled at the big man.

"Are you heading for the inn, Lord Ravenhead?" Scolop asked but, by the time he had spoken, the small party had stopped in front of the butcher's table. Three women who were waiting there turned and, seeing Balliwick, moved away but stayed within earshot in order that they might listen to what was said. It was clear from the chamberlain's determined countenance that he was not there to buy meat. Anyway, there were servants to do such menial chores, so whatever Balliwick's purpose was, it would be worthy of gossip. Seconds later, the three women were joined by the Rypan sisters and Mistress Byrgan, all wishing to witness what was about to happen. If any more women of the village gathered with them, then there would be nobody to tell the gossip to.

"What would you recommend for us today, Master Gripple?" Balliwick asked loudly and the women began to lose interest. They muttered questions between themselves, wondering why on earth the chamberlain was undertaking servants' duties for the castle.

"Mutton would seem to be plentiful," he added. "Did you purchase this from his lordship's stock at Four Thing Farm?"

"I did, Sir," came the nervous response.

"And when did you buy this particular sheep?"

"Last week, Sir."

"Boy," said the chamberlain to a small child who was standing by his mother's side with the other women. "Go and fetch Master Cotes for me. I saw him a few moments ago at the churchyard, gossiping."

The boy did not need to be asked twice and he set off as fast as he could run, as a look of grave anxiety appeared on Gripple's face.

The stout figure of Abel Cotes approached the table as quickly as he could, arriving just after the boy.

"You summoned me, Master Balliwick," he said as he doffed his hat.

The chamberlain directed the farmer's attention to the various cuts of lamb on the table.

"Maggoty Gripple here tells me that he purchased this sheep from you last week. Can you confirm that, Master Cotes?"

"Yes, Master Balliwick; well, the week before last to be correct."

"The week before," Balliwick repeated loud enough for everyone to hear, for he knew it was a relevant fact in the case. "And when did you sell him the previous one?"

"Three weeks before that, Sir."

The chamberlain looked back at the butcher and asked why he was selling mutton that was a month old.

"But it is not, your Worship," Gripple replied, confusing his titles.

Balliwick turned to the small boy's mother and asked her how much she had paid for the mutton that she was holding in her hand. After she had replied, he commented on how cheap this was.

"Less than you charged us at the tower for mutton last week, Master Gripple."

"I paid less for it," replied the butcher and Abel Cotes went to intervene. But before the farmer could speak, Balliwick had slammed his fist on the table, making the pieces of meat bounce into the air.

"Either you are selling mutton that is one month old, Master Gripple, or the sheep you purchased from Master Cotes here last week had five legs." He looked back at Abel Cotes. "Do your sheep have five legs?" he asked, without the hint of a smile.

The farmer took his question seriously and shook his head. "Of course not, Master Chamberlain, they all have four, I am certain of it."

"Maggoty Gripple," declared Balliwick. "I am charging you with stealing a sheep."

The gathering crowd stood in silence and Gripple was clearly trying to think of something to repudiate the claim. The best he could do was not good enough.

"With respect, Master Balliwick, it is not for you to make such an accusation."

The chamberlain glared at him and noted the insolent remark for a later time.

"If a crime was committed then there is a victim," said Gripple. "And it is up to the victim — or the victim's family — to seek justice. Let us hear what Master Cotes has to say on the matter, for it is his sheep that you speak of."

As he finished speaking the butcher glared at the farmer and raised his eyebrows. But Cotes was trapped between the two men.

"Master Cotes," shouted Balliwick. "Do you so accuse Maggoty Gripple?"

The farmer looked nervously at the chamberlain and then looked back at the trembling butcher. It was a question of which one he feared most. And, though the fear of violence was great in his mind, his concern about losing his livelihood was even greater.

"It is true. I have lost a sheep."

"You have had a sheep stolen," replied Balliwick. "You said it yourself to me yesterday."

Cotes looked at both men in turn.

"I do so accuse him," came the reluctant reply.

"Come with me, Master Gripple," ordered Balliwick. "And you must come too, Master Cotes," he added, as he paused while Gripple called to one of Byrgan's sons to pack away the table and its contents. But Balliwick stopped the boy and gave him new instructions.

"Deliver that mutton to the tower," the chamberlain ordered. "Until this matter is resolved, it is evidence in the case."

"Now come, Gripple. If you have broken your oath and committed a serious crime your entire kin may be punished too."

"Is this not a case for the hundred court?" Gripple asked, hoping to defer the matter.

"We have had no hundred court since Maeldun, as you very well know. This is a matter for his lordship or, at his pleasure, for me as the shire reeve to pass judgement on."

As the party walked past the churchyard, a thought came to the accused.

"Aldwyn Byrgan will testify my innocence," declared Gripple, pointing towards the gravedigger who had stopped his toiling to see what all the fuss was about.

Byrgan stepped anxiously towards the chamberlain and his friend the butcher.

"Take care, Master Byrgan," Balliwick cautioned him. "Think ahead before you stand witness in this case. As you well know, it is a serious offence in itself to bring wrongful witness."

"Why should it be wrongful witness?" asked Byrgan timidly.

"Well, to begin with, Master Byrgan, you have not yet heard what the offence is, or when it was committed, or whom it was committed against. So how do you know whether you may stand witness for your friend, Maggoty Gripple here?"

"Then tell him what the charge is against me," demanded Gripple, growing in courage. "And let my good friend here repudiate it." There was an emphasis on the words 'good friend', as if they were intended to remind the gravedigger of his relationship.

"It is the law," Balliwick said in a quieter tone to the gravedigger. "If you are found to have given false witness then you shall never stand witness again and you must pay a thirty shilling penalty to the King."

"The shire reeve speaks truthfully, Master Byrgan," said Father Shriver, stepping forward. "He who chooses to swear a false oath cannot be considered oath-worthy again, nor even be buried in hallowed soil."

The penalties for speaking in defence of his friend mounted up in front of him as Byrgan took a step backwards, trying to melt into the crowd, wondering as he did so where he might be buried instead of the very graveyard in which he worked.

"Let me hear the charge first, then," he replied nervously, adding, "and the time, place and offence."

Between them, Balliwick and Cotes structured the details of the charge, while Byrgan listened attentively.

"I cannot say for sure where Maggoty Gripple was on Friday night, but I did spend most of the evening with him," Byrgan answered. "I drank with him at the inn until late and then we went to our beds."

The shire reeve recalled the men's absence from the vigil mass that evening and thought about calling for Leland Hoop to give evidence of what time they had left the inn. But he chose not to, leaving it to the accused to order his own defence.

"Did anyone witness this?" asked Balliwick.

"Leland Hoop and Cyrus Scolop saw us leave the inn."

"And who saw you return home?" the shire reeve asked.

"There was nobody. Everyone was in church at the vigil mass of Saint Lazarus."

"Then your testimony is void, Master Byrgan," Balliwick replied and pointed towards the two dead bodies that lay in the church yard. "Get you back to your work or those two lost souls will not be buried today."

So Byrgan remained in the graveyard with his sons and the accused was escorted to the castle by Chamberlain Balliwick in the company of Father Shriver. It was not uncommon for a parish priest to act as counsel for the accused in such cases and so Friar Sopscott was enlisted to say morning mass.

On their return to Scullion Tower, Maggoty Gripple was led into a room adjacent to the great hall by his lordship's servants and left standing there, in the company of Father Shriver, to await his trial. In the meantime, it was left to Balliwick to explain to his lordship what had occurred in town. Scullion was furious to have lost the wager he had laid with Ravenhead and was enraged even further by being proved wrong at the hands of a complete stranger. It was agreed that Balliwick would conduct the hearing and his lordship would listen to the events from the adjacent room.

While he waited for proceedings to commence, Gripple asked Shriver what the priest thought he should do. The answer was predictable.

"Always tell the truth. If you are guilty, then admit your offence and submit yourself to the mercy of Lord Scullion."

"What is the penalty, Father, for the theft of a sheep?"

"Five shillings and you must swear again your oath not to steal."

"And if I cannot pay the penalty?"

"You *must* pay the penalty, Master Gripple, for you will be hanged if you are found guilty and fail to do so."

An extensive list of penalties was in existence at this time, some created by the King, others by the eorls and some by the Church. The only penalty that most peasants knew was the fifty shillings payment if you were to lay with a virgin of the royal household. It was the subject of many bawdy comments at inns around the land and was made funnier if the royal household in question contained any particularly unattractive ladies.

It took the servants only a few minutes to rearrange the chairs in order that those present could be questioned by the shire reeve, who chose to stand and walk about the room. Balliwick thought much better on his feet and needed to ensure this tribunal reached the required conclusion.

As the trial began, Gripple was thinking less about the gravity of his offence and more about how he might get Byrgan to pay all, or most, of the fine. His mind was certainly not on any greater penalty than five or ten shillings. Nevertheless, he denied the charge strenuously but was challenged on every word by the shire reeve.

The repeated loud pleas of innocence from Maggoty Gripple were eventually dismissed by Balliwick, who reminded him of the requirement to bring forth two men to repudiate the offence and testify to his innocence.

"I have no sons," he declared, as if only family members would suffice. "I lost my son at Maeldun. He would be the same age as Lord Scullion for he was born the same year. I have already lost a son to the Crown and now I am to lose my own life, too, if I fail to pay the fine? That's not right, Master Balliwick."

As the defendant spoke, loud banging could be heard from the next room. This was immediately interpreted by Balliwick as a signal from his lordship, so he halted the proceedings and went into the adjacent room, closing the door behind him.

"This is an opportunity, Balliwick," declared Lord Scullion, as if a great idea had suddenly occurred to him. But the look that greeted the statement indicated the chamberlain required an explanation.

"It is an opportunity," Scullion repeated. "The butcher must hang."

"Hang, Sir? But he will almost certainly pay the required penalty and avoid such a terrible consequence. I am sure if he does not have five shillings he will have no difficulty raising it."

"He must hang, Master Balliwick. Then Lord Ravenhead shall know that we are not to be meddled with. This northern lord shall witness, first hand, the strength of our authority. He must see we do not flinch in exercising our judgement."

Balliwick tried by every means possible to mediate on behalf of Maggoty Gripple and reminded his lordship of the butcher's great sacrifice, for when all the tenant farmers had been accounted for, old Lord Scullion was short of his quota for Maeldun. One man for every five hides of land was the requirement of the Crown. Byrgan's twins had been only eight years old, Scolop had no children, nor did the Goodlyheads. So it had fallen to Gripple to submit his only son to join the others at Maeldun. The boy went willingly, convinced of great glory, armed only with a butcher's axe to defend himself with. It was never used in battle, for the boy had been stationed at the centre of the battle wall and was felled by a spear thrown in the first Norse attack.

Lord Scullion was angry that he should have to explain himself at such length to his shire reeve.

"Hang Gripple," he whispered with as much force as he could muster. "Do I want to be known as Morcar the merciful or Morcar the merciless? The man must hang, all must know of my unflinching justice."

"It is not justice to hang a man when he may repay the debt."

Scullion did not even answer the last point, for when you lack honour you can justify anything. But what Balliwick knew was that when you justify anything with a power that lacks justice, you have misrule and dishonour.

Balliwick appealed one last time for a reasoned decision from the eorl, but his lordship was adamant on the matter. This, in his view, was too good an opportunity to miss. Someone who might prove an enemy at some time in the future must be shown the unflinching vengeance of the Scullion household.

The delay and the angry but hushed voices from the next room increased the anxiety that now gripped the butcher. So great was his apprehension that he blurted out his admission the moment Balliwick re-entered the room.

"I will pay the five shillings," declared Gripple, with a relieved sigh.

"And I will have you hanged, Master Gripple."

For a moment, neither Gripple nor Father Shriver could understand the devastating statement that had just been made.

"What do you mean, you shall have him hanged?" asked the priest. "Master Gripple here will pay the fine."

"By the power invested in me, I shall have this oath-breaker hanged."

"Power?" questioned the priest. "The responsibility of power is to protect the weak and to administer justice. True power can only be found in humility. And for true justice to prevail it must be clothed in integrity, for corruptible justice leads to the oppression of the weak."

"You call my justice corruptible, Father Shriver, but choose to defend one who would breach his oath, steal other's property and, then, deny the charges and try to enlist an innocent man to break his oath also."

"But it is the law. Master Gripple may pay punitive compensation as demanded by his lordship."

"Subject to the mercy of this court," the chamberlain corrected him.

"Then demonstrate that mercy, I beg you," pleaded Shriver.

Balliwick knew the weakness of his case, but knew also that a return visit to the next room to seek mercy would be fruitless. So he resigned himself to defend the indefensible.

"Gripple is not simply guilty of theft, Father Shriver. He stole from his lordship himself."

"I did not," declared Gripple, almost in tears.

"You did," bellowed the chamberlain.

"But I stole from Abel Cotes," the accused whimpered.

"Specific ordinances made by his lordship require each tenant to pay him an annual tithe of one-tenth of their harvest income. Other additional tributes are added through the year. Four Thing Farm is a fee farm with a fixed annual payment in addition to the tithe. The farm is owned by his lordship, not Cotes, and the sheep was therefore the property of his lordship. Stealing his lordship's sheep is the same as stealing his deer and is punishable by hanging. No monetary penalty may compensate for the damage done to a member of the royal household."

Gripple fell to his knees and pleaded for mercy, but Balliwick called the servants to remove him.

"Take him to the cell in the yard. He shall hang on Apparition Hill tomorrow morning."

"I need to confess my sins before I depart this world," Gripple called as he was led away.

Balliwick asked Father Shriver to accompany the prisoner to the cell to hear his confession but, as he was led away, the butcher asked if he might confess his sins to the visiting friar.

"I will ask Friar Sopscott if he will visit you," Shriver called to him as he followed him out of the building.

~~~~~

It was getting late and what little sun there had been on that December day was now falling beyond the dense forest that covered the western horizon. It was getting dark inside the barn and Willem hurried himself to finish his work before he had to light a candle. He stepped back and admired the tidy product of his labours. Then, looking outside, he decided it was still light enough to resolve something that had been on his mind all day.

Willem felt drawn back to the place where the Watchman Darrayne had died. There were issues that he could not dismiss, nor could he discuss them with others until he had reached some conclusion in his own mind. So he returned to the inn, looking about him as he went, trying not to appear conspicuous and stopped where he had done before.

The red stain had disappeared and what was left of the snow was coloured only by the muddy surface it now covered. The boy immediately recognised the rock he had examined previously. The bloodstained snow may have vanished, but there was still blood on the rock. He turned it over, looking at the roughly hewn shape of the thing, then walked over to the trunk of the tree, where he believed the rock had rested for many years. He leaned over, lowering the large stone and it fitted the indentation exactly. He turned the object over and over, examining its surface in detail. Of course, the insects he had seen previously had disappeared, but it was clear from the green mould on one side and the colouring of the stone that it had been moved. He convinced himself of it, for it was too much of a coincidence that it should have been moved before the alleged accident had occurred.

In any case, why was the blood stain on the darker side of the rock, the side that was also marked with mould and earth? Why was the blood not on the dry side, the upper side of the stone? Surely, if Darrayne had fallen onto the rock as Mistress Goodlyhead had said, then the earth and mould would be underneath it, on the other side, not on the top where the man allegedly fell.

When he had first examined the stone there had been insects there too, on the mouldy side of the rock. Everyone knows that insects crawl under the stone, not on top of it. There was only one conclusion he could reach. This stone had been lifted up and used as a weapon to strike Darrayne on the head. But who would do such a thing? By all accounts, he had just arrived at Ebbsweirmouth. He knew no one and had spoken only to Hoop about a room at the inn for the night.

The consideration for Willem now was whether to tell anyone else about his suspicions. It was nearing sunset and he had been invited to join the Goodlyheads for supper with Friar Sopscott that evening.

Willem rushed back towards Mardyke House to prepare himself for the meal. Might this be the right opportunity to raise his suspicions? The Goodlyheads had appeared very disappointed by his obtrusive questioning at the last supper he attended. And he couldn't be sure of the friar who, apart from himself and the couple staying at the inn, had been the only other visitor to the town when Darrayne was killed. It was unlikely that a Benedictine monk would kill someone, but then, nobody had met Friar Sopscott before and they had only his word that he was a holy man. The boy tried to clear his head of the supposition and conjecture that clouded his judgement on the matter.

When Friar Sopscott arrived for supper, he was surprised to find such affluent surroundings and had not appreciated the family connection, albeit some two generations past, with Eorl Æthelstan. Mardyke House was indeed a pleasant home, cheerfully adorned with unusually bright fabric and not at all like the peasant single-room homes found in most villages of this size.

The Goodlyheads had no servants, a decision taken as much on principle as affordability. Mildred enjoyed cooking and keeping the house clean, and her endeavours were visible in the pleasant ambience that greeted him.

Willem arrived shortly after the friar and his appearance interrupted a discussion that Edwin was enjoying with the learned man on the subject of the nativity and how it was celebrated in Fleury, where Sopscott had studied.

"Noel, noel," the friar was saying to Edwin, as he related the angels' message to the shepherds.

"Is that Latin?" interrupted Willem in an effort to join the conversation, for he was eager to do so.

"No," replied Sopscott emphatically. "It is French. It is the traditional Christmas greeting in France, for it was the angels' declaration of joy at the Saviour's birth."

"Were the angels French, then?" the boy asked.

"No," replied the friar. "Their greeting was written in Latin so that the world may understand it."

Willem failed to see how the world would understand Latin, when the vast majority of the people he had met did not speak a word of it. He paused for a moment, wondering whether he was asking too many awkward questions again. And yet there were so many important matters he wanted to raise. Even on the subject of angels, he was anxious to tell them all about his own visitation by an angel. But it was such an implausible story that he suspected he would simply upset the evening for his hosts. Perhaps he would save the episode, he thought, in case he was asked to tell another story.

The boy particularly wanted to seek the holy man's advice about the mysterious old crone he had met in the yew tree wood on his way to Ebbsweirmouth; of the strange things she had said and the markings she made on the floor. However, this encounter seemed even more bizarre than his meeting with an angel and neither tale would lead him any further towards the real issue that continued to occupy his mind. What he really wanted to do was raise the matter of the strange shadowy figure he had met in the church and again in the barn. But he kept his own counsel and, in the end, the friar's words about the angels' Christmas greeting hung in the air.

"This is Willem," Edwin said, introducing the friar to their other guest and making great capital of his wife's generous nature to the poor in general, and to homeless boys in particular.

As Sopscott took the boy's hand, he held his grip for a few seconds and, noticing the missing fingertip, examined it with a questioning aspect. Mistress Goodlyhead looked into his eyes suspiciously and wondered if he had noticed the same abnormality on the boy Eldrik. She thought for a moment about raising the matter and asking for the holy man's opinion on the coincidence of the missing finger tips. But she truly did not want to cause anxiety to the boy, so she remained silent on the subject.

Willem simply looked up at the friar and wondered why he was taking so much interest in his hand. He wanted to enquire why the holy man should be so attentive to such a minor defect, but he hesitated too long, distracted by the cuts and bruises that marked the man's face. Both parties knew in their hearts that these distinguishing features, although temporary in the friar's case, each concealed an interesting tale. Strangely, although he had kept the matter secret from those he ate with at Scullion Tower, Friar Sopscott felt able to talk to the boy candidly. He considered that the young should never be deceived, or their learning might be impaired. And he certainly wouldn't lie. So, convinced that the boy would ask about the injuries anyway, he explained how he had come by them.

"My work has made me somewhat unpopular amongst some priests. I am charged by the monasteries with the removal of secular priests from the parishes. It generates great enmity towards me and, by some misfortune, I happened to meet two former priests on my journey to Ebbsweirmouth the other day."

"Who are these men?" asked Edwin.

"It matters not, but I think they left me for dead on the roadside, so I must pray to God that I do not meet them in such circumstances again."

"We shall pray for it also," replied Mildred.

"Thank you for that, Mistress Goodlyhead. And also for your kind hospitality," he added, directing his gratitude to both the Goodlyheads. "I was fortunate enough to be invited to dine with Lord Scullion last evening and the generosity of this village to a poor, travelling mendicant is greatly appreciated."

"It is our pleasure," answered Mildred and directed her guest to the chair at the head of the table.

The friar was surprised to learn that the couple had not dined at the castle and, furthermore, that the business Edwin conducted with the castle was often through Oswald Balliwick. On those few occasions that Edwin did meet his lordship, it was in the counting house, where both he and his chamberlain preferred to receive most visitors.

The polite conversation that controls most introductory meetings continued and was interrupted at intervals by overly long periods of silence whenever the subject touched on the events of that day. Everyone knew the source of the awkward pauses. They had all witnessed or heard of the events in town and yet none seemed willing to introduce it into the conversation. Eventually the subject that hung in the air above the table was brought crashing down by Willem.

"I heard some talk in the town today about Master Gripple," the boy said. "Some say he is to hang for the theft of a sheep."

"There have been no hangings in this town for many years and I am sure it shall remain so," Edwin Goodlyhead assured Willem. "There is a charter of penalties to be paid and, if he is guilty of such an act, then he shall pay the price demanded."

"When I journeyed here on Friday," replied the boy, "I saw the gallows to the north of town. It seems to me that it is situated on the ridge of a high hill, so that all who live nearby may see the product of a guilty man's offence."

Both the Goodlyheads wanted to counter the dark nature of the boy's comments, but were interrupted by Friar Sopscott, who joined his hands and offered a prayer in thanks for the food they were about to receive. As soon as he closed with the sign of the cross, Edwin spoke up.

"As I said, Willem, the gallows has not been used since we were last troubled by the sea wanderers, before Maeldun. In those days," Edwin continued, in the hope of deflecting the subject, "Lord Scullion's father, Eorl Æthelstan, would write death warrants in poison. He made the potions himself. I was invited once to the counting room where I met his son, young Morcar as he was then, for the first time. But, since those distant, belligerent times, I am pleased to report that the people of this village live in continued peace."

"And, yet, there have been two sudden and unexplained deaths in the town this very week," commented the friar, much to the surprise of his hosts.

"Unexplained?" questioned Mildred as she served the food at the table. "Whatever do you mean?"

"Is it not strange that two such deaths should occur within as many days?" asked Sopscott, thinking back on the chamberlain's tirade on the subject the previous evening. "After all, your husband has already said that the town has enjoyed a long period of peace."

"There are still deaths," declared Edwin.

"The man was a visitor to the town," added Mildred. "He fell and struck his head on a rock. His death is not unexplained, for I have just explained it." Her voice was becoming a little more determined in its tone, as she was hoping that such an unfortunate discussion would be brought to a close.

"And the fisherman's boy?" responded the friar. "The serf, Eldrik?"

"The boy drowned," replied Edwin. "It was a stormy winter night, it was unfortunate and yet a common outcome, I imagine, for those who work at sea."

"Such deaths cause great sadness," Mildred interrupted. "But no one is suspected of foul play and, therefore there will be no hanging. All this talk of hanging," she stuttered, not knowing how best to express her frustration. "Nobody is to be hanged in Ebbsweirmouth," she declared.

"I beg to disagree with my host," replied Sopscott. "But I must tell you that I am attending Scullion Tower tomorrow to hear the confession of a condemned man. For the butcher, Maggoty Gripple, is indeed to be hanged for the theft of a sheep. As we speak," he added, "Gripple is held at the tower, awaiting his execution."

The others stopped eating and considered his words. Clearly, none of them had heard the outcome of Gripple's hearing.

"Is there nothing that can be done to dissuade the shire reeve from this course of action?" asked Edwin.

"I fear not," replied Sopscott. "Yet I fear it is not the shire reeve who favours such action, for I see mercy in his eyes. I can only assume that his lordship is resolved on the matter."

Mildred suggested that someone should speak to his lordship, pointing out that Gripple was not the best of men and yet he was not the worst of them either.

~~~~~

In the great hall at Scullion Tower, the two men of whom they spoke had just finished their own supper. Balliwick had exhausted all mitigation on behalf of the butcher and resigned himself to the determined resolve of his lord. In fact, through the perseverance of Lord Scullion, eventually Balliwick was almost persuaded towards the merit of such a decision. It was true, the men agreed, that Ravenhead might prove a difficult neighbour once he was granted the earldom of Haeferingas. So a show of force might leave a lasting impression on him. And yet there was cruelty in their digression from the charter of penalties.

"Do not be angry with me, Oswald," pleaded his lordship, as he walked to the other side of the table and rested his good hand on the chamberlain's shoulder.

"Do you not fear for your soul?" asked Balliwick. "For I certainly do."

"There is no place for us in heaven, my friend," came Scullion's reply, as his comforting hand slid along Balliwick's shoulder and caressed the back of his neck.

Balliwick stood up and walked to the door.

"I am going to check on the prisoner. And then I think I shall take to my bed, for we have a busy day tomorrow."

As the chamberlain left the room, Scullion lifted the bottle of wine and shook it. He poured what remained into a chalice and slumped back into the chair.

The courtyard outside was sheltered from the wind but the cold night air had frozen the ground. Patches of snow lingered by the wall where the sun never shed its light. Balliwick walked to the corner of the castle where the counting house was and checked that the door was locked. Then, crossing to the other corner, he could hear the butcher in selfish prayer, pleading for his life to be saved.

Largely unused for two generations, the soil and gravel that formed the cell had moulded itself into a solid mass and patches of moss were the only indication of the material that formed it. The door was encased by earth and the interior was pitch dark. Those imprisoned here could draw no comfort from the delusion of freedom. For them, there was only the inevitability of that long walk up Apparition Hill towards a certain death. This was a tomb for the forsaken, a place where hope had never visited and prudence was a forgotten virtue.

Balliwick waited for a moment before calling through the small metal grill in the door.

"Gripple, have you been fed?"

"I am not hungry, my Lord Chamberlain. Has the eorl been persuaded of my innocence?"

"He is persuaded of your guilt, for you are guilty."

"Why should I, alone, hang? Was it just one person who stole the sheep? Was it me, alone, who carried it from the field?

"Take care, Master Gripple," warned Balliwick, "for you will hang tomorrow whatever you say."

"I can name others who were conjoined in this enterprise."

The chamberlain stepped back from the bars.

"I do not wish to hear this," Balliwick shouted back, hoping to stop a declaration that would have appalling consequences. "Has the friar been to hear your confession?" he added, hoping to change the course of the conversation.

"No," Gripple answered and he appealed not be hanged until his sins had been forgiven.

"I'll do what I can," Balliwick called as he turned to leave, thinking and indeed hoping that the butcher would now remain silent. But it was not to be so and a loud voice echoed around the courtyard as the condemned man shouted after the shire reeve.

"It was Byrgan; Aldwyn Byrgan, aye and his sons too. All four of us are as guilty as each other. Are we all to hang? What unmerciful lord would hang four men for the theft of a single sheep?"

Balliwick turned and walked back to the door of the cell. "You fool!" he shouted through the grill. "Your treachery provides further reason for his lordship's irrational will. If the hanging of one man might prove his unmerciful power, then you have increased such validation fourfold."

The chamberlain walked back towards the castle with hesitant step, wondering whether it was possible to keep this information from his lordship. What purpose would it serve to tell him? Another three deaths in addition to one that was already unjust. And yet he could not keep silent. The implications for his own position were too great. What ails a man, he thought, that he might endure his own death only through the condemnation of three others with him?

Desperation was the answer, of course. Gripple was desperate to avoid the gallows and would do anything to escape such an end.

His lordship was not drunk enough to forget what Balliwick might tell him. The chamberlain could not use that excuse again. Anyway, it was his duty, not his lordship's, to take action when an accusation was made, even one by a condemned man.

When he returned to the great hall, the table was being cleared by the servants and he learned that Lord Scullion had retired to bed. So, he had the night to dwell on it, but there seemed little way to avoid the inevitable consequences of Gripple's indictment.

Balliwick slumped into a chair and wondered how many more citizens might be immersed in this iniquitous affair.

Willem went to his bed that night convinced that he had seen the last of Watchman Darrayne. His mind had been enlightened by his mentor and his heart emboldened by courage. But prudence now rested in his soul so, whilst his thoughts questioned what action he should now take, the virtues now guided him towards justice. The Watchman had suggested that his own desire for a just outcome was linked to the boy's journey. Now that journey took Willem on a path towards justice for Eldrik and perhaps the Watchman too. It was apparent to the boy that Darrayne did not simply seek revenge for his own death; there was something of greater meaning that drove the former soldier. That quest must now be Willem's to take forward. Through the gift of prudence, he knew that the next step must be preceded by consideration, for had he not learned that the signs to truth are often unheeded?

Wisdom teaches the importance of prudence and justice. It is impossible to find true good in every circumstance and, yet, sometimes it is difficult to find it in any.

Chapter Twelve

Justice

Sit and abide with me awhile if you will, dear reader, for your understanding is required of how justice was served in these days. You will appreciate, of course, that there were no prisons at this time and justice was rudimentary at best, and more often harsh and pitiless. A freeman needed only to pay compensation to his victim to retain his liberty, or would be hanged for failing to make such restitution.

These were the only two outcomes permitted by law and authorised by the Crown. Even crimes against our fellow man were the subject of a schedule of compensation, although most could not stand sound examination. To shave a man in such a manner as to expose him to derision required a payment of ten shillings and yet to break a person's arm resulted in a fine of just six shillings. The list of fines was extensive, but none applied to offences against slaves or serfs, for their owner could treat such individuals as mercilessly as he desired.

The process, whilst not in the least arbitrary for the penalties were well known, was adopted at the discretion of the Crown, or the King's appointed one. So the only exceptions to the general *rule of penalty payments were offences against the Crown or, in the case of parochial matters, the elderman.*

The eorl, as elderman, sat in judgement of anyone who lived within his shire, although most crimes fell under the auspices of his shire reeve, a man you will recall of utmost virtue. Precisely what that virtue was is unclear, but often it did not include prudence, discretion or wisdom, all three of which would seem to be a prerequisite for such a position and entirely necessary if justice was to be dispensed.

Scullion Tower had, in the not too distant past, been little more than a keep or a stockade, built to repel invaders, or the sea wanderers as Lord Scullion's grandfather had called them and the term had held since then. It was this same ancestor who rebuilt that old wooden fortress and created the grey stone castle that now stands there.

Most of the land inside the fortress was occupied by his lordship's living quarters, including the great dining room and several large bedrooms. Outside, surrounding a square courtyard, were other buildings, such as stables for the horses, a well that provided the tower's water supply and two other important structures. The first was the counting house and the second was little more than a mound of earth, as high as a man could create, which stood in one corner of the yard. Two generations had passed since it was constructed and the turf and soil, over time, had transformed to a solid mass. At the front of the mound a hole had been dug, deeper and deeper, and timbers placed inside to ensure it did not collapse. Then a sturdy door had been erected and placed facing the courtyard, which contained a barred window, a grill just large enough to permit someone to peer through, with a slot below it in order that food may be passed to those incarcerated there.

At this time, it was unusual for a castle to have a dungeon for, as I have already attested, there were no prisons in these dark days. But, this building served a different purpose; this was built before Maeldun to house captured sea wanderers, until they were hanged at Gallows Ridge, high on Apparition Hill and left there for all to see.

For these cut-throat libertines, the noose that was used to hang them was left long, so they would hang just above the earth's surface, their feet flailing above the ground that could save them from a slow death. There they would dangle, where first the birds and then the wild beasts of the forest would gorge upon their bodies, in order that all those travellers of a stout heart and doughty stomach who passed that way might look upon them and know what misfortune lay ahead if they attacked the village of Ebbsweirmouth.

The twelfth virtue of destiny is justice and it rightly dwells between prudence and mercy for, without such chaperones, revenge might disguise its true self and, through deception, supplant itself in its place. For revenge and justice are not kindred spirits. You have heard it said that an eye may be taken for an eye and a tooth for a tooth, but such words are born of Babylon and yet the gateway to God was destroyed by such beliefs. Justice must never be mistaken for retribution, nor used to demonstrate might or power. Yet this was, indeed, the motive that drove the Eorl of Ebbsweirmouth on this sorrowful advent morning.

※※※

Lord Scullion sat in the cold counting house and lifted the lid from the container of poisoned red ink. He held it to his nose to smell the deathly odour of the monkshood and hemlock. He smiled to himself and, replacing it on the table, he rolled out one sheet of parchment, placing a weight on each corner to hold it in place. At the top, he wrote 'Death Warrant' and paused to think, trying to recall the words that needed to be written. He had not performed the task for some years, but the words did not need to be precise; there was nobody to challenge him, no higher authority to dispute his judgement on the basis of a misspelt word, as might happen today. The document simply required his signature and the statement 'by warrant under the eorl's sign-manual' and that would be sufficient for the bearer to hang Maggoty Gripple on Apparition Hill just six days before Christ's mass was to be held.

Each of us has a duty to ensure that no evil goes unpunished in this world and, for the most part, the cardinal virtue of justice persuades us to moderate our anger in the dispatch of such duties. Cardinal virtues are praised under other names in many passages of the Good Book. But all such considerations had been dismissed by Lord Scullion in his objective. Fairness, integrity and honesty were swept aside as he dated the warrant and pressed the red ink dry. The shadow of justice is revenge and yet, if revenge is mitigated by honour, then prudence and mercy may prevail. But, little honour dwelled in the world inhabited by Lord Scullion and it was certainly absent on this particular day. For, if any doubt had lingered in the darkness of his heart, it was dispelled by the arrival of Oswald Balliwick.

"My Lord," he announced as he walked into the counting house. "It was too late to report this to you last night but the accused has citied others in his crime."

Balliwick explained how Gripple had implicated Aldwyn Byrgan, the gravedigger, and his two grown sons.

"All four collaborated in the theft and, in his own words, each is as guilty as the others. As a consequence of this the butcher's hanging will not take place until tomorrow."

Scullion seized on the opportunity to elaborate on his previous plan. If the hanging of one man might enhance his merciless reputation, then four would do his purpose an even greater service. His instruction to the shire reeve was to arrest the three men as publicly as he could, in order that his authority may be demonstrated to all and word of it spread as widely as possible.

"We shall hang all four of them on Apparition Hill, Balliwick, for all must see how we deal with those who cross us."

"There is room for only three on the gallows, my Lord," replied his chamberlain. "And we must question them first."

"And then hang them," Scullion interrupted.

"It is for their accuser to declare their guilt, my Lord, not us."

His lordship ignored the irritating pedantic utterings of his chamberlain.

"We shall hang the butcher tomorrow, after he has indicted the others, then the Byrgans shall follow the next day, so that all may see. What better way have we to provide a spectacle of our strength to this northern shire upstart?"

"Is such a brutal demonstration essential, my Lord?"

"I am my father's son, but I am eorl by might, not just inheritance. And my might must be demonstrated if it is to be maintained."

Balliwick wanted to respond. What duplicity, he thought. A public demonstration of might by a very private eorl seemed cowardly in the extreme. An eorl unknown to his people, kept hidden for fear they should see his true self. The loud roar of a timid animal, kept incarcerated by his own fears. Such a man would hold unimpeachable rule by his own invisibility. Such a man, whose father adopted the fearsome sobriquets 'lion' and 'wolf', and yet, in reality is a sheep in a wolf's coat and the most fearful lion to walk this earth. All these thoughts he would have laid bare if Balliwick thought it might remedy the situation, but he knew Lord Scullion was resolved on the matter.

Lord Scullion would play his part in spite of his torn character. Not with the arrogance or vanity one might normally find in one of high office, nor the modesty or humility that one would wish to find, but only through the self-loathing, the contempt he held for himself, which was even greater than that of his own people, manifested in revulsion of self.

Balliwick bowed and started off on foot towards town. As the weeping sun rose on such a dishonest day, it was for him to deliver the awful vision of death that might flatter his lord. As he went, he came upon Friar Sopscott on his way to see Maggoty Gripple.

"This day worsens before it has begun," the shire reeve said dejectedly.

The friar remained silent, waiting for Balliwick to explain his comment.

"Gripple has named three others who took part in the enterprise. I am going to arrest Aldwyn Byrgan now, along with his two elder sons. They must face their accuser and present their defence."

"Shall I await your return?" asked the friar.

"Someone must impress reason on an unreasoned mind. Unfortunately, my own appeal for clemency has fallen on stony ground."

Sopscott knew what he meant. He knew where the true power of Scullion Tower rested and it was not with Chamberlain Balliwick.

Balliwick had forewarned his master that Friar Sopscott would be attending the castle today to hear the last confession of Maggoty Gripple.

The friar was uneasy with the butcher's request. As an ordained priest, as well as a follower of the order of Saint Benedict, it was quite within his authority to hear confessions, but he normally did so only when a parish priest was unavailable. Nevertheless, he felt as uncomfortable about refusing the wish of a dying man as he did about supplanting himself for Father Shriver. And greater still than these misgivings was the friar's opinion on the efficacy of a deathbed confession.

"But this is not a deathbed confession," Father Shriver had pointed out. "This is the confession of a condemned man."

Yet, Sopscott's beliefs were deep rooted, the product of dutiful studies at Fleury Abbey and his many years as a novice to Abbot Oswald. For him, a deathbed confession, whether that of a dying man or indeed one condemned to die for his crimes, was insufficient to warrant eternal life in heaven. Eternal life, many believe, depends on the state of our soul at the moment of death and, yet, the good friar was not convinced by the merits of such a tenuous standpoint. For Friar Sopscott it was not enough to die in a holy state but to have lived a holy life too. There must be reparation, some compensation for the sins. It was not sufficient, for him, that the soul should be on the road to holiness, it had to have rested and abided there to warrant the gift of heaven.

"What about the thief on the cross?" Shriver had asked. "And what of the parable of the labourers in the vineyard? Do they not provide authority for a deathbed confession?"

Friar Sopscott had served men of a different mind. His Benedictine masters, particularly his mentor, Oswald, saw a more onerous path to eternal life. A path of sacrifice, poverty and strict holy rule. Had he not spent the past five years ridding the church of married priests?

"In an ecclesiastical church, there can be no room for secular priests," Oswald had demanded. And Sopscott had implemented those demands, making many enemies in the process. A great number of married priests had lost their homes, their employment and a comfortable life. And many of those were the younger sons of noblemen. Yet their wrath could not reach the great Oswald, for those who ran the monasteries held power and the gift of eternal life remained in their remit. Yet the servants of the monasteries, like Sopscott, were sent into the world to rectify it and it was they who felt the harsh tongue and indeed acts of violence at the hands of the deposed priests.

Gripple needed to make his confession before he was hanged, that was the friar's only consideration at this time. Whether it became a deathbed confession through the actions of someone else was not of his making. The

Benedictine monk rarely went into a confessional box expecting the ordinary. He had been surprised too often by common folk who had done dire and appalling deeds to foretell the manner of someone's sins.

Friar Sopscott entered the castle gate and a maid directed him to the dark grotto of a cell in one corner of the yard. Gripple heard the words of someone in prayer and pressed his face against the bars on the door. The friar called towards a shadow that knelt in the darkness.

"I am here, Father Friar. I do thank you for attending."

"Kneel on the other side of the door, my son."

Sopscott knelt as close to the door as he could and looked over his shoulder at the maid. The look turned to a glare and she walked off, back to the kitchen.

Gripple's confession was the product of a heart filled with sorrow. Not, perhaps for his sins, thought Sopscott, but for his own circumstances. Yet the man's mind was focused on his past faults, there was no doubt about that. He did not wish to forget any previous shortcomings for, if he failed to record them now, they might be presented to him by a higher authority in the days to come.

He confessed to the theft of the farmer's sheep and to another that Cotes had not even missed. Unsurprisingly for a butcher, he had also killed his lordship's deer and sold this at a profit. None of this was a surprise to the friar. However, the sworn vengeance that Gripple had carried in his heart for several years was unexpected and as heartfelt as his confession itself. It was the Scullion family who had sent his only son to his death at Maeldun, just to make up the number required to meet the shire's pledge.

The friar was an astute and worldly man, and when Gripple had finished his supplicant plea for forgiveness, he paused, reflecting on whether it was reasonable for him to remind the penitent of something he may have forgotten. He could not resist the opportunity to move the man closer to God by laying bare his other failings.

"Are you not the author of the stories told hereabouts on the subject of the spirits that haunt the corpse road?"

Gripple hesitated, wondering what the holy man was referring to. "The author, Sir?" he questioned, not fully understanding the friar's meaning.

The perceptive Sopscott had married these ghostly stories to the theft of the sheep when Balliwick had told him about Byrgan's involvement earlier that morning. His only consideration was not whether he was correct, but whether Balliwick had himself made the connection.

"Did you, Master Gripple, conjure up and circulate the untruthful phantoms that people spoke of as haunting the corpse road and drove roads at night?"

"It was the people themselves that said as much," Gripple replied.

"Yes, but it suited your purpose for it to be propagated, did it not?"

"Is it a sin to have done so, Father?"

"Of course it is a sin, my son. For your own material gain, you allowed your neighbours to believe that the drove roads were inhabited by evil spirits. People were deterred from going about their business because of your deceit. Your falsehood caused others anxiety and fear. Why should this not be considered a sin in the eyes of God?"

"You are right, of course, Father Friar, and I humbly add it to the list of my sins and failings."

"Are there others that you have not spoken of?" asked the friar.

"I hope not, Father."

"What about your sin against Master Byrgan and his sons?"

Gripple gasped, wondering how the friar knew of his accusation so soon after he had spoken with the chamberlain.

"I spoke only the truth."

"And in doing so, you chose to forsake an opportunity to alleviate your own sinful heart, did you not?"

"How so, Father?"

"By keeping good counsel, you may have tempered the judgement that will be made upon you."

"I will accept and undertake any penance you provide, Father."

"Not the judgement of I," sighed Sopscott. "I refer to the judgement of the Almighty."

Gripple explained that he had accused Aldwyn Byrgan and his sons only in order that he might be spared the death sentence.

"Surely they will not hang four men for the theft of one sheep."

In the kindest terms possible, Sopscott tried to explain the butcher's dire circumstances and how Lord Scullion would need to renege on his previous judgement if he was to defer the hanging of all four men.

"What new evidence or information could cause him to do this?" the friar asked. "Can four men not be guilty of a single crime? Did the eorls not hang many Nordic sea wanderers for a single crime in the past? All you have done," he continued, "is to incriminate your friends in your act." He fell silent but, when Gripple began to speak, he interrupted. "Do you wish to repent this sin?"

"I do, Father, but I know not what to call it."

"It is wrong to find a fault in others that is just as apparent in thine own self, Master Gripple. That is the sin."

"Then I do confess it, Father."

Friar Sopscott then pardoned those sins that he had mentioned and others that he may have forgotten.

"For your penance, say the Lord's Prayer three times, and now make a sincere act of contrition."

Gripple said the act of contrition aloud and, as the priest began to rise from his knees, the butcher spoke again.

"I do not have a prayer book, Father."

"Do you not know the Lord's Prayer by heart?"

"I do, Sir, but I do not want to omit a word, or recite a phrase wrong."

The friar realised that the man was clearly afraid that any such error might revoke the purging of his sins, so he opened his own prayer book at the required page and passed it through the slot below the grill on the door. As he waited, Sopscott walked about the yard, leaving Gripple to complete his penance. It took a few minutes for, whilst the butcher could not read very well, he did indeed know the prayer by heart and yet he followed and spoke each word deliberately, so as not to forego his chance of redemption in heaven.

When he had finished, Gripple passed the book back through the bars. As the friar took it, the butcher gripped his hand.

"Will you speak for me, Father Friar? To his lordship? Will you ask for mercy for me, Father?"

"It is not for the Church to interfere in such secular matters. I cannot plea to his lordship on your behalf, but I will do so to your heavenly judge."

Gripple took little comfort from the holy man's words. It was Balliwick or his lordship who needed to hear his plea for, if he found himself before the Almighty judge, it would be too late.

As he approached the town, Balliwick saw Ravenhead, who dashed across the street to meet him.

"When might I receive the blessing of Lord Scullion for my proposed marriage to the Lady Una, Chamberlain Balliwick?"

"There is much to attend to, Lord Ravenhead."

"But what is there to consider?"

"Not in this matter," Balliwick corrected the nobleman. "There is much to address in town matters today. The man we arrested for the theft of the sheep has accused three others in the enterprise and I must see them without delay."

"Obtain the five shilling penalty for their offence, Balliwick, and advise his lordship to pass it on to me in settlement of our wager." He laughed aloud as he spoke the words.

"We do not accept such payments for crimes against the eorl in this shire, Sir. The butcher will hang and his accomplices shall follow soon after."

At first, Ravenhead was shocked at the declaration. Then he paused and mumbled something about what great wisdom Lord Scullion had shown.

"Come to dinner tomorrow night and you shall have his lordship's word on the marriage."

"Tomorrow night," Ravenhead called back as the chamberlain walked away.

Balliwick tossed Ravenhead's mumbled words about in his head. Great wisdom he had said, the shire reeve thought. The visitor's words convinced Balliwick that he knew that his lordship's true motive for the hanging was simply to impress.

What is wisdom? It is idealism, thought Balliwick, the gift of the visionary, and Lord Scullion is certainly not that.

It was less than one week from the Christ's mass and the account of Maggoty Gripple's arrest was the source of discussion at every market stall on that cold morning. There was no meat for sale, of course, because the butcher was held at the tower and his wife had no time to sell the wares that had not been confiscated by the shire reeve. Indeed, she was too busy raising the money for his freedom. Those who owed her husband money were the first to be tracked down and then there were others, like her brother, Aldwyn Byrgan, who she considered obliged to contribute. In fact, the five shillings she required was produced before she had found her brother, but now she had been told by some busybody that this was not enough to secure his release.

The Rypan sisters were now saying that the fine was three times the cost of the stolen goods, for what deterrent would it be to make someone simply repay the cost of the sheep?

"How much is three times five shillings?" she asked them, for they seemed to know much more than she did on the matter.

Eventually they found enough hands and fingers between them to calculate the sum required. Now, it seemed, she needed to raise more money than even her gravedigger brother could give her, so she brought out the table and furnished it with what meat her husband had left to sell, including some of the salted meat that he was storing for later in the winter. There was no mutton, of course, because this had been seized by Chamberlain Balliwick.

Word soon spread from the Rypan sisters that Mistress Gripple was in charge of the meat stall, causing a crowd to form, as they all knew she had a poor head for figures and it seemed a good opportunity to seize a bargain. Mistress Gripple was a stout, brawny woman who was deaf to all but the loudest of voices. So, handicapped by a frequent desire to eat, her deafness and an absence of even the most elementary ability in addition and subtraction, she set about raising the necessary funds.

Before noon the goods had all been sold and the stout butcher's wife set about counting her money. The crowd had left by then and had it not been for the kindness of Edwin Goodlyhead, who happened to be passing, she would still be there counting her money long after her husband had been hanged.

"Thirteen shillings and nine pence," Edwin declared.

"Is that more or less than fifteen shillings, Master Goodlyhead?"

He shook his head despairingly and almost wept in the face of such innocence. It took him less than a minute to consider the matter and he made up the difference from his own pocket, holding his hands up as she protested and assured him it would all be repaid.

As they were still talking, Oswald Balliwick came out of the graveyard and walked towards them, calling.

"Have you seen your brother, Aldwyn, Mistress Gripple?" he asked Gripple's wife, but his unheard question was ignored by her as she looked towards Edwin for assistance. Goodlyhead walked forward to meet the chamberlain and simply held his cupped hands out, offering Balliwick the money. Edwin had both heard and understood what Friar Sopscott had said over dinner last evening, but chose to ignore it and see if the shire reeve would accept the coins.

"What is this?" Balliwick asked as he finally arrived in front of them.

"Payment of Master Gripple's fine," he answered. "Mistress Gripple here has raised fifteen shillings, which she believes to be three times the cost of the sheep."

Balliwick explained that his questioning of her husband still continued and no penalty had yet been set by his lordship.

"Why are you here then?" asked Mistress Gripple. "If it is not to receive the payment?"

"Your husband has named your brother in the crime, along with his two older sons, and they need to accompany me to the castle to face their accuser."

"Aldwyn? My brother, Aldwyn?"

"Yes, Mistress Gripple, do you know where I might find him, for he is not at the graveyard."

"He will be here shortly, for I have sent word to him already. I hoped he might contribute towards the fine as it has emptied my purse and was produced only by the benevolence of Master Goodlyhead here."

Balliwick agreed to wait for his arrival and, as he did so, Edwin Goodlyhead took him to one side to ask why this straightforward case could not be resolved through the payment of a fine. The chamberlain explained that a full enquiry must be made, for it was a serious offence to steal his lordship's sheep.

"This may yet result in a hanging, Master Goodlyhead," he continued.

"A hanging?" the businessman answered, a little too loudly, although it did not seem he had been overhead by the condemned man's wife. "But they have the money to pay the fine."

"As I say, Master Goodlyhead, this is the theft of his lordship's property. It is for him to decide whether a penalty is sufficient to settle the issue."

"But, who will salt the meat for the remainder of the winter? What will we do with the meat now? Who will salt it?"

At first, Balliwick couldn't comprehend why the salting of meat for the winter had suddenly become the primary consideration in this case, but it soon became apparent, as Edwin Goodlyhead's normally generous nature turned to one of a more mercenary persuasion.

"I have twelve sacks of salt in my barn and Gripple has already agreed to purchase most of it from me. What am I to do with twelve sacks of salt, Master Balliwick?"

"Gripple has accused Byrgan and his sons, so all may yet hang for this offence, Master Goodlyhead, and you ask who will salt the meat?"

Suddenly, they both stopped speaking as they saw Byrgan and his two sons approaching with spades over their shoulders, heading towards the graveyard. Balliwick called to him and told them all to accompany him to the castle.

Byrgan remonstrated with the shire reeve and Mistress Gripple came out of her house to join the heated conversation.

"Do I accompany you also?" she asked.

"You do not have any involvement in this matter," declared Balliwick.

"But I am the wife of the accused."

"You have no involvement in this matter," he repeated, even louder than before, then demanded that the gravedigger and his two sons walked with him to the tower. The men handed their spades to the woman and told her to keep them for their return.

The low sun in the southern sky flickered and flashed through the empty boughs of the thinly canopied forest. The last snow had fallen overnight and had not yet melted under the barren trees, so Balliwick could trace the footsteps he had pressed into the pathway on his journey into town earlier that morning.

Aldwyn Byrgan and his two sons traipsed behind and the crunch of their feet on the icy surface was the only sound that disturbed the birdless wood. The silence had been interrupted on several occasions at the beginning of the journey, but the chamberlain's response to any questions had been the same.

"Wait for your hearing, Master Byrgan."

The gravedigger heeded the instruction and, what is more, counselled his sons on the merit of their own silence too, for he could see it annoyed the shire reeve to be challenged on the matter.

As they approached a fork in the road, Seth Wainthrop came walking towards them, heading into town for the first time since Sunday, when he had attended mass and witnessed the recovery of the serf's body from the beach. He was anxious to find out more news of the events, or rather his wife was, and seeing the chamberlain with the three Byrgan men seemed to suggest that there had been developments. The farmer was convinced that Cyrus Scolop had something to do with Eldrik's death and quickly came to the premature conclusion that the Byrgans had seen something of the incident too. Perhaps they had accused Scolop of the boy's murder, but where was the fisherman if they had?

Balliwick was in no mind to provide an explanation when Wainthrop stopped to ask the purpose of their journey.

"Go about your business, Master Wainthrop," was all Balliwick would say, yet it was enough to silence any further enquiry. Although, after the chamberlain had walked on, the farmer looked at Aldwyn Byrgan for an explanation. He didn't receive one, which only served to provoke his curiosity still further. The fearsome look on Byrgan's face suggested that he and his sons were in trouble.

But Wainthrop could not possibly know the seriousness of their plight.

The farmer rushed off towards the town as quickly as his legs would carry him, hoping to meet one of the widows on the way, for he was certain that they would know more about events.

When the group arrived at the tower, Balliwick signalled to a servant to fetch Maggoty Gripple from the cell, before leading the three Byrgan men into the room where he had interviewed the butcher previously. Whilst the Byrgans waited for the arrival of Gripple, the chamberlain went into the adjoining room to make sure his lordship was in there preparing to listen to proceedings.

Once all was set, the shire reeve instructed Gripple to repeat his accusation that the three Byrgan men were party to the theft of the sheep. The butcher wiped his hands against his leggings, as if trying to wipe blood from them, like he did when he was carving meat. Then, looking directly at Aldwyn Byrgan, he made the required declaration.

Unhesitatingly, Balliwick told the accused that, if he was to counter the charge, he needed two persons to attest to his innocence.

"Then, I will call on my sons to speak so."

"You fool!" shouted Balliwick impatiently. "They are arrested with you. They cannot testify."

For a few moments, the gravedigger babbled on about his long service to the church and how he had attended mass regularly, but not once did he declare his innocence.

"This is mitigation of guilt," said Balliwick. "Are you innocent or guilty?"

"We are guilty," he replied. "All four of us," he added, looking directly at his accuser, Maggoty Gripple. "And we will pay the penalty."

"Aye, Master Shire Reeve," called Gripple. "We shall pay the five shilling fine, and more if you see fit."

Balliwick took a scroll of notepaper from a desk and read from it. "If a freeman steals from an elderman, let him make threefold compensation; and let the elderman have the punishment penalty."

"But we stole from Abel Cotes, not the eorl."

"The sheep is the property of Eorl Scullion," replied Balliwick.

The four men all spoke at once, insisting it was Cotes they had stolen the sheep from.

"Cotes," replied Balliwick, "is a tenant farmer. The farm and therefore the stock of that farm is the property of his lordship."

The men fell silent for a moment, wondering what was meant by the elderman holding the punishment penalty.

Aldwyn Byrgan spoke up first and hesitatingly asked the question.

"The punishment for theft from the royal household is death," Balliwick declared, causing a chorus of gasps from the accused. A few moments elapsed as the four men wondered how they could answer such an alarming announcement.

"But, who will bury the dead, Master Chamberlain?" asked Aldwyn Byrgan. "Indeed, who will bury our bodies if we are hanged, for we are the town's gravediggers?"

"You are an idiot, Byrgan," replied Balliwick. "Your wit and intellect will not be a loss to this town."

"Are there not enough widows in Ebbsweirmouth already?" asked Gripple, before adding that it was the Byrgan boys who had spread rumours in town about the spirits of the dead who walked the corpse road.

"Why do you accuse us so?" Byrgan screamed at Gripple.

"Why should I, alone, hang for the offence?" he replied indignantly.

The two slow-minded boys stood looking at each other as the reality of their sentence suddenly took hold. One began to cry and was followed immediately by his brother, who fell to his knees and pulled at his hair.

Accusations were called back and forth, with each man trying to minimise his own involvement in the deed. The shire reeve was interested in Gripple's statement, though, and called above their voices for silence.

"You," he said, pointing at the two teenage boys. "Is this true? Did you spread evil rumours of ghostly spirits haunting the drove roads, frightening the populace with such stories?"

The brother that was now prostrate on the floor, sobbing, had not heard the question and could not answer for his crying anyway. The other, who had stopped sobbing and now stood glassy-eyed at the proceedings, spoke for them both.

"Master Gripple told us to do it, Sir," he replied, with the honesty of youth in his voice. "He said it would empty the roads and give us leave to steal whatever we wished. We also enticed our younger brothers to mark the lychgate with the bloody sign. But it was at Maggoty Gripple's behest."

The butcher's face was inflamed and he racked his memory for some other treachery he could accuse the Byrgans of.

"These two brothers have had dealings with the widows, Master Chamberlain," he finally shouted, pointing at the boys. "They told the widows of the cheap mutton, for they had dealings with them."

"Dealings?" bellowed Balliwick loudly.

Gripple moved a little closer to the chamberlain, as if he wanted to whisper in his ear. But Balliwick would have none of it.

"Speak up," he declared, stepping back away from the advancing butcher.

"Dealings, Master Chamberlain. I shall say no more on the matter."

He looked at his judge and smiled, wondering if he had secured his own freedom in his accusation. But Balliwick shouted back at him when he realised the nature of his accusation.

"This is a tribunal, Sir, not The Salutation Inn. I will admit none of your idle gossip, Master Gripple." He hesitated, looking disappointedly at each of them. "Dealings, indeed," he repeated.

"My sons are just boys, Master Chamberlain," pleaded their father. "Their only guilt is that they did what they were told to do and that is no guilt at all. They are boys," he continued to say, before he was silenced by the authoritative voice of the shire reeve.

"And as such," Balliwick replied, "they swore their oath no more than three years ago. It is fresh on their lips. They undertook to forsake criminal acts. They swore not to steal,

Master Byrgan, but they did so. And they did so under your authority, Sir."

He then ordered them all to remain in the room whilst he left to consider his judgement.

When he arrived in the great hall, he found his lordship beaming a smile. "It fits perfectly," Scullion declared happily.

"My Lord," pleaded Balliwick, "what purpose will it serve to put to death a man who is no more than the village idiot? And then, his two sons and Gripple too?

"No," he replied. "What better opportunity is there to prove my strength of character and resolve to Ravenhead? He is a spy of the northern shires, I am sure of it. This will demonstrate the power of the East Seaxe people."

"My Lord, that spy, as you refer to him, is coming to dinner tomorrow night to receive your blessing on his planned marriage."

"Good, then we shall hang them in the morning. It will be the subject of great conversation over dinner."

"My Lord. Four men will die," Balliwick declared, wondering if Scullion had measured the consequences of his decision.

"You said it yourself, my Shire Reeve. If a freeman steals from an elderman, let the elderman have the punishment penalty. Then I shall have my punishment penalty, Master Shire Reeve, I shall have my hanging."

"I forged the wording. The law actually refers to theft from the royal court, rather than an elderman."

"Am I not a member of the royal court?"

"The court, my Lord, is in Wessex."

"Is the King not my cousin?"

"Many times removed, Sir."

Lord Scullion was determined to have his way on the matter and seized on the other line of prosecution.

"Did they not admit to causing the terrible rumours of ghostly apparitions in the drove roads around town?"

"That, my Lord, was irresponsible but not, as far as I am aware, an offence."

But Scullion's sudden elevation from an impotent power to one whose word might strike fear into all was complete, at least in his own mind. Those frustrations, held in abeyance since childhood, were to be unleashed. The opportunity to put right the feeble and frail image that had accompanied him through manhood was not to be missed. A heart that had fermented since boyhood with the wrath of anger was to be opened, like the abyss that so many spoke of in such fearsome tones.

"They are responsible for the theft and also they are responsible for spreading vile and dispiriting rumour. Hang them! You have my decision."

~~~~~

There were more people than usual in The Salutation Inn that day. Gossip abounded and the best place to uncover the truth, or indeed to propagate the rumours further, was at the inn. Most wanted to invest their own opinion on the various events that had overtaken the town, yet none saw those events as a fulfilment of the prophecy. The arrest of Aldwyn Byrgan and his two sons had, in the view of the men who were standing at the bar finishing their ale, nothing to do with the coming of the devil. The devil was a figure, maybe not a human one, but a physical being all the same. To them, the arrival of Satan could not be a series of events. When the abyss was opened it would be the anti-Christ, the angel of darkness, who would be revealed, not the clever handiwork of his devious soul.

Lord Ravenhead and the Lady Una sat in quiet conference by the door, discussing their forthcoming dinner engagement at Scullion Tower. They were as close as could be to their prize. Nothing appeared to stand between them and their inheritance of Haeferingas. What possible objection could Lord Scullion raise against the only surviving daughter of his now departed cousin receiving her due inheritance? They considered well what gift of enticement could be offered to him to secure the final blessing on their marriage, but Ravenhead had not yet settled his mind on the matter.

It was mid-afternoon and those who had visited the inn for a midday drink before setting off home were casting their view through the casement window at the darkening sky and preparing to leave. Their talk had been about the prophecy, for, in spite of the two recent deaths, it was still the augury of foreboding that cast its long shadow on this pitiful day.

It was no longer a discussion on whether the devil would come but, moreover, when he would arrive. Opinion was divided on the matter. Some thought that, as Christ arrived on the twenty-fifth day of December, why would Satan not do the same? Others said it must be at the year end. They were all still loudly arguing the point when the door opened and Seth Wainthrop stumbled over the threshold, panting for the want of breath.

"What has happened now?" cried Leland Hoop above the noise.

Everyone stopped talking and waited for Wainthrop to gather himself.

"I have just seen the shire reeve marching Aldwyn Byrgan and his boys towards the castle."

"We know that, Wainthrop," called Hoop. "They have been arrested for the theft of the sheep."

"I thought Maggoty Gripple stole the sheep," he replied, still taking deep breaths.

"All four of them conspired to steal the sheep."

The farmer was sorely disappointed that news of the gravedigger's arrest had spread so quickly around the town, mainly by the womenfolk who had been in the market when the act had taken place. Speculation had quickly grown that the Byrgans had been named as accomplices by Maggoty Gripple, otherwise why would Balliwick have arrested the gravedigger and his sons?

"Everyone knows that Gripple and Byrgan are as thick as thieves," said one woman, although she immediately regretted the discourteous pertinence of her words.

The arrest of Aldwyn Byrgan prompted much scandalous talk. Many could not believe that one as stupid as him would attempt to commit such a crime, as he was sure to fall foul of the law. The news prompted the retelling of many anecdotes about the man's stupidity. Hoop recalled the most frequently told story, of when Byrgan had been faced with a similar task to his present one, the simultaneous burial of two bodies. And everyone hoped he would not make the same mistake again.

"He buried them on a Friday and set about carving their headstones. A week later, he had forgotten which body had been buried in each grave," laughed Leland Hoop to his customers at the inn.

"That was not the only time he buried a body and forgot where the grave was," replied Seth Wainthrop. "Two years ago he buried old Widow Peascombe and forgot where she had been laid. He spent days digging holes in the graveyard until he uncovered the bones of a dog. He then asked the priest what could have happened to the woman because her bones had shrivelled to such a small size."

"And, on another occasion," said Hoop, "he buried his lunch with a body after leaving it on the shrouded corpse."

None of the revellers in The Salutation Inn that day even considered the possibility of a hanging. They had seen Mistress Gripple recovering her debts and counting the money with Edwin Goodlyhead. And, now that Byrgan had been indicted too, there were two families to pay the penalty. Nor did anyone consider that the men had done anything more than steal a sheep. The curious coincidence of two deaths in as many days was just that, a coincidence, a strange twist of fate.

The argument that had earlier ensued on the subject of the prophecy was a quiet debate compared to what followed on the subject of the penalty. Five shillings or fifteen shillings was a considerable sum, although many believed Gripple capable of paying it without the need to solicit help.

"The price he charges for a rabbit is a greater crime than the theft of a sheep," said one of the Rypan sisters, although that family's reputation had never been held in the highest respect. The Rypan sisters had been married five times between them and had enjoyed many illicit affairs both before and during those marriages. In a small town like Ebbsweirmouth, such matters could not remain secret for long. But they had been widowed by Maeldun and their sojourns to the more lustful days of their youth were now confined to clandestine meetings with the Byrgan boys at dusk, when most residents of the widows' hides had already taken to their beds. The curly-haired brothers were less like their father than they were like Maggoty Gripple whose lecherous ways were well known and ignored by his deaf and largely dumb wife. The boys' clothing was often threadbare and worn, and yet their mother never noticed how they would return from a day's work with patches sewn into their clothing by the grateful widows.

Everyone was so engrossed with the events that nobody considered whether two untimely deaths were, in any way, a sign that the prophecy was being fulfilled. Nobody suspected that the abyss was about to open. Yet few could know that the sensitive hearing of the widows who attended the inn simply to gather such gossip would lead to just that event. Nobody could have guessed that the Rypan girls, those champions of the tittle-tattle, might prise open the closure to the abyss.

It had been Ravenhead who had unintentionally placed that ruinous seed in the younger Rypan sister's mind. He had been whispering furtively to Una about their good fortune. The events taking place did, indeed, seem to favour them, for such matters distracted almost everyone from their own enterprise.

"It suits us well," he said in a hushed tone, "that Gripple and the others should be arrested and not only because it makes me five shillings the richer. Scullion has other things on his mind this advent, my dear. Our blessing will follow as a formality. It would not surprise me," he added, perhaps a little louder than he intended, "if the four men charged are responsible for these ridiculous rumours of spirits in the drove roads about the town. I mean, one of them is an undertaker and the spirits are said to have carried a coffin."

This innocent piece of speculation was overheard and then passed from one Rypan sister to the other. And when Ravenhead and the Lady Una departed to their rooms, the sisters claimed the theory for their own. The supposition that Gripple and the Byrgans had clothed themselves in white sheets and carried a coffin along the lanes outside the town began as a possibility. However, once the plausibility of such a mischievous prank had been considered by those attending the inn that day, it soon became a probability, until a presumption of truth took root and it became a fact.

The protracted lunchtime session at the inn continued into the evening and finally ended as the sun began to fall slowly towards the treetops of the forest beyond town. Cyrus Scolop left before the others, unhappy that his normally quiet afternoon drink had been disrupted by the raucous gossiping of women and men who acted like women. The remaining customers stayed until the rumour had become fact and they had acquired sufficient scandal to slander the most pious of men. By an hour before sunset, the bar had emptied.

The tables of the inn were littered with empty tankards but Leland Hoop had not yet considered cleaning them away. Instead, he stood at the unshuttered window, gazing out at the fading light and an empty street. He seemed distracted, engrossed in a single thought, a particular comment that had been made. It overwhelmed him and he could think of nothing else. So he just stood there, gazing out into the lonely world, as his heart pounded harder and harder, and his mind became seduced by rage.

Even when young Willem hurried from Mardyke House and ran past the houses towards the church at the other end of town, Hoop took no notice. He was impervious to all matters other than the one that now so fully occupied his thoughts.

~~~~

In that tiny place between day and night there lies a moment in time that we call dusk. It is neither one nor the other. In like manner, there is a place near Ebbsweirmouth where there abides neither day nor night. Nor is the place either land or sea, but a cavern sculpted and shaped by the endless tides that tear land from the earth and make of it a place where the stilled sea sleeps.

That place seemed to Willem like the tiny space between life and death; an eerie, spectral place where the constant clamour of the sea deprived the cove of even an instant of silence. And yet, when the tide had departed to its farthest point and the ocean's mighty roar became just a distant murmur, there was an intimidating calm about it.

Hollow Hole Cove was a resting place for the sea, built by the sea and owned by the sea. It was an imposing chamber, dark in more ways than the word commands.

Willem heard a familiar clump and thump of a small fishing boat being forced against the rocks by the foaming waves. There, too, was the rattling chain that he had heard on that Friday night.

He clambered down the sloping hillside, slipping on the wet rocks that led from the cliff top and disturbing some sea gulls, which flew off at his approach. A small stony-eyed hawfinch seemed impervious to the sudden commotion about him and remained, undaunted as he observed events. A distant sun was setting on the land above the beach and the weak shadow of the overhanging crag stretched out to sea. At the foot of the hill, a rock had been worn towards a flat surface by the frequent footsteps of fishermen over the centuries, mooring their wooden boats at the harbour built by nature. There, where the rocks met the sea, a wooden post had been set in the seabed with chain links attached in order that a vessel could be secured.

Against that post, a small wooden boat was being rocked violently by the incoming waves. On board were coils of wires, nets and boxes of hooks. On the top of the wooden anchor post where Cyrus Scolop moored the boat, there was a distinct and recently cut notch that revealed new wood beneath it. And in this groove the residue of blood still rested, resisting the occasional splash of sea water that reached that high. It was as if someone had held a hand there and chopped off a finger; or, at least, that was what Willem imagined in his mind. Everyone would consider this to be more speculation, he thought, yet somehow he knew it to be true.

For a moment he wondered if the victim may have been his own brother, born of the same mother and sent into slavery by the wicked hand of providence.

In his heart, he believed someone had killed both Eldrik and the Watchman. He looked again at the bloodied wooden post. There has been no accident here, he said to himself. A reckoning had taken place here and yet he couldn't bring himself to think about that right now. He needed to hurry. Night was falling quickly and the path up the cliff face was treacherous. He had been invited to dinner again at the Goodlyheads.

Perhaps it was the full moon, or the shaping of the stars, because it could not be a coincidence that both Willem and Seth Wainthrop felt compelled to relieve their burdened minds of suspicious thoughts and declare their secret convictions that night. If they had known the consequences of their actions, perhaps they may have chosen to keep their own counsel on the matter. The child, Willem, might be forgiven for his unshaken belief that power and responsibility are constant companions, which they are not of course. The more experienced farmer, however, should not be so easily excused for such naivety.

None of the townsfolk who had seen the boy these past few days knew him, nor did they recognise him from his infancy at the castle. Not that he had ventured outside the tower very much, for Lord Scullion's undertaking had amounted to no more than the provision of food and shelter, along with a little education.

As the boy neared Mardyke House, the purple clouds of winter were turned an orange gold by the departing sun and the day's final minutes melted into darkness. That same low hanging sun hovered on the western skyline, dissipated by its own brilliance, as Seth Wainthrop left his home to walk the short distance to Scullion Tower. He could not live with the aching thought of what he had seen any longer.

The day had passed and the evening light of the setting sun reflected on the empty branches of the holly thicket as he made his way along the path. Its berries had already been consumed by the hungry blackbirds in search of winter food. Yet its bright green leaf still shone and put the ivy to shame as it signalled the coming of Christ's mass.

Wainthrop's mind wandered as he quickened his pace and ran through what he was going to say to the shire reeve.

All the lusty foliage of summer was lost to the oak and the tree's crusty leaves now lay protecting the ground from the harsh frost of December, making an oily mess of the snow-covered path. Wainthrop's thoughts were distracted by a sudden rustle in the hedgerow. He thought he had seen a jay that morning, its colourful plumage set like a pastel rainbow against the pale white snow. And here it was again, except it was not a jay, it was a much smaller bird of the finch family. But the farmer was preoccupied, for he had a difficult decision to make.

"It's not right, Master Chamberlain, Sir," he mumbled to the cold night air, reminding himself to call Balliwick 'sir', for he held himself in high office and appropriate respect was due to him. "There are greater evils done this day, Chamberlain Balliwick," he muttered. "Take the fishmonger, Cyrus Scolop. He has done far worse deeds than the four men you have arrested."

Occasionally he stopped in his tracks and thought about turning back. But he continued each time and practised the eloquent speech he would deliver to the shire reeve.

"I don't know what I am doing here," was what he actually said when he arrived at the door, as all the well-rehearsed dialogue was flushed from him by nerves.

"Well nor do I," Balliwick replied, as curtly as you please.

And then the story came out in patches; small pieces of dislocated, incongruous, incoherent comments that made little or no sense to the listener until the time was taken to reconstruct some relevant parts into a sequential order. Then, and only then, did Balliwick begin to understand that Wainthrop had witnessed a crime. Not, as he had first thought, the theft of a sheep but another crime, which nobody knew had been committed.

"He killed Eldrik," Wainthrop said. And a moment later he made reference to Cyrus Scolop being the perpetrator of the aforementioned offence. And he did actually say 'aforementioned offence', an expression he had practised at length on his way to the castle, having heard it spoken by Mistress Goodlyhead recently.

Eventually, Balliwick managed to silence the farmer and repeated to him, with greater articulation and less wasted time, the essence of what he had just declared. Wainthrop had seen Scolop moor his fishing boat at Hollow Hole Cove on Friday morning. He had been on the coastal path because the main drove road into town was flooded at the ford. Then, seeing Scolop arrive from his night's fishing, the farmer had begun to walk down the slippery cliff face to offer his help to carry the catch. But halfway down he had stopped, shocked and appalled at what he saw. He hid himself from view, behind the large reed bushes that sprang up on the sandy ledges of the cliff, and he observed something that he could not believe and, indeed, wished he had not seen.

Cyrus Scolop appeared to instruct his serf, Eldrik, to jump into the shallow waters by the boat, perhaps to secure the anchor or tie the vessel to its mooring post. Wainthrop could not hear what was said above the roar of the waves, but he could see how the events unfolded.

As the child lifted the rope around the wooden post, Scolop leaned into the boat and retrieved a large knife or axe. He then grabbed the boy's wrist and planted the tiny hand firmly on the top of the timbered pillar. With one mighty blow, he smashed the cleaver down, severing the tip of the smallest finger on the boy's right hand. There was no scream of pain, for in one swift movement, Wainthrop saw the fisherman hold the boy under the water, pressing down on the back of his neck. Eldrik thrashed away with his arms but it was to no avail and, after a few minutes, Scolop dragged the limp body up and wrapped a chain about the boy's torso before securing it to the boat. The body sank beneath the incoming waves and Scolop began to ready himself to leave.

"What did you say or do?" asked Balliwick.

"I ran, Master Chamberlain, Sir; I ran."

"And you told nobody?"

"Not until this moment, Sir."

By this time, Wainthrop had turned to tears at what he had witnessed and Balliwick could see the man was torn and ashamed by the fear that had prevented him from intervening or indeed speaking of the brutal murder until this moment.

"Go home, Seth; go home and leave this matter to me."

It felt to Balliwick as if a light had been shone on all the appalling events of the past few days and a much greater abomination had been exposed beneath these dreadful acts, putting the theft of a sheep into perspective. Yet, even so, the chamberlain was convinced that this latest discovery would only add to the slaughter not, as it should do, deter such wanton brutality.

Earlier that day, Balliwick had met with Edwin Goodlyhead in the counting house. There were candles and other goods to be ordered and he wanted Edwin's advice on what problems may ensue if Gripple was hanged.

"The townsfolk will be upset, I am certain of that," Edwin had replied. But Balliwick was not referring to how people might react, he was considering the more practical aspects of life without a butcher.

"Most of the people who keep stock attend to it themselves, Master Balliwick," Edwin answered. "But I am not sure about salting and other such skills. And, since Maeldun, there are not many young men around now to take over."

"There will be even fewer if Lord Scullion has his way," replied Balliwick. "He wants me to hang Aldwyn Byrgan and his two sons for their part in the theft of the sheep. If the gallows was big enough, he would hang all four together but, fortunately it is not, so we are spared such a spectacle."

"Why is he so resolved?" asked Edwin. But the chamberlain did not answer.

"Gripple will hang in the morning and the others the next day. May God have mercy on their souls, Edwin."

When he returned home, Edwin was reluctant to introduce such a subject to the dinner table, but he could not keep such news to himself. Mistress Goodlyhead pleaded with him to intervene in the matter.

"It is not the shire reeve who needs persuading," he replied. "It is Lord Scullion who is resolved on the matter and it appears that nothing will change his mind."

"Why is Master Gripple to hang first and the Byrgans not until the following day?" asked Willem as politely as he could.

"The only reason is the size of the gallows," Edwin sighed. "Although I think Master Balliwick is pleased to have an excuse to postpone their deaths."

"Is Master Gripple's crime greater than theirs?" the boy asked.

Edwin confirmed that their crime was one that could be punished with a financial penalty.

"Fifteen shillings could settle this matter. But his lordship will have none of it. It is a crime against the Crown, he says. And they all must hang."

"What if someone was to have committed a greater crime still? Would their punishment be deferred?"

Edwin looked directly at Willem, wondering what he could mean by such a question.

"What greater crime has been committed?"

Instead of answering Edwin's question, Willem turned to Mildred Goodlyhead, who was preparing the meal by the stove.

"Do you recall when I visited you first on Saturday, Mistress Goodlyhead? The fish I delivered to you, do you remember?"

"Well of course I remember, young Willem. It was only a few days past."

"Do you remember the note we found inside the fish?"

Mildred stopped what she was doing and joined them at the table. She nodded.

"I believe," he said, "that somebody killed Eldrik and they also killed the stranger who was in town that same day, the chandler who visited here to meet with Master Goodlyhead."

"Killed them?" Edwin and his wife replied in unison.

"I believe the chandler was struck on the head with a rock and killed."

"For what purpose?" Mildred asked.

"I don't know," confessed Willem sadly, as if the words undermined his allegation.

"The chandler fell and struck his head on the rock, Willem. If he had been murdered, why did he still have money in his pocket? Who would kill someone and not steal from the body?"

"Perhaps the killer was disturbed."

"But who would do such a terrible deed?" asked Edwin.

"Master Scolop killed both of them," he answered, without a shred of doubt in his voice.

"Why would Scolop kill the slave boy and the chandler? How are those two deaths connected? It makes no sense at all, Willem."

"The note in the fish," answered Willem. "It said 'pay me'. Master Scolop ordered me to deliver two fish that morning. One had to be taken here to Mardyke House and the other to Lord Ravenhead at The Salutation Inn. Master Scolop was most precise about which fish to deliver to each person. But I fell on the snow and dropped the fish. They must have been switched and you received the fish destined for Lord Ravenhead."

Willem was speaking faster now, as if the whole incident was taking on a new clarity in his mind. But there was nothing clear in his rambling, fragmented thoughts.

"The message," he continued, "was meant for Lord Ravenhead. The note instructed him to pay Master Scolop for murdering the chandler."

"Why would Lord Ravenhead want Scolop to kill the chandler?" asked Edwin. "And why would that have then resulted in the killing of poor Eldrik too?"

Willem shook his head, but went on to tell the Goodlyheads about the rock he had found near the blood-stained snow. The rock had been turned over and not replaced where it was originally resting on the ground.

"Someone had clearly picked it up, struck the chandler on the head and put it back on the ground, but failed to put it back where it had previously rested," he explained to them.

"The message might simply have been an instruction for Lord Ravenhead to pay for the fish," insisted Mildred.

"And what has the death of a stranger to do with young Eldrik?" asked Edwin.

The challenges to Willem's suspicions mounted.

"I went to Hollow Hole Cove today," Willem said abruptly and before Mildred could say 'whatever for', the boy told them about what he had seen. It was dismissed of course. And it could easily have been the blood from a fish, as Mistress Goodlyhead said. But, in his heart, Willem knew what the marks on the mooring post meant and he dwelt on it throughout the meal.

The virtue of justice now rested heavily upon the boy's shoulders. So, at the end of the evening, Willem stood up from the table and thanked his hosts for their kind hospitality.

"I do not wish to offend you, nor do I wish to alienate you from your neighbours, but I must be true to myself in this matter. I believe that Master Scolop murdered his slave Eldrik and also, in all likelihood, the visiting chandler too. I therefore intend to call at Scullion Tower in the morning and tell the shire reeve."

Mildred looked at the boy and then at Edwin. She didn't need to speak.

"Very well," declared Edwin. "I shall go with you. After all, Chamberlain Balliwick hardly knows you, young man, and he will probably at least listen if I accompany you."

"Once you have spoken of the matter, you will have cleared your conscience," said Mildred. "And, whether or not Master Balliwick takes any notice of the accusation, you will have done your duty."

Willem smiled.

"Now, off to bed with you," Mildred added and the boy wished them goodnight.

~~~~~

Balliwick was reluctant to tell Lord Scullion about Wainthrop's visit as his lordship had been drinking wine since dinner and, though not drunk, he was still inclined towards a demonstration of authority. This news would only add to his rancour. And yet there was a small possibility, perhaps, that it might serve to postpone the hanging of the others. So he relented and told the whole story to the eorl.

"Hang the fisherman along with the others," Scullion demanded after the chamberlain had related Wainthrop's testimony.

"If it was up to me, I would hang the man in preference to the others," Balliwick answered, hoping for some sign of mercy in reply. But his lordship simply continued sipping his wine.

"In truth, Cyrus Scolop is guilty of nothing," said Balliwick, "as it is no crime to kill one's slave. But, in the eyes of the town, his is a much greater sin than those of Gripple or the Byrgans."

"You're in charge," shouted Scullion. "Hang them in any order you like. Just get on with it. Ravenhead is coming to dinner tomorrow night and someone needs to be hanging from that gallows by then. Do you hear me, Balliwick?"

"Yes, my Lord," he said and rang a bell that stood on the hearth.

A servant arrived and Balliwick instructed him to take Gripple from the cell before dawn and hang him on Apparition Hill before the sun has risen.

"Hang him high, so all may see. And, on the way back, arrest the fishmonger, Cyrus Scolop, and bring him to me." The chamberlain paused. "Take three or four men with you for he may put up a fight."

Chapter Thirteen

Mercy

Pity the man who shows no mercy, for compassion will be his eternal desire. Mercy is a twofold gift, for few virtues are so equitable, since every kindness shown is a kindness received. Thus twice holy is mercy, for it is a blessing on both the giver and the receiver.

Yet, mercy and wisdom are worthless jewels if they are not fixed upon the crown of wise counsel. We are told that the wisdom of this world is mere foolishness in the eyes of heaven. And nowhere is this in greater evidence on this dark advent morning than at that place of harsh retribution upon Apparition Hill, where our story now leads us, through the early mist of dawn.

False prophets have come into this world. Not that simple augury, Abel Cotes, but those who would mislead through their actions and words. Wise counsel is to be sought like a treasure buried amongst the counterfeit baubles and beads that are set to deceive those in search of the truth.

In the dark days of which our tale is set, all freemen, on reaching manhood, are required to swear a common oath. This oath requires everyone to denounce and abstain from all criminal acts. As a consequence of the oath, any crime is therefore seen as an act of disloyalty. Such disloyalty reflects not only on the offender, but on their kin also and so the entire family may face punishment in equal measure.

Our story now takes us to a frozen winter morning at the northern edge of Ebbsweirmouth village. Frosty fields and hedgerows are bathed in feathered crystals of hoar frost dew, left frozen by the drifting easterly wind that howled through the night. The byways and country lanes that curl and carve their way through the empty fields and that remain in silent awe of each new day now capitulate to the raucous sound of men's voices. And the blackbirds and robins who have signalled that new day on this spot for all time are silenced in their leafless branches by the uncommon sound of man.

A hermit once lived high up on Apparition Hill, way above the ridge that now houses the gallows. He turned his face from Christendom when the monasteries became too wealthy and the men he knew grew too comfortable in their elegant homes, whilst others lived in abject poverty. Destiny had no power over this man, for he needed nothing, wanted nothing and lived the most frugal of lives. The sea wanderers left him alone, because he had no possessions. A tributary that ran from the mountain towards Pryklethorn Bay supplied him with water and he lived from the produce that nature provided around the small cave that was his home. He was seen infrequently, yet always after a hanging, kneeling and looking down towards the ridge as he prayed for the condemned soul. He could be seen by the whole town and, more importantly, by his lordship, who would observe him from the turret room of the castle. Of course, the old Lord Scullion had assumed the man was praying to him, such was the eorl's arrogance. Nobody had seen the man since the time of Maeldun. There had been no hangings on Gallows Ridge since then, so perhaps he lost his purpose in life. No body was ever found and the eldest member of the execution party wonders if the grey-bearded hermit might yet appear in the light of day, praying for the soul of Maggoty Gripple.

The men themselves yield to the finger-biting wind that bids farewell to night and they shield themselves amongst the rocky hillside, sheltered against the drifting, cavorting wind that speeds its way through the stripped boughs that mourn their second life. What God created as the proud oak now stands half hidden by the last breaths of the darkened night in its own new life on Gallows Ridge.

Mercy is absent from Apparition Hill this night, for destiny requires this great gift to be delivered elsewhere.

※※※

The widows' hides rested in silence and a hazy grey fog lay suspended above the fields that surrounded the village. So low did the mist lie that Apparition Hill stood above it in the distance to the north of the village, like a lofty giant's kingdom that rested above the clouds. As Aurora's glow appeared out to sea, an orange tinge began to settle on the land and, through the cold haze, a cockcrow from Four Thing Farm signalled the beginning of another day.

Hidden by the slowly departing shadow of night, a wooden trap door was released on Gallows Ridge and Maggoty Gripple's body dropped through it. The timbers above him creaked under his weight and the taught rope groaned as his legs thrashed in the cold, moist air. Any sound he made was drowned by the crows and ravens that flew up suddenly from the branches of the nearby trees, disturbed by the trap door slamming against the wooden frame of the gallows.

Four men, servants from Scullion Tower, were sitting on some rocks nearby and each took some food from their pouch and waited for the condemned man to die. As they enjoyed their breakfast, they speculated on how long it would take the butcher to utter his final gasp. As they spoke, their icy breath slowly became visible in the dawning light. Between mouthfuls of bread and cheese, one of their number recalled how easily the sea wanderers had fared when they were hanged in this place some ten years past.

"That was his lordship's mistake, you see," pointed out one of them, with the voice of assured experience. "Your long-drop hanging might serve to feed the villain to the beasts of the forest, for the body hangs much nearer the ground. But then, it is often the long drop from the gallows that kills them. Their necks break in the fall, you see, for they have farther to drop. 'Tis no punishment at all in my mind, for they don't feel the beasts chewing at their bones, do they?"

His words were spoken in a reasonable and practical manner, with no hint of condolence for the dying man whose passing from this world was accompanied not by his own screams, for these were throttled from him, but by the creaking and grinding of the rope and loose timbers of the gallows. It is an extraordinary thing to witness, although only the youngest of the men looked upon Gripple's agony, for he had not seen it before.

"He is right," replied another of the men, who now turned to point at the thrashing body. "Look at Master Gripple there. He fell only a few inches and now he is left to die by strangulation. He'll be there for twenty minutes, I'd say." For the youngest member of the group, his colleague's nonchalant words grated against the awful sight that he beheld.

In truth, it was nearly thirty minutes before the butcher stopped wriggling, with his hands tied behind his back and his eyes now bulging from their sockets. The men were not waiting to take Gripple down, for he would hang there until tomorrow. They simply needed to confirm that he was dead before they returned to inform Master Balliwick. It wouldn't do to have the condemned man released from his punishment by some good Samaritan who happened to be passing by.

Their second duty of the day, on their way back to the castle, was to arrest Cyrus Scolop and so, as they finished their breakfast, their speculation changed from the butcher to the fisherman.

One of the servants prodded the legs of Maggoty Gripple and told the others he was dead.

"Now," he said as the men set off, "Master Scolop isn't going to come without a fight, so I hope you are all up to the task in hand."

As the men walked down towards the village, they spoke about how they might tackle the heavily built fisherman.

At the other end of town, Edwin Goodlyhead and young Willem were walking past the churchyard, making an early start and setting off towards Scullion Tower. If they had turned around they might have seen the four men in the distance behind them; they may even have seen, farther behind those same men, up on Gallows Ridge, the body of

Maggoty Gripple sending his lordship's posthumous message to the slowly waking villagers.

Oswald Balliwick looked as if he was expecting someone else when he stepped out of the main door and found Edwin Goodlyhead and a boy standing before him. He ignored them at first and looked towards the gate of the castle as if someone was approaching. Edwin and Willem looked too, but they were the only visitors to the castle on this damp morning. The chamberlain thought about asking Goodlyhead if he had seen a party of men on the way from the village, but decided not to, for he was sure Edwin would have mentioned it to him. Balliwick would have visited the turret room to witness the hanging, but it was still too dark to see more than a few paces.

Edwin explained that he and Willem had called to see Balliwick in his official capacity as the shire reeve.

"Willem here has some information on the two recent deaths."

Balliwick looked at the boy and recognised him as the one Abel Cotes had accused in the street recently. He waited for the boy to speak, but the boy waited to be invited to do so.

"Well?" asked Balliwick. "Who do you accuse? What have you seen?"

"He believes that the two persons died not as a result of accidents, but at the hand of foul play," said Goodlyhead.

"Let the boy speak for himself," shouted Balliwick, who was clearly distracted by the pending arrival of someone else.

"I think the chandler, who was visiting the town, was murdered, Sir. And the serf Eldrik, I believe he was also murdered, Sir."

"Who do you accuse? What did you see?" Balliwick bellowed impatiently.

"I believe it to be Master Scolop, the fishmonger," the boy replied meekly.

Willem's words secured the chamberlain's attention.

"What did you see?" he demanded.

"In the case of the chandler, I saw a rock on the ground and some blood in the snow."

Oswald Balliwick stared with a curious expression at the boy. He repeated the boy's words back to him.

"You saw a rock on the ground and blood in the snow?" Then he looked at Edwin Goodlyhead for some further explanation.

"Tell him what you believe," Edwin instructed the boy, although he was sure the shire reeve was losing his patience.

"The rock had been turned over. The blood was underneath the rock and the soil and insects were on the top. And the patch of blood in the snow was in a different place to where the rock rested."

"What is the boy jabbering on about, Goodlyhead?"

But Willem did not wait for his friend to respond.

"If the chandler had fallen and struck his head, then the blood, the rock and indeed, the chandler's head, would have been situated in the same place. But the rock was three paces away from the blood. So he could not have fallen and struck his head on the rock."

Balliwick listened to the boy but shook his head.

"Did you see anyone strike the chandler with the rock?"

"No," Willem replied.

"Then why do you believe Master Cyrus Scolop killed the chandler?"

"I do not know, Sir. I can only assume the chandler saw Master Scolop kill the boy Eldrik."

"And what evidence do you have that Master Scolop killed Eldrik?" Balliwick asked.

"None," replied the boy. "Well, only the blood on the mooring post at Hollow Hole Cove."

As they spoke, Seth Wainthrop arrived, looking extremely pale.

"Are you unwell, Master Wainthrop?" asked Edwin.

The farmer nodded his head and mumbled that he had been sick, worrying about the events of the day.

"Which day?" asked Edwin.

"This day," he replied, before standing directly before the chamberlain and telling him that he was here to do his duty, for Balliwick had summoned him to attend and make his accusation to Cyrus Scolop.

As they stood in the castle yard, a noise could be heard outside the gate. A few moments later, the four servants entered, pushing and shoving Scolop, looking like a rabid dog with his arms tightly secured to his body with the aid of a strong rope. Two servants each held one end of the rope and they pulled their captive reluctantly towards Willem and the other three men, shouting and cursing as they came. Three of the servants had cuts and bruises to their faces, as did the fisherman.

"He refused your order to attend the castle, Sir," stated one of the servants.

"What have you to hide, Master Scolop, that you do not wish to meet with me?"

"I have nothing to hide. I am innocent of all the charges."

"What charges?" asked Balliwick. "I have not yet mentioned any charges."

"If I am not charged, then why am I bound?"

"I did not say you were not charged, Master Scolop. Just that you have not yet heard the charge."

Balliwick turned to Wainthrop and told him to make his accusation.

Scolop could not think what Wainthrop could possibly know of events, but this did not stop him firing a fearsome look at the farmer, which left his accuser in no doubt about the consequences of his actions.

Wainthrop put his hands to his stomach and bent over a little. Wondering whether he might vomit on the floor, Edwin Goodlyhead took a step backwards and pulled Willem in the same direction. After a few seconds, the farmer raised himself up and looked directly at Balliwick before speaking.

"I saw Cyrus Scolop kill the boy Eldrik. It was on Friday morning at Hollow Hole Cove, soon after dawn. He struck him with a cleaver and then held the poor soul under the water until the life was drained from him. As God is my witness, I swear this to be true." The farmer sighed heavily as the final word rushed from his mouth and then stepped backwards as Scolop leaned towards him menacingly. The ropes pulled him away and he turned to face the shire reeve.

"Two people must condemn me if I am to be found guilty of such an offence," shouted Scolop, for if anyone knew anything of the law it was this one, important point. It required two men to accuse and two to acquit, too.

"This boy here accuses you also," Balliwick said confidently, pointing at Willem.

"I gave you work," Scolop screamed at the boy. "I gave you employment. And this is how you treat me. Treachery, treachery, I say."

"You gave me work, but you did not pay me," replied Willem.

"You see," boomed Scolop, "he accuses me out of spite. Anyway, the boy is a slave and only a freeman may accuse a freeman."

"I am a freeman," declared Willem indignantly and he removed a small piece of paper from his pocket.

Balliwick took the note from him. It said 'Free man' and a mark had been scrawled beneath it. The chamberlain wanted to dismiss this irrelevant piece of evidence and he would have done in any other case. But he knew that Lord Scullion was in the mood for a hanging and, as shire reeve, he saw some merit in substituting Scolop for the Byrgans. If the fisherman wasn't guilty of this crime, he was guilty of others and yet had not suffered the consequences of his actions.

"The boy is a freeman," the chamberlain declared.

"But he is a boy," shouted Scolop. "He is the same age as Eldrik, too young to have sworn the common oath. And so, he cannot accuse me."

"Have you sworn the oath, boy?" asked Balliwick and the boy shook his head.

There!" screamed Scolop. "The boy is not yet twelve years old and cannot give witness for he has not yet taken the oath to denounce crime."

Scolop looked at his captors to release the ropes that still bound him, but Balliwick said he should be detained while he considered the evidence. Before instructing the servants to take him to the cell, he invited the fisherman to tell him what had happened to the boy Eldrik.

"The boy drowned at sea on Saturday night, or early Sunday morning. I returned to Hollow Hole Cove and the body was washed up on the shore. I ran to the church to tell everyone. There are many witnesses to these facts."

Willem stepped forward and held up his right hand for all to see.

"Then, how did Eldrik end up with the tip of his smallest finger missing from his right hand, just like I have?"

"The boy is right," said Wainthrop. "I saw Eldrik many times and his finger tip was not missing."

"It is true, Master Balliwick," confirmed Goodlyhead.

Before the chamberlain could ask the question, Scolop was answering it.

"A fish must have bitten it off when his body was in the water."

Wainthrop reminded the shire reeve that he had seen Scolop with a cleaver at Hollow Hole Cove. "There were no cleaver marks on Eldrik's body, Sir," he added, "only the tip of his finger missing. It is clear that Scolop must have cut the finger off."

"Why would I do that? What purpose would I have for such an act?"

"Why would you kill the chandler?" asked Willem in a rhetorical tone.

"Oh, I have killed the chandler too, have I?" Scolop screamed back. "I did not kill the chandler. These are accusations born of spite, Master Balliwick."

"But you did kill Eldrik," replied Wainthrop.

"The boy drowned at sea when we were fishing together on Saturday night," Scolop said, refuting the claim. "His finger must have been bitten off by fish."

Balliwick interrupted, insisting it would be easy to determine who was telling the truth.

"Wainthrop says Eldrik was killed early on Friday morning. Let us see if anyone saw the boy between Friday morning and Saturday night, when Master Scolop here says he went fishing with him."

Scolop squirmed and spluttered, knowing very well that nobody had seen Eldrik in that time, for he had lain beneath the waves at Hollow Hole Cove for two days.

Before the fisherman could speak, Willem intervened. "If Eldrik was alive, why did you engage me to make deliveries of fish to the Goodlyheads and Lord Ravenhead on Saturday?"

The boy had barely finished speaking when Scolop began to condemn himself.

"Friday, Saturday, what does it matter? Alright, alright, Eldrik drowned before first light on Friday morning, but I didn't feel it was necessary for me to mention it. After all, he was only a slave. Where does it say that I must report the death of a slave?"

Balliwick was about to concede and release the prisoner when, suddenly, something occurred to young Willem.

"So, you went fishing with Eldrik before dawn on Friday?" he asked. And, before Balliwick could object to the boy asking questions, Scolop answered.

"Aye, I did and that is when the boy drowned. Can we leave it there now?"

Balliwick went to agree, but Willem spoke up again. "On Friday morning, there was an ebb tide. What fisherman goes to work on an ebb tide?"

Scolop looked at the boy angrily. But again, before he could speak, the boy continued his verbal attack.

"And, what is more, if Eldrik drowned on an ebb tide, why was his body not washed out to sea?"

"Of what consequence is that?" shouted Scolop.

"Of great consequence," Willem replied, "because you did not go fishing on Friday morning. You went to Hollow Hole Cove for one purpose and one purpose alone, to kill Eldrik and to remove the tip of the smallest finger on his right hand."

Scolop's anger was diluted to a sullen look as he considered the consequences of the boy's words.

"Very well," he screamed at Balliwick. "I killed the slave boy, Eldrik. So what? He was my slave and I may do what I like with his life. The law only applies to crimes against freemen, not against slaves."

Balliwick took some papers that were rolled up under his arm and began to read from them.

"If a finger be struck off, let compensation be made with eight shillings. If the middle finger be struck off, let it be made with four shillings. If the gold finger be struck off, let compensation be made with six shillings. If the little finger be struck off, let it be made with eleven shillings. Where does it speak of freemen, Master Scolop?"

"Murder of a serf requires no punishment and Eldrik was a serf," shouted Scolop as he saw the gallows looming.

"We all serve somebody, Master Scolop," replied Balliwick. "No one is master of all. To kill a serf is no crime at all, you say? But I think not."

The chamberlain could see an opportunity in this moment. Gripple had already been hanged, but if he condemned the evil Scolop, he might yet free the Byrgans from an unjust death.

"The punishment for murder is death by hanging," stated Balliwick. "You shall hang at dawn on Gallows Ridge."

The servants standing close by smiled and a loud sigh of relief from Wainthrop could be heard by all.

"I plea for your mercy, my Lord Shire Reeve, Chamberlain Balliwick, Sir," cried Scolop. "I plea for your mercy and pray to God for his pardon."

"Is it not correct," replied Balliwick, "that a true penitent must pray for pardon all the days of his life?"

The chamberlain's words, indeed any words, held some hope for the sobbing fisherman. But his hope of mercy was short-lived. "I will pray unremittingly to God, all the days of my life, if you grant me mercy, my Lord."

"Then let me reduce your labour," shouted Balliwick to the servants. "Hang him! Hang him at dawn when you remove the body of Maggoty Gripple from the gallows."

Edwin Goodlyhead, Seth Wainthrop and Willem were taken aback at the chamberlain's final words. Gripple had already been hanged, they thought to themselves, as Scolop was led away to the same fate. But Balliwick dismissed them before they could ask any further questions. And, as the three of them walked away, they could barely utter the thoughts that disturbed their minds at that time.

Balliwick wasted no time in finding Lord Scullion. The only accuser of the Byrgans was now hanging on Gallows Ridge. And more importantly there was another, more worthy, case for hanging than the idiot gravedigger and his sons.

Lord Scullion was in the turret room. He stood by the large open casement window and looked across the village towards Apparition Hill. The patches of mist that had lingered, hovering just above the fields, were lifting and he could now see the gallows on the ridge. It was too far to distinguish who the poor creature was, but it was certainly clear that his soul had departed this world.

"If we leave Scolop in the same cell as the Byrgans, who knows what might happen?" Balliwick told Scullion. "They might collude to conjure up a defence between them. Or, worse still, Scolop might kill them himself."

Lord Scullion was in no mood for an argument and gave Balliwick leave to take whatever steps he thought fit.

"Provided Scolop hangs in the morning," he conceded. "For Ravenhead is coming to dinner this evening and the hangings of today and tomorrow will be the subject of worthy discussion, I think."

As he left the room, the chamberlain stopped and walked back towards Scullion.

"There is something bothering me in all this, Sir," he said, quietly and thoughtfully. "I cannot make sense of the matter and yet I am certain it has some significance in the case."

"Speak up, Oswald," replied Scullion. "What is it you cannot understand?"

"There is a boy," he said, speaking cautiously, as he was still trying to fathom its consequence in his own mind. "His name is Willem, a waif who arrived in town only a few days ago."

"What of him?"

"It is he who accuses Scolop of the murder."

"Yes, yes," answered Scullion impatiently.

"The boy has a missing finger tip, the smallest finger on his right hand."

"And what is the significance of this?" asked Scullion.

"The dead boy, the boy murdered by Scolop, he had the very same finger tip missing from his right hand, too."

"A coincidence," Scullion said, with more certainty than the answer could merit.

"Perhaps," replied Balliwick, but he was not convinced by the reply.

Balliwick had Scolop thrown into the cell and he released the Byrgans with instructions to them to pay their fine.

"Go to town, gather a sum of fifteen shillings and meet me at Four Thing Farm in two hours," he told them.

Aldwyn Byrgan agreed willingly, doffed his cap and hurriedly gathered his sons about him. The fisherman hurled abuse at them, assuming they had given evidence to the shire reeve to secure their freedom. He could not think what Byrgan might know of his activities and yet it seemed a strange coincidence that the three men had been set free just as he was imprisoned.

"I said nothing about you," shouted Aldwyn as he led his sons away. And then he mumbled to the boys that he could have said something, yet he was pleased he had not been forced to do so.

"What do you know, Father?" asked one of them.

"Scolop lied about when the boy died. I could tell that from how the body felt. Young Eldrik had been dead for more than a few hours when he was recovered from the shore at Hollow Hole Cove.

And so Scolop's misery was balanced threefold by good fortune, for as with mercy, good and bad fortune are equally shared. The Byrgans had their liberty returned, Lord Scullion had his multiple hangings and Abel Coles would receive payment for his stolen sheep, rather than have the enduring misery of four deaths on his conscience. In addition, Balliwick would not need to worry himself about who would bury the bodies of Gripple and Scolop. And Seth Wainthrop had cleared his conscience of what he had seen that Friday morning.

Willem waited until he and Edwin parted company with the farmer before speaking further on the matter of Scolop's guilt. He could see that Master Wainthrop was still unwell and to prolong his discomfort by continuing the conversation would be unkind.

"Do you not think," Willem finally asked, as they took the right-hand fork towards town, "that Master Scolop seemed scrupulously sincere in pleading his innocence in killing the chandler?"

Edwin agreed and said he was as convinced of the man's innocence in this death as he was of his guilt for the murder of young Eldrik. As he spoke, he was entirely aware that it destroyed Willem's theory that Scolop was guilty of both killings and, perhaps more importantly, that the two deaths were connected in some way.

"Of course," replied Willem, "if you start from that premise, it presents the note that Mistress Goodlyhead and I found in the fish in quite a different light."

"How so?" questioned Edwin.

"If the note was not a payment demand from Master Scolop for killing the chandler, then it suggests that it was a note demanding a payment for the killing of the boy Eldrik. And yet," he continued, "if it was, indeed, a note to Lord Ravenhead and not yourself or Mistress Goodlyhead, then why would a nobleman from the northern shires wish a poor servant boy to be killed? And, indeed, wish his death so fervently that he would pay someone to murder him?"

"Perhaps we should have mentioned the note to Chamberlain Balliwick," replied Edwin.

"I am sure he would simply dismiss it, for he has what he wants," replied the boy, disheartened by the wanton lust for a hanging.

"Take heart, Willem, the man who holds himself in high office and all others in disdain is set for a great fall," replied Edwin, who immediately regretted speaking ill of his fellow man.

As they approached the town, they could see Mildred Goodlyhead talking with Father Shriver as they stood amongst the graves of the fallen warriors in the churchyard. Today she wore black, but for her it was a choice, for she had clothes for each occasion and today was an occasion for sorrow.

The townsfolk of Ebbsweirmouth weaved their own clothes and most could afford a change of clothing only once or twice in their adult life. And yet, everyone who had not already owned a black dress eight years ago had taken on that colour. Everyone had weaved in black following Maeldun and those who could not afford new dresses and cloaks had simply dyed what they had the colour of mourning.

There wasn't a single person in the town who had not lost a father, brother, son or cousin at Maeldun. Only the craftsmen and tradesmen had remained at home, to defend the village if it was raided. It had been August, nearing the busiest time of the year in the fields, when the household regiment of Ebbsweirmouth had marched off towards Maeldun. The ragged unit had consisted mainly of farmers and their sons, armed only with what sharp tools they could carry.

There was a purpose to Mildred's visit to Father Shriver that day. As they stood by the newly dug graves of young Eldrik and the visiting chandler, she asked for the priest's advice on a matter of some concern to her.

She reminded Father Shriver that she had already drawn his attention to the fact that young Eldrik had lost the tip of the smallest finger on his right hand. Nobody had noticed this deformity before and, yet, several people had done so after his body was recovered.

"I was assured that it was bitten off by a fish," the priest responded.

Mildred shook her head. "We may only speculate on that, Father. But it is not how it occurred that worries me."

"Then what is it that distresses you, my dear?"

"You are aware of a boy, of similar age to Eldrik, coming to town recently?"

The priest confirmed that he had seen the boy of whom she spoke.

"His name is Willem, Father. Look, there he is," she said, pointing towards the approach of her husband and the boy.

The priest nodded. "And what of him?"

"He is marked with the same missing finger tip."

The boy of whom she spoke drew nearer to the churchyard and she was anxious that he did not hear she was speaking of him to the priest.

"Ignore me, Father. I was just wondering if there was some significance to it. But, please, don't speak of it in front of the boy."

And so he did not speak of the matter, but he looked strangely at the boy, trying to see the hand of which Mildred spoke.

"What news from the tower, my dear?" asked Mildred as her husband stood before her.

"Cyrus Scolop murdered Eldrik," he declared. "That much is certain, but we cannot be sure of anything else, for we know not why he killed the boy."

"Where is Scolop now?" asked the priest.

"Detained at the tower, awaiting his hanging."

"For the death of a slave?" questioned Shriver. The indifference in his voice shocked Mildred.

"The boy belonged to God before he belonged to Scolop, Father," she replied indignantly.

As the priest considered how he might counter Mildred's rebuttal, Abel Cotes, whose farmhouse rested on a hill to the northwest of town, came running towards them shouting something about Maggoty Gripple and Apparition Hill. By the time he reached them, the fragmented pieces of information had formed in their minds. So, when he told them what he had seen, they were already looking upwards towards the ridge where the gallows stood. Above the tops of the tiny houses dotted about close by, up beyond the ford, set between the estuary at Pryklethorn Bay and Four Thing Farm, stood the wooden platform, a tree-turned-gallows upon the ridge of Apparition Hill. The figure hanging there could not be made out through the hazy grey mist that still lingered. Cotes said it was Maggoty Gripple and all that had gone before seemed to make complete sense to the group standing in the churchyard.

"I never intended for him to be hanged," Cotes said pleadingly to the priest, as if he had committed a mortal sin. "A sheep was stolen and I only wanted to be recompensed for my loss. It was not I who asked for Maggoty to be hanged."

Father Shriver tried to console the poor man and Edwin Goodlyhead was just about to predict that Aldwyn Byrgan and his two sons would be likely to follow the next day, when his wife intervened in an attempt to prevent further anxieties to Abel Cotes.

"Someone must speak with the shire reeve. Chamberlain Balliwick is a reasonable man." She was just about to suggest that perhaps the Byrgans would not follow in the same fashion as Maggoty Gripple when, all of a sudden, the gravedigger and his sons came along the path, as jauntily as you please, towards them.

"I was just saying how Chamberlain Balliwick is a reasonable man and I am proved right by your presence, Master Byrgan," Mildred said in a happier tone.

When Byrgan began to relate to them the events at the castle, everyone was pleased that a settlement of sort had been reached and Mildred was anxious to remove Willem from any further talk of hangings. She whispered to Edwin and he ushered his wife from the churchyard, suggesting to Willem that he returned to finish his work in the barn.

"Scolop is sentenced to hang," declared Aldwyn Byrgan as they left and then he turned to Abel Cotes. "And I am to meet the shire reeve at Four Thing Farm with fifteen shillings as quickly as my feet can take me there."

"Why are you going to my farm, Aldwyn, for I am here?"

"Well, clearly Chamberlain Balliwick wants to settle this matter and expects to find you at the farm too. We shall go there together, Abel, and let him witness the payment."

With that, the men set off to do as they had agreed, but stopped at intervals to tell people of the arrest of Cyrus Scolop and the hanging of Maggoty Gripple.

From that moment, a variety of stories reverberated around the town. Seth Wainthrop was slandered for telling Balliwick that Gripple had stolen the lamb; Aldwyn Byrgan was condemned for accusing Scolop of the same crime. Almost every piece of tittle-tattle was incorrect, altered and embellished with each telling. Calumny and defamation of character continued into the afternoon and was stoked by a diet of ale and wanton gossip at the inn.

As the Goodlyheads and Willem walked back towards Mardyke House, now well ahead of Cotes and Byrgan, the boy stopped in his tracks.

"I must go back," he declared suddenly.

"To Shire Farm?" asked Mildred Goodlyhead.

"No, no," answered Willem. "Back to Scullion Tower."

"Whatever for?"

"I must tell Master Balliwick about the note from Master Scolop to Lord Ravenhead. It implicates Lord Ravenhead, do you not see?"

The pair shook their heads and he repeated what he now firmly believed in his heart. "Lord Ravenhead commissioned the murder of Eldrik and Master Scolop carried out the foul deed."

"But why would..." Mildred's words tapered off as the boy ran away, back the way he had come, and disappeared behind the church.

~~~~~

One week ago, self-doubt and nervousness may have overpowered Willem but then, one week ago, he had been working at Shire Farm, removed from contact with anyone other than the Cuddlewicks. There had been little to generate fear at the farm except, perhaps, an unfamiliar noise in the depth of the dark night. Even then, if his strange bedfellows had not stirred, then there was probably little to fear. Chickens and goats were particularly fearful beasts, unlike the ram, who feared nothing and for whom a noise in the night was an opportunity to demonstrate his fearlessness.

And yet, it was the fearsome heart of an imaginative boy that had altered this past week. It had not been hardened by the grisly tone of Cyrus Scolop, nor had it agonised at the mysterious appearances of the shadowy Watchman, but was now steeled by the alchemistic wonder of the virtues of destiny.

In those lonely nights spent in the barn behind Mardyke House, he had thought much about the words of the old woman who dwelt in the yew tree wood. And he had considered, too, the judicious meanderings of Watchman Darrayne. Even on that Friday night, on the snow-driven coastal path, he had considered the fairy's words when she summoned up the first gift of courage.

Willem soon arrived at Scullion Tower and could hear the sound of Cyrus Scolop snoring as he walked gingerly past the cell in the castle courtyard. He rapped his small fist as hard as he could on the large wooden door and heard voices calling from inside. Suddenly it creaked open and an elderly man stood in front of him, with eyes made dim by age and hard work. His throat gurgled as he spoke and Willem struggled to understand what he was saying.

"May I speak with Chamberlain Balliwick, please?"

The boy listened closely to the reply and could just make out that the chamberlain had gone to Four Thing Farm on business. Willem stood there, wondering whether he should wait, or walk to the farm in the hope of meeting the shire reeve on his way. As he stood there, the servant moved back from the doorway and an elegantly dressed man stepped out. He had a black cloak pulled tightly about his person as protection against the cold air and prying eyes.

"What do you want, boy?" asked Lord Scullion in a stern voice, as he walked away from the building and headed towards the counting house, leaving the boy to scuttle after him in order to answer the question.

"I have some important information about Master Scolop, Sir."

Scullion walked on, ignoring the boy, for he assumed it was some waif or stray who had come to plead the man's innocence in order to retain their livelihood. But he stopped in his tracks when Willem added three more words.

"And Lord Ravenhead," the boy said and these words seized the eorl's attention.

"What of Lord Ravenhead?" his lordship demanded to know as he turned quickly to take a better look at the boy.

"Well, Sir," the boy began, before Scullion thought better of the matter and stopped the boy speaking. The eorl looked directly at his servant who was waiting nearby.

"That will be all," he shouted, before ushering the boy off towards the counting house.

"Come," Scullion told Willem as they walked across the courtyard and entered the room.

Lord Scullion pulled his cloak tightly to his body and sat down at the desk. The largely empty room was as cold as it was quiet and Scullion wished he had put his gloves on. Willem remained standing in front of him as his lordship ordered the boy to continue.

"I arrived at Ebbsweirmouth on Friday evening, Sir, and on Saturday morning I was engaged by Master Scolop to make some deliveries of fish. He ordered me to deliver two large fish."

"Go on," replied Scullion, wondering what this had to do with Lord Ravenhead.

"One had to be taken to Master and Mistress Goodlyhead at Mardyke House and the other to Lord Ravenhead at The Salutation Inn. Master Scolop was most precise about which fish to deliver to each. But I slipped on the snow and dropped the fish. I must have mixed them up and the fish destined for Lord Ravenhead was delivered to the Goodlyheads."

"Is that it, boy?" Lord Scullion shouted.

"No, Sir. The fish that I delivered in error to Mistress Goodlyhead contained a note."

"A note?"

"A note, Sir; a message inside the fish," answered Willem. "It said just two words, 'pay me'. This same note, Sir, was instructing Lord Ravenhead to pay Master Scolop for killing the boy Eldrik."

Scullion sat for a moment, considering the boy's comments.

"So, the message delivered to the Goodlyheads was actually meant for Lord Ravenhead and it said 'pay me'?"

"Yes, Sir. And the note instructed Lord Ravenhead to pay Master Scolop for murdering the serf, Eldrik, Sir."

"Surely it was a note demanding payment for the fish," replied Lord Scullion.

"No Sir, it was not. At first I thought it was a note asking for payment for killing the stranger who arrived in town on Friday, a chandler named Darrayne, Sir. But it wasn't. I am certain of it, Sir. Lord Ravenhead paid Master Scolop to kill Eldrik."

"But, why would Lord Ravenhead want Scolop to kill the slave boy?" asked Scullion.

"I do not know, Sir, but I am convinced it is so."

Lord Scullion scrutinised the boy and asked how old he was. The eorl could not conceal his disappointment in receiving confirmation that the boy was several years short of adulthood. He stood up and paced about the room, all the time holding his cloak tightly about his person. The boy would make a very poor witness against this upstart lord from the northern shires, thought the eorl. It suited Scullion to implicate Lord Ravenhead in a murder, but there would need to be greater evidence to hand before he could hang a lord and he certainly could not do so on the word of this boy alone. The easiest solution, of course, would be Scolop, but then he would probably say anything to save his own skin.

"Do you still have the note?"

"It is at Mardyke House, Sir," the boy replied.

Scullion assured Willem that he had acted correctly in reporting this matter to him.

"We need to discuss this matter with the shire reeve when he returns. Wait here," he told the boy. "Here, sit in this chair and I will send for you when the chamberlain comes back."

After Lord Scullion had left and the door had been shut, Willem looked about the well-lit room, examining, but not touching, the pots of ink and newly trimmed quills.

As he did so, Lord Scullion headed across the sunlit courtyard towards the cell and pulled his cloak about his shoulders to conceal his withered arm as he grabbed the bars that separated him from Cyrus Scolop.

"Do you know me?" called Scolop, for the low-hanging sun glared directly into the fisherman's eyes and blinded him. "If you are my confessor, then you have had a wasted journey," he shouted. "For my soul was damned before I reached manhood."

"It is Lord Scullion who speaks," said the figure hidden by the haze. "The only person who may pardon your crimes."

In his heart, Scolop still harboured the foolish thought that Ravenhead would save him from the gallows so, when Scullion asked why the fisherman had killed the slave boy Eldrik, he was reluctant to accuse his fellow conspirator in the act.

"I killed the boy when fishing. It was the act of a flared temper, my Lord, no more than that."

"And yet, you wanted to conceal it. Why would you wish to hide the fact?"

"Can you not see where it has put me? I am jailed for it, Sir. I am to be hanged for the death of a serf. That is not right, Sir, that is not right. A freeman cannot be hanged for the killing of a slave."

"I am not interested in the what and where of it, Master Scolop. I am interested only in the why and the who."

"The who is me," replied Scolop. "I killed Eldrik."

"The why and the who are the same thing," replied Lord Scullion. "Somebody instructed you to kill the boy. Tell me who that was and what their purpose was and you may yet retain your liberty."

Scolop did not understand the subtlety of the word 'may' as well as his lordship did and, in that instant, the fisherman saw an opportunity to secure his freedom. What debt did he owe Ravenhead? Any debt had been settled when the deed was done and a fee paid.

As Scolop hesitated, Lord Scullion played his final card. "Take care, Master Scolop," he said. "I have a note in your own hand asking for payment for the killing. You just have to confirm who the note was intended for."

But the fisherman had already decided to place his last hope on the eorl.

"It was Ravenhead," he shouted. "He paid me to kill the boy."

"Why?" asked Scullion. "Why would a nobleman from the northern shires wish to kill a slave boy who worked for a fisherman in Ebbsweirmouth? Tell me that and you may yet go free."

Scolop realised it would serve no purpose to elaborate on the circumstances of Eldrik's death.

"You must ask him," declared Scolop. "Ask Ravenhead why the boy had to die, for I do not know the reason."

Lord Scullion walked off towards the counting house but Scolop called to him. "I have done thy will, Sir. I have given you the answer. Set me free as you promised."

"You have made an accusation. Lord Ravenhead will stand before you and you must repeat that accusation to his face. Let us hear what he has to say. Then we will consider your part in the crime."

Inside the counting house, the boy could hear the sound of raised voices but could not make out what was being said. As he stood by the door, listening, he heard footsteps crossing the courtyard and the door swung open.

"You must wait here," Lord Scullion told the boy and asked him again what his name was.

"Willem, Sir, Willem the waif, although I am now a freeman, Sir."

"Willem, you say," answered Scullion, recalling Balliwick mentioning the name. "Show me your hand."

The boy held out his right hand, for he was certain in that moment that it was his missing fingertip that the eorl was interested in seeing.

"Wait here, Willem," his lordship replied. "I will instruct a servant to bring you food. But don't leave this room. Do you understand?"

The boy nodded and Lord Scullion left, closing the door behind him.

Hearing the raised voice of his lordship in the courtyard, the servants inside the main building readied themselves for his instructions. And those instructions were given as soon as the main door swung open. Four men were sent to arrest Lord Ravenhead, another was instructed to deliver a tray of food to the counting house for a boy who was waiting there. And another was told to leave at once to find Chamberlain Balliwick and return with him immediately to the castle.

"No one is to tarry. Do you hear? Go now, for the day is passing all too quickly."

There was no sign of Balliwick in town, so the four servants returned to the castle with Lord Ravenhead. In that short time, Lord Scullion had considered carefully all that had occurred in the absence of his shire reeve and he fashioned a way in his mind to capitalise on the situation.

Lord Ravenhead insisted that Lady Una accompanied him to the castle in order that she might provide witness to his actions since they arrived at Ebbsweirmouth.

Fearing that they might conspire to avert his plans, Lord Scullion had them each taken to separate rooms to be questioned by him on the untimely death of Eldrik. But he had little to fear on that part because Lady Una now saw the need to disassociate herself from her companion. After all, Ravenhead had brought this situation on himself with his ill-considered five shilling wager. It was he who had pointed an accusing finger at Gripple who, in turn, had accused Scolop. And now it was Scolop who had led his lordship to the source of the plot.

Lord Scullion kept Ravenhead waiting, hoping that Balliwick would return in time to oversee the questioning. In the meantime, he proceeded to entertain Lady Una and put subtle questions to her in the hope of securing a reason for the killing of Eldrik. He told her of Scolop's allegation that Ravenhead had conspired with him to kill the boy.

"Are not two accusers required for this purpose?" she asked.

"They are," replied Scullion, "especially if you are to testify on behalf of your betrothed." He paused, wondering whether she would confirm her allegiance, but she did not speak. "A second witness stands ready to do this," he added. "A boy, around the same age as Eldrik, is waiting in the counting house outside to further accuse Lord Ravenhead."

"What boy is that?" she asked.

"A boy who once lived in this very castle," he answered. "And a boy who shares a strange and particular semblance with the dead boy, Eldrik."

He waited to see if Una was yet ready to speak against Ravenhead.

"This boy," he continued in a patient tone, "has the tip of his smallest finger on his right hand missing, just as Eldrik did when his body was recovered at Hollow Hole Cove."

The surprised look on the woman's face was visible to anyone who watched her reaction. And Scullion was certainly doing that.

"Now, Lady Una. I shall make you the same offer I have made Master Scolop in this matter. Whoever tells me first why Lord Ravenhead paid Scolop to kill Eldrik might well secure their freedom. But, mark my words," he added sternly, "my patience wanes."

Una thought on his words, yet she knew well the cunning and guileful nature of Lord Ravenhead. She realised that the next words she spoke might easily condemn her.

"Lord Ravenhead and I have journeyed here, in deferential regard to yourself, Cousin, in order to seek your blessing on our marriage. We have nothing to do with the death of a slave boy."

Scullion was disappointed by her response. Perhaps, he thought to himself, Lady Una was subject to this conspiracy, the same as all the other victims. Could it be, he wondered, that only Ravenhead himself knew the truth of the matter and all others were merely victims of his crime?

And so he left the room and, after asking if there was any news of Chamberlain Balliwick, he then went into the great hall to speak with Lord Ravenhead.

"Why have I been brought here in such a manner? Hopefully it is to receive your blessing on our forthcoming marriage, but I fear that is not the case, having been summoned and marched here under guard."

The eorl dismissed the guards for he did not want them to hear the nature of his questions to another nobleman.

"You are aware, I am sure," began Scullion, "of the events that have taken place in our town this past week."

"The theft of a sheep and the hanging of the offender. Yes, I am aware of such matters, but I do not see how this concerns me."

"There have been two deaths; a chandler, who visited the town to sell candles and a serf boy, who carries a strange mark on his right hand."

"Two accidental deaths, so I am given to understand by the talk in The Salutation Inn, my Lord."

"Perhaps," his lordship replied, as he turned his back to his guest and adopted a relaxed but knowing pose. All the time he kept his cloak wrapped about him to hide his withered arm. The manner in which this was done had attracted the attention of Lord Ravenhead on each occasion they had met. He had seen the victims of many battles against the sea wanderers, for they lived and many begged in the towns and villages along the sea coast. And, by now, he was convinced of Scullion's desire to conceal some physical defect. He had never seen his left arm and his right hand more often held tight on to his tunic or cloak to ensure it did not fall open.

"What have these deaths to do with me?" Ravenhead asked.

"You stand accused of one or both of them, my Lord. Firstly by the man you commissioned to murder the boy Eldrik and secondly by a boy who now waits in the counting house; a boy who, like Eldrik, has the tip of a finger missing;

a strange coincidence, which I am determined to find the reason for."

"Then presumably I will be given the opportunity to face my accusers and repudiate their claims. And Lady Una will testify in my name too. I am innocent of such allegations."

Scullion ignored his guest's confident defence and returned to the subject of coincidences.

"It is strange," he said, "how one person's disposition, complexion, marking or countenance distinguishes them from another," Scullion added, gaining in confidence with each word. "I recall, for example, the many stories I heard of Maeldun, when those few survivors returned to our village. Chamberlain Balliwick would tell their stories to me each night after supper, of all that had occurred at the battle and of the sad tales that the survivors told."

Lord Scullion looked at Ravenhead to see if he could distinguish any change in his demeanour, but there was none.

"They were stories of gallantry and courage," Scullion continued. "And some of faint-heartedness, cowardice and treachery, too. And I recall the story of a nobleman named Godric, the son of Odda, who fled the battle almost before it had begun. And had it been but one man whose courage had failed him, then it would have mattered little. But that man chose to steal Byrhtnoth's horse. Then, seeing what they thought to be their leader's steed fleeing the fight, panic set in amongst the East Seaxe army and hundreds of those at the rear of the battle joined the coward and they turned and ran from the enemy. All of this happened because Godric had feared for his life."

As he spoke he could see the same look of nervousness appear on Ravenhead's face as he had seen on Una's.

"I was a young man at the time," Scullion continued. "And it is strange what simple elements of each story you recall. I remember, you see," he said in a soft voice, looking directly at Ravenhead. "Everyone described Odda's son Godric in the same way, as the one with flame red hair and trimmed moustache and beard to match. Just like your own, in fact, Lord Ravenhead."

Before Lord Scullion had finished speaking, Lord Ravenhead held out his right hand in a gesture of friendship.

"Take my hand, Cousin. Let us not be enemies. Red hair is more common than you think. The fact that I share such a distinguishing mark with this coward, Godric, does not make us of the same faint heart."

At that moment, Ravenhead knew that if he could not take Haeferingas by guile and falsehood, he would do so by force. And in that moment, an error of judgement was made. Lord Scullion, thinking he would gain Ravenhead's confidence and lure the truth from him through artfulness and cunning, stepped towards him. He took Ravenhead's hand with his and looked deeply into his eyes to see if he could detect the guilt that he suspected dwelled in the man's heart. As he did so, Ravenhead drew the dagger from the belt around his host's waist with his left hand and plunged it fully into Lord Scullion's stomach. As he suspected, Scullion made no attempt to defend himself with his free hand and fell to the floor, grasping the wound that was now haemorrhaging blood.

With the dagger still in his hand, Ravenhead crept from the room and, in the absence of the guards, was able to make his way to the main door of the building. Slipping outside, he looked about him and saw nobody in the courtyard.

The sun was beginning to disappear behind the main castle building and the counting house was draped in shade. The room had grown cold and the boy had long since eaten the food that his lordship had sent. Willem sat looking at the pots that stood on the desk and dipped a quill in the bright red ink. Just then, the door burst open and in the dark shadow Willem could not make out who had entered the room. He assumed in that brief moment that it was Lord Scullion. But, as the door slammed shut, the figure took two or three steps forward and Willem recognised the man he had delivered the fish to a few days before. Strangely, at that moment, the boy's heart was not filled with morbid fear but with courage and faith.

The boy replaced the quill in the inkpot and boldly stood up from the chair. Three more steps and the man was now almost in front of him. In that instant, Willem saw a glint of steel from something held in Ravenhead's hand. It was the dagger, still bloodied from the attack on Lord Scullion and it was now going to be used for the same purpose on the boy.

Willem raised his hands to defend himself but Ravenhead simply grabbed his wrists and pushed the boy back on to the desk. Willem was pinned to the wooden surface by a strong hand that now wrapped itself around his neck. The boy was no match for the powerful attacker, who held him down with just one hand. Blood dripped from a dagger that Ravenhead raised above his head and was now about to plunge into the boy. Willem's arms flailed about in the space between them, but he was not strong enough. Courage and faith alone could not help him now. He thrashed at the man with his closed fist, but his punches were simply not strong enough to have any effect. As the boy kicked at his attacker with his feet, Ravenhead positioned himself against Willem's legs and was about to thrust the knife down into the child's heart.

The boy's hands swung towards his attacker's face and then back down again, striking the desk that his back rested upon. Suddenly he felt something on the desk touch his hand and he grabbed at it in desperation. The inkpots crashed on to the stone floor and Willem could feel he was holding a quill, dripping with red ink, in his left hand. From the corner of his eye he could see the same bloody red colour of the dagger as it descended towards him. He flashed his closed hand again at Ravenhead's face and thrust the inky quill into his assailant's neck. Then, leaving it there, he managed to grab his assailant's wrist with his other hand, expecting it to be too strong to withstand. And yet it wasn't. As the red ink, poisoned with the monkshood and hemlock, entered Ravenhead's vein, it sapped all the strength from his body, almost as quickly as the courage had been taken from it that day at Maeldun.

The crashing of the inkpot and the screams of the boy were heard by Oswald Balliwick, who had just returned to the castle. He called towards the main building for help as he ran towards the counting house.

As Ravenhead's limp body slumped to the stone floor, Balliwick rushed through the open door, followed by a group of servants, shouting about the attack on Lord

Scullion. The boy appeared to be unharmed and Ravenhead lay motionless on the floor.

"If Ravenhead is not dead, then throw him into the cell with Scolop," shouted Balliwick to the servants. "And then bring the boy to me."

With that he rushed across the courtyard to see what could be done for Lord Scullion.

As the limp body of Ravenhead was dragged away by the servants, Willem waited for them to return to collect him, not knowing what punishment might befall a boy who had somehow managed to summon enough strength to slay a nobleman

The scene that surrounded him was not a vision of justice, nor did he feel any sense of retribution. And yet, as he stood awaiting his own trial, the gift of mercy rested upon him.

Chapter Fourteen

Wise Counsel

A*las, how easily a fool does fool himself. Proverbs say that the way of a fool is right in his own eyes, but a wise man listens to wise counsel. Yet, through want of humility, seeking advice is a path chosen by the few. Understanding is the product of knowledge, wisdom and wise counsel, yet all are rejected by the fool whose heart has strayed from the true path of destiny.*

Many thought Aldwyn Byrgan a fool and his sons to be fools-in-waiting. And he was indeed a fool, of course, to allow himself to be cajoled and corrupted by the mendacious Maggoty Gripple. He and his sons were victims of misplaced confidence, unable or unwilling to seek advice.

For the citizens of Ebbsweirmouth, as with anywhere that humankind exists, there is no need to summon the devil incarnate, for he is ever present. He is the morally blind, the spiritually incontinent and the misguided fool. Thirteen virtues we have considered thus far and yet the Byrgans and Master Gripple could not conjure up one between them. Now, wise counsel is endowed and destiny shall be fashioned accordingly.

For Maggoty Gripple, his transgression is met with equal hostility. Just as mercy is twice blessed, so his crimes were to be punished twofold. Earthly vice is the mirror of the heavenly virtue of mercy and an intemperate anger is its sudden manifestation. The silent indifference of Leland Hoop was also the product of his own foolishness. Beguiled and led astray by tales of haunted drove roads and spirits returning from the other side, which were simply stories that he wished to be true. And, when he found them not to be so, his anger could not be contained. Wise counsel is rarely found at The Salutation Inn or anywhere of its like.

Even Chamberlain Balliwick, the most virtuous and wise man of the shire, can be deceived, for no man is immune from imprudent folly.

Wise counsel is to be found in unlikely places; by an attentive ear to the wisdom of age, or in the innocent musings of youth; in the magnificence of kings and in the simplicity of nature.

The sound of a robin's footsteps upon the ground is like the pit-a-pat of the gentle rain. When it is heard, the worm beneath the earth fears that it will soon drown in the wet soil; so, rising to the surface, it is then snapped up by the hungry bird. And so it was with Scolop. The pit-a-pat of Willem's questioning caused the truth to surface and Scolop was condemned by its righteous light.

And now, never has wise counsel been more greatly needed in Ebbsweirmouth, as its people look into the gaping abyss. Lord Scullion lies dying and a man lies dead outside the counting house. Another hangs on Gallows Ridge and unrest abounds. In the town, a quickly erected bonfire glows and people gather around it to consider their fate and assert their own pale imitation of wise counsel on matters that they cannot possibly understand. Whilst at Scullion Tower, where we now return, the murderous stain of blood can be seen in many rooms and none less than his lordship's bedroom, where he now lies amidst the bloody gore.

The room, which is normally filled with silence, vibrates with the confused movement and noise that now echoes about the place. It is a large space, unhindered by furniture and, apart from the large four-poster bed, only a wooden dais holding a washing bowl occupies any space in it. The stone walls are bare and the bed is placed next to the only source of light and air, a small arrow-loop slit that has been extended to form a cross. There is no hearth in the room and it is cold. It is to this room that our story now turns, as Oswald Balliwick, benumbed and almost paralysed by the tragedy that unravels before him, stands at the bedside of his bloodied friend and master.

The large room was shrouded in darkness as Balliwick stood, wondering what steps could be taken to save Morcar Scullion. Candles flickered on either side of the bed and the floor was stained with smears of blood that had been trodden in by the servants who ran hither and thither about the frenzied scene, carrying water, torn sheets to be used as bandages, messages and questions.

Beneath the heavy woven covers on the bed that same blood continued to seep through the dressing that Mildred Goodlyhead had wrapped around his lordship's body. She had gone downstairs to prepare a poultice. The bandages would need to be removed again, she told the chamberlain, as she rushed away.

"I shall be as quick as I can," she assured him.

In his heart Balliwick knew her efforts would be in vain. He stood there looking at Lord Scullion's bloodied face, wondering why Mistress Goodlyhead had not questioned

Scullion's limp arm and then wondered how many people actually knew about it, but had never made reference to the injury. Scullion's red-stained hands thrashed about as the agony gripped his mind, transferring the blood from his body to his face, flicking and dripping it on to the sheets and drapes, until nothing and nobody remained untouched by its crimson mark.

There was a deep wound to the stomach, Balliwick had been told. And yet there was blood everywhere. Scullion had pressed his hand to the wound, hoping to stem the flow of blood, but Ravenhead had done his work well. As Morcar writhed in agony, the red stains began to congeal and Balliwick took a cloth to wipe the drying fluid from his lordship's face.

At that moment, moonlight streamed through the lancet window into the room, casting a bright whiteness shaped like a crucifix across the awful scene. Lord Scullion stirred and looked in wonder at what seemed like a beam of eternal light. Something was preventing him from speaking and he tried to spit the gory saliva from his mouth. Balliwick held a chalice of water to his mouth and he drank from it, groaning as he leant upwards towards it. The tiny movement took much from him and his appetite to speak waned under the effort.

"Listen to me," said Balliwick forcefully. "Ravenhead is dead. The waif Willem killed him. You will get well," he continued, drawing as much positive tone to his voice as he could manage. He waited, but his lordship breathed heavier still and his chest rose and fell beneath the covers.

"Everything falls well, my Lord," Balliwick began again. "Ravenhead is dead and you shall marry the Lady Una.

Your house will be united with that of Haeferingas. The future is bright for us all. All you must do is recover. Do you understand?" His voice was pleading now and the tone was all misplaced hope and little expectation.

"Mistress Goodlyhead is preparing a poultice as we speak. The wound will mend and you shall marry Lady Una. Can you hear me, my Lord?"

Unable to lift his head from the pillow, Lord Scullion tilted it slightly to face his chamberlain.

"Marry, my friend?" he muttered questioningly, spitting more blood from his mouth as he spoke. "I will not make a greater mockery of my life than it already is. Do not pity me, Oswald, for I have met love and though it treated me harshly, I knew it well."

As he spoke his eyes brightened and he gazed at his loyal servant and good friend. Balliwick leaned down and kissed his master on his bloody cheek. "You marry her," Scullion whispered in his ear.

"I serve only one master," he replied and as he spoke the door to the bedroom swung open. Mildred Goodlyhead rushed into the room accompanied by a young servant maid.

"I have made a poultice of sticklewort and creeping tormentil," she told the maid. "Now stop arguing with me and make some more for later. Remove the dark green leaves of the sticklewort and macerate its roots with the tormentil and some red wine."

The maid was nodding and wondering whether to continue taking her advice or proceed downstairs to carry out the instructions.

"Well, go then, girl. Why are you here?"

As the maid left, Mildred called after her. "Not too much wine, you understand. It mustn't be runny. It needs to thicken."

"Yes, Mistress Goodlyhead," the girl called back as she rushed into the hall outside.

"Now," said Mildred looking directly at Balliwick. "Remove that bloodstained dressing. Here, I have torn some more from the sheets."

Balliwick took the strips of white cloth from her and wound them into a ball before pulling the bed cover back. The mattress was saturated in blood.

"We must move him," the chamberlain said.

"We cannot move him, Master Balliwick. For each time we do, it will open the wound more. Remove the dressing."

He did as he was told and once the pressure of the soaked bandage was removed, blood oozed from the wound even more freely than before.

"Lift him up," she called and the patient groaned loudly as the chamberlain did so. Mildred pushed the new dressing under his back and collected it from the other side. She then slapped the poultice on the torn skin and quickly covered it with cloth and tied it tightly with the bandage. Balliwick and Mildred were now covered in blood themselves and it was clear they were fighting a lost cause.

Mildred sighed heavily, placed her hands on the bed and bowed her head in despair. She walked slowly to the door and opened it slightly. A servant stood close by in the hall.

"Fetch Father Shriver," she said. "Tell him it's urgent."

She went to turn round but found Oswald Balliwick standing directly behind her.

"Is it over?" he whispered and she nodded.

"The bleeding will not stop," she said.

"Can we move him to a clean bed? Balliwick asked. "Or perhaps wrap a clean sheet around him? We can't let him die like this, wallowing in his own blood."

Mildred called to one of the other servants and told her to prepare another clean bed. She then called two others for assistance in removing Lord Scullion from his bed. They did as Balliwick ordered and wrapped the long linen sheet around the flailing body of the dying man. His pleas for mercy were ignored for the benefit of dignity, for they could not send him to his maker in such a bloodied state.

As they settled his lordship into the adjacent bedroom, he coughed up several cupfuls of blood and the cushions needed to be changed immediately. Eventually, with a heavy blanket covering his body, he at least looked presentable. He lay there, his breathing shallow now and his eyes dimmed, until Father Shriver arrived but, on seeing his face, Eorl Scullion breathed his last.

The gurgling sound of Scullion trying to speak but managing only to cough blood had become a monotonous background sound and, when it suddenly went silent, Mildred Goodlyhead slumped, exhausted, into a chair. As she did so, Oswald Balliwick collapsed on the floor, mourning the loss of his great friend and master. Father Shriver called for assistance, thinking that the chamberlain, too, was injured.

"Get out, get out!" Balliwick called to the servants as they rushed into the room, not wishing them to see him in such distress.

Father Shriver administered the last rites to Lord Scullion and then, once he had spoken at length with

Balliwick, he accompanied Mildred Goodlyhead back to the town. Oswald Balliwick went to his room to clean himself and change his clothes. He still had to speak with Lady Una to see if he could make any sense of all that had happened on this saddest of days.

It was almost midnight before Balliwick came out of his room and he was hoping his guest had gone to bed by this late hour. A servant asked if he required supper but he could not think of eating.

"Bring me some wine in the great hall," he said dejectedly as he walked away. "Oh," he called as an afterthought, "have Father Shriver and Mistress Goodlyhead left?"

"Yes, Sir," the servant replied, "two hours ago."

"Did they take the waif, Willem, with them?"

"No, Sir, he has been left in the counting house with the body of the dead man, Sir."

"Send the boy to one of the bedrooms for the night. I will speak with him in the morning."

The servant bowed and went to walk away.

"And what of the Lady Una?" Balliwick called to the departing servant.

"She is waiting on your attendance in the great hall, Sir."

A heavy sigh needed no forcing from his chest, for he did not require company at this moment. This was a time for reflection, recollection, not labouring his way to the truth. Whatever the truth was, he thought, it would not change anything now.

And yet, in spite of the yoke that straddled his tired shoulders, Balliwick knew he must continue in his duties.

"Good evening, Lady Una," he said as he arrived in the great hall. "I apologise for keeping you waiting."

"I understand," she replied. "I am sorry to hear about the death of Lord Scullion. And I am pleased his killer has lost his life also."

She wanted to continue but a servant entered the room with a tray containing wine and two chalices. He placed the tray on the table and stood looking at Balliwick for further instructions.

"That will be all," the chamberlain said.

"Sir," the servant asked. "What of the prisoner, Cyrus Scolop?"

Though exhausted by his labours, anger and bitterness dwelt in the heart of the chamberlain and it had to be burned away or he knew it would not leave him.

"Take three men and hang him on Gallows Ridge at dawn."

"You are right to seek revenge for his part in the murder of Lord Scullion," Lady Una said as she stood up and walked over to where Balliwick sat.

"It is not revenge, Lady Una. It is justice. I am lord chamberlain, the shire reeve, not some rancorous, vindictive child."

She apologised, but Balliwick was still angered by the loss of Lord Scullion. As the servant walked towards the door, he called after him. "And take the body of that vile northern lord and hang him alongside Scolop, so all might see the result of their heinous joint enterprise."

When the servant had left the room, Balliwick poured the wine and gave one chalice to Lady Una, asking her to recount to him the details of Ravenhead's plot and all that had happened since she met him.

Lady Una did as she was asked, beginning with the death of her aged father, who she said had never recovered from the loss of his son, Osmund, reminding the chamberlain that he had fought alongside Lord Scullion's own father and older brother, Æryk, at Maeldun.

"I was too easily persuaded by the charm of the man. I was, after all, alone in the world, with no father or brothers to protect me. Lord Ravenhead wished to inherit the Haeferingas estate much more than he desired me, I can see that now," she added. "But he required some independent approval of the marriage in order to avoid any future dispute over his right to it. So he told me we should visit Ebbsweirmouth to see my cousin, Lord Scullion."

Balliwick sat in front of the raging fire in the hearth and sipped the wine. His mind was distracted from the course of her story as he was still thinking about his master and wondering what might happen now that he had died.

"When we arrived at The Salutation Inn, another guest recognised Lord Ravenhead. He was, by all accounts, a travelling chandler and yet he was familiar with my lord and went into a fiery rage at the sight of him. Lord Ravenhead sent me back to my room, but I heard much of what was said because their voices were raised. It seems the chandler had fought at Maeldun and recognised my fiancé from that past day. I listened as Lord Ravenhead encouraged the man to step outside the inn in order that he might placate him."

"Did nobody intervene in their dispute?"

"No, my Lord Balliwick. The noise inside the inn was even louder than their shouting, so nobody heard what was being said."

"What was their argument about?" Balliwick asked her.

"It was difficult to fathom at first," she replied. "But then it became apparent that Ravenhead was not who he said he was. Indeed, the visiting chandler was entirely sure that Lord Ravenhead was actually a man named Godric and I remembered that name well from those who had fought and recalled the events at Maeldun."

"I know the name too," replied Balliwick. "It was Godric who fled the battle and caused others to retreat with him. Godric brought shame on his family name, so it is no surprise that he changed it and adopted a new identity as Lord Ravenhead."

"When the shouting stopped," she continued, "Ravenhead, or Godric, returned to the inn and took me inside where others were gathered."

"And where did the chandler go?"

"I dared not think, my Lord. For I knew of my fiancé's short temper and assumed the man had been beaten for his trouble. I did not know what had happened until I heard others talking of the stranger's death later that day."

"And what of the boy, Eldrik?"

Lady Una hesitated, as if she was trying to gather her true recollection of events.

"The boy witnessed the killing," she replied hesitantly. "He knew that Ravenhead or Godric, as we now know him, had killed the chandler. So Scolop was engaged to drown the boy and was paid ten shillings for his wickedness."

"And what of the missing finger tip?"

Lady Una seemed startled at the question.

"The missing fingertip?" she asked.

"The boy Eldrik had a fingertip missing after he drowned," said Balliwick, wondering why she did not seem to know what he was talking about.

"As everyone said," she replied. "It must have been bitten off by a fish."

~~~~~

The bonfire that had been erected by the villagers as dusk fell continued to crackle and burn as the sable pall of night enveloped the street outside The Salutation Inn. At first glance, it had the appearance of a party to celebrate a fine harvest and yet, on closer view, there was neither jesting nor jubilation to be found there. It was past midnight and yet a large crowd of people were still gathered there, full of forlorn looks, wondering what their fate might be and complaining amongst themselves that the inn had not yet opened.

"It is not safe to be here," declared Abel Cotes for all to hear. "The light is dying." For him, the prophecy was being fulfilled on this starlit night. Others listened as they warmed themselves by the fire and all agreed that it had begun. One widow had noticed that a rowan tree had disappeared on the corpse road, providing a gateway to the underworld, and all were convinced that the abyss had been opened. Bloodied bodies, not corpses, had been seen entering the village from Apparition Hill and from behind the church graveyard, too. Abel Cotes swore he saw the very likeness of Leland Hoop, walking trance-like into the town, covered in blood. And now there was no answer from The Salutation Inn, which was locked and shrouded in darkness. And one of the Rypan sisters had seen Mildred Goodlyhead in the same condition entering the town from behind the graveyard, drenched in the same blood of Satan. Someone else had seen Father Shriver with bloodied hands, too.

Rumours were rife that Maggoty Gripple had been accosted by the devil's dark angels in the drove roads and had aided them in the theft of a sheep. And everyone knew the symbolic significance of sheep. So that was surely the beginning of the prophecy, Abel Cotes told everyone.

"Take care of my sheep," recited one of those standing close by. "That is what we were ordered to do. It is a sign, for it was one lost sheep that signalled the abyss opening."

"I will strike the shepherd and the sheep of the flock will be scattered," said Abel Cotes. "That is what is written in the Bible. And I am the shepherd," he added in a fearful voice.

"Jesus said we should rejoice when he found the lost sheep, for there will be more joy in heaven over one sinner who repents than over ninety-nine righteous people who need no repentance," said the older Rypan sister.

"Are there ninety-nine people living in the town of Ebbsweirmouth?" asked Mistress Byrgan.

"Perhaps that is it," replied Abel, as if he had discovered the cause of all the town's ills. "Are there ninety-nine people living here?"

Some of the crowd turned on the farmer, for it was his stolen sheep that had given Satan leave to take hold of their souls. The farmer could have approached Gripple himself, they thought and sought recompense for his loss.

"Am I wrong to seek restitution for the crime against me? Restitution is justice only in part. He that steals is bound to pay and much more than he who only borrows," the old man said in his defence. "And, in repenting, the wrongdoer must seek pardon for his offence. But he did not, he did not," Cotes shouted back at the crowd. "And to suffer no more than one who borrows is not justice at all, I say."

Cotes was shouted down by the growing crowd who had taken to the street in order that they would not be alone when the devil called.

"But it is the law," replied Mistress Byrgan, in defence of her husband's lenient penalty.

The argument continued long into the night and one thing was certain, nobody was going to bed. Consternation rapidly turned to terror and the only comfort to be found was in prayer. Half were praying ceaselessly and others were counting those present and trying to recall those who had not joined the throng. Did they amount to ninety-nine righteous people, they wondered? If so, was Satan coming for them all whilst God saved but one? And, who would that one be?

Ravenhead was not the devil incarnate as Abel Cotes had told everyone, but simply a man running away from himself, or at least his past. He was not the devil, he was not even Lord Ravenhead; but Godric, the coward of Maeldun, the man despised by everyone.

As the long night crept by, Leland Hoop sat, as he did each evening, in the chair by the casement window of the inn, gazing out down the street, hoping for the return of his beloved wife. No candles burned inside the inn and his presence was masked by the darkness that surrounded him.

His troubled mind was oblivious to the shouting outside, or to the occasional banging on his door.

As the new day appeared from a distant land beyond the sea, the sanctuary of daylight signalled safety to those who had feared the night. No vainglorious devil would exit the abyss in daylight and night was now edging away. The crowd fell silent as dawn approached and they became both sombre and elated at the same time. Then, just as the bonfire petered out and the subdued mob prepared to leave, the sound of people could be heard, approaching the town from the path that led past the graveyard. There was a distinct sound of muffled voices coming from a group of men who arrived from behind the church. The largest of the men was being forced to carry another over his shoulder and the other four were prodding him with sticks as he cursed them.

At that very moment, Father Shriver and Friar Sopscott approached the lychgate from the other side of the church and stopped to question the men about their business.

"These two men are to be hanged at dawn," shouted one of the men, who Shriver now recognised as servants from Scullion Tower.

"But that man is already dead," said Friar Sopscott, pointing at Ravenhead.

"We act in accordance with the shire reeve's instructions," replied the man.

All the time, Cyrus Scolop was calling on the priest for mercy. The two holy men wanted to intercede but did not doubt that Balliwick had instructed the men as they said, so they let them proceed. As the party approached the remains of the bonfire, some people gathered rubbish from the street and threw it at Cyrus Scolop as he was led past them on the way to Gallows Ridge. They shouted abuse and condemned him as the one responsible for the horrors that had beset the town.

As the servants set off out of town towards Apparition Hill, the crowd followed them, as did Father Shriver and Friar Sopscott, who felt in some way obliged to offer prayer and supervision to the unruly proceedings, for it was little more than a lynching.

With the sun not fully risen and the crowd now standing at the foot of the hill, Gallows Ridge could not be seen. The way up to the ridge was a single-track path, so a servant led the party, followed by Scolop, who was carrying the body of Godric, who the crowd still called Ravenhead because none knew the full story of the events.

When the lead person reached the ledge, he stopped suddenly and gasped at what greeted him. At first he thought they had perhaps hanged the body of Maggoty Gripple too low, because the ground around him was covered in blood. But as the servant stepped forward and others followed, it became clear that the wounds had not been inflicted by animals. Someone had taken a sharp weapon to the hanging body. The butcher, who had slaughtered many animals with a cleaver and knife, had been subjected to a similar fate himself.

Gripple's body was still dripping with blood, so whoever was responsible had not long finished their horrific work. The body had been hacked and torn to pieces, even though it had not been hung low like a sea wanderer. The fact that the body was nearly a man's height from the ground meant it had not been eaten by wild animals. As it was, the birds had taken their fill from the innards that had been exposed by the blade that had cut the body, but their work was incomplete and the figure of Gripple was still recognisable.

"This is the devil's work," cried Abel Cotes as one of the servants cut the body down.

The party of servants set about their work, firstly hoisting the body of Godric up on to the gallows.

"Now get Scolop up here beside him," the servant called. "For the shire reeve wishes the two to be hanged together, so all may see the consequence of their foul works."

Scolop cursed and bellowed abuse until the moment the boards fell from beneath his feet, dropping him less than half his own height. It was not enough to break his neck and he thrashed his legs at the bystanders for five or more minutes before the flailing stopped. The rope creaked under the strain, but the fisherman's burly hulk of a body speeded his death, for a lighter man may have taken three or four times as long to leave this world. When he finally breathed his last, the crowd cheered and continued to do so in spite of Father Shriver's appeal for greater charity.

The servants from the tower wrapped the bloodied body of Maggoty Gripple in a sheet and carried it back to the cemetery. The sun was now rising and the crowd began to disperse, returning to their homes after an extraordinary night.

A servant had shown Willem to a large bedroom that he referred to as the turret room. The boy did not understand what this name meant and, having not yet spoken to Chamberlain Balliwick, he was still uncertain whether he might expect to be punished for the killing of Lord Ravenhead. Recent events seemed to suggest that there would be a reckoning, but word had spread among the servants and when the maid Mary brought his supper she seemed convinced that Willem had done nothing wrong. Indeed, it appeared he had delivered retribution to the man who had killed Lord Scullion. Nevertheless, Willem slept uneasily that night and, whilst he was sure he would never see Darrayne again, he felt his presence in the cold turret room. Even the howling wind that buffeted the shuttered windows sounded like the shallow voice of the Watchman.

Of course, the spirit of the Watchman never left the boy's side, for wise counsel received with an open heart is never lost.

Chapter Fifteen

Understanding

Simonites, the monasteries called them, hawkers of holy relics. And they were as common as wandering minstrels, storytellers, herb beaters and healers. There was barely a market day that passed without one or all of them appearing alongside the regular tradesmen. Finger nails from saints, teeth from the disciples, pieces of the holy cross and plumes from angels' wings. They were somebody's finger nails, someone's teeth and the rest were simply fragments of wood or swans' feathers. Yet, who could resist them at this perilous time? The abyss had been opened and everyone needed protection.

Sometimes, more often than we know, the subtle nuance of irony is lost upon the world; overwhelmed by garish conspicuousness, which is strange for a world that continuously looks for a symbolic meaning in all things, as this one does. Indeed, for the people of Ebbsweirmouth, this past night has been spent with watchful eye at the shaping of a star and the movement of the moon for just such a sign. But the irony of this moment was not lost on the educated soul of Friar Sopscott, who sat gazing at the awkward figure of Aldwyn Byrgan, praying to the saint of the day for mercy.

The friar had been thinking of something else; someone else, in fact, who, like him, prepared the altar that early December morn, for the feast of Saint Themistoeles.

With care and due attention, Sister Philomena lit the advent candles and walked off into the adjacent room to write a short note for the priest who would be celebrating mass at the convent that day. She dipped the nib of the quill into the inkpot and began to write. 'Saint Themistoeles refused to betray his friend, Dioscorus, and suffered persecution and execution by the Emperor Valerian'.

Friar Sopscott had been thinking about Eling Priory and his mind was now resolved on the matter. All things are washed away on the ebb tide of life and only the most resolute of memories persist. But that most distant of memories haunted the friar's thoughts and urged him to change the course of destiny.

A little knowledge is a greater evil than a little ignorance, for of all the ills known to man, nought captivates and consumes the soul more easily than vanity. Faith is not belief, for faith had little to do with the belief that the people of Ebbsweirmouth held on the events of these past few days. Where belief is no more than misplaced conviction, it is indeed a greater evil than ignorance itself.

Yet, matters were not as methodical in these dark days. A hide of land, for example, was a poorly defined area; sufficient to feed a family was its intention, yet the size of it was determined as much by the generosity of the shire elderman as the length of a man's stride as he marked out the earth beneath his feet. Imagine, in the same manner, the minds of so many with such ill-defined knowledge of events; certain, yet misinformed. Gossips would be negligent to have no opinion in such catastrophic times and so, opinions were soon rooted in myth and spoken with misplaced authority.

The premature death of Lord Ravenhead revealed little of the plot to depose Eorl Scullion from his East Seaxe shire. Other than the fact that he was actually the coward Godric, who had fled the field at Maeldun, his motives were as certain as the wayward words of the Rypan sisters as they exchanged their thoughts. Those thoughts, though falsehoods, became facts and soon began their rampant erosion of truth.

Wisdom might easily be mistaken for the first and highest gift, and yet it is no more than the root of understanding, for it provides only the desire to contemplate all things. Understanding grants the ability to comprehend the truth. Yet few had made the journey towards such a worthy virtue.

Understanding is the final step of all journeys. Understanding the purpose of Ravenhead's plot would indeed give Lord Scullion's soul rest and allow his loyal servant Balliwick some peace of mind in knowing the impious purpose of such violent intent. And yet, once again, it is a child who is granted the penultimate gift of understanding; it is Willem who must apply his own will upon the world.

The dry-stone wall that surrounds the graveyard around the Church of the Virgin Mary was moved after Maeldun, in order to extend the land that it occupied. Trees were cut down to increase the space and yet one particular tree was spared. An unusual lime tree, with a heart-shaped leaf and chocolate-coloured bark on its lower trunk, remained untouched and stood alone, inviting speculation as to why the priest and his lordship had wished it to remain unharmed. The tree's grey-green branches, which had been sheltered by the woodland for many years, were turned red in colour by the now unhindered sunlight.

A local herb beuter made a soothing tea from its leaves and many swore of its medicinal properties. The tree provided nesting for birds, fed the honeybees in summer and many claimed that it *was a great symbol of fertility. So, in order that the town may thrive again, it was left standing as a tribute to those who fell at Maeldun.*

And yet, owing to the decision of the King to pay the Norse warriors off, there had been no other battles since Maeldun. So, apart from a few deaths from illness and old age, the graveyard remained sparsely filled. That was, until these six days past, when village life became a cortege for the bereaved.

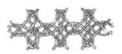

It was now morning in the town of Ebbsweirmouth and the doom-mongers had had their way. The self-fulfilling prophecy had been made a reality by the auguries of apocalyptic woe. Yesterday eve, the day turned to night, just as it had done since the beginning of time and yet, it was met with the awe of an eclipse. This was no ordinary night, they all said. Lord Scullion had been murdered; his killer had been unmasked and suffered death himself at the hands of a strange boy. The limp body of the coward Godric was hanging on Gallows Ridge alongside the murderer Cyrus Scolop. And the violently torn body of Maggoty Gripple lay covered by a cloth in the churchyard awaiting burial alongside the slave boy Eldrik. But there was no grave being dug, for the soil was like stone. In any case, Aldwyn Byrgan was distracted from his work by thoughts of greater import and his sons wandered about the graveyard looking for softer earth to dig.

The rumour-mongers were certain. The abyss had been opened. None could deny it and yet the priest would certainly try.

When it came to his homily, Father Shriver berated the many parishioners who had gathered for the dawn mass.

"Saint Themistoeles did not betray his friend," he told them. "And neither must we betray our God." He took the fourth, unlit candle from the altar and held it aloft.

"When we light this fourth candle of advent in three days' time, it is this that will signal the great coming, not the auguries and prophecies of the ignorant masses. It is not Satan who is coming, but God made man, who has dwelt among his people these thousand years past."

The priest's voice boomed and echoed around the small church.

"Though our bodies are laid down for but a short time, there is no circumstance in life that is not soured by death. It is manifested in so many ways and yet, so often, violent death provides the greatest sorrow. But what we see today is not the work of the devil; this is the work of man, beguiled by the devil." The priest stared into the eyes of each one who knelt there and looked into their souls. "Pray!" he declared loudly. "Pray to our merciful maker that we may understand his purpose for each of us."

None of those who listened to his words dawdled or gathered outside the church as they normally did after mass. Each went their own way, only to gather in small groups about the town, to discuss what had taken place, for nothing could stop the gossiping. And yet it was hearsay and calumny that had kindled the events of yesterday.

It was the elder Rypan sister who had sown the seed of viciousness in Leland Hoop's mind when she had repeated the words she had overhead in The Salutation Inn during that long lunchtime session.

"It would not surprise me," she had said in a convincing tone, as if it was her own idea, "if it isn't Maggoty Gripple and perhaps the Byrgans who are responsible for the rumours of spirits in the corpse road. I mean," she continued, mimicking Lord Ravenhead's words, "one of them is an undertaker and the spirits are said to have carried a coffin. And now we know their purpose for doing so," she declared. "The theft of a sheep."

The image of Gripple and the Byrgans clothed in white sheets and carrying a coffin along the lanes outside the town may have been sufficient on its own to turn the innkeeper's sanity. But then there had been the empty nights spent alone, gazing through that casement window towards the street outside, hoping to see the spirit of his beloved and departed wife.

Then, last night, when the crowd gathered outside, he had sat there alone, imagining how Gripple must have laughed at the success of his deception. Hoop could not have killed him, of course. But, seeing him there, hanging on Gallows Ridge was too great an opportunity to resist. All the anger at the loss of his wife was gathered up into one unchecked moment of wild abandon.

"You're not laughing now," Hoop had screamed at the dangling body as he hacked at it with the very same scythe that Fanny had been using that day in the field, before she dropped dead beside the garnered sheaths of barley.

In every undertaking, the wise man both considers his motive and reflects upon its purpose. If that motive seeks the benefit of self, then those actions are in themselves the purpose. In his anger, Leland Hoop had not seen this shining truth.

Friar Sopscott was made of more virtuous stock. Before mass began, he took his leave of Father Shriver and set off for Scullion Tower, resolved in his own mind on what must be done.

When he arrived there, Balliwick repeated to the friar the full account that Lady Una had given him and he informed Sopscott that a messenger would be sent to the King, seeking his advice on what course of action should be taken for the two parts of the East Seaxe shire that were now without leadership.

"Will they not promote you from shire reeve to elderman?"

"I am not that man, Friar."

"Perhaps a marriage to Lady Una is not out of the question in order to unite the shire. Everyone would rejoice at such news, I am sure."

"It was something I discussed with Lord Scullion before he died. He rejected the idea and I must honour his name by doing the same. Like him, I cannot enter into a marriage of convenience and make a lie of my life."

He looked at the friar with a watchful eye and wondered whether he had understood his true meaning.

"I loved Morcar and was happy to serve him all the days of my life. I would be pleased to do so for Lady Una too, but I doubt that the King will allow a woman to reign over such a strategically important shire. Whilst the sea wanderers continue to raid our shores, the East Seaxe shire must defend those shores against them."

"Your duty is done," the friar told him.

"It was never a duty," he replied and Friar Sopscott saw the fear of change in his eyes.

"You think the Crown will impose a stranger as elderman?"

"It is likely, I think. We shall see," replied Balliwick.

"Chamberlain," the friar said, seeking to secure the man's utmost attention. "May I beseech you to defer your actions until after the Christ's mass? Four days, I ask, before a messenger is sent to the King."

"What difference will four days make?"

"I need to go somewhere, to take advice, to seek counsel."

"Where will you go?"

"I need to travel to Eling Priory at the Ford of Reeds near Haeferingas. The truth of this matter lies there, I am certain of it."

"Haeferingas is two days' journey from here."

"If I leave this morning, I will return in time for the midnight mass on Christmas Eve."

"The opening of the abyss," replied Balliwick in a cynical tone.

"You do not believe it," replied Sopscott.

"After all that has happened, I do not know what to believe."

"Keep Lady Una safe and the waif Willem too, until Christmas Eve. I am sure the truth will be revealed on my return."

"They will remain in the castle as my guests. I have already written a note confirming that the boy is a slave no more. He is now a freeman as his owner at Shire Farm intended."

"All men are free in the sight of God," answered Sopscott. "As long as we are free in our heart and in our mind, we cannot be enslaved."

"I spoke to the boy this morning," replied Balliwick. "He is deserving of some compassion I think and yet, he believes he already has it. He said he is favoured with the blessing and protection of the Blessed Virgin. He was certain of it, he said, for there are too many coincidences for it to be otherwise."

"He is a strange boy," the friar commented. "He has an inquisitive mind."

The turret room of the tower provided a comfortable shelter for our pilgrim child Willem, who sat gazing through the lancet window. Across the misty, unploughed fields stood Apparition Hill with its deathly symbols of the prophecy plainly exhibited for all to see. Hearing the sound of footsteps in the courtyard below, the boy watched as the friar walked off, not knowing that providence was to take another turn.

The virtue of understanding is not measured by the awareness or discernment of this mortal world, but by the acceptance and application of the greater gift of love. Willem knew he must confess the sin of murder, for he had indeed killed the man they now called Godric. Yet, whether it was the sharp nib of the quill that killed him, or the poison that it had been dipped in, might never be known. The boy thought about his friends, the Goodlyheads and wondered what they now thought of him.

Whilst they were greatly distracted by events, neither Edwin nor Mildred had forgotten the plight of young Willem. For different reasons, the Goodlyheads had both been inattentive during the mass; well, at least until the outburst that Father Shriver delivered in the guise of a homily. In addition to Willem, Edwin Goodlyhead was still worrying about who would take responsibility for salting the meat. And he could now add to that concern over who might catch the fish. In a business sense, they both presented opportunities for a tradesman of his particular expertise and financial position. However, he could now dismiss his concerns about who might bury the dead, as Aldwyn Byrgan had not been hanged along with the butcher and fishmonger.

At least his wife's unholy musing had no mercenary motives. Mildred Goodlyhead had no head for business, but was more easily distracted by people. She paid attention to changes in their manner and disposition. She noticed nuances that other people missed; and not only in those people she cared about, but in just about everyone she knew. So it was no surprise that she could account for all who were missing from this Thursday morning mass. She noticed who was absent and concluded that it must have been these godless individuals who had been making all the noise in the street last night. How wrong she was, for Mistress Byrgan was there for sure and the Rypan sisters, sitting alongside Abel Cotes, just to be sure they did not miss any gossip that might be forthcoming. Nor did Mildred miss hearing the details of last night's events.

Of course, Mildred noticed the absence of Willem from mass and this caused her some distress, in spite of the assurances given to her by her husband that she should not worry. He was a strange child and it seemed to her that he had travelled here on ancient tides, driven by some meaningful purpose, the roots of which were grounded in the past.

The congregation dispersed quickly after mass, not wishing to be subjected to any further reprimand by the priest. Everyone, that was, except Abel Cotes, who loitered there to listen to a message sent from the castle to Father Shriver. Always wishing to gather gossip, he stood as close as he could as the priest was told of the visiting friar's plans to visit a distant land called Haeferingas. Convinced of its significance, the farmer took himself off towards the inn.

On her way home from the church, Mildred overheard some gossip too. The Rypan sisters were talking in great detail about how the body of Maggoty Gripple had been mutilated. She had not been asked to examine the body. In fact, Aldwyn Byrgan had cautioned her against it when she saw him working in the graveyard after mass.

As she neared Mardyke House, Mildred looked towards The Salutation Inn and beyond to Apparition Hill. It was then that she felt the eyes of someone watching her and, suddenly, all her suspicions fell into place. He wasn't watching her, of course, just staring into the distance, and hopelessly waiting for his lost wife to appear from the corpse road.

Mildred banged on the door of the inn and, when he failed to answer, she went to the small casement window where she had seen him sitting.

"Leland! Leland Hoop!" she called through the open window. "Let me in. You may lock the door behind me, if you don't wish to see anyone else. But you will need to talk to someone and it may as well be me as anyone else."

The innkeeper had moved away from the window to an alcove where he couldn't be seen.

"Leland! We all miss Fanny, all of us. What Maggoty did was wrong, Leland. He should not have misled his friends with those tales and, if he had any sense at all, he would have realised the effect such tales would have on you." She stopped speaking and listened for the sound of movement. "He's paid the price now, Leland. Now, open the door."

A moment later she could hear the door of the inn being unlocked and she followed Leland into the room, making sure she locked the door behind her. It hadn't crossed her mind that she was locking herself in a building occupied solely by a man who had brutally mutilated the body of Maggoty Gripple with a scythe.

Hoop had not changed out of the blood-soaked clothing and his face and arms were splashed with congealed blood that had dried into flecks that appeared like freckles on his pale skin. Mildred filled a bucket with water and told him to wash and change his clothes. He did as he was instructed and twenty minutes later he returned to the bar area and sat in the chair opposite her.

"I suggest," she said in a positive tone, "that you say nothing of this matter to anyone. Except for the priest, of course," she added. "You will need to confess what you have done. But there is no need to speak of it to anyone else, for nobody will speak of it to you, or they will have me to answer to."

Mildred stood up and paced about the room. "No crime has been committed. I shall speak privately with Chamberlain Balliwick and the matter will be closed. For the benefit of all, this whole episode needs to be forgotten."

"And what of Lord Scullion?" he asked, remembering how often his lordship had overruled Balliwick's more merciful gestures.

"Lord Scullion is dead, Leland. He was murdered by the gentleman you had staying here. The man who called himself Lord Ravenhead." She sat down again and looked directly into Hoop's eyes. "He was Godric, the man they say ran from the enemy at Maeldun; the one they call the coward."

"Godric? Here, at my inn? Who is the woman?"

"She is, as she told you, Lady Una, only daughter of the recently deceased Lord Haeferingas and now the only heir to the eorldom."

"But she is a woman."

"Yes, which is why, I suppose, she allowed herself to be seduced by the handsome face and smooth tongue of her deceiver." She paused for a moment to look around the room they were sitting in. It was untidy and steps needed to be taken to correct this.

"Now," she said, taking his arm and lifting him up from the chair. "Let us get this place tidied up. You need to open up this evening, or there may be another riot in the street tonight."

As the contrite Hoop rose from his seat to join Mildred as she began cleaning the inn, there were similarly forlorn faces at the other end of the town. The only people left outside the church were Aldwyn Byrgan, Abel Cotes and Seth Wainthrop. Byrgan's two sons had returned to their home to collect their spades, for there were many bodies to be buried and they had found a suitable patch of earth for the graves. All three men and the boys, too, had confessions to make for their part in the events of yesterday. Byrgan for his conspiracy with Gripple in the theft of the sheep; Wainthrop for telling Balliwick what he had seen last Friday morning at Hollow Hole Cove; and Cotes for his incessant raving about the opening of the abyss. Of these, only Wainthrop could find any virtue in his part in the events, but he was still troubled by it.

"Mine was the darkest deed," said Byrgan. "I know how fortunate I am not to have accompanied my friend to the gallows. And, for my penance, I am resolved to repay my widowed sister the fifteen shillings she had to pay to you, Abel."

"I would gladly forfeit it, but I am accountable, you see. They are not my sheep, but Lord Scullion's; I am but a tenant farmer, as is Seth here."

"And now Lord Scullion is dead," replied Wainthrop. "What will become of us now is unknown."

As they spoke, the two boys returned carrying spades and walked to the area that they had marked out.

"You have a busy day's work, Aldwyn," said Abel Cotes.

"And so do I," replied Seth Wainthrop as he began to walk back towards his farm. "One of the widows reported travellers building a camp on the south of the estate and I must go there and send them on their way. Whoever our elderman might be, he will still expect his rights to be honoured."

~~~~~

Now, at this time a stranger appeared in town. The quality of his clothes, though dishevelled, suggested he was from a noble or clerical background. And though he spoke little, he had a good knowledge of Latin. He was either a minstrel, a healer or a simonite and yet he demonstrated no eagerness to part with his talent or wares. He arrived early in the morning, having slept overnight in someone's barn. Then he wandered the streets, observing the people gathered about, but spoke to none of them.

Later that day, he enquired about a room at The Salutation Inn but, on checking his pockets, decided not to stay there, deciding instead to purchase a bowl of vegetable soup for his lunch. Mildred Goodlyhead had left the inn by this time and Hoop lit a fire in the hearth before warming the soup for his first customer of the day. He spoke little to the traveller, who was pleased to sit by the crackling fire. Edgar, he said his name was; Edgar Binbind, although he did not reveal the purpose of his visit to Ebbsweirmouth.

A few moments later, Abel Cotes came in and tried to engage Hoop in a conversation, but the innkeeper simply filled the farmer's tankard and made himself busy to avoid any talk about the events that had taken place. Cotes spotted the stranger and, hoping to hear some news, he sat close by him, near the hearth.

Hoop did not notice the weariness on the face of the stranger, but Abel Cotes did. It seemed to him that mortality weighed heavily on the man, like unwilling sleep. He seemed a lonely soul resigned to involuntary exile. An oppressed heart compelled by adversity to live apart from his fellow men.

As he sat as close as he could to the fire in the hearth, the stranger examined, at intervals, the content of his pockets. This consisted of a few coins and a small cloth purse containing some objects that he didn't remove from it. But, from time to time, he looked into the bag and moved the contents about with his finger.

"What have you there?" asked Abel Cotes.

"They are the bones of a saint," Edgar explained reluctantly, but the farmer pressed him on the matter, asking which saint's bones they were and how he had come by them. All the man would say was that he had purchased them from some travelling Norsemen who he had shared a camp with one night. Yet, the way he told the story was hesitant and fragmented, as if he was trying to replace the truth with some other account of how the holy relic had come into his possession.

When pressed further on the matter, he told of how the bones had been stolen from a church that the sea wanderers had ransacked. This seemed an unlikely tale, thought Abel Cotes, as the Norsemen would have had no interest in Christian artefacts. They stole metal objects like candlesticks or, more often, the church bell, in order to melt them down to make swords or shields. So, the farmer challenged him on the point.

"It is a sad truth," replied the man, "that the footgear of battle is indeed made from the religious sentiment of sacred objects." But he agreed that it was a strange item for the sea wanderers to have stolen. And, for a small price, the man had been able to purchase the bones from them.

"Do they ward off sin?" asked Cotes, with a despairing look about him. But the man did not know what the farmer meant.

"The bones," said Cotes firmly. "Do they ward off sin?"

The stranger looked into his eyes and back down into the purse. He saw an opportunity in that look and guessed the cause of that fear.

"Better still," the man replied, "the relic bones of Saint Stephen can resist the devil himself."

The name Stephen, he explained with a learned tone, means crown, because Saint Stephen is crowned as the first martyr of Christ.

"And Saint Stephen's day is the day beyond Christmas, when the abyss shall open," added the man wryly.

The words startled the farmer.

"Have you not heard that the abyss is to open?" he asked Cotes, who nodded and drew a little nearer to the man in order not to be overheard.

"Anyone in possession of one of these bones," the man said, holding up the purse, "will be protected."

Cotes reached into his pocket and removed what coins he had there. But the stranger did not want money. It was information he sought and he had tapped into a fruitful source.

And so, for the sake of a bogus phalanx bone of an early saint, our story is turned. As the fairy crone had told Willem, fate is not something that happens by accident. Events may be moulded by anyone with sufficient desire and guile to make it possible.

That evening the man was not to be found and Abel Cotes saw another opportunity to extol the privileged information he had gained from a passing stranger. He had been the first to comment on the divine revelations of Saint John. It was he who had warned of the opening of the abyss.

And now it fell to him to offer protection against that same cataclysmic event.

The finger bones of Saint Stephen were shown to all who would listen to the farmer's words. All, that was, except Father Shriver, who insisted that the bones had not been stolen by Norsemen, but had been taken from Saint Stephen's church on the Anglian shire border by a defrocked priest. But even the pious Father Shriver had to agree, under pressure from the townsfolk, that they should retain the bones until after the Christ's mass, just in case they possessed the power of the first martyr. Even the saintly Mildred Goodlyhead could see no harm in delaying their return, if only to appease the rowdy crowd that gathered about the priest after mass the next day.

With the bones safely deposited behind the altar, the feast days of Saint Flavian and Saint Servulus passed more quietly than anyone had expected. Attendance at the dawn mass increased as the days grew closer to the Christ's mass, which began with the midnight bell. Most heeded the priest's words and spoke less of the devil's coming, at least in public. But the joy of Christmas had dissolved along with the snow that had fallen one week earlier.

Chamberlain Balliwick had spoken to only a few people about the events of that past week and had kept his promise to await the return of Friar Sopscott before taking any further action. He shared his thoughts with only the Goodlyheads and Father Shriver. The priest could not enlighten the chamberlain on what information the friar was hoping to retrieve from Haeferingas and Balliwick still needed the priest's support in controlling any insurrection among the townsfolk.

Taking Edwin and Mildred Goodlyhead into his confidence seemed entirely appropriate too. After all, they were distant relatives of Morcar Scullion and the Crown may wish to see their support for the newly appointed elderman. For all he knew, the couple may be the closest living relatives to the deceased lord.

Willem spent those three days confined to the turret room in the tower, with little more to do than witness activities on Gallows Ridge on those occasions when the mist cleared. Balliwick visited the boy occasionally and allowed the Goodlyheads to do so too, but little was said about events. The chamberlain had no clue as to what Sopscott's aims were, but the friar had seemed very sure of a positive outcome. In a like manner, the shire reeve spoke only a little to Lady Una, preferring to join her for dinner and never referring to the events of recent days.

Through his visitors, the gift of understanding enabled Willem to comprehend the series of events that had led to his incarceration in the turret room. He had been assured that he was not a prisoner, but clearly everyone was still shocked by events and were anxious to find a suitable resolution.

On Christmas Eve morning, which fell on a Sunday, Balliwick arranged for Father Shriver to celebrate mass in the tower chapel and invited Lady Una, Willem and the Goodlyheads to join him. This would ensure that they were all present when Friar Sopscott returned from his visit to Haeferingas. Of course, nobody could be certain about what time he would arrive, but he had assured Balliwick that the matter would be resolved before the midnight mass on Christmas Eve.

After the chapel mass, the guests retired to the great hall to partake in lunch. Then it was agreed that after the friar had returned, they would all journey together to attend midnight mass.

After lunch, Balliwick continued to avoid any awkward conversation about recent events, but this unnatural course could not be sustained and it was not long before the post-lunch discussion moved on to questions about the possible motives of Friar Sopscott. Balliwick managed to deflect the conversation, not wishing to prejudice any evidence that the friar might produce. Then, as they sat and returned to discussing matters of little or no consequence, there was a loud banging on the outer door. Balliwick accompanied a servant into the hall, expecting to find that Friar Sopscott had returned.

Instead, it was Seth Wainthrop, out of breath from a strenuous run to the castle.

"You must come, Sir," he shouted at Balliwick and pointed towards the castle gate. "It is Friar Sopscott." He paused again, regaining his breath only slowly. "He lies dead by the pathway through the forest."

Chapter Sixteen

Love

The immeasurable gift of love stands above all things and its eminence is made so by wisdom, counsel and understanding. Love is infinite in its design and in its divisibility too. It can separate and divide and yet is never diminished by this process, as anyone will testify who has loved a husband or wife so completely and yet found greater love still for the children of that union. Love is not replaced by love for, like the loaves and fishes that were fed to the multitude, love is unending. It is the infinite wonder of mankind and the greatest gift of God.

And yet, it may be argued that love, by its very nature, never ends well, because everything must end and all things must perish. Even requited love ends badly, for all earthy love results in death and is therefore a tragedy in the eyes of the lover. Saint Paul said that the greatest of all virtues is love and, as we have already heard, the sixteenth and final virtue of destiny stands above all others.

The Watchman Darrayne, Lord Scullion, Cyrus Scolop, the slave boy Eldrik and the coward Godric in the guise of Ravenhead are all now dead. The minor sins of Maggoty Gripple were enough to add his name to this list. And now it seems that Friar Sopscott is dead too and with him his secrets are lost and his attempt to change the course of destiny lays rough-hewn in a frozen meadow. I began this story by referring to it as a tragic tale and seven deaths suggest it can be judged as nothing else but a tragedy. And in this dark, circumscribed age of man, there are only two possible conclusions to any story. It is not enough for a tale to involve love or hate, admiration or envy, for each tale must a comedy or a tragedy be. All comedies are graced with a happy ending and all tragedies with a death. You may have surmised already that this story will not end well. Nor could it, with such a copious number of deaths, be considered a comedy. So, let us then move towards its tragic ending.

It is a little more than one week since Willem journeyed here and so much has happened in that time. It is as if Satan himself has been unleashed upon this small town. The natural enemy of good is evil. And to prevail it must become the predator of truth; it must overcome fortitude and, when it has succeeded in these precursors, it must overpower hope. Hope gives the past purpose, the present joy and the future beauty.

And so, each tragedy must have its tragic ending. Yet death holds no monopoly on tragedy. One boy's search for truth rested on another man's journey to find that truth. A journey that ended prematurely for here we find, amongst the budding snowdrops at the wood's edge, another body. The brutal death of Friar Sopscott, who now lies still by the pathway, augers badly for our pilgrim hero. How often truth presents itself too late and even then, it stands unrecognised in our midst, masked by its high celestial veil.

Just before the path turns northward and heads between the castle and Holm Farm, the well-trodden route is bordered by a green verge, which itself is sheltered by an ancient hedgerow that separates the track from the most south-westerly part of the

Scullion estate. In summer, the meeting of two full-laden hedgerows protects a barley field and, in this corner of land, a small copse provides a shady bower, filled with the fragrance of a dog rose that stretches forth from the blackthorn hedge. This was the same hedgerow that Willem had passed in the blizzard that Friday evening and the same one that he had dreamed of and where he had met an angel on some distant summer day of his childhood.

And so it is with destiny; where dreams are made, they may also be extinguished. Fate is to be feared above all things. For had Friar Sopscott not met Oswald and had he not undertaken the purging of the secular priests, he would not have been attacked that dark December night and the destiny of a young boy would have changed beyond recognition. But then, the friar may not have heard the confession of the young novice. And if Morcar had not fallen from his horse, or if Æryk had not been so brave, or Byrhtnoth had been less bold, less foolhardy. Or indeed, if Una had not been so smitten by her young lover, or her father had been less belligerent in the face of destiny. But then, of course, Willem might just as easily have taken a different path in the yew tree wood.

When the group arrived at the point where two hedgerows converged at the most distant point of Lord Scullion's land, it was growing dark. Balliwick had left Lady Una, Father Shriver and Willem at the castle, and taken with him Edwin and Mildred Goodlyhead, together with two servants.

No more than a hoar frost was left where the snow had rested these past few days. And there, beneath the narrow trunks of the sparse hedgerow, lay Friar Sopscott's frozen body. In summer, this was a scene of happy picnics, a place where the fragrant dog rose grew amongst the leafy blackthorn. But, today the hedge consisted of no more than spindly bare threads of twigs that stood shrivelled by winter, and the only fragrance one of premature death.

The group set off back to the castle, led by the servants carrying the friar's body with all the dignity that they could muster. As they walked, the chamberlain struggled to decide what he should do next.

When the party arrived back at Scullion Tower, Willem and Lady Una retired to their rooms. Father Shriver accompanied the body of Friar Sopscott to a small room where he administered the last rites and then knelt in silent prayer. Balliwick was grateful to have been left alone with Edwin and Mildred Goodlyhead, and led them through to the great hall, as he had something he needed to discuss with them in private. The chamberlain needed to confide in someone he could trust because, at this very moment, it seemed that every event conspired against his good office.

Oswald Balliwick related to the couple what Friar Sopscott had told him before he had left Scullion Tower on his journey to Haeferingas. The friar had met the Lady Una some seven years ago, but had not actually seen her because her identity had been shielded by the grill of the confessional. Because of the circumstances, the friar was unable to divulge anything that had been said that day, so Balliwick knew only as much as the friar could tell him before returning to Eling Priory, where he had met Lady Una previously.

"Friar Sopscott wanted," said Balliwick, "to find the truth behind Godric's plan and to determine why Lady Una had come to Ebbsweirmouth. And he could only do this by returning to the convent where he had heard her confession."

"But why did he have to return there?" questioned Mildred.

"I don't know, but there was clearly something that needed clarification in his mind."

"Then, what did he tell you before he left?" asked Edwin.

"Yes," added Mildred. "Tell us every word, for we might find something that has not occurred to you."

And so the three of them sat down and Balliwick repeated the story just as the friar had told him.

The friar's tale began at Eling Priory, a convent near Haeferingas, at a place called the Ford of Reeds. The friar had visited there on the anniversary of Maeldun, exactly one year after that day when so many had laid down their lives. It was not chance that had led him to this place, for he had been summoned to attend there by his order. A child had been born there that spring and the boy was about three months old at that time. Being so young, he was being raised by the virgins who lived there and who dedicated their lives to God.

Friar Sopscott had heard the confession of the mother, who was a novice there. The boy should, he believed, have been raised by the person he knew to be the young woman's father, but the Eorl of Haeferingas wished it to be otherwise.

The prioress had told the friar that the child might be ill-treated if it was ever discovered that he was the son of a postulant. And so, a plan was agreed by all parties. The neighbouring shire was East Seaxe and the child was to be taken there to be raised by Morcar, who had become Eorl of

Scullion on the death of his father and older brother at Maeldun. The friar offered to take the child to Ramsey Abbey and to instruct him personally in the divine word of God. This suggestion was dismissed by the abbess on the instructions of Eorl Haeferingas and a few days later, a servant was despatched with the child, who was to be raised by Lord Scullion until he reached an age where he could work on the land. The friar's own journey took him north to the old Roman city of Camulodunon and his varied travels had not taken him to Ebbsweirmouth until this past week.

"And now," said Balliwick, "it seems that whatever information it was that Friar Sopscott was seeking, it was never found."

"Do we know how long the friar had been lying by the roadside?" asked Mildred, who was wondering whether he had died at the beginning of his journey, or on his way back to the castle.

"It is difficult to say," replied Balliwick, "for he had been lying in the snow and freezing conditions. There was nothing on his person to give us any indication of what it was he was seeking or, indeed, whether he found it." It mattered not in Balliwick's mind, for whether the friar had learned something or not, it had been taken to the grave with him.

"If Ravenhead was not who he said he was," suggested Mildred, "then could it be that Friar Sopscott suspected that Lady Una is not who she says she is?"

"I think you may be right, Mistress Goodlyhead," Balliwick replied. "But I am unsure how we can find that out, now that the friar is dead."

"We can question her," replied Mildred. "And, if she is not who she says, she will certainly not know what was revealed to you by Friar Sopscott before he left."

"What was the name of the priory?" asked Edwin.

"Eling Priory."

"Then, an imposter would not know that, would she?"

And so it was agreed, with renewed enthusiasm, that the three of them would ask Lady Una Haeferingas to join them in the great hall in order to question her and invite her to provide an explanation of events.

To their great pleasure, the story she recounted to them corresponded precisely with what the friar had told Balliwick.

Eight years ago, just before the Battle of Maeldun, Una had fallen pregnant and when her father discovered she was with child, he lost his mind. Una was sent to Eling Priory to submit herself to the life of a nun and her son was sent away, for Lord Haeferingas could not bear to look upon the child. He sent the baby to his cousin, Lord Scullion, to be raised.

More recently, when news came to Una at the priory of her father's death, she returned to the family home to settle her father's estate. A few days later, Lord Ravenhead had arrived, wishing to offer his condolences. When Una had told her story to Ravenhead he was full of sympathy for her plight and suggested that they travelled to Ebbsweirmouth to find the long-lost child and restore him to the throne of Haeferingas. And so, they travelled there together and arrived last Friday. But, on that first evening, her companion had met a man outside the inn who had recognised him as Godric, son of Odda, the coward of Maeldun. Godric had murdered the man, crushing his skull with a rock and left him for dead outside the inn. It was then that Una had learned of Godric's true plan.

"Godric wanted to kill my son, in order that there was no male heir to Haeferingas," explained Una. "Then he intended to force me into marriage and, with Lord Scullion's blessing, he could seize the throne for himself. It was probably his plan to claim this land also, upon the death of Lord Scullion."

Una began to cry, but composed herself and concluded her sad tale.

"I had already identified Eldrik as my son and, as I now know, Godric arranged for Scolop to kill the boy when they went fishing together."

Her version of events agreed in every respect with Friar Sopscott's account and explained, to a great extent, why the friar had suspected something was wrong. Quite what he had hoped to find at Eling Priory, however, was still unknown. But there was little comfort that those present could offer to the poor young woman who had lost her only son so soon after the death of her father.

Oswald Balliwick assured Lady Una that her son would be reburied and given a new gravestone, and then suggested that his guests should begin to prepare themselves to attend midnight mass at the Church of the Holy Virgin. It was agreed that the Goodlyheads, Willem and Lady Una would spend Christmas night as the guests of the chamberlain, in order that they might assist in the writing of a letter to the King to seek his advice on what action should now be taken to settle the eorldom of the East Seaxe shire.

As the party returned to Scullion Tower after mass, they eventually came to the point in the road where it divided and went to the castle in one direction, and to Holm Farm in the other. From a wooded copse in front of them a shadowy figure appeared and seemed to be approaching them. The person seemed poorly wrapped against the damp night air as he or she came closer and closer towards them. It was too small to be Seth Wainthrop, thought the chamberlain, who by now had convinced himself that it was nobody he knew.

Balliwick felt for the sword by his side and told the others to make their way to the castle, while he waited for the stranger to approach. Nobody had yet established how Friar Sopscott had been killed so there were still fears that a killer may be at large.

Edwin Goodlyhead ushered his wife, Una and Willem along the pathway, looking behind him at regular intervals to try to see what was happening. Through the poor light he could see the two people talking and, although he could not make out who the other person was, there was no sign of any animosity or argument and Balliwick had certainly not drawn his sword from its scabbard.

Willem and Una went off to their rooms, whilst Edwin and Mildred waited in the great hall for their host to return. Willem was unable to sleep and stalked around the Turret room wondering about the events of the day. From there he had seen Balliwick arrive back at the castle with the shrouded visitor, but the stranger was too small to be Darrayne. In truth, in spite of all the boy had witnessed and heard, he still believed that Darrayne might be alive.

In the Great Hall downstairs, Mildred and Edwin stood in speculative anticipation and when Balliwick entered the room, that speculation grew in their minds. Alongside their host was a woman, whose face they could just make out beneath a cloak which the chamberlain had thrown about her to stop her from freezing, for she had been walking for many hours. She was led by Balliwick to one of the large, high-backed chairs by the hearth to warm herself and a jug of mulled wine was ordered for everyone.

It was only when the cloak was pulled from her head that the Goodlyheads saw she was a nun, a sister of the Benedictine order, for her tunic was black and her scapular white. She lifted the crucifix that hung about her neck and kissed it.

"This is Edwin and Mildred Goodlyhead," said Balliwick, introducing her to his other guests.

"My name is Sister Philomena," she eventually responded. "And I have travelled this long day from Eling Priory, near the Ford of Reeds. I have come to pray at the grave of my only son, who was brutally murdered here one week ago."

The Goodlyheads looked stunned by her comment, as did the chamberlain, but their tired visitor failed to notice their questioning expression.

"How can that be?" questioned Mildred, but Balliwick quickly intervened and ordered a servant to place two large logs on the fire. For her part, Sister Philomena believed Mildred's confusion about her being a mother arose from the fact that she was a nun. But Balliwick felt otherwise.

All three knew, of course, that Sister Philomena referred to young Eldrik and each of them wondered whether she knew of the brutal way in which the boy had lost his life. Edwin and Mildred struggled to contain themselves and both wanted to tell her about Lady Una's claim to be the boy's mother. But Balliwick sensed that they should not reveal their hand too soon in this matter and gave Mildred a knowing look.

So, as the four of them began to thaw, Sister Philomena was encouraged to tell them more about the purpose of her journey and why she had decided to travel so urgently to their village. Soon, both the Goodlyheads realised that their host wished them to remain silent about Lady Una, who slept upstairs.

"The journey I made today represented only the last few steps of a much longer journey, which began many years ago," she replied.

"Then, please begin there, for none of us are able to take to our beds until we have heard what you have to say."

Mildred's words reflected the feelings of her husband and Oswald Balliwick.

Like the stories of so many who had lived in these parts at that time, Sister Philomena's tale began in those blessed summer days before Maeldun, for everyone had been affected by that conflict and it had become a milestone for everyone and a millstone for many.

"When word came to us that the sea wanderers had landed, my brother, Osmund, and the leader of the watch began to prepare the household for battle. Lord Æthelstan Scullion arrived from Ebbsweirmouth with his son, Æryk, and twenty fighting men. They rested at our home for two nights, as our household retainers made the preparations to travel to Maeldun. Æryk was a handsome and charming young man and he quickly became good friends with

Osmund and our watchman. I was completely beguiled and fell deeply in love with him."

Sister Philomena's countenance changed at these words and it was clear that tears would have had their way had she not been in the company of strangers. Mildred encouraged her to take her time and to feel no shame for her feelings.

"Of course," explained Sister Philomena. "All of this took place before I took holy orders and I was still subject to the authority of my father, Lord Haeferingas."

"Lord Haeferingas?" questioned Edwin loudly and the sister nodded.

"And your brother was Osmund?" he added.

"He was," she replied, wondering why the man was so shocked by her declaration.

"And did you have a sister named Una?" he then asked.

"I have no sister," she answered in a confused tone. "I am Una, or I was before taking holy orders. I am the only daughter of Lord Haeferingas."

Edwin went to ask another question but he was prevented from doing so by Balliwick, for the chamberlain feared he would reveal something to this second claimant who now sat before them.

"Continue, Sister Philomena," said Balliwick, hoping that she might say something to either prove or disprove her claim to the title.

"Those three days," she continued, "were the sweetest of my life, although as each day passed, we grew more anxious about the danger that awaited our brave men at Maeldun."

The sister blushed as she tried to explain how desperately she and Æryk had fallen in love with each other.

"When Æryk returned from Maeldun, we planned to marry and were certain that our parents would welcome such a union. But it was not to be. Of all the men who made that fateful journey to Maeldun, only our watchman and a few men of the household returned to Haeferingas. Many were wounded and those men whose injuries could not be seen were greatly tormented by the bloody event. A short time later, I went to my father and told him that I was with child. He was already destroyed by the death of his only son and welcomed the opportunity, I think, to lash out at someone, anyone, for what he had suffered."

She then explained how he had arranged for her to take holy orders at Eling Priory. It was a decision that she had welcomed, because she wished to be taken from the world. Her life had ended when Æryk did not return from Maeldun. Una was told that her son was to be sent away, to be raised in a strange place and she would never see him again. When her maid, Lizy, came to take the child, she begged her to tell her where the boy was being sent and, in her desperation, asked the maid to mark the boy in some way that he may be recognised, for she had resolved at that time to find him, wherever he was, when the opportunity arose.

"I never dreamed she would do what she did and when I learned of it my heart was broken by the pain my son must have suffered, for she removed the tip of the smallest finger on his right hand with a cleaver."

One month ago, Sister Philomena had been informed of her father's death by a stranger who had come to the priory. Lord Ravenhead had said he had the blessing of both the King and her father to become the new eorl and it was the dying wish of Lord Haeferingas that his only daughter should remain in Eling Priory seeking forgiveness for her sins.

"By now I was resigned to both my life at the priory and to not seeing my son again. So I accepted the dying wishes of my father and re-dedicated my life to God."

Then, she explained, three days ago, Friar Sopscott had visited her at Eling Priory with the saddest of news. Not only had she lost her beloved father but now her son had died at the hands of a violent man named Cyrus Scolop in the town of Ebbsweirmouth.

"The friar explained to me the circumstances behind my son's death and, when I told him of the missing fingertip, his demeanour changed quite suddenly. It seemed to me that he found great significance in the missing fingertip and promised to return after Christmas with further news. I am certain he did not wish to encourage unwarranted hope on my part, but clearly there was something that he still needed to resolve."

Sopscott had then instructed Una to wait at the priory whilst he returned to Ebbsweirmouth to settle this outstanding matter, saying he would return and seek some solution with the Crown on the matter of her estate. But Sister Philomena had no interest in her inheritance and was inconsolable after the friar left. So the following day she was given special permission to visit the grave of her lost son. Even the hardened heart of the redoubtable prioress was softened by the awful consequences that had befallen the devout young Sister Philomena.

Her emotions left Sister Philomena in no doubt that life's greatest tragedy is the loss of life out of its prescribed order.

When her father had suffered the death of his son at Maeldun, he was lost to the world and the years since had been no more than a posthumous existence for him. Now, his only daughter, Una, had suffered the same loss.

"The watchman of the Haeferingas household, a good man named Darrayne after his father, was one of the few survivors of Maeldun. When he arrived at my home, all battered and torn from the battle, he first reported to my father, telling him of the sad loss of my brother, Osmund. Later, when my father had received an elixir to sedate him, Darrayne came to me. He stood in the doorway, unable to approach me, for he knew how much I truly loved Æryk. 'Don't say it', I begged him loudly, because all the time he did not speak the words, then it had not happened. And for those brief moments I lived in a world where my love still lived, at least until the watchman spoke the words. 'Don't say it', I repeated, hoping the moment would last forever. But, of course, he did speak the words, for it was his duty to do so. I could tell from the tone that he knew about my love for Æryk Scullion. What he could not know, nor could I know at that moment, was that I carried Æryk's child in my womb. And, when that moment came, he was the first person I told; not my father, but the Watchman Darrayne."

Una explained how Darrayne had then adopted a self-imposed exile from his previous life. He became a chandler, making candles. It was the Watchman who she named as her son's godfather and it was he who swore an oath and continued to visit the boy, from time to time, to learn of his new life of serfdom. He visited Shire Farm under the pretext of selling candles, as he did when he visited Ebbsweirmouth on that fateful day after he had called at Shire Farm and learned that the boy had left.

Balliwick told her about the chandler's violent death at the hands of Godric. It was now obvious that Darrayne had recognised Godric at The Salutation Inn that evening and, fearing his plan would be revealed, Godric had killed him by striking him with a rock from behind.

By this time it was nearing dawn and through the eastern casement Aurora's faint glow appeared beyond the ocean. Only Willem and Lady Una, or more correctly one of the two women who claimed to be Lady Una, had slept that Christmas night. Balliwick, along with the Goodlyheads, had chosen to stay up listening to their visitor's tale and so the servants had not slept either.

Sister Philomena's tears left the chamberlain very confused. He had been completely convinced by the other Lady Una's tale and yet the sudden appearance of this nun now suggested that her story had been part of a great hoax devised and almost executed to perfection by her and the coward Godric.

Edwin and Mildred, too, were as convinced by the sister's version of events, just as they had been with the other woman who claimed to be Lady Una.

Balliwick paced the room, stopping at the casement to watch the rising sun. He was convinced that things had to be put in order, or at least addressed in a particular order, if he was to resolve the situation. If only Friar Sopscott had made those last few steps back to the castle, thought the chamberlain. The friar had many enemies, mainly married clergy who had been displaced by the monasteries in general and Friar Sopscott in particular, so it was unlikely that his murder had been anything to do with the case of the two women claiming to be Lady Una. Rumours of a strange man in town, selling holy relics and asking for information about Friar Sopscott, added to the chamberlain's belief that the holy man had been murdered by a defrocked priest.

There was only one way to resolve the mystery, thought Balliwick, and whilst he had suffered more than sufficient confrontation these past few days, a further conflict was inevitable. The chamberlain resolved that it was now time to introduce the woman claiming to be Una to Sister Philomena. And so, he ordered a servant to wake the Lady Una and ask her to join them in the great hall at her earliest convenience.

She did so with great haste, of course, and was shocked to come face to face with her former mistress, the true Lady Una, who she was well aware had been Sister Philomena for these past eight years. Confronted by the truth, Lizy confessed everything. Lizy Herbbeater was the daughter of an apothecary and had been raised on the Haeferingas estate. When she was fourteen years old, she had become Lady Una's private maid and served her until she took holy orders. It was Lizy who had taken Una's baby to Ebbsweirmouth all those years ago and it was she who had removed the tip of the baby's smallest finger in order that he may be recognised if the child was ever to be united with his mother again.

During her time at Eling Priory, Sister Philomena, the true Lady Una, had learned the worthiness of mercy and she forgave her maid for everything that had happened. Love is more than an emotion and certainly greater than its misshapen sisters, idolatry and lust. It is, as we have heard, the greatest of the virtues, for all things in this world crumble except love.

It was Christmas morning and the servants began to prepare the great hall for lunch.

"I shall need to write to the King about this matter and seek his judgement," announced Balliwick. "But, for now, we must all prepare ourselves for the dawn mass of Christmas, as Father Shriver will be here shortly to celebrate it in the tower chapel."

"There is just one other matter to resolve before we do that," replied Mildred.

Balliwick gave a questioning look, but Mildred was intent on resolving certain matters that concerned her greatly.

"Lizy," she asked. "When Cyrus Scolop was instructed to kill Lady Una's son, how was the boy identified?"

"Lord Ravenhead, or Godric as we now know he is, asked if Scolop knew of a boy in Ebbsweirmouth with a missing fingertip. At first, the fisherman said he knew of nobody with such a mark. But, once he learned that Ravenhead was prepared to pay for such information, he changed his mind and told us he knew the boy well. The two men then conspired together to kill the boy," Lizy told her.

"But in truth," replied Mildred knowingly, "Scolop knew of no such child."

Lizy was surprised by this statement, but before she could interrupt, Mildred continued.

"What Scolop did, however, was to trick you both by cutting the finger from his own slave boy, Eldrik, who happened to be about the same age as the boy Godric was looking for. Little did he know," she continued, "that on the very day he carried out that evil deed, the actual boy you were seeking would arrive at Ebbsweirmouth; the boy with the missing fingertip."

Nobody was sure of what Mildred was asserting, least of all Sister Philomena. But Edwin had realised what his wife was about to reveal.

"Are you suggesting," asked Sister Philomena, "that Scolop cut a finger from his slave boy and passed him off as my son? Does this mean that my son still lives and is out in the world somewhere?"

Mildred held her hands up and asked Sister Philomena to be patient for just a little longer.

"It is clear to me," the old woman said, "that if Godric was to succeed with his plan, he would need to ensure that any other claimants to Haeferingas were disposed of, and your son was certainly a possible heir."

By this time, Edwin had left the room and gone to find the boy, Willem. He returned a few moments later with the boy following behind.

"We wish to ask you some questions," Edwin explained to Willem and then asked him to describe his earliest memories and what he had been told about his childhood.

"I remember nothing before Shire Farm."

"What is your earliest memory?" asked Sister Philomena.

"My earliest memory is a day in the countryside. It seems to me now very much like the fields that surround Scullion Tower, except this day was at the onset of summer, not as the fields are now, covered in snow. It is a memory so worn by recollection," he confessed, "that I am not entirely sure it isn't a dream. But in the dream I am playing in a field of barley, accompanied by an angel. It is a place where two ancient hedgerows meet and the delicate velvet pink flowers of the dog rose rise above the blackthorn on its precarious stems of arching briars. And the air is filled with the intoxicating scent of green apples, overpowering the gentle fragrance of honeysuckle, wild violets and cow parsley, signalling that summer has arrived. It was a picnic sheltered by the scented hedgerows and filled with birdsong. And yet I am certain it is just a dream."

Sister Philomena took out the small ornate box she had carried with her from Eling Priory and opened it.

"Is this the fragrance you recall?" she asked, holding the box towards the boy.

Willem held the box to his nose and nodded.

"Are you an angel?" he asked the strangely dressed woman, for he had never seen a nun before. As he spoke, he slowly realised that it had not been a dream.

But, before the true Lady Una could answer the boy's question, Mildred Goodlyhead intervened.

"This," said Mildred with a large smile on her face, "is your son Willem. Show her your right hand," she added, directing her comment to the boy.

Willem removed the mittens and stretched out his right hand, so that everyone could see that the tip of his smallest finger was missing.

"When did you lose your fingertip?" asked Una.

"I cannot remember," he replied. "I think it has always been like this, Mistress…" Willem hesitated, wondering what to call the strangely dressed lady. "What do I call you?" he added.

"Mother," she replied.

"Then, who am I?"

"You are Willem," answered Mildred. "But you shall be William, Eorl of two shires. Eorl of Haeferingas and of East Seaxe, although Chamberlain Balliwick here will be required to act largely on your behalf until you come of age."

Balliwick seemed utterly relieved that he would not be forced to assume the eorldom of East Seaxe.

"An eorl?" replied Willem. "But I am only a child of the land and I still find wonder in it; in the spring lambs that gambol in the meadow and in the golden glow of the forest in autumn. All of these things are of greater value to me than thrones and kingdoms."

"You love this land, Willem. Now you must love its people in the same way and rule with justice," replied Una.

~~~~~

As the true Lady Una knew too well, time takes our breath away too easily. Its immeasurable days stretch out before us and those who pass from this world are missed for a very long time. So, the following morning, Una and Willem visited the graveyard to place flowers on the graves of the Watchman Darrayne and Eldrik. On the way, she told her son all about his father, Æryk, and his good friends, Osmund and Darrayne.

"Was the Watchman a brave and fearless man?" Willem asked.

"No man is both brave and fearless," she replied, "for to be brave you cannot be fearless. It is in overcoming their fears that a person is made brave and this is the product of courage."

Una then explained how Darrayne had pledged his allegiance to her son even before the child was born and he had stood as Willem's godfather at the child's baptism. It was Darrayne who had made frequent visits to see Willem, without ever making contact during the past eight years.

For his part, Willem explained about the strange discussions he had had with his godfather after he arrived in Ebbsweirmouth.

Their arrival at the graveyard disturbed some pigeons nesting in the two oaks that loomed overhead, but a yellow-billed hawfinch rested, indifferent to their arrival, among the grey-green branches of the old lime tree and maintained a watchful scrutiny of their conversation.

Willem looked curiously at the headstone. "This stone says that Darrayne died on the very day that I arrived at Ebbsweirmouth. But this cannot be true, for he visited and spoke with me for three nights after this. How can that be?"

Of course, nobody could answer the boy's question, because it was impossible to make sense of the events that the boy recalled. That was how it came about that, whenever the story was retold, it was suggested that perhaps the Watchman visited the boy in his dreams. Others, particularly those who have traced the sixteen virtues of destiny, will tell you otherwise.

Did you solve the riddle?

Why does the book have this title?

One Christmas Past

Remember the clue in Chapter One?

'Start at the beginning and read each chapter'

If you have solved the puzzle, tweet your solution directly to the author.

**Follow the author on Twitter
Peter Larner@OpusWriter**

Made in the USA
Charleston, SC
06 October 2015